"I wonder if that is how Sor Noris sees all of us, pieces in a game, sterile sanitary images that have shapes and textures, but no intruding convenient smells and noises. Not quite real. No one quite real. No, I'm wrong. I was real for him awhile. Cluttering, demanding, all edges some days, all curves another. Maybe that's why he wants me back—to remind him that he's real too. He wants the touch he remembers, the questions, the tugs that pulled us together, yet reminded each that the other was still other. He doesn't want me as I am now, only the Serroi he lost. And he doesn't even know that the Serroi he wants never quite existed, was a construct out of his clever head. . . ."

JO CLAYTON
has also written:

# CHANGER'S MOON

## Duel of Sorcery # 3

## JO CLAYTON

**DAW BOOKS, INC.**
DONALD A. WOLLHEIM, PUBLISHER

1633 Broadway, New York, NY 10019

DAW Collectors' Book No. 638

### DEDICATION

*For the nurses and teachers of this world
who do impossible things under impossible
conditions with little reward or recognition.*

First DAW Printing, August 1985

3  4   5   6   7   8   9

PRINTED IN U.S.A.

# FOREWORD

Once upon a time there were a Sorcerer and a Goddess, and the World they each claimed for their own; the Game they invented to settle the question amused them awhile, but was not so good for the World and the folk who lived on it.

## WHAT HAS GONE BEFORE

For many generations there was peace in the land; a man knew what his son's life would entail, knew the path his son's son would walk. And a woman knew the same of her daughter and her daughter's daughter. Those who had food to fill their bellies, a bit of land or a trade to keep them secure were content to have it so, but there were more and more who were frustrated and restless, younger sons, unmarried daughters, tie-children whose parents could not feed or clothe them, people without place or hope. Under the calm surface turmoil was building toward explosion.

Into this volatile mix stepped Ser Noris. He had long since halted the processes of growth and decay within his body and passed the time he had thus acquired honing his skills, gathering knowledge, dueling with other norissim until there was none left with the power or skill to challenge him. The day came when he looked about and found himself with no more worlds to conquer within the limits allowed him; he eyed those limits with distaste and speculation but found no way around them. More years passed. He grew bored, monumentally, extravagantly, disastrously bored. Thus, the Game.

In MOONGATHER, the challenge is issued, the pieces are selected, the long Game begins.

In MOONSCATTER, the Game continues, the pieces are maneuvered to set them up for the final confrontation, each Player trying to take out or somehow nullify the other Players' pieces, to gain advantage in position or strength or both.

# THE MAJOR PIECES

## SERROI

She is a misborn of the windrunners, saved from a death by burning and taken by Ser Noris to his Tower, raised and taught by him, her gifts used by him to create new types of life (the child his gate into the forbidden), life he could command, something he could not do with the World's life, for that was outside his limits. She was abandoned when she was twelve in a desert east of the mijloc, when his disregard for her feelings and her understanding made her useless to him, her gifts inaccessible; abandoned because he didn't understand his own emotions, ensuring that he'd spend futile years trying to retrieve her—because he'd unexpectedly come to love her, something he had not thought possible. She is a sliding piece, first his strength, then his weakness.

   Having walked out of the desert to a tribe of nomadic pehiiri she is welcomed by their janja or wisewoman, Reiki (who is also the form of flesh the Goddess puts on when she visits the World), then makes her way to the Biserica Valley where she lives in peace for a number of years, studying and learning the skills of a meie and refusing to hear about her talents for magic.

On her second ward—this time as a guard to the women's quarters in the Plaz of Oras, watching over Floarin and Lobori, the Domnor Hern's two wives, and his multifarious concubines—she and her shieldmate Tayyan learn of a plot against the Domnor. Tayyan is killed and Serroi runs. When her panic dissipates, she returns to Oras, acquiring a companion called Dinafar, meeting the Gradin family on their way to celebrate the Gather in Oras.

In Oras, with the aid of Coperic (thief, fence, smuggler, Tavern owner and Friend to the Biserica in his spare time), she thwarts the plot against Hern, but only in part because he is driven into exile by Floarin and the Nearga Nor. She returns to the Biserica taking Hern and Dinafar with her.

But even that quiet place is no longer a refuge for her. Ser Noris sends her dreams, using her to disrupt the peace of the Valley. Because she is a weakness in the defenses of the Biserica, she is forced to leave it; because Hern is also a storm center there, disturbing the order Yael-mri works to preserve, the prieti-meien sends them on a quest with two purposes, to remove them from the Valley, to acquire a weapon to help them all in their struggle against Floarin and her forces, against the Nearga Nor.

In the midst of the unnatural heat—sent by Ser Noris to wear them down—Serroi and Hern ride in uneasy partnership on their quest to find the Changer who also calls himself—or itself—Coyote.

Under attack by Ser Noris whenever he can find her—Serroi is protected from nor longsight and nor spells by the tajicho, the crystallized third eye of a Nyok'chui, a lethal giant earthworm—they cross the continent, attacked by minark soldiers after they humiliate a minark lordling, attacked by Sleykynin, chased and nearly killed by Assurtiles for what they did to those Sleykynin, forced onto an eerie plateau where they meet small flying people and great glass dragons and are so affected by the magic there that they walk in each other's bodies, share each other's dreams, where Serroi finally succumbs to the magic that is her nature, the magic she has denied so long.

Given shelter by Hekotoro to the fenekel in Hold Hek, she learns the imperatives of her newly acquired talent for healing while she and Hern reach a tentative peace with each other.

Attacked in Tuku-kul by ambushing Sleykynin, she learns the other side of her healing power, that what heals can also kill. She and Hern quarrel and make peace again.

They cross the Sinadeen to the southern continent, then sail out on the Dar, a great featureless swamp where their only enemies are the leeches and biting bugs. And the boredom. On the far side of the Dar they climb a mountain, meet the Changer, have a confrontation with Ser Noris. Serroi touches Ser Noris's hand and that frightens him so badly he is driven into instant flight and at the same time loses the concentration that has been holding off winter and focusing heat on the Valley and the mijloc. As Serroi and Hern are taken into Changer's Mountain, the weather reverts to normal for the time of year and the first flakes of snow come drifting down on Valley and mijloc.

## HERN HESLIN

Fourth domnor in the Heslin line since Andellate Heslin united the mijloc and established the Biserica.

He is nearly yanked out of his skin and replaced by a demon, is rescued by Serroi, a poison knife, small horde of rats and roaches and his own skill with the sword.

He is a man who likes women (definitely in the plural) who has wasted his abilities because there is no real call to use them, who has been as bored with his life as Ser Noris, who finds he likes to stretch himself to meet challenges, who is possessive even of that which bores him, who learns in the long journey the value of letting go.

## TULI GRADINDAUGHTER

Twin sister of Teras Gradinson, the Gradinheir. Tuli and Teras have been inseparable since birth, but biology and custom are catching up with them. Tuli resents the changes in her body and in her brother; though she has always been the leader, able to best him whenever she wanted, now her brother is inches taller, stronger and faster and he won't listen to her as he used to though she can still talk him into things. In addition to that, the time is coming when she will not be permitted to run the night like a wild thing and will be expected to settle into courtship and marriage.

One night around the middle of autumn the twins climb from their bedroom windows to spy on their older sister Nilis. To their astonishment and horror, they hear her betraying their father's plan to conceal a part of his harvest so his ties and family won't starve, they hear her betraying her blood to the Agli and the Followers of the Flame. After a series of setbacks they get away and ride to warn their father that a noose waits for him in Oras where he is going to try convincing Floarin to abate part of the grain tithe. On the way they come across an ex-meie named Rane who recognizes them and helps rescue their father.

Tesc takes his family—except for Nilis and his youngest son, Dris, who has been named tarom in his place—into the mountains where he joins other outcasts to set up a Haven where they will have shelter and a base from which they can harass the forces of Floarin.

Teras goes off with Hars (an old Sankoise stockman who taught them a lot about hunting and stalking and the habits of beasts) to seek information and do a little sniping at the Guards and the tithe collectors.

Left forlorn and more than a little angry at her brother, Tuli feels more than ever an outsider; she doesn't like ties, especially to the girls; she isn't allowed to wander far from camp and feels that she is going to smother at the constraint; she can't take teasing and is the more teased because of that; she doesn't want to be forced into the female mold she despises; trying to find a replacement for her brother, she plots a night hunt with a newcomer, a boy called Fayd who is a few years older, a neighbor, but he mistakes her interests and forces sex on her, too involved with his own sensations to realize that she is trying to stop him, to fight him off.

Rane comes by Haven to pass on information and gather what news they have for the Biserica and when she is finished there, she takes Tuli away with her; they stop at the Biserica where Tuli learns more about Rane, where a healwoman confirms her worst fears—she is pregnant by Fayd, only two weeks but the woman is sure—and where she makes up her mind that she is neither old enough for motherhood nor temperamentally suited to it so she flushes herself out with a series of herbal drinks, then leaves the Biserica with Rane to continue the ramble about the mijloc, gathering information about the mind-state of the mijlockers and about the strength of Floarin's forces.

## MINOR PIECES (Ser Noris)

LOBORI who thinks she's the instigator of the plot against Hern and who is very surprised by dying at the moment she expects to triumph. FLOARIN who thinks she's running her country and her war and in charge of the nor working for her. The NEARGA NOR who are slaves to the will of Ser Noris.

Assorted Sleykynin, Plaz guards, Sankoise, Majilarni raiders and their shamans, NEKAZ KOLE, Ogogehian general and his mercenary army, the two Aglim of Cymbank, all the Followers of the Flame, assorted demons and demon beasts. NILIS GRADINDAUGHTER and the DECSEL MARDIAN are sliding pieces, first serving Ser Noris, then the Maiden.

## MINOR PIECES (Reiki janja)

CREASTA SHURIN (small brown intelligent teddy bears) COPERIC (general purpose rogue and news source for Yael-mri) and picked members of his troupe. His co-conspiritor, the fisher Intii VANN, the Ajjin TURIYY and her son (shape changers), assorted other fisherfolk, Stenda, fenekelen, tiny fliers, glass dragons large and small, ship masters, outcasts, keepers, all the Meien, YAEL-MRI, HARS, the SHAWAR, BRADDON of Braddon's Inn, ROVEDA GESDA (thief, smuggler, busy entrepreneur of Sel-ma-Carth and news source for the Biserica), assorted small folk dwelling in the cracks and crannies of the mijloc. And the CHANGER'S GIFT: JULIA DUKSTRA, GEORGIA MYERS and his raiders, ANGEL and his bunch, the Council, and the men, women and children with various talents Hern brings through the MIRROR.

Comes the CHANGER'S MOON and the endgame begins that will determine the winner of the World.

# AT THE CUSP THEY CAST LOTS

With the forefinger of his left hand he stirred the dodecahedral dice. His right was a withered claw, gray like dirty chalk, held curled up against his chest between the spring of his ribs. His face was thinned, worn, yet grown stronger since the game had begun. The ruby was gone, that vestige of youthful flamboyance that had dangled, a drop of fire, from the small gold loop piercing his left nostril. He gathered up the dice, tipped them into an ivory cup.

"Your pieces are scattered, janja," he said. "Shall we throw for time?"

She knelt on an ancient hide, the coarse wool of her skirt falling across the rounds of her thighs in stiff folds. Her face had thinned also and that which was mortal and human had grown more tenuous. The Dweller-within showed through the smoky flesh, stern and wild and tenderly terrible, without the sheen of Reike's smiles to temper its extravagance.

"Time does not exist. There is only now."

The corners of his mouth curled up. "Granted, Great One." There was wry laughter in his dark eyes, a touch of mockery in his voice. "I would offer you another *now* to put your pieces on the board." His hand closed tightly about the cup. "You're losing the janja, Indweller. You give me an edge you might not want to concede, not having her touch with detail."

Reiki smoothed the yellowed ivory of her braids. "You're an impudent rascal, my Noris." Under their white brows her brown-green eyes twinkled at him.

He lifted the ivory cup as if he toasted her. "Are you displeased, Janja?"

"You know more than you should, my Noris. Surprising for Soäreh's get."

He shrugged, distaste on his lean face. "I use Soäreh, I don't follow him," he said impatiently. "Shall we throw for time?"

"No. I am permitted a warning, Ser Noris. Consider carefully the consequences of each move. You have the dice. Throw."

The gameboard sat on a granite slab which thrust through shag and soil like a bone through broken flesh and fell away a stride or two behind the man, a thousand feet straight down to a broad valley white and silent under heavy, moonlit snow. The board was a replica in miniature of the world below them, complete to the placement of trees and structures but empty for the moment of moving forms.

He rattled the dice in their ivory cup, cast them on the stone beside the board. The moonlight waking glitters from their facets, emerald and ruby, amethyst and topaz, they tumbled through a staggering dance and landed with four sigils up: The Runner, the Sword, the Sorcerer, the Eye.

"Ah," he breathed. "My army begins its march." He drew his long slim finger along the line of the Highroad, clearing the snow from it and from the land on either side, then he brushed the snow from the fields around Oras. Gravely he contemplated the cleared space. "The order," he said. "Yes." He began arranging on the board tiny figures of men-at-arms, on foot and in the saddle. When he had them set out to his satisfaction, he set half a hundred traxim hovering in the air above them, then added supply wains and their teams of plodding hauhaus, the double-

teamed war wagons piled high with gear and the parts of
siege engines. Last of all he set down tiny black figures,
scattering them about the periphery of the army, norits to
serve as shields and alarums, transmitting what the traxim
saw. He looked over what he'd done, made a few minor
adjustments then spoke a WORD and watched the figures
begin marching south along the Highroad. Smiling with
satisfaction, he scooped up the dice, dumped them in the
cup and handed the lot to Reiki janja. "Your throw."

She grasped the cup, shook it vigorously, sent the dice
skittering over the stone with a practiced flip of her wrist.
"Interesting. Kingfisher, Poet-warrior, Priestess, Magic
Child. The mix as before with a factor added." She touched
the Poet-warrior sigil with a fingertip. "And one change."
She tapped the Priestess.

"There's no center to the mix; it'll never serve against an
army. You don't even have leave to mass your meien
against me." He frowned at the dice, running the fingers
of his good hand over the chalky skin of the crippled other.
"Cede me the mijloc," he said. "And I'll turn the army
from the Biserica."

"The mijloc is not mine to give. Take it if you can, go
elsewhere if you wish. Nothing changes." The Indweller
spoke through a janja gone smoky again. The wildness was
flaring, weighed down a little by a compassion as cold as
the stone they sat on.

"To the end, then," he said.

"To the end." She bent over the board and began setting her figures in place.

# I

# THE JANJA'S PLAYERS MOVE

## KINGFISHER

Hern woke disoriented, coming out of dreams not quite harrowing enough for nightmare. He reached out for Serroi, not wanting to wake her but needing to be sure she hadn't evaporated as had his dream. His hand moved over cold sheets, a dented pillow. He jerked up, looked wildly around, the not-quite-fear of the not-quite-nightmare squeezing his gut.

She was curled up on the padded ledge of the window Coyote had melted through the stone for her comfort, moonlight and starlight soft on the russet hair that had a tarnished pewter sheen in the color-denying light. Relief washed over him, then anger at her for frightening him, then mockery at his dependence on her. He sat watching her, speculating about what it was that drove her night after night to stare out at stars that never saw the mijloc. What was she thinking of? He felt a second flash of anger because he thought he knew, then a painful helplessness because there was nothing he could do to spare her—or himself—that distress. Not so long ago he'd shared dreams with her and learned in deep nonverbal ways the painful convolutions of her relationship with Ser Noris. Love and hate, fear and pleasure—the Noris had branded himself deep in her soul. If he could have managed it, he'd have strangled the creature. Not a man, not in the many senses of that word. Creature.

He got out of the bed and went to her, touched her shoulder, drew his finger down along the side of her face. "Worried?"

She tilted her head back to look up at him. For a moment she said nothing and he thought she wasn't going to answer him. Then she did, with brutal honesty. "No. Thinking, Dom. Thinking that this is the last time we'll be together."

He wrapped his arms about her. Her small hands came up and closed warm over his wrists. "You aren't coming back with us?" He heard no sign in his voice of the effort he'd taken to speak so calmly.

"That's not what I meant," she said. "I meant whole to each other, one to one, with everything, everyone else left outside the circle."

"I see. The last time until this is over."

She said nothing. He felt her stiffen against him, then relax, knew she had no belief in any afterwards even if they both survived. And he knew with flat finality that there was no place for her in his life as long as he continued Domnor of Oras and Cimpia plain. And knew, too, that each passing day made going back to that pomp more distasteful to him—that shuttered, blinded life where no one and nothing was real, where the courtiers all wore masks, faces pasted on top of faces that were no more real than masks. Like peeling the layers off an onion: when you got down to the last, there was nothing there. He looked over her head at the scatter of moons. He had to see his folk and the mijloc clear of this, but that was all he owed them. I'm tired, he thought, they've got enough years out of me. He shifted so he could slide his hands along her shoulders, moving them up her neck to play with her earlobes, back down again, flesh moving on flesh with a burring whisper. "There will be an afterwards for us," he murmured. "If you'll come with me, vixen. The world has another half to it, one neither of us has seen. You heal, I'll heave, and we'll end up as wizened little wanderers telling stories to unbelieving folk of the marvels we have seen, the marvels we have done."

She moved her head across his ribs, sighed. "That feels good."

He dropped a hand to cup her breast, moved his thumb slowly across her nipple, felt it harden. "Can't you see us, me a fat old man with a fringe of mouse-colored hair, feet up on a table—I've forgotten all my manners, you see, gone senile with too much wine, too many years. Where was I, oh yes, feet up on the table, boasting of my sword fights and magic wars fought so long ago that everyone's forgotten them. And you, little dainty creature, bowed by years, smiling at that old man and refraining from reminding him how much more necessary to the winning of those wars you were." He slid his arm under her knees, scooped her up and carried her back to the bed.

Serroi woke with Hern's arm flung across her, his head heavy on her shoulder. The window was letting in rosy light, dawn well into its display. She lay a few minutes, not wanting to disturb him. He had enough to face this day. Coyote was growing increasingly impatient because Hern hadn't yet selected any of the mirror's offerings. Today would be the last—he hadn't said so, but she was sure of that. Today Hern had to find his weapon, the weapon that would someday turn in his hand and destroy him, if what Yael-mri hinted at was true. Or destroy what he was trying to protect. The Changer. Ser Noris feared for her, but she discounted that, not because she thought he'd lied but because his passion was for sameness not change; he wanted things about him clear-edged and immutable. At the peak of his power, any change could only mean loss. She sighed, eased away from Hern. His body was a furnace. Her leg started to itch. She ignored it awhile but the prickles grew rapidly more insistent. Carefully she lifted his arm and laid it along his side. For a moment her hands lingered on his arm, then she slid them up his broad back. She liked touching him, liked the feel of the muscles now lightly blanketed with fat, liked the feel of the bone coming through the muscles. She combed her fingers very gently through his hair, the gray streaks shining in the black. Long. Too long. You ought to let me cut it a little. Clean and soft, it curled over her wrist as if it were a hand holding her.

The itch escalated to unendurable. She sat up, eased the quilts off her and scratched her leg. She sighed with pleasure as the itch subsided, glanced anxiously at Hern, but he was breathing slowly, steadily, still deep asleep. She smiled at him, affection warm in her.

The light was brightening outside with a silence strange to her. All her life she'd seen the dawn come in with birdsong, animal barks and hoots, assorted scrapes and rustles, never with this morning's silence as if what the window showed wasn't really there. Magic mirror. She smiled, remembering the mirror Ser Noris made for her that brought images from everywhere into her tower room anywhere, anything she wanted to see it showed her, tiny images she never was sure were real, even later when she'd seen many of those places and peoples with her own eyes, heard them, smelled them, eaten their food, watched their lives. *I wonder if that is how Ser Noris sees all of us, pieces in a game, sterile sanitary images that have shapes and textures, but no intruding inconvenient smells and noises. Not quite real. No one quite real. No, I'm wrong. I was real for him awhile. Cluttering, demanding, all edges some days, all curves another. Maybe that's why he wants me back—to remind him that he's real too. He wants the touch he remembers, the questions, the tugs that pulled us together, yet reminded each that the other was still other. He doesn't want me as I am now, only the Serroi he lost. And he doesn't even know that the Serroi he wants never quite existed, was a construct out of his clever head.*

She sighed, looked down at Hern and wanted to wrap herself about him so tight he couldn't ever leave her, but she knew far better than he how little possibility for realization there was in those dreams he'd described to her. She smoothed her hand over his shoulder. He muttered a few drowsy sounds of pleasure, but did not wake, though his hand groped toward her, found her thigh and closed over it. *Ah*, she thought, *I won't say any more to you about that. I won't say don't count on me, love, I might not be around.* "I'm a weakness you can't afford, Dom Hern," she whispered.

As if in answer to that his hand tightened on her thigh; he still slept but he held onto her so hard, there'd be bruises in her flesh when he woke. His hands were very strong. Short, broad man who'd never be thin, who was already regaining his comfortable rotundity with rest and Coyote's food. She laid her hand over the one that was bruising her and felt the punishing grip loosen. Deceptive little man, far stronger and fit than he looks. Fast, stubborn, even quicker in mind than he was in body. Tired little fat man, gray hair, guileless face, bland stupid look when he wanted to put it on. She stroked the back of his hand and heard him sigh in his sleep, felt the grip loosen more. A snare and a delusion you are, my love. Mijloc didn't appreciate you when they had you, won't appreciate you when they get you back. She eased the hand off her thigh and set it on the sheet beside him. He didn't wake but grew restless, turned over, his arm crooking across his eyes as if the brightening light bothered him, then he settled again into deep slow breathing, almost a snore. She slipped off the bed, kicked the discarded sleeping shift aside and began the loosening up moves that would prepare her for more strenuous exercising.

# POET-WARRIOR

She thought she was calm, resolute, but she couldn't get the key in the keyhole. Her hand was shaking. Fool, she thought, oh god. She flattened her right hand against the wallboard, braced herself and tried again. The key slid in, turned. "That's one." Two locks to go. She took a deep breath, shook the keys along the ring. The Havingee special was easy enough to find, a burred cylinder, not flat like the others. She got it in, managed the left turn and started the right but for a moment she forgot the obligatory twitch and tried to force the key where it didn't go.

Again she sucked in a breath, let it trickle out, then leaned her forehead against the door's cracking paint, trembling as if someone had pulled the plug on her strength.

"You all right?" A quiet voice behind her, not threatening, but she whirled, heart thudding. "There something I could do?"

The young man from the apartment by the head of the stairs—he'd come down the hall to stand behind her. Only a boy, can't be more than early twenties. He looked tired and worried, some of it about her. She remembered, or thought she did, that his friend worked as a male nurse and had a bad moment wondering if he'd seen the disease in her. But that was nonsense. Even she wouldn't know about it if the photogram hadn't shown lump shadows in her breast, if the probe hadn't pronounced them malignant. She tried a tight smile, shook her head. "I was just remembering. When I was a little girl living on our farm in the house my great-grandfather built, we kept a butterknife by the back door. I learned to slip locks early." She smiled again, more easily. "We locked that door when we went to town and opened it with that knife when we got back. No one'd even seen the key for fifty years. The farm was between a commune and a cult, you see, and no one ever bothered us." She held up her key ring. "Triple locked," she said. "Sometimes it gets me down."

He nodded, seeming tired. "Yeah," he said. "I know. Well, anytime."

She watched him go back to his apartment. He must have followed her up the stairs. She hadn't noticed him, but she wasn't in any state to notice anything that didn't bite her. She twitched the key, finished its turns, dealt with the cheap lock the landlord had provided, pushed the door open and went inside, forgetting the boy before the door was shut behind her.

In the living room she snapped on the TV without thinking, turned to stare at it, startled by the sudden burst of sound, the flicker of shadow pictures across the screen. She reached out to click it off, then changed her mind and only turned the sound down until it was a meaningless burring that filled the emptiness of the room. She kicked off her shoes, walked around the room picking things up, putting them down, finally dumped the mail out of her purse. The power bill she hadn't had the courage to open for three days now. A begging letter from the Altiran society, probably incensed about the PM's newest attack on the parks. She sent them money whenever she could. Money. Her hand shook suddenly. She dropped the rest of the mail. A brown envelope slid from the table to the floor. A story. Rejected. One she thought she'd sold, they kept it six months, asked for and got revisions of several sections. She pressed the heels of her hands against her eyes and fought for control. "Oh, god, where am I going to get the money?"

With a small impatient sound, she took her hands from her eyes and dropped onto the couch to stare blankly at the phantoms cavorting on the TV screen. After a minute she swung her feet up and stretched out on the lumpy cushions.

She wasn't afraid, not the way her doctor thought. Jim wasn't really good at passing on bad news. Cancer. Still a frightening word. Caught early, as he'd caught hers, no big problem. If she had the money for the operation. If she had the money. Jim wanted her in the hospital immediately, the sooner the better. Hospital. She closed her hands into fists and pressed them down on her betraying flesh. Money. She didn't have it and could see no way of getting it.

Her independence, her comfortable solitude, these were hard won and fragile, all dependent on the health of her body. There was never enough money to squeeze out insurance premiums. Never enough money for anything extra. Not for a car, though public transit here was an unfunny joke. (Even if she could afford to buy the car, she couldn't afford the rent on an offstreet lockup, and any car left on the street overnight was stripped or stolen by morning.) Not enough for vacation trips; those she did take were for background on books so she could write them off her taxes. But with all that, she liked her life in her shabby rooms, she needed the solitude. No lovers now, no one taking up her life and energy. And she didn't miss that . . . that intrusion. She smiled. Her dearly unbeloved ex-husband would be shocked out of his shoes by the way she lived, then smugly pleased. He'd been pleased enough when she stopped alimony after only a year. Not that he'd ever paid it on time. She'd gotten sick of having to go see him when the rent came due. She started her first novel and got a job in the city welfare office, wearing and poorly paid, testing her idealism to the full, but she liked most of the other workers and she liked the idea of helping people even when they proved all too fallibly human.

The last time she saw Hrald, she sat across an office table from him and smiled into his handsome face—big blond man with even, white teeth and melting brown eyes that promised gentleness and understanding. They lied, oh how they did lie. Not trying very hard to conceal her contempt for him, she told him she wanted nothing at all from him, not now, not ever again. He was both pleased and irritated, pleased because he grudged her every cent since she was no longer endlessly promoting him to his friends and colleagues, irritated because he enjoyed making her beg for money as she'd had to beg during the marriage. While she was waiting for the papers, she studied him with a detached coolness she hadn't been sure she could achieve, let alone maintain. How young I was when I first met him. Just out of college. There he was, this smiling handsome man on his way up, moving fast through his circumscribed world, expecting and getting the best that life could offer him, taking her to fine restaurants, to opening nights, to places she'd only read about, showing her a superficial good taste that impressed her then; she was too young and inexperienced to recognize how specious it was, a replica in plastic of hand-made elegance. It had taken her five years to learn how empty he was, to understand why he'd chosen to marry her, a girl with no money, no family, no connections, supporting herself on miserable shit jobs, yessir-nosir jobs, playing at writing, too ignorant about life to have anything to say. Control—he could control her and she couldn't threaten him in anything he thought was important.

He was brilliant, so everyone said. Made all the right moves. No lie, he was brilliant. Within his narrow limits. Outside those, though, he was incredibly stupid. For a long time she couldn't believe how stupid he could be. How willfully blind. Will to power. Willed ignorance. They seem inextricably linked as if the one is impossible without the other. His cohorts and fellow string-pullers—couldn't call them friends, they didn't understand the meaning of the word—were all just like him. There were times at the end of the five years when I'd look at them and see them as alien creatures. Not human at all. I was certainly out of place in that herd. Vanity, Julia. She smiled, shook her head. Vanity will get you in the end.

She stared at the ceiling. Fifteen years since she'd thought much about him. Since she'd had to think about him. Recently, though, he'd been on TV a lot, pontificating about something on the news or on some forum or other. He was into politics now, cautiously, not running yet but accumulating experience in appointive positions and building up a credit line of favors and debts he could call in when he needed them. Rumor said he was due to announce any day now that he was a candidate for Domain Pacifica's state minister, backed by the Guardians of Liberty and Morality. Book-burner types. She'd gotten some mean letters from GLAM, letters verging on the actionable with their denunciations and accusations of treason and subversion.

She thought about embarrassing Hrald into paying for her operation. A kind of blackmail, threatening to complain to the cameras if he didn't come through. The fastest way to get money. It would take time to get through the endless paperwork of the bureaucracy if she applied for emergency aid and she had little enough time right now. He had money in fistfuls and he'd get a lot of pleasure out of making her squirm. His ex-wife, the critically acclaimed, prize-winning author (minor critics and a sort-of prize, but what the hell). Authoress, he'd call her, having that kind of mind. He could get reams of publicity out of his noble generosity—if he didn't shy off because her books were loudly condemned by some of his most valued supporters. She thought of it, started working out the snags, but she didn't like the price in self-respect she'd have to pay. I've heard people say they'd rather die than do something. Never believed it, always thought it was exaggerated or just nonsense. Not anymore. I'd really rather die than ask him for money. She rubbed her eyes, sat up, running her hands through short thick hair rapidly going gray.

No use sitting here moaning, she thought. She looked about the room. Not much use in anything. She glanced at the TV screen. What the hell? Gun battle? Police and anonymous shadows trading shots. She thought about turning up the sound, but didn't bother. No point in listening to the newsman's hysterical chatter. They were all hysterical these days, not one of them touching on the root causes of much of this unrest. The rich getting richer, the poor getting poorer and more desperate. When you've got nothing to lose but your life, what's that life worth anyway? In recent months she'd thought about leaving the country, but inertia and a lingering hope that this too would pass away had kept her where she was. Hope and the book she was finishing. It exhausted her and was probably a useless expenditure of her energy. There was still a steady market for her books, loyal readers, bless their gentle hearts, but her editor had begun warning her the House was going to make major changes in anything she sent them, even in the books already published, so they could keep them on the shelves. "You're being burned all over the country," he said. "The money men are getting nervous."

She watched the battle run to its predictable end (blood, bodies, clouds of teargas, smoky fires), and thought about her life. Most people would consider it bleak beyond enduring but it suited her. A half-dozen good friends (ex-lovers, ex-colleagues, ex-clients that she called now and then, whenever she felt the need to talk), who called her when they had something to say, had dinner with her now and then. Sometimes they met for a night of drinking and talking and conjuring terrible fates for all their enemies. Those friends would help all they could. If she asked. But she wouldn't ask. They were as poor as she was and had families or other responsibilities. And there were a few acquaintances she exchanged smiles with. And a handful of men not more than acquaintances now, left over from the time just after the divorce when she was running through lovers like sticks of gum, frightened of being alone. They sent flowers on her birthday and cards at the new-year Turn-fete, invited her to parties now and then, slept with her if they happened to meet her and both were in the mood.

And there was Simon who was something between an acquaintance and a friend, a historian she'd consulted about details she needed for her third book. He'd got her a temporary second job as lecturer and writer-in-residence at Loomis where he was tenured professor and one of the better teachers. He'd asked her to marry him one night, grown reckless with passion, liquor and loneliness, but neither of them really wanted that kind of entanglement. He'd groused a bit when she turned him down, and for over a year refused to admit the relief he felt, his vanity singed until she managed to convince him she simply didn't want to live with anyone, it wasn't just him she was refusing.

That was the truth. It pleased her to shut the door on the world. And as the years passed, she grew increasingly more reluctant to let anyone past that door. I'm getting strange, she thought. She grinned at the grimacing face of the commentator mouthing soundless words at her from the screen. Good for me. Being alone was sometimes a hassle—when she had to find someone to witness a signature or serve as a credit reference or share a quiet dinner to celebrate a royalty check (few good restaurants these days would serve single women). But on the whole she lived her solitary life with a quiet relish.

A life that was shattering around her now. She contemplated the ruin of fifteen years' hard slogging labor with a calm that was partly exhaustion and partly despair.

# THE PRIESTESS

Nilis sat in the littered room at the tower's top, watching moonlight drop like smoke through the breaking clouds. The earth was covered with snow, new snow that caught the vagrant light and glowed it back at the clouds. Cold wind came through the unglazed arches, coiled about her, sucking at her body's heat. She pulled the quilt tighter about her shoulders, patted her heavy sleeping shift down over her feet and legs, tucked the quilt about them.

For the first time since she'd joined the Followers she was disobeying one of the Agli's directions, disobeying deliberately. A woman at night was to be in her bed; only an urgent call of nature excused her leaving it. Nilis smiled, something she'd done so little of late her face seemed to crack. Being here *is* a call of nature, she thought. And urgent.

A tenday ago the sun changed and the snow began to fall. About that time she gave up trying to scourge herself into one-time fervor and admitted to herself how much she missed her family, even Tuli who was about as sweet as an unripe chays. Dris didn't fill that emptiness in her. She sighed, dabbed her nose with the edge of the quilt. Dris was a proper little Follower. Treated her like a chattel, ordered her about, tattled on her to the Agli, showed her no affection. She'd ignored that aspect of the Soäreh credo; at least, had never applied it to herself. The ties, yes, but she was torma now, didn't that mean anything? Certainly, Dris was Tarom, but that shouldn't mean she was nothing. He was only six. She whispered the Soäreh chant: *to woman is appointed house and household/ woman is given to man for his comfort and his use/ she bears his children and ministers unto him/ she is cherished and protected by his strength/ she is guided by his wisdom/ blessed be Soäreh who makes woman teacher and tender and tie.* She'd learned the words but hadn't bothered to listen to what she learned. *Given to man for his use.* She shivered.

She'd always been jealous of the younger ones: Sanani, Tuli, Teras, even little Dris who could be a real brat. They all seemed to share a careless charm, a joy in life that brought warmth and acceptance from everyone around them, no matter how thoughtless they were. Life was easy for them in ways that were utterly unfair. Easier even from conception. Her mother had had a difficult time with her, she'd heard the tie-women talking about it, several of the older tie-girls made sure she knew just how much trouble she'd given everyone. She'd been a sickly, whining baby, a shy withdrawn child, over-sensitive to slights the others either didn't notice or laughed off, with a grudging temperament and a smoldering rage she could only be rid of by playing tricks she knew were mean and sly on whoever roused that anger. She hated this side of her nature and fought against it with all her strength—which was never strength enough. And no one helped. Her mother didn't like her. Annic was kind and attentive, but that was out of duty, not love. Nilis felt the difference cruelly when the other children were about. Sanani was shy and quiet too, but she was good with people, she charmed them as quickly and perhaps more effectively than Tuli did with her laughing exuberance. Year after year she'd watched the difference in the way people reacted to her. She was quiet and polite, eager to please, but so clumsy and often mistaken in her eagerness that she put people off.

She stared at the opaline shift of the moonlight, sick and cold. Try and try. Fight off resentment and anger and humiliation and loneliness. And nothing helped, no one helped, nothing changed the isolation.

Soäreh caught her on a double hook, offering her the closeness she'd yearned for all her life and a chance to pay off old scores—though she'd blinded herself to the second enticement. The old fault in new disguise. The tiluns left her exalted, warmed, enfolded in the lives of the others there as the Maiden fetes had not, had only made her feel all the more left out. She was the kind deed, brought into the celebration by a generosity that was genuine and not at all mocking, but it was a generosity that she bitterly resented. She burned at the careless kindness of young men who swung her now and then into the dance but never into the laughing mischievous bands of pranksters winding through the crowds. She convinced herself she despised such lawlessness even as she gazed wistfully after them.

As the years passed and the disappointments piled up, she grew mean and hard and resentful, renouncing the fruitless struggle to fight that wretched spiteful side of herself. But she hated what she'd become.

Then Soäreh and then Floarin's edict and then her rivals were swept away. Sanani and Tuli and Teras, they were swept away. Father and mother swept away too. She regretted that but would not let herself grieve for them, told herself it was their fault not hers. At first she watched the changes at the tar with triumph and satisfaction. There was calm and order within the House. Tie-women were grave and quiet and submissive; there were no more resentful glances, mocking titters, no more flirting with tie-men and wandering day laborers. No more groups that closed against her..

As the months passed, she gradually realized that she was still outside of everything. The groups never closed against her but never really incorporated her. She had no friends. It was all fear. It took a while for her to acknowledge this but she was neither stupid nor blind and certainly not insensitive to atmosphere. She could fool herself only so long. Then the rebels turned the Agli into a dangling clown doll and another was sent to replace him. The new Agli merely tolerated her and avoided her when he could. The tilun became a kind of agony for her. She no longer went to the confession fire, and because she did not she soon realized that the exaltation was born from drugged incense and the Agli's meddling. She saw in the faces around her all that she despised in herself and felt a growing contempt for them. And for herself.

There was no laughter left in Cymbank or at Gradintar. The fist of Floarin and the Agli closed so tightly about her she choked.

She stared at the shifting shadows and pearly light and saw the clouds being stripped from the face of Nijilic TheDom as a paradigm of the way illusion had been stripped from her. It was hard, very hard, to admit to herself she could no longer submit to Soäreh. It meant she could no longer deny her responsibility in the betrayal and outlawing of her family. During the last passage she'd flinched repeatedly from this admission. She looked out at the naked face of TheDom and let the last of her excuses blow away like the winds had blown away the clouds.

This morning (the Agli standing beside him, hand on his shoulder) Dris had called the tie-men into the convocation Hall. She had watched from the shadows high up the stairs, forbidden to be present, forbidden to speak. Watched as Dris read names of tie-men from the list and told them they were being sent to Oras to fight in Floarin's army. Fully half the men. Rations would be continued to their families as long as they were obedient and fought well for the manchild in the cradle in Oras. They were told to rejoice in their calling as their absence would serve their families as well as Soäreh's son-on-earth, Floarin's child, since they would no longer be eating at Gradintar's tables, and those left behind would be less apt to starve. Nilis watched the still faces of the chosen, the still faces of the not-yet-chosen. This was the second levy on the already culled tie-men. No one knew if or how soon another levy would come.

When the Hall was empty, both sets of men filing out without having uttered a single word, the Agli turned to Dris, "Halve the rations for the women and children of the chosen," he said. "Order the torma to see that none of the other families give from their tables. The men must be kept strong to serve Soäreh should he require that service."

Hearing this, she knew what was going to be required of her. Prying into larders, visiting the tie-houses to make sure there were no extras at table, more . . . and if she refused, she'd be turned out herself. She could go into the mountains after the outcasts, or be forced into the House of Repentance. Either place was death for her now; in spite of everything she did not want to die. The load of guilt she carried frightened her. There had to be some way she could redeem herself. Had to be.

Something moved in the corner not far from her. She

heard the rustle of clothing, the soft scrape of a sandal against the stone. She swallowed hard but didn't move.

An old woman walked around her and groaned as she sat down facing Nilis. She leaned forward, held out a broad strong hand. Nilis reached out, hesitantly, not sure why she did so. The old woman's hand closed about hers. Warmth flowed into Nilis, a love greater than any she'd known to yearn for. She smiled and wept as she smiled. She laughed and the old woman laughed with her. They sat as they were a timeless time. The Jewels rose, crossed the open arch, vanished. Somewhere a hunting kanka vented a portion of its float gas in a hungry wail. Finally Nilis spoke. "What must I do?"

"Cleanse the Maiden Shrine."

Nilis licked dry lips. "That sounds such a little thing. Can't I do more?"

The old woman said nothing; her large lustrous eyes were warm and encouraging, but gave Nilis no more help than that.

Nilis fidgeted. Then she bowed her head. "Forgive me."

"Forgive yourself."

"I can't." The words were a broken whisper. Nilis stared at hands twisting nervously.

"Look within."

"I can't, I can't bear what I see."

"Learn to bear it. You are no more perfect or imperfect than any other. How can you bless them for being if you can't bless your being?" The quiet voice became insistent. "Daughter, you asked for something harder but you did not know what you were asking. Cleanse the shrine. Make a sign for the people. It won't be easy and it won't come quickly; it may take the whole of your life. But a sign can be far stronger than many swords." The old woman looked gravely at her. "You'll be cold and hungry, you'll feel the old rancors and invent new ones, you'll doubt yourself, the Maiden, the worth of what you're doing. Some folk from both sides of the present war will spit on you, will never forgive you for what they call your treachery, will remind you day on day on day of what you have done. Know that before you take up what we lay on you."

"I know." She calmed her fingers, flattened them on her thighs. "Nothing changes, it will be as it was before."

"There will be compensations. But you'll have to be very patient."

"You mean me for Shrine Keeper."

"Yes. The first of the new Keepers." The old woman smiled. And *changed*. Suddenly standing, she was a wand-slim maiden, young and fresh and smelling of herbs and flowers, pale hair floating gossamer light about a face of inhuman majesty and beauty, translucent as if it had been sculpted from the night air. That air thrummed about her, shimmered with the power radiating from her. At first her eyes were the same, smiling, compassionate, a little sad, then they shone with a stern, demanding light. Then she faded, melting into the night, leaving behind the delicate odors of spring blooms and fresh herbs.

Stiff with cold, Nilis went slowly down the stairs and into the dark empty halls of the House. She went to the chests in her mother's room, found the old white robe she remembered. She stripped off her sleeping shift, pulled the robe over her head. It hung on her. She found a length of cord and tied it about her waist, pulled the robe up so it bloused over the cord and swung clear of the floor.

She went back to her room, walking quickly, the floors were icy, drafts curled about her booted ankles and crawled up her legs. She sat on her bed and took off her fur-lined boots, frowning down at them as she tried to remember what the Keepers of the past wore on their feet. With a sigh she stood, put the boots away and got out her summer sandals. She strapped them on, got her fur-lined cloak from the peg behind the door, held it up, smoothed her hand over the soft warm fur. Forgive yourself, she thought, smiled, and tossed it onto the quilts. Sacrifice was one thing, stupidity another. She laughed suddenly, not caring whether she woke anyone or brought them to find out what was going on. Joy bubbled in a glimmering golden fountain from her heels to her head, burst from her in little chuckles. She stood with her head thrown back, her arms thrown out as if she would embrace the world. She wanted to shout, to dance, to sing. She loved everything that was and would be and had been, even the aglis. All and all and all.

When the excess of joy boiled out of her, she went back to collecting things she'd need at the Shrine. She found a worn leather satchel with a broken strap that Tuli, for some reason, had rescued from a pile of discards then forgotten. With quick neat stitches she repaired the shoulder strap, then laid the bag on the bed and began packing it with what she had collected, from her comb to a pack of needles and thread. Then she rolled a pair of quilts into a tight firm cylinder about some changes of underthings and an old pair of knitted slippers, tied it together with bits of cord and made a long loop from end to end so she could carry it as she did the satchel and leave her hands free. Then she took the ties from the braids that skinned her fine brown hair back from her face, ran her fingers through it with a sigh of relief and pleasure.

The fur cloak bunched under her arm, the satchel and quilt bundle slung from her shoulder, her hair flowing loose, she went through the silent sleeping House and down into the kitchen.

Ignoring the startled disapproving look from the old woman Tuli and Teras called Auntee Cook, she took a fresh-baked loaf of bread from the rack where it was cooling, put it in the satchel, went into the pantry, took a round of cheese from the shelves that seemed to her to be emptying far too fast, added a cured posser haunch, smiled, fingered a crock of the chorem jam she liked above all the others. *Forgive yourself*, she told herself, *take pleasure in the good things of the earth so you won't grudge them to others*. The words came into her head as if someone whispered them to her. She tucked the jam in beside the other things, went back into the kitchen. She found a canister of cha leaves, added them to her hoard. The leather was sagging and creaking under the weight. She began to worry a little about her stitching, hoping it would hold. She collected a mug and a plate, other supplies she thought she might need, packed these into a bucket with a large pumice stone and some rags. The sides of the satchel bulged so that she could not buckle down the flap, but it closed enough to keep snow out if the sky clouded over again and a new storm started. She looked around the kitchen, her tongue caught between her teeth, but there was nothing she could see that would be worth the difficulty in hauling it with her.

Auntee Cook watched all this, dazed. As Nilis started for the door to the outside, she gulped and burst into rapid speech, "Torma, it's against the rules, you know it is, I'm just a poor old tie-woman, I can't go against you, but how can I go against tarom Dris or the Agli, Soäreh grant him long life? You know it's against the rules, what can I tell him, them, anyone? What can I say? What can I do? Tell me. What? You tell me, you. . . ."

Nilis burst out laughing, a joyous sound that stopped the old woman in mid-sentence and made her eyes bulge. Still chuckling, Nilis kissed the withered cheek, patted the rounded shoulder. "Just tell them what happened," she said. "Don't worry, little Auntee, you couldn't help it, it's not your business to tell me what to do." Humming an old tune, she danced down the steps and plunged into the drifts outside, plowing toward the barns and the macain sleeping in the stalls.

# THE MAGIC CHILD

The snow fell, flake by flake, drifting softly onto withered half-burnt foliage, a strangely unemphatic break from the unnatural heat. It didn't even seem cold, though the macain they rode were beginning to complain; they had to wade through those feathery nothings that were suddenly more clotted and obdurate than frozen mush. Tuli brushed snow off her face, glanced at Rane and was startled to see the ex-meie only as a fuzzy shadow; she was barely visible through the thickening curtain of falling snow. There was no wind and sound continued to be sharp and clear, she could hear the crunch of her macai's pads, his disgusted snorting, the creak of the saddle, the jingle of the chains and other metal bits. She wiggled her fingers. They were starting to get cold. "Rane," she called. "Don't you think we should camp?"

"No." The ex-meie's voice sounded close, almost in Tuli's ear. "Not a good idea. Lower we go, more likely the wind is to pick up. We need cold-weather gear. I have to admit, I didn't expect so much so soon."

Tuli rode in silence for a while. The snowfall thickened yet more, blotting out everything around her, the trees and the rutted road and Rane. According to the feel of the saddle against her thighs and buttocks they were still going downhill, but that seemed a chancy thing to rely on for guidance. "Rane."

"What?"

"We still on the road?"

"Yes."

"How can you tell?"

"You running your nose into any trees? Trust your mount, he'll keep you to the road." Her voice crackled with impatience. "Stop fussing, just ride."

Tuli closed her lips tight over the words crowding on her tongue. When Rane got like that, there was no use talking to her. She shook the snow off her head, brushed at her shoulders and thighs; the stuff was starting to pile up everywhere it could get a hold.

The snow fell in copious silence, there was still no wind, and the ride went on, down and down and down, getting colder the lower they went. The macain kept up their moans and whiny roars, voicing their distaste for the footing and the weather and their riders. The beasts were tired and hungry like their riders and like their riders they hadn't had time to change for the change in the season. The prolonged unnatural heat conjured by the Nearga-Nor had kept them unnaturally long in their summer hides and this sudden drop in temperature was triggering the winter-change far too quickly, putting strain on their tempers and their strength. Her macai began jerking his head about, trying to get his teeth in her leg, his hoots turning angry when the bridle hurt his mouth as she pulled his head back around. Once, he started to kneel, but she coaxed him up and urged him on though she wasn't sure Rane was right about going on. Maybe it would be better to find a sheltered spot, get a fire going and wait out the storm. But that depended on how long the storm was going to hang about; some stopped in one day, some went on for a tenday. The way things were messed up, there was no telling about this one. Snow crawled down her neck and into her boots. It spilled onto her shoulders and down the front of her shirt, got into the pockets and cuffs of her thin jacket. Her body heat half-melted it, it froze again as soon as more snow piled on. Her shoulders and back, her thighs and arms were all damp, shirt, jacket, trousers and hair were sodden and clinging clammily to her. Her feet were growing numb, her hands burned from the chill, and still there wasn't much wind, just enough to make the snow slant a bit. She pulled her jacket cuffs down over her hands, crooking her arms inside the sleeves to give her some extra length; that helped a little, shut out some of the freezing wet. She hunched her shoulders and tried to trust Rane, though it was seeming more and more stupid to ride away from the Biserica in only their summer clothes when they knew the weather was going to break. She drew her mouth down. Be fair, she thought. I didn't think of it either; I didn't open my mouth and say go back. Anyway, who'd have thought the snow would come so fast once the sun was right?

The road flattened out and the snow grew thicker, wetter. The wind was suddenly blowing into their faces with stinging force. The quiet vanished and the cold got worse, fast. Tuli started shivering so hard she thought she was going to shake herself right out of the saddle. Rane left her side and rode in front, blocking the worst of the wind's force.

After another eternity of straining to follow the seen-unseen shadow in front of her, Tuli heard the rush of running water, then they were on a low humped bridge. Creeksajin, she thought. It can't be too much farther before we stop.

Tuli's macai bumped his nose into the haunches of the beast Rane rode, stopped. Rane dismounted and came to stand at Tuli's knee. "There's a turn we have to make just ahead." She was shouting but Tuli had to bend down and listen hard to catch the words the wind was tossing and shredding. "I'm going to walk awhile, feel my way, but I could miss it in this mess. Keep your eyes open for a hedgerow. You see one on your right, we've gone past the turn and will have to come back. You hear?"

Tuli shouted her acknowledgment, felt a pat on the thigh, then the lanky figure faded into the whirling snow.

And came back a moment later with the end of a rope. "Tie this someplace," Rane shouted. "Keep us together, this will." She shoved the rope at Tuli. Her fingers were clumsy and as cold as Tuli's.

They went on, it seemed forever, the wind battering them, the cold numbing them, but this eased a little when Rane found the mouth of the lane and they turned into the meager protection of the lines of trees that grew thickly on both sides of the rutted track.

A long time later Rane stopped again. As Tuli's mount stomped restlessly about, she caught glimpses of stone pillars and a wooden gate.

Moving again—along a curving entranceway similar to the one at Gradintar. Tuli felt a surge of homesickness. Tears froze on her eyelashes as she blinked.

Stopped again. Behind a high flat surface that kept the wind off. Rane leaned to her, pinched her arm. "Wait here. You hear me?"

Tuli nodded, croaked, "I hear."

Time passed. An eternity of black and cold. Hoots of misery from her macai. Nothing to measure the moments against, just darkness and wind noise and slanting snow.

Then someone was beside her. Rane. Someone beside Rane, a long thin shadow.

And the beast under her was moving, Rane's macai moving beside her.

And there was a grating sound—not too loud but she could hear it over the roar of the wind.

And they were out of the wind, going down a long slant into darkness—but the snow was gone and the air was warmer. As she woke out of the numbness, she began to shiver without letup.

The darkness lightened as they turned one way.

Lightened more as they turned another.

They stopped.

A stable of sorts, straw on the floor, water and grain, a fire off in the distance filling a long narrow room with warmth and a cheerful crackling.

She felt the warmth but she couldn't stop shivering.

Hands pulled at her.

She was standing rubber-kneed on the stone floor, hands holding her.

A MAN'S VOICE:   Hot cha, I think.

RANE:   Any chance of a hot bath?

MAN:   Depends on how many people do you want to alert you're here?

RANE:   No one would be best. Other than you, Hal. I suspect everyone now, old friend, everyone I don't know as well as I know you.

MAN:   (chuckling) Eh-Rane, you sure you know me well enough?

RANE:   Fool.

All the while they talked they were helping Tuli stumble closer to the fire. They eased her down on a pile of old quilts and cushions and Rane knelt beside her, rubbing her frozen hands.

RANE:   Is it too much to ask for the cha you offered?

MAN:   Hold your barbs, scorpion. Have it here in a breath and a half.

Heat. Hands stripped soggy clothes off her. Hands rubbed a coarse towel hard over her. She protested. It hurt. Rane laughed, dropped the towel over her head. "Do it yourself then, Moth."

They were at one end of a windowless room with roughly dressed stone walls. The loudest noise was the crackling of the fire; Tuli caught not the slightest hint of the storm outside. At the other end of the long room one of the macain had his nose dipped into a trough, sucking up water. The other was munching at a heap of corn. Both made low cooing sounds full of contentment.

A contentment Tuli shared. When her short hair was as dry as she could get it, she dropped the towel and pulled the quilt up over her shoulders. She stretched out in front of the fire on the pile of cushions, soaking up the heat until she wanted to purr.

Later. Dressed in boy's clothing, long in the leg and tight about the buttocks, she sipped at the steaming spiced cha and struggled to keep her eyes open as Rane talked with the man she called Hal.

RANE:  How are the Followers taking this weather change? Asking questions of the Agli? Blaming us? Angry? Confused? What?

HAL:  Hard to say. Most of them are dupes. Agli doesn't tell them anything, keeps them happy with a tilun now and then and promises of a better life. We have to sit through interminable sermons on the virtues of submission and the evils of pride. Soäreh's will. I wonder how many times I've heard that over the past few days. I want to spit in their faces. Very disconcerting for a placid soul like myself. That's about all I've got for you, gossip from the rats in my own walls. I've stayed away from Sadnaji since the heat broke. Followers there've turned nasty, bite off any head that pokes out. I'm exceedingly fond of my head.

RANE:  We came through Sadnaji a few days ago. Looked dead.

HAL:  Might as well be. None of the fête-days being kept, no one laughing. We've all forgotten how to laugh.

RANE:  Braddon's Inn was shut down, torch out. I never

thought they'd go that far. What happened? Where were all his friends? Is he all right?

HAL: Friends. (He shakes his head.) Those of us nearby keep our mouths shut and don't look him in the eye. He's alive, doing well as could be expected. (He goes silent a moment, the lines suddenly deeper in his long ugly face, a gentle face, mournful as a droop-eared chinihound.) His son's in the mountains somewhere, I expect you've got a better idea about that than I do. Somewhere's close as I can get (a sigh). Shut Braddon down, put him in the House of Repentance. For a while it looked like the Agli was going to burn him out, but he backed off, Sadnaji was tinder dry. The little meie, she managed to burn a good bit of hedge (sigh). Had to spend a tenday setting posts and planting hedge sets. Which will probably freeze if this keeps up.

RANE: Little meie? What happened?

HAL: It was just after the sky went bad. The little meie showed up at Braddon's, you know who I mean, Serroi, a man with her. Braddon says he tried to hold her there but she got suspicious and tunked him on the head. He won't say else to anyone. He says he didn't know the man with her, never saw him before. Whispers say it was Hern (shrug). She tangled with a norit staying there, turned the attack back on him somehow, she and the man both got away, traded their worked-out macain for a fresh pair, took the norit's mounts which steamed him some to hear tell. He went after them, wouldn't wait for anyone, anything. Agli rounded him up a mob, took three guards from the Decsel in the Center, sent them all after her. What happened to the norit, Maiden knows, but there's a man-sized charred spot in my pasture grass. Guards came chasing her through the gap in my poor abused hedge. First one through was an airhead carrying a torch. Soon's he was on the grass his macai went crazy, threw him and tromped on him. He let go the damn torch and it landed in my hedge. Agli's mob, they had to stop being a mob and fight the fire or Sadnaji could have gone up too. The two guards left followed the meie and her friend, got back a couple days later, hungry and tired, scratched up and scratching—idiots didn't know enough to stay away from ripe puff-balls—feeling mad and mean. Lost the meie in the foothills past the ford.

RANE: Yael-mri thinks she's the one turned the weather for us (laugh). For such a little thing, her efforts they do multiply. I'd like to be around when she tells the tale of the past few months. Well, enough of that. To business. Guards. How many here now?

HAL: Three decsettin. One in town, the others quartered on the tars. I've got one here, Decsel sleeping in the house, his men in the tie-village. And a resident norit (he holds up a hand). No worry. He's a smoke eater who hates the cold. I looked in on him an hour ago. Room stinks of the weed and he's lost in his private heaven.

RANE: Sleykynin?

HAL: They've been trickling into the mijloc by twos and threes, see some of them almost every day. A few large bands of young ones, just hatched from their houses (smile). Was a break in the trickle shortly after the little meie went through here. Coincidence?

RANE: (laughing) I wouldn't bet on it. Do they stay around Sadnaji or move on?

HAL: Three or four are quartered on the Agli, been there for a while. Those coming through lately keep on without stopping. Going north.

RANE: Anything else?

HAL: Got a vague report of Kapperim busy in the hills east of Sankoy. Before the snow started. I went on a ride to check my hedges, make the circuit like a good tarom.

RANE: Hal! You?

HAL: Uh-huh, Anders was trying to convert me, following me around preaching at me. Eh-Rane, he's such a block. You suppose Marilli played me false? (he grins)

No, probably not. She was too proud a woman to tarnish her perfection that way. I suppose he's a throwback to Grandfather Lammah who had just two ideas in his head. If it was game, chase and kill it, if it was female . . . (he catches Tuli watching and does not finish the sentence). Where was I? Ah. Anders. Had to get away from him before I strangled him. Not a thing you want to do to your son and heir. So I rode the hedges. Smuggled a book out with me, *Dancer's Rise* writ by Mad Shar the poet, you should know it, Biserica's got a copy, that and a skin of a nice little wine. Point of all this—I was sitting in the shade near the east end of the tar. Half-asleep. Maybe a little drunk. A pair of shurin came out of the shadows and squatted beside me. Said to pass this on: Army massing in Sankoy, waiting to join the one Floarin's bringing down from Oras. And the Kapperim tribes are getting thick in the hills, might be going to start raiding the outcast Havens, might be joining up with Floarin too, when the time comes. That was a tenday ago. I was thinking maybe I'd have to carry the news myself if somebody didn't come by. Not a good idea sending message fliers, too many traxim about.

RANE: So Yael-mri said. Tuli and I, we're going looking the long way round Cimpia Plain, see what's happening firsthand.

HAL: You're taking the child?

RANE: Peace, Hal. Tuli stopped being a child awhile ago. (she stares at the fire, runs her hands through hair like short sun-bleached straw). There are no noncombatants in this war, my philosopher friend.

HAL: Why is this happening? (He looks from Rane to Tuli, back at Rane, then stares into the fire as she does). What have we done to bring this death and desolation of the spirit?

RANE: (Smiling at him, reaching over to put her hand on his.) Ah, my friend, I have missed this, sitting with you in front of a fire and solving the problems of the world.

Seriously, why does it have anything to do with us?
Perhaps it's five hundred years of stagnation. All things
die sometime, now it's our time. From our death something new will be born.

HAL:    The Maiden? Rane. (Shakes his head.)

RANE:    We dance at the Maidenfetes, but when they're
done the Keeper dowses the festfire. We're tired, happy,
flown on wine and hard cider, ready to find our beds, so
we forget what the dowsing means. Eh-Hal, all that makes
lovely symbols for scholars to play with while the rest of
us mundane souls go our ways looking for what comfort
we can find in life. I've been thinking for several years
now that the mijloc was ripe for trouble. Forget about
symbols. Think about this. Too many ties for the land to
support. Too many tar-sons and tar-daughters. Oldest son
gets the tar, but what do his brothers do? Hang around,
get drunk, make trouble with the ties, the other taroms, do
some hunting. If he's got any intelligence and ambition,
then he's got a chance. Go into the Guards, get an ap-
pointment as a court scholar, get himself apprenticed to a
merchant if he's got that kind of interest and ability. Some
just drift away, losing themselves in the world outside the
mijloc. You didn't have to worry about that, Hal, only one
living son and two daughters, one married, one with us at
the Biserica. But what about your grandsons and grand-
daughters? How many children does Anders already have?
His wife is young and healthy. How many more children
will she have? How will he provide for them? If he's lucky
his extra sons will find their own ways, Guards, merchants, scholars, artisans, even maybe a player in the
bunch. What about his daughters? Some will marry. The
others? Let me tell you, the valley is bursting with girls.
We've been taking care of excess daughters for generations
but there's a limit to the numbers we can support. There
are other limits. Some girls just aren't happy with us.
Many of the girls that come to us don't stay more than a
few years. Some go home, find husbands, or work for
their keep in the homes of their married sisters. Some drift
into the cities; the best of them find work, the others walk

the streets. Think about it, Hal. All the discarded children. Thieves, vagabonds, drunks, bullies, prostitutes, landless laborers, drifters of all kinds, a drain on the resources of the mijloc, a constant source of discontent. Think about the bad harvests this year and last, the Gather and Scatter storms. People getting hungrier and hungrier, watching the taroms and the rich merchants and resenting them, the taroms and merchants growing frightened, hiring bravos to protect them. The Heslin peace falling apart. Well, all that's irrelevant now, Hal. The mijloc is going to be chewed up so thoroughly there'll be no going back to the old ways. Change. There's no stopping it and no knowing what direction it will take.

HAL(sighing): And no room in it for peaceful souls like me. Back to the bad old days before Andellate Heslin knocked the belligerence out of the warlords. Every man's hand raised against his neighbor and the landless left to starve. Eh-Rane, if the Nor do me in, I'd almost thank them.

RANE: Back to business, old philosopher. Practical things have their charm. How are the ordinary folk feeling? Not the converted, the others.

HAL: All this happened so fast, most folk were stunned; it came on them boom-boom, they didn't have time to react or work themselves up to resisting. They're beginning to stir now, just need a leader. With Anders putting on the black so fast, it took a while before the ties would talk to me, but I've picked up a few things. Example: Our folk grumbled when the Gorduufest was cancelled, then they got together and made a little Gorduufest out in the orchard. I was rather afraid I'd scare them off, but I joined them anyway with a jug of hard cider to liven the night for us. Another example: Some of the tie-wives are starting to seethe at the way they're being treated. They work damn hard. Used to be they had a say in what happened to their families. The Agli and his more rabid Followers, they resent and fear women for tempting them from what they see as higher things, and the women are beginning to resent back hard. (He chuckles, then shakes his head.) Though there's little they can do about it. If they open their mouths to protest even the most outrageous nonsense, even if it's to protect their children, they're hauled off to the House of Repentance to be schooled in submission. Repeat the offense and they're publicly flogged. (His brows come together, he stares down at his hands, sighs.) There are a lot of floggings these days, my friend. Fools. The Followers, I mean. They don't see that they're not beating sin out but rebellion in. What else? Ah. Yes. Folk are angry about the defiling of the Maiden Shrines and the treatment of the Keepers. The Keeper in Sadnaji was quite old, she taught most of us our letters and the chants, delivered a good many of the babies the past fifty years. She disappeared after the Guards led her out of the Shrine and took her to the House of Repentance. One rumor is the Agli had her whipped to death. Other rumors say worse. It doesn't sit well in the bellies of our folk, even some of the Followers. Um. Floarin's levies are making trouble for her; she's taken half the men off the tars to fight in that army of hers. A lot of the men don't want to go, but what can they do? The tithing is another thing. She's starting to dip into the seed grain. Lot of folk going to starve that shouldn't need to.

RANE: Any resistance organized?

HAL: Getting there. Tesc Gradin has sent some young ties down from the mountains to sound things out, his son too, good lad from what I've heard. There was some resentment of his attacks on the tithe wagons, but he's defused this by sending young Teras Gradin around with some of the grain he took and promising more. Rumor says he's defied the more conservative outcast taroms and brought ties into the governing council of that Haven. When they heard that, my ties got a fire under their skins. There's a lot of talk about after the war, how things are going to be different. I only get snippets of that, they won't talk much around me, well, can you blame them? And there's Hern. (The words are a question, there is a hint of a twinkle in Hal's faded brown eyes.) A clever man, they say. There's almost as much talk about Hern as there is about Tesc. Though I might just be hearing more of that. There's a large reservoir of good will for the Heslins. I've heard men say he's a lazy layabout too keen on women, almost fond talk as if they admire his weaknesses as much as his strengths; it's as if he belongs to them. They tell stories about his skill with a sword and what a fox he is at settling disputes. Funny, a lot of stories I haven't heard for years are surfacing again. How he got the truth out of twisty Jagger; the time he settled that marriage business at Cantintar; how he led a decset of guards after that rogue band that was burning tars, backed them into a corner and whipped them though they had five times his fighters. (He chuckles.) First time I heard the story, there were only a dozen raiders. Now there's fifty. By the time Hern returns (he raises a brow, his smiling eyes fix on Rane's face) he'll find a space waiting for him no man could possibly fill.

RANE: What about you, Hal? Any danger?

HAL: (shrugging) They've tolerated me so far because they see me as an amiable nothing. They've taken the tar from me, did you know? Anders is tarom now, good little Follower that he is.

RANE: Does anyone suspect you're sending information to the Biserica?

HAL: (chuckling) Oh no, my long friend. Sweet Hallam, he's a harmless fool. Let him potter about grinning at people, he's entertaining now and then, cools things down sometimes. They burned my books, did you know? Took them all out and put them on a pile. Even the *Keeper's Praises*, illuminated by Hanara Pan herself. Anders carried them out with his own hands and put them on the fire. (He broods at the fire, his anger so intense it was palpable; Tuli felt it powerfully.) Barbarians. They're all barbarians. (His voice is very soft, very even, the words are flat, floating like leaves in the crackling silence.)

RANE:  Hal, you don't have to stay here. This storm will close the pass to wagons, but a man on snowshoes could get through if he had a reason to.

HAL:  Oh, I think I must stay. There are still ways I can help my ties. Anders is too thick to notice when he's being led about by the nose. (He ran a trembling hand through his silverwhite hair.) If by chance I do survive this nonsense, I'd like to live in your guesthouse and work in the Biserica Library. You might mention that to Yael-mri when you see her next.

RANE:  (putting her hand over his) I will, be sure of that. Hal?

HAL:  What is it, my friend?

RANE:  Could you dig into your stores, get us some winter clothing? Blankets (she makes a rueful little sound, bites on her lower lip) and food; meant to get that from you anyway, grain for our macain, they'll find little enough to eat, groundsheets, a tent, a firestriker, we'll be sleeping out until we hit Sel-ma-Carth. It's a lot to ask.

HAL:  A lot, but not too much. It's late. Anders and his soulmate will be sleeping the sleep of the self-justified. The attics will be dusty but deserted. Come with me. (He nods at Tulie.) The youngling should stay here. You know the bolt holes if we run into trouble. By the way, I've never gotten round to telling Anders about the little secrets in the walls so you needn't fear he'll be poking around down here. If it's still snowing tomorrow you'd better stay. That won't be a problem. (He gets to his feet, stretches, pats a yawn.)

Rane unfolded from the pillows, stood looking down at Tuli. "Eh-Moth," she said. "Kick some of that straw together and stretch out between those quilts. You're pinching yourself to keep awake."

Tuli yawned. She nodded, got shakily to her feet. Yawned again.

Rane chuckled. "We won't be leaving until tomorrow night at the earliest. Sleep as much as you need."

They stayed in the secret cellar for three days while the storm raged outside. Tuli grew heartily bored with the place. This wasn't what she'd expected, wasn't the kind of adventure the old lays sang of.

She and Rane worked over the gleanings from Hallam's attic, got them sorted into packs for each of the macain, then cut up old worn blankets and sewed them into coats for the macain—no time to let them finish their winter changes. Tuli spent a good part of her days scrubbing a stiff-bristled brush across the itching thickening skins of the beasts, raking away the dead slough. What should have taken a month or two was being pushed into a few days and the good-natured macain were miserable and snappish. The brushing helped. And it kept her temper more equitable, gave her something to do with the long empty hours.

Though Hal seldom visited them during the day, he would come strolling in late at night, usually after Tuli had crawled into her quilts and slid into sleep. Sometimes she woke and saw the two of them head to head by the dying fire, talking in low tones, always talking, more of what she heard the first night. She didn't bother listening, it was all too boring. She'd enjoyed hearing about her father and Teras, had glowed with pride when Hal praised them, the rest of it seemed a waste of time.

She didn't quite know what to make of Hallam. He wasn't like her father, or her uncles, or even old Hars. He seemed a lazy man, too indolent to tend to anything but his own needs, drifting indifferently along as the Agli and the Followers took away everything he had. When she thought about it, though, she saw he was defeating them in his own way by not letting them change him. If they caught him spying, he'd go to his death mildly appreciating the absurdity of what both he and his murderers were doing. Gentle, shambling, incompetent in so many things, he was right, he had no place in the world that was coming. She liked him well enough, but she was glad she didn't have to live around him, could even understand why Anders had done his best to be as different as he could from his father.

It was easy to let her mind wander as she scrubbed at the macai's back, scraping loose the fragments of dead skin. Might meet up with Teras as Rane and she wandered about the Plain. She felt a sudden pang of loneliness. She missed Teras more than she wanted to think about, wished he was here, now; it would be so good to have him along, sharing all this, she'd have someone her own age to talk to. She began to see what Rane meant when she said Tuli was too young to interest her any way but as a friend and daughter. Rane was about Annic's age. Tuli thought about her parents up in the mountain gorge, wondered how they were coping with the snow and the cold. It was interesting to hear from Hallam that her father had got the ties onto the council in spite of the Tallins, seemed things were getting settled in odd ways up there, but settled for sure and in the way her father wanted. Teras and old Hars shuttling messages back and forth between the tars and the gorge. What would Sanani be doing with her oadats, how would she keep them from freezing? Seems like a hundred years since I saw Da and Mama and Sanani. The Ammu Rin, she said it took ten years to be a healwoman. I don't know if I could take that. I think I'd like being a healwoman. The two men she'd killed, she dreamed about them sometimes, though she didn't want to. They'd almost forced her to kill them, but they wouldn't get out of her head. If I can't be a healwoman, I could always work in the fields; I wouldn't mind that, I like making things grow, or maybe the Pria Melit would let me help with the animals. She shivered as she heard again the soft whirr of the sling, the faint thunk the stone made against the temple, saw again the guard crumpling with loose slow finality, saw the young acolyte swing round and stretch out on the ground, felt against her palms the empty flaccidity of his legs as she helped carry him to the fire, saw the grime on his feet, the crack in the nail of a big toe, his shaven head, the round ears like jug handles sticking out from his head. She scrubbed at burning eyes with the back of her hand. I won't cry, not for them, they asked for it. She sniffed again, swallowed, and scrubbed fiercely at the macai's back.

Late on the third night, Rane woke Tuli. "Wind's gone down," she said as Tuli rubbed sleep from her eyes. "Some snow still falling, but that's just as well, it'll cover our tracks when we leave here." Tuli crawled out of the quilts and started putting on her winter gear.

Carrying a lantern Rane walked ahead of her, plowing through the drifts, vanishing repeatedly in the swirls of gently falling snow. There was no wind but tiny flakes kept drifting down and down, with the persistence of water wearing away stone. Hal followed with another lantern, leading the two macain and leaving behind him a wallow a blind man could follow, but when Tuli looked back, she could see that the snow was already filling it. By morning there would be no sign anyone had ever passed this way.

Tuli plodded along between the two lights; in spite of her heavier clothing she was beginning to shiver. So much snow. There ought to be more sound with that much falling, but there was only the crunching of all their feet, a hoot from a macai, the soft hiss from the lanterns.

Rane stopped outside the gate, took the lead rope from Hallam and gave him her lantern. "You can get back all right?"

"I'm not in my dotage, woman. Have a care, will you. Who have I to talk to if you get yourself killed? And give my best to Yael-mri when you see her again."

Rane watched him disappear into the veils of falling snow; when he was gone, she pulled herself into the saddle, waited until Tuli was mounted, then started east along the lane. The rope tied between them tugged Tuli's macai into a slow dance, crunching through the drifted snow. She slumped in the saddle, tucked her gloved hands into her sleeves and, half-dozing, followed the shapeless blot in the darkness ahead of her.

# NIGHT CAMP

Silence between the woman and the girl.

The snow had stopped falling about an hour before they made camp. In the small clearing it came nearly to Tuli's knees, under the trees it was about half that, where the wind blew the drifts were almost to her shoulders. Using Hal's shovels they dug away the snow between two trees and put up the tent, dug out another space for the fire and a place to sit by it, fried some bread, made a stew and some cha for supper, the hot food a warm comforting weight in their bellies. Now they sit on piles of brush by the fire, sipping at the last of the cha. Rane is staring at the coals, her reddened, chapped hands wrapped about a mug. Her face is drawn and unhappy. Tuli watches her, wondering if she is grieving again for her dead lover or worried about Hallam or even looking with despair at the future she sees for the mijloc.

Tuli watches the fire in between the times she stares at Rane. She thinks about Teras. About her father. She sees their faces looking at her from the coals. Ties on the council, she thinks, and wonders how she feels about that. She has never been comfortable with ties. We share a shape, but that's all, she thinks. She can't follow their jokes and when they laugh, more often than not she feels that she is the butt of their jokes. Even when she finds out this is not true, the feeling still lingers and doesn't help her like or deal well with them.

She looks at Rane, wonders if she should say something, but has a feeling it would be an intrusion into places she has no business poking into, so she says nothing.

Still not speaking, Rane stands, kicks snow over the coals, gathers up the supper things she and Tuli have already cleaned and piles them before the tent. She waits for Tuli to crawl inside, wriggles in after her. They share the blankets and the quilts, sleeping side by side in their clothes, their boots under the blankets with them so they'll be wearable in the morning. There are some awkward moments at first, working out wrinkles in the covers, finding a comfortable way to share the narrow shelter of the tent. Rane sleeps almost immediately, but Tuli stays awake for some time, listening to the ex-meie breathing. The feel of the lanky strong body pressing against hers disturbs her in ways that remind her too much of what Fayd had done to her not so long ago. She is growing up in her head, that doesn't bother her, in fact she's rather pleased by it, a lot of the confusion is clearing away, though more mysteries are still appearing. But she is gaining confidence in her ability to deal with those. What worries her is growing up in her body. The rages she gets are beginning to be more manageable, it is as her mother said, she is growing out of them, but there are other things, things she doesn't want to feel. It isn't just the menses, she never has much trouble with those, not like other girls, they are just a mess she hates having to deal with. Sometimes she is so restless she can't stand herself, sometimes she can't stand anyone else either, she isn't mad at them; she just doesn't want anyone around her, especially boys. Not Teras, he is different, he doesn't make her feel funny. She wishes he were here now, it would be a lark, they could race with each other, hunt lappets with their slings, maybe spy on people as they did before. Was a time they worked together so well, they didn't even have to talk much. But that is gone. Teras isn't that way anymore. He's changed. Well, that isn't quite right. He acts like she's the one changed. Rane can be fun, but she needs to explain things to Tuli and Tuli needs to ask questions and have things explained to her. That is interesting sometimes, learning about people and places and other ways, but Rane is so much older she sometimes forgets how it is to be young and not sure of anything and too proud to ask. Tuli begins to feel depressed, but she is very tired, even the turmoil working in belly and brain has to retire before the waves of exhaustion that roll over her. She sleeps.

## II

# A REPORT FROM ORAS

Two men sit at each end of a narrow table, hunched over a shallow lamp, a wick floating in oil and burning with a fishy stench. Blankets are hung over every aperture, the air is thick with smells: old fish, the oil in the lamp, man-sweat, a lingering hint of incense too redolent of norit for the comfort of either. Outside, the wind is blowing hard; the boat rubs against the wharf, breathing and flexing and creaking, caught by the tail of a storm passing out to sea and flicking at the edges of the estuary.

Coperic smoothed a hand along the thin tough paper (a waterproof membrane, the innerskin of a kertasfish, and the small closely packed lines of glyphs on it written in waterproof ink) and read in a low drone the words written there. The fisher Intii, Vann, was illiterate by choice, but his memory was phenomenal. If he had no chance to pass on the written report, he could whisper it into the ears of that member of Coperic's web who came for it. He listened, eyes hooded beneath brows like tangled hedges.

"The Army is complete. No arrivals for the past three tendays. These are the numbers. Five bands of youngling Sleykinin. About a score in each. Say a hundred, hundred-ten in all. Full Assassins, hard to say, scattered like they are, no more than two or three in a bunch. Maybe another hundred. I have to depend on remembering mask patterns and can only count those I happen to see. In the streets and around the camp, maybe a hundred as I said, probably more. Small band of Minark nobles and their attendants, three sixes of nobles, five attendants each, three-score ten in all, keep to themselves except when they go roaring through Oras, chasing whomever they take a notion to hunt. Wild card, might break through where more seasoned and disciplined troops can't. Watch 'em. Four bands of mounted archers, majilarni from the eastern grasslands. Their rambuts are fast and maneuverable, give a steadier seat to bowmen than macain do. Disciplined within the band; outside, it's ragged. Very apt to take offense at a look or a word and start a brawl. So far Necaz Kole has them under control, but it's a weakness that might be exploited. Nekaz Kole of Ogogehia has taken over as Imperatora General of the army. From what I hear, Malenx, whom Floarin appointed Guard General after Hern took out Morescad, resents the man and would work against him if he dared but he's terrified of the minark norit who's running Floarin. Kole brought two thousand picked men across the Sutireh Sea with him, the best, I hear, from the mercenary bands of Ogogehia-across-the-Sea. They're going to be the toughest to face, got their own officer cadre, sappers, engineers expert at building and working siege engines. Two thousand light armed foot soldiers, fast and flexible, many of them competent archers and slingers, all of them expert with those short swords they carry, handle a pike better than a master reaper swings his scythe. Been watching them work out and got a shiver in my belly. Expensive, too. Floarin's beggaring the mijloc to pay them. Next most dangerous, the Plaz Guards. They're being used mostly to officer the conscripts from the Cimpia Plain. About two thousand of these. Farmers, clumsy and unskilled, just meat to throw against the Wall, far as I can tell. A few exceptions. Two bands of slingers, ragged slippery types, look to me like landless poachers, but they're good and accurate. Just how much use they'll be in a battle is hard to say. About thirty of them. A few others are archers, can hit a target before it bites them. Maybe another thirty. The rest they give pikes to and shields and set to marching until they sweat off a lot of suet and can more or less keep together. About a third of these look sullen and slack off when they can, maybe wouldn't fight if their families weren't hostage for their good behavior. The others are convinced Followers. Won't stop before they're dead. Norits and norids. I didn't bother trying to separate these; it's hard to tell them apart unless you see them in action. Anyway, of the Nor, there are maybe five hundred. One last thing, the army goes through food like a razimut gorging for its winter sleep, so Floarin keeps the tithe wagons rolling, the butchers up to their necks in blood, the fishers hauling their nets. The outcasts up in the mountains are really hurting her when they take the wagons. If we could free the fisher villages, that would be another telling blow against her. She rides out in her warcar whenever she gets worried, harangues some of the men about the moral principles they're defending. They hear her patiently enough, considering that most are there for her gold and don't give a copper uncset who rules in the mijloc or why. Oras-folk get out to listen, that's about the only time we can pass the gates, officially at least; generally me and the others, we're out to see what we can and only listen for the look of it." He lifted his head. "That's all that's on here." He looked a last time at the paper, rolled it into a tight tube and passed it across the table.

Coperic was a small wiry man, shadow like smears of ink in the deep lines from his nose to the corners of a thin but shapely mouth, in the rayed lines about eyes narrowed to creases against the wisps of greasy smoke rising from the lamp. There was a tired cleverness in his face, a restrained vitality in his slight body. "How soon before you can leave?"

Vann slid the tube back and forth between his thumb and forefinger. "Soon as the storm passes." He was a lanky long man with gray-streaked brown hair and beard twisted into elaborate plaits, thin lips pressed into near invisibility when he wasn't speaking. "This norit fights wide of storms and the blow out to sea, he's a monster, too much for trash to handle. Norit likes him; a nice following wind and a flat sea and that's what he give me when it's him I'm taking south." He moved his long legs, eased them out past Coperic's feet. His mouth stretched into a tight smile. "He's got a queasy belly."

"Your usual ferrying job, or is this one special?" Coperic leaned farther over the table, his smallish hands pressed flat on the boards, his eyes narrowed to slits.

The Intii stroked his beard. "They don't talk to me." The oiled plaits slid silently under his gnarled hand. "Norit's been buzzing back and forth between here and up there," he nodded his head toward the walled city on the cliffs high above the wharves where his boat was moored, "grinding his teeth because the storm kept hanging on. I'd say this one was important. To him, anyway. What's happening with the army?"

"Gates been closed on us the past three days, traxim flying like they got foot-rot, there's a smell of something about to happen round the Plaz and the Temple. I'd say they're getting set to move. I wouldn't wager a copper uncset against your norit taking word to Sankoy to get their men moved to the passes so they'll be ready to join up with this bunch. You better walk careful, Vann. Shove that," he flicked a finger at the paper tube, "down deep in the mossy cask the norit won't want to drink from. If what we think's right, he'll be twitchy as a lappet in a kanka flock."

The Intii shifted his feet again, plucked at his eyebrow, his face drawn, the anger in him silent but all the more intense for that. "They think they got me netted." He reached out to the paper tube, rolled it with delicate touches a few inches one way, then the other. "Kappra Shaman living in my house. Norit leaning on my son when he go out with the boats. Figure I got no way to move, so they forget about me, don't even see me these days."

The fisher villages on the tappatas along the coast south of Oras had been built by families determined to live their lives their own way, calling no man master, sheltered from most attack by the mountains and the sea, sheltered behind their village walls from attack by the Kapperim tribes who came up from the Sankoy hills on stock and slave raids when the spring thaws opened the mountain passes. The fisher-folk made for themselves most of what they needed; anything else they traded for in Oras, the various families of each village taking turns carrying fish to Oras to sell for the coins the whole village shared. They worked hard, kept themselves to themselves, exchanged daughters between the villages, managed to survive relatively unchanged for several hundred years.

Now there were Kapperim inside the walls, a Kappra Shaman watching everyone. The women and children and old folks were held at risk, guaranteeing the tempers of the men and older boys who were sent out day after day to bring back fish for the army. Norits rode the lead boats in each village fleet; a captive merman who wore charmed metal neck and wrist rings swam ahead of the boats locating the schools so the fishers wouldn't come back scant. Day after day they went out, and most days nothing was sent to the villages. One boat in each fleet, one day in five, was permitted to take its catch to the women and children so the families wouldn't starve. The fishers worked hard, not much choice about that, but they were sullen, their tempers smoldering, especially the younger men. The older men kept watch and stopped revolts before they started, but the norits wouldn't have lasted a day in spite of their powers if it weren't for the hostage families.

The Intii Vann was looser than the others. He was used by the norits to ferry them up and down the coast; though a noris could pop across space by the potency of his WORDS and gathered power, the norits were limited to more ordinary means of travel. They had a choice between taking a boat or riding the Highroad where they'd have to face snow-blocked passes and attacks by outcasts. The boats were faster and more comfortable and a lot safer. To ensure their safety, the norits he ferried made the Intii handle his boat by himself, helping him (and themselves) by controlling the wind and water as much as they could.

The Intii had a tenuous association with Coperic going back a number of years, doing a little smuggling for him, carrying the men and women of his web up and down the coast and occasionally across Sutireh Sea. When the trouble began at the Moongather and the Intii found himself chosen as ferryman by the norits, Coperic and he wasted little time working out their own methods for passing messages south and handling other small items. At Sankoy, Vann gave these messages to men or women he knew from times past, who relayed them on to the Biserica, a slow route but the only sure one. The norits suspected nothing of this; they didn't understand people at all well, they'd had too much power too long, they were too insulated from the accommodations ordinary folk had to make to understand how they managed to slid around a lot of the pressures in their lives. In their eyes, a powerless man could never be a danger to them.

Vann took up the roll. "If the army moves south, what do you do?"

Coperic sat back, his face sinking into shadow. "I move with them, me and my companions. We hit them how and where we can, we stay alive long as we can."

Vann scratched at his beard. "I would come with you, my old friend, but I've got a wife and sons and a stinking Kappra Shaman with a knife at their throats."

"You better figure a way to change that. If the battle goes bad for Floarin, well, you're dead, your folk are dead."

"I know." Vann reached over, pinched out the wick. In the thick rich-smelling darkness, he said. "Take care going back. Norits see in the dark."

## III

## THE SPIRAL DANCE—MOVING TOWARD THE MEETING

## KINGFISHER

The light bounded along before them through the winding wormhole in the mountain, leading them once more to the Mirror. The way to the mirror-chamber changed each time they went there as if the room they slept in were a bubble drifting through the stone. Or perhaps it was the mirror chamber that moved about. Or did everything here move, bubbles blown before the Changer's whims? However many times Serroi followed their will o' the wisp guide to meals, to meet Coyote in one of his many guises, to walk beside the oval lake in the ancient volcano's crater, she never managed to gain any sense of the ordering of Coyote-Changer's home. If it had rules, they were written according to a logic too strange or complex for her to understand.

After a dozen more twists and turns they stepped into the huge domed chamber that held the mirror.

Coyote's Mirror. An oval bubble like a gossamer egg balanced on its large end, large enough to hold a four-master under full sail. Color flickered through the glimmer, a web of light threading through its eerie nothingness. A long low divan was pulled up about three bodylengths from it, absurdly bright and jaunty with its black velvet cover embroidered with spangles and gold thread, its piles of silken pillows, the gaudiest of greens, reds, blues, yellows and purples. In that vast gloom with its naked stone, sweating damp, its shifting shadows and creeping drafts, the divan was a giggle that briefly lifted Serroi's spirits each time she came into that chamber and warmed her briefly toward Coyote.

He wasn't there. That rather surprised her. She'd expected him to be titupping about, hair on end, his impatience red in his long narrow eyes, tossing an ultimatum at Hern. She began to relax.

Hern looked about, shrugged and walked to the divan. He settled himself among the pillows, leaned forward, hands planted on his knees, waiting for the show to begin. Serroi hesitated, then perched beside him, her hands clasped loosely in her lap, her feet supported by an extravagantly purple pillow. The Mirror whispered at them, shapeless sounds to match the unsteady shapes flowing through it.

"Begin." It was a staccato bark, loud enough to reverberate through the great chamber. As it died in pieces about them, Serroi twisted around, trying to locate the speaker, but it was as if the rock itself had spoken, aping and magnifying Coyote's squeak.

When she turned back to the Mirror, there were excited voices coming from it, a great green dragon leaped at them, mouth wide, fire whooshing at them, then the dragon went round the curve of the Mirror and vanished—but not before she saw the dark-clad rider perched between the delicate powerful wings. More of the dragons whipped past, all of them ridden, all of them spouting gouts of fire at something Serroi couldn't see. They were intensely serious about what they were doing, those riders and the beasts they rode, but Serroi couldn't make out what it was they fought. She looked at Hern.

He was frowning thoughtfully at the beasts, but when he felt her eyes on him, he smiled at her and shook his head. "No," he told the Mirror. To Serroi he said, "Think about those infesting our skies. The sky is one place the mijlockers don't need to watch for death. We've got nothing here that would keep beasts that size from breeding until they ate the world bare."

Serroi sighed. "But they were such marvelous creatures. I wish. . . ."

"I know."

The gossamer egg turned to black glass with a sprinkle of glitterdust thrown in a shining trail through it. Silvery splinters darted about in eerie silence eerily quick, spitting fire at each other. They were odd and rather interesting, but so tiny she couldn't see why the Mirror or Coyote had bothered with them—until the image changed and she saw a world turning under them, a moon swimming past, then one of the slivers, riding emptiness like a sailing ship rode ocean water, came toward them, came closer and closer until only a piece of it was visible in the oval and she knew that the thing was huge; through dozens of glassy blisters on the thing's side she saw men and women sitting or moving about like parasites in its gut. As she watched, it sailed on, began spitting fire at the world below, charring whole cities, turning the oceans to steam. Power beyond any conception of power she'd had before. She looked at Hern.

"No," he said. "Ay-maiden, no."

The Mirror flickered, the black turned green and blue, a green velvet field, a blue and cloudless sky. Small pavilions in bright primary stripes, triangular pennants fluttering at each end of a long low barrier woven with silken streamers running parallel to the churned brown dirt. Beneath the pennants, gleaming metal figures mounted on noble beasts with long elegant heads, flaring nostrils, short alert ears with a single curve on the outside, a double curve on the inside, a twisty horn long as a man's forearm between large liquid eyes, long slender legs that seemed too delicate to carry their weight and that on their backs. A horn blared a short tantara. The metal riders spurred their mounts into a ponderous gallop, lowering the unwieldy poles they'd been holding erect, and charged toward each other, each on his own side of the barrier. Loud thumps of the digging hooves, cries from unseen spectators, huffing from the beasts, creaks and rattles from the riders, a general background hum. They charged at each other, feather plumes on the headpieces fluttering, the long poles held with impossible dexterity, tips wavering in very small circles. Pole crashed against shield. One pole shattered. One pole slipped off the shield. One rider was swaying precariously though still in the saddle, the other had been pushed off his beast and lay invisible until the viewpoint changed and they saw him on his back, rocking and flinging arms and legs about as he struggled to get back on his feet.

"No," Hern said, though his gaze lingered on the riding beast fidgeting a short distance off, neck bent in a graceful arc, snorting and dancing from foot to foot with an impossible lightness as attendants dived for the dangling reins. "No," he said and sighed.

The Mirror flickered. A forest. Gigantic trees with skirts of fragile air-root lace arching out near the ground. A woman standing among and towering above brown glass figures that danced around her, crooning something exquisitely lovely and compelling; Serroi could feel the pull of it as she watched. A woman, bright hair hanging loose about a frowning face, a face alive with something better than beauty, a powerful leonine female, visibly dangerous. She lifted a hand. Fire gathered about the hand, a gout of gold flame that flowed like ropy syrup about it. She pointed. Fire leaped out in a long lance from her finger. She swept her arm in a short arc, the lance moving with it to slash deep into the side of a tree. The forest groaned. The hypnotic chant broke. One of the glass figures cried out, agony in the rising shriek, a deep burn slanting across its delicate torso. "I want my friend," the woman cried. "Give me back my friend; bring her out from where you've hid her." She cut at another tree. A spun gold crown appeared on her head, a band woven from gold wire, flowers like flattened lilies on the band, the petals made of multiple lines of wire until the petal space was filled in. The centers of the blooms were singing crystals whose pure sweet chimes sounded over the moaning and screaming from the little ones, the hooshing of the trees. "I want my friend or I'll burn your forest about your ears." She took a step forward, the fury in her face a terrible thing. Once again she slashed at a tree.

"No," Hern said. Hastily but definitely.

"Why?" Serroi turned from the fading image to examine his face.

"I've got enough trouble coping with the women in my life." He chuckled. "You, Yael-mri, Floarin, even the Maiden. Fortune deliver me from another. Remember my number two, Lybor?" When she nodded, he jerked his thumb at the Mirror. "A Lybor with brains. Give that one a year and she'd own the world."

"If she wanted it."

He shrugged. "Why take the chance?"

The Mirror flickered. The gloom about the trees changed, deepened. The giants shrank to trees that were still great, but great on a more human scale. The ground tilted to a steeper slope. The view shifted until it seemed they hovered over a red dirt trail. A line of men came trotting along it—no, not all men, about half were women. Serroi counted twenty, all of them lean and fit, moving steadily down the mountainside, making no sound but the soft beat of their feet and the softer slide of their clothing. Dark clothing. Trousers of some tough but finely woven cloth more like leather than the homespun cloth she knew. Some of them wore dark shirts that buttoned down the front, heavy blousy shirts with a number of buttoned-down pockets, others had short sleeved, round-necked tunics that clung like fine silk to torsos male and female. Some had wide belts looped across their bodies, others had pouches that bounced softly and heavily against their hips. They all carried complicated wood and metal objects, rather like crossbows without the bowstaves. Well-kept weapons, handled with the ease of long use. Down and down they went, moving in and out of moonlight that was beginning to dim as clouds blew across the sky. They reached a dirt road, only a little wider than the trail but with deeper ruts in it. Without hesitation they turned onto it and loped along it, still going down.

A purring like that of a giant sicamar grew slowly louder, died. A blatting honk. The band split in half and vanished into the brush and trees on both sides of the road. The throaty purr began again, again grew louder. Again it stopped. Serroi heard a sharp whistle. Three bursts, then two. The purr again—coming on until Serroi at last saw the thing that made it. A large squarish van rather like the caravans of the players. This one had no team pulling it, yet it came steadily on, its fat, soft-looking wheels turning with a speed that started Hern tapping his fingers. The purring muted to a mutter as the van slowed and stopped; the man inside the glassed-in front leaned out an opening by his side and repeated the whistle signal. His face was strained, gaunt, shadow emphasizing the hollows around his eyes, the heavy lines slashing down his cheeks and disappearing under his chin.

An answering whistle came from the trees on his left.

He opened the side of the van, jumped down and trotted around to the back, put a key into a tiny keyhole, turned it, then pulled down the two handles and opened out the doors. The viewpoint shifted so she could see inside, but it was a disappointment; nothing there but thin quilted padding on the floor.

The men and women came swiftly and silently from the trees and began climbing inside, fitting themselves with quick ease into the limited space. The driver and the leader of the band, a stocky blond man, stood talking by the front door.

"Rumor says they're close to finishing new spy satellites and shooting them up." The driver's voice was soft, unassertive, a hoarse but pleasant baritone that blended well with the soughing of the wind through the conifers, the brighter rustling of the other trees. "When they do, they'll be going over the mountains inch by inch until they find you." He passed a hand across his brow, stirring the lank thin hair hanging into his eyes. "Unless you can take them out again."

"Through a fuckin army? Hunh! Well, we won a year. They took their time." The stocky man rubbed a fist across his chin. "We can hold out." A quick swoop of his arm included the fighters. "But the rest, the old folks and the kids. . . ." Hand fisted again, he jabbed at the unseen enemy, eyes narrowed, cheekbones suddenly prominent, catching what was left of the moonlight. "Shit, man, what else we fighting for?"

The driver smiled, a nervous twitch of his lips. "All of us, we'll have to go deeper underground or cross the border and raid from there. Tell you, Georgia, I've about gone my limit in town. Getting so I grovel to shadows. Had a couple blackshirts go through my store records a week ago, they came back yesterday, didn't do anything but stand around. Still, I was sweating rivers."

"You suspect?"

"I don't think so. Not for this." He patted the side of the van. "It's what I sell, electronic games, the mini-computers, the rest of it, all that second-hand gear. And I was a wargamer before they got that outlawed. Devil's work, you know." He shrugged, swiped again at the hair falling in his eyes. "Be really ironic if they pull me in because whatever they've got instead of brains is twitching at shadows like that. It's getting so it's anybody any time, all the cops need is a funny feeling. Hunh! The Dommers, they located a collection of drop-outs a couple hundred miles south of here. What I hear, all they were doing was scratching a few patches of vegetables out of the mountain-side, living on what they could catch or kill. Dommers rounded them up, the ones left alive, brought them in for trial. Was on TV last night, showing us the horrible examples. Rumor says trial's rigged, they're going to shoot them first of the week." He shrugged again. "They're starting to ration gas. Guess you'll have to lift a few cans so I can fill up again. I damn sure don't want them coming down on me asking questions I can't answer. Constitution suspended till the emergency's over. Over!" The last word was a barking snarl. He thrust his hands in the pockets of his jacket and scowled into the night. "It'll be over when the fat cats get themselves dug in so deep we'll never root them out; little man can wave good-bye to any rights he thinks he's got."

Georgia said nothing, put his hand on the driver's shoulder, squeezed. Still silent, he moved to the back of the van and looked inside, nodded with satisfaction, and closed the doors. He pulled at the handles to make sure the latches had caught, took the key from the lock without turning it (Hern nods, good sense not to trap the fighters inside should something happen to the van) and went to the front, climbed up beside the driver and settled back so his face and torso were lost in deep shadow. The driver busied himself with small, quick movements Serroi found puzzling until she heard the purr grow louder. The man backed and turned the van in the narrow space with a skill both Hern and Serroi approved, then started down the winding road.

The viewpoint lifted so she could see out over the land, over the wild rugged mountains with their heavy covering of trees and many small streams, mountains much like the Earth's Teeth on the western rim of the mijloc.

The Mirror blinked. The van was out of the mountains and moving along a paved road through intensively cultivated farmlands, past clumps of houses and outbuildings (more vehicles in many shapes sitting in driveways or open sheds, some farms have several varieties), herds of beasts vaguely like hauhaus in some fields, in others a smaller number of beasts somewhat like the majilarni rambuts—or the mounts of the metal men, minus the horn between the eyes. The van went through many small villages, huddles of glass-fronted buildings plopped down beside the larger roads, most of these brightly lit by globes that neither smoked nor seemed to need refueling. A prosperous fertile land that apparently had never known war. There were fences but only to keep the beasts from straying. No walls about the farmhouses, no walls about the villages, no place to store food against siege or famine—yet, from what the men had said, there was much wrong here. She frowned at the tranquil night pictures before them and thought about that conversation. A good deal of it was simply incomprehensible though she understood the words; apparently the Mirror gifted them with the ability to understand all the languages spoken within its boundaries. However, she did not have the basic knowledge to comprehend things like *spy satellites*, *electronic gear*, *mini-computers*. They were blurs in her mind about a vague notion of communications. What she did understand was the similarity between the situation there and the one in the mijloc, folk being driven off their land and into the mountains to escape persecution by another more powerful group that had seized control of the government. And the *feel* she got of the usurpers was very much like that of the Followers, repression, denial of pleasure, demands for submission. And there was something else. A sense of impending doom. Not so very different from the mijloc with Floarin's army gathering, getting ready to march.

The Mirror blinked. A glow spread across the sky, a steady shine that turned the clouds yellow and sickened the face of the single moon. They flew above a vast city, a sleeping city. Glass everywhere, lights everywhere, those cold-fire globes that burned as brilliantly as the sun, turning night into day on the empty streets. Countless houses and communal dwellings, all sizes and shapes, from the ragged crowded slums to sprawling elegance spread on beautifully landscaped grounds. Toward the center of the city there were rows and rows of great square towers, their hundreds and hundreds of windows dark and empty, made mirrors by the perfection of the plate glass, and among the towers were shorter structures, stores heaped with goods of all kinds, some recognizable, most incomprehensible, such a heaping up and overflowing of things that Serroi felt dizzy with it all.

Then they were back with the van, watching it turn and twist through the silent streets until it reached a blocky black building surrounded by a high fence of knitted metal wire. The van moved slowly past it then went around behind some other buildings and stopped. Georgia was at the back doors almost before the vehicle was completely stopped, turning the handles, dragging the doors open. A tall thin woman, her skin a warm rich brown with red-amber highlights, her hair a ragged bramble, was the first out, looking sharply around, then beginning a rapid series of bends and stretches. The rest of the fighters came out with equal silence and followed her example, then Georgia held up a hand. The others snapped straight, eyes on him. He pointed to the dark woman. She waved a casual salute, gave him a broad glowing smile, brought up a hand and waved it at the van, a fast gesture.

The fighters split into two unequal parts, fifteen staying with Georgia, five climbing back into the box. Georgia closed the doors, thumped on the side. A moment later it rolled away, moving slowly, the purr kept to a minimum.

The others followed Georgia along the street, bunched in groups of two or three spaced at varying intervals. To a casual glance they were night shift going home and not too anxious to get there—an illusion that would vanish if anyone took a long look at them, but Hern nodded and smiled his appreciation at the intelligent subtlety of the move; there was little about the band to attract such close scrutiny.

They rounded a corner, crossed the street and went along the knitted fence until they came to a brightly lit gate flanked by thick pillars of red brick. There was a small guardhouse inside the gate but it was dark and silent, its shuttered window locked tight. The largest of the fighters took a clippers longer than his forearm from his belt, unsnapped a leather cover, set the cutting edges against the chain that held the two parts of the metal gate together. Others were busy at the pillars taking down metal plates and doing things that had no meaning to Serroi but much meaning to them if she judged by their intentness, the tension evident in workers and waiters. The wait was short; in less than a minute the gate was open and the small band was inside.

Running on the grass, they reached the building a moment later and went round it to a small door at one side.

More intense working, intense waiting, then the door

was open and they were inside, fading into shadows along the walls of the storehouse. Piles of boxes, rows of vehicles and other large objects angled out from the walls, the place was filled and overflowing. Silent and hard to see in the darkness, the fighters moved in and out of alcoves, a dance of shadows in shadow.

Voices. The shadows stilled, then began converging on a door whose bottom half was solid wood, top half opaque glass.

The watchers' viewpoint shifted. They hovered in the room on the other side of the door, saw four armed men in sloppy gray-green shirts and trousers, heavy laced boots, broad belts each with a metal object where a sword would hang—a weapon of some sort—a small cousin of the larger weapons the raiders carried. These men were playing a card game of some sort, sucking on white cylinders that glowed on the end, breathing out streams of gray-white smoke. One man took the cylinder from his mouth, plucked a bottle filled with amber fluid from a bowl of cracked ice, twisted the top off, threw his head back and drank with noisy gulps, put the bottle down beside him, two-thirds emptied, and picked up his cards.

The door slammed open. One of the invaders was inside. A woman. Small, wiry. Her face was hidden in a black stocking with holes for her eyes. She stood tense, balanced for quick movement, silently begging the guards to move.

The four men had started to roll away and bring their weapons up, but froze before the threat of that eagerly quivering weapon. Only their eyes moved—shifting from the woman to the other raiders, the stocky man, masked like the woman, another, taller man, a fourth raider just visible behind him. The stocky man pointed a gloved finger at one of the guards. "Stand," the woman said, her voice like cracking ice.

The guard got slowly to his feet. The fourth raider came quickly and silently into the room, a stubby man with muscles on muscles, arms, neck and chest straining the thin knit shirt he wore. His hands were gloved, supple leather gloves he wore like a second skin. He pulled a coil of wire from his pocket, jerked the guards arms behind him, wound a bit of wire round his thumbs, snipped it off the coil, twisted the ends together. He came round in front of the man, pushed him in the chest with a deceptively gentle shove that sent him staggering against the wall then down onto the floor. He squatted and wired the man's ankles together.

One by one the others were immobilized, quickly, efficiently, with no unnecessary moves or sounds. The raiders didn't bother with gags. Apparently they didn't care how much noise the guards might make once they were gone. The woman who'd given all the orders was last from the room. At the door, she turned. "Yell and I'll be back. You won't like that." She vanished after the others, pulling the door neatly and quietly to behind her.

She joined two of the smaller women who were standing guard. The rest of the raiders were moving back and forth between a large vehicle—like the van but broader, bulkier, a brutal mass to it, a canvas top stretched over ribs. They were packing boxes and metal containers into it, filling it with supplies of all sorts, breaking open the larger boxes and distributing the contents in the cracks and crannies between the smaller boxes. One man was working over a number of two-wheeled vehicles, installing bits and pieces, pouring something that sloshed from a can into the small tank on each of the vehicles. The work went on and on, silent and quick and impressively efficient. No questions, no fumbling about, no hesitation over what to take.

When they were finished loading, they pulled uniforms like those of the guards over their own clothing, took off their masks and put on shiny black helmets whose smoked visors hid almost as much of their faces. Georgia looked around, made a soft hissing sound. "Almost forgot," he said. "Fill a couple cans for our friend. Put them up front, that's the only space left."

The short, powerful fighter brought back two large metal containers painted the color of the uniforms. While he stowed these in the front, the others wheeled the small vehicles into place around the large one, six in front, six behind; they mounted them, feet on the floor holding their metal mounts erect. The guarding women swung the great double doors open, then ran back to the big brute, scrambled inside the cab, two sitting in view, one crouching behind the seats. The riders on the two-wheelers stamped down, the warehouse filled with a coughing throbbing roar much louder than the purr of the van. Moving with ponderous majesty, the procession edged out of the building. The last two riders closed the doors and after they were through the gates, closed those, replaced the sheared padlock with another lifted from the warehouse, then they rolled on, leaving the place looking much as they'd found it.

They went unchallenged through the silent streets. A few drunks stumbling along muttered curses after them, several night-shifters looked curiously after them, but no one seemed to question their activities, no one tried to stop them; what was visible of their faces was disciplined, their bodies were alert but relaxed; they were soldiers about an everyday task, nothing to fuss about.

The Mirror blinked.

There was a glow of pink low down in the eastern sky and the convoy was rumbling along a broad empty highway, moving in and out of patchy fog without slackening speed. The ocean was close, a few hundred yards on the far side of a line of scraggly sandhills high enough to block the view of the water. A little later they came round a broad shallow bend and into a clear patch of road, then slowed abruptly enough to startle Serroi.

On one of the higher and weedier sandhills a rider sat his beast like a statue carved from the darkest cantha wood, his hands crossed on the saddle in front of him, his long black hair lifting on the wind. He waited until the convoy turned onto a drifted, broken side road that slanted off from the highway a short distance past his knoll, then he brought his mount around, galloped recklessly down the slope and clattered ahead of the machines onto the main street of a desrted and half-destroyed coast village. More clatter of hooves—half a dozen others came riding down the street to meet him, short dark youths, long black hair held out of their faces by beaded leather bands or strips of bright cloth. They wore black trousers, skimpy knitted tops with no sleeves and scuffed, high-heeled boots, and rode like demons, as if they were sewed, to their mounts; they came swooping around him waving their weapons, but maintaining a disciplined silence all the more impressive when taken with their exuberantly grinning young faces. They slowed to a calmer pace and rode ahead of the convoy along the shattered street.

Many of the houses and stores were smashed into weathered splinters, a deep layer of dried muck cracked into abstract shapes, graying every surface to a uniform dullness, drifts of sand piled against every semi-vertical wall, sand dunes creeping slowly over the wreckage, beginning to cover what was left of the town. Here and there, by accident of fate and the caprice of the storm that had wrecked the town, a building stood more or less whole. The riders dismounted in front of the open loading door of one of these, an abandoned warehouse, and lead their beasts inside.

Georgia held up his hand, stopped the convoy, dismounted and wheeled his machine after the dismounted riders. In a few minutes the street was empty, the big machine and the little ones tucked neatly away into the empty interior of the building.

Georgia walked over to the lounging youths, tapped the leader on the shoulder. "Angel." He raised thick blond brows. "Run into trouble? Where's the other half?"

"Heading home with a new cavvy. We lifta buncha good horses from ol' Jurgeet's; don' worry, boss, they scatter and go way round. Nobody going to follow 'em through the brush. Us here, we each got a spare horse; seven of us c'n haul as much stuff as the dozen, yeah." He grinned suddenly, his pitted face lighting into a fugitive comeliness. "And boss, we leave his prizes alone; don't want his goons on our tails, besides they too delicate, not worth shit except running."

Georgia chuckled, shook his head. "Long as you're loose and considering it's Jurgeet. Take your horse thieves and brush out the tire marks from where we turned off the highway to here. I want to get this place neated up before the sun's out and they maybe send choppers after us."

"Uh. We go." Another flashing grin. Whistling his companions to him, Angel trotted out of the large room.

Georgia wiped his smile away, turned to frown at his raiders. Several were working together to peel the canvas off the ribs, the rest were stripping off the uniforms, folding them neatly and putting them aside against future use. "Liz," he called.

The small intense woman who'd done all the talking at the armory ran a bony hand through her mop of coarse black hair, came over to him with short quick steps. "What is it?"

"Pick up a pair of binoculars and head back to the highway; find a place where you can get a clear view down the road. Dettinger should be along fairly soon. If he's got lice on his tail, I want to know it."

She gave a quick assenting jerk of her head, rummaged through a stack of supplies and snatched up black tubes with a neck strap (Binoculars? Serroi wonders), slung her weapon over her shoulder by its webbing strap and went quickly out of the warehouse and along the street. She climbed the sandhill and settled on her belly in the weeds, brought the binoculars to her eyes, fiddled with them a while, then settled to her tedious watch.

Inside the building the raiders continued unloading the big vehicle, strapping packets on the back of the two-wheelers. As soon as one was ready, a raider mounted it and roared off into the foggy dawn. Before the sun was fully up, all twelve two-wheelers were gone, Angel and his band were gone, spread out on separate routes so they could be sure at least some of their captured supplies would get through to their base.

Silence settled back over the ruins and the dunes. Liz lay quietly among her weeds, Georgia and the strongman strolled along the street, using an ancient broom and some brush to scratch out wheel and hoof marks, apparently relaxed but keeping a close eye on the sky. Dawn was fading, the fog was fading, there were few clouds in the sky, it promised to be a warm pleasant day. The two men went back inside the warehouse, muscled the sliding door along its rusted track, leaving a crack wide enough for a man to walk through.

The Mirror blinked.

The sun leaped toward zenith, settled at about an hour from noon. A loud whopping sound. A speck in the sky grew rapidly larger. Two men sitting in a bulging glass bubble in a lattice of metal, rotors whirling overhead. The thing swept low over the wrecked village, slowed until it was almost hovering, moved in a tight circle and swung away, moving south along the highway until it vanished into the blue.

The Mirror blinked.

The sun flashed past noon, slowed to its usual pace. Liz thrust her head through the crack. "Van's coming. Far as I can tell, he's loose. No copters."

A short while later, a familiar muted purring—the van came down the street, stopped while Georgia shoved on the sliding door, then drove in beside the military vehicle and stopped.

The dark woman came out the back, one arm hanging useless, a wide patch of drying blood on the shoulder of her tailored shirt. As the rest piled out after her, she lifted the dangling arm with her other hand and hooked her thumb over her belt so the arm had some support. Walking slowly so she wouldn't jar her shoulder, she crossed to stand beside Georgia.

"We had to fight loose," she said. "We got Aguillar and Connelly out. Catlin's dead. He couldn't make it, too far gone, asked me to shoot him. Did. Ram's got a bullet in him, a crease on his leg, bled a little but he could run and did. Rest of us, well, we're mobile. As you see, we picked up a couple other prisoners. Connelly says he knows them both not just from the introg center, vouches for them. Woman's a doctor. Orthopedic surgeon. Man's a history professor at Loomis. Asked about Julia, says he knows her. Feisty dude for an academic type, saved my life just about. Hauled me up when the bullet knocked me off my feet, half-carried me till we reached the transport." She grinned. "We jacked ourself a copcar. Bit of luck, got us in smooth enough. It was getting out the shit started flying. Took us awhile to get loose enough to connect with Det. Doc there did get the worst of the bleeding stopped with stuff in the copcar, but she didn't have much to work with."

"Liz says you're clean."

"Yeah, or I wouldn't be standing here flapping my mouth." There was sweat on her forehead and her rich brown had gone a dull mud-gray, but the spirit in her was a wine-glow in her light eyes.

Georgia touched her cheek, his stolid face deeply serious. "You go sit down before you fall down." Then he grinned at her. "Picking up a medical doctor." He looked over her shoulder at the battered, middle-aged woman bending over a wounded man, a medipac already open beside her. "Anoike's luck."

"Ain' it de trut'." Refusing Georgia's arm, she went over to the military vehicle, sat down on the flat ledge that ran between the wheels, resting her head against its metal side, waiting her turn for treatment.

The Mirror blinked.

Night. Fog or low-hanging clouds. Trees swam in and out of the fog as the Mirror's eye swept along. A creek cut through a small clearing. Condensation dripped off needles and leaves, off rocky overhangs. A man came from under the trees, another, two more, carrying a third on a stretcher—Ram, the doctor walking beside him. Another two, another stretcher, Anoike on it. A man in his fifties with thick unruly gray hair. Liz. More of the raiders, the strongman, finally Georgia. A soft whistle came from somewhere among the trees; he answered it without breaking stride.

As they moved into the trees again Serroi began seeing small camouflaged gardens, the plants growing haphazard in the grass and brush, then some lean-tos and crude pole corrals with horses in them, more shelters, tents huddled close in to trees, more and more of them, heavy canvas tops with walls and floors of rock or wattle and daub. Faces looked out of some, some men and women came out and watched the raiders pass, called softly to one or the other, getting soft answers. A whole little village under the trees, hidden from above, a portable community able to pick up and move itself given a few hours warning, leaving only depressions and debris behind. Thick, netting stretched overhead, open enough to let in some moonlight and certainly any rain. The Mirror's eye swept up through the web and circled over it, showing her, showing them both, the hillside below them, empty except for vegetation and trees, the tent village wiped away as if it had been a dream, nothing more.

The Mirror blinked.

The sun shone with a pale watery light through a thinning layer of clouds. The Mirror's eye roamed about the village, showing them children playing, laughing, chasing each other among the trees and tents, others gathered around a young man, listening as he talked to them, writing in notebooks they held on their knees. Some women and men were washing clothing in the stream, others were cooking, working in the gardens, talking and laughing, some stretched out on mats, sleeping. There were sentries keeping a desultory watch on the approaches to the camp, young men and women, mostly in their teens, perched in trees or stretched out under brush. They weren't exactly alert, but there were enough of them to make it very hard for any large group of men to catch the villagers off-guard.

A whup-whupping sound. Serroi remembered it and wasn't surprised when the Mirror's eye swept above the camouflage netting and focused on the sky. Huge and metallic, twice the size of the searcher she'd seen before (copter, Georgia had called it, she remembered that after a moment; copter, she said to herself as if by naming the thing she could draw some of the terror out of it), it slowed in the air, hovered over a slope some distance from the camp. Fire bloomed under it, it spat out darts so swift she guessed at them more than saw them until they hit the hillside and exploded, blew a hole in the rock with a loud crunch, a fountain of stone and shattered trees.

The copter hovered over its destruction until the reverberations of the explosion had died, then a loud voice boomed from it, a man's voice, many times magnified. "Terrorists," it trumpeted, metallic overtones and echoes close to defeating the effect of the volume, turning the words into barely understandable mush. "Surrender. Save your miserable necks. We coming after you, gonna burn these hills down around you. Defoliants, you scum, remember those? Napalm. Rockets. We gonna scrub these hills bare. Ever seen third-degree burns? Want your kids torched? Surrender, scum. You got no running room left."

Before the last echoes died out, the copter was moving on along the range. Serroi held her breath as it passed over the village, but the men in the machine were blasting slopes at random intervals without any real hope of hitting anyone. They blew a chunk out of the next mountain over, repeated the message with a few added descriptions, and flew on, the whump-crump of their assault on stone and dirt and living wood fading gradually to silence.

The Mirror's eye dipped back under the webbing. Shaken, angry, excited, afraid, the folk from the tents converged on the largest of the camouflaged clearings. Some were silent, turned inward in their struggle to cope with this new threat. Others came in small groups, talking urgently, voices held to whispers as if they feared something would overhear what they were saying. At first it was a confusion of dazed and worried people, but gradually the villagers sorted themselves out and settled on the dirt and grass while three men and two women took stools to the far edge of the clearing, set them in a row and climbed up on them so they could see and be seen. The low buzzing of the talk grew louder for a short while, then died to an expectant silence as one of the five, a lean tall man with thick glasses he kept pushing up a rather short nose, came to his feet and walked a few steps toward the gathered people. "We got a little problem," he said. His voice was unexpectedly deep and carried through the clearing without difficulty.

Laughter, nervous, short-lived, rippled across the assembly.

"We also got no answers." He clasped his hands behind him and ran milky blue eyes over the very miscellaneous group before him. "Seems like some of you should have some questions. Don't want to drag this out too long, but . ." he smiled suddenly, a wide boyish grin that took years off his age, ". . . .your elected councellors need to do a bit of polling before we make our recommendations." He glanced at the timepiece strapped to his wrist. "You know the rules. Say your name, say your question or comment, keep it short and to the point. You want to argue, save it for later. You stand, I point, you talk." There was a surge as a number of the listeners jumped up. He got his stool, climbed up on it, looked them over and snapped a long forefinger out. "You. Tildi."

The dumpy gray-haired woman took a deep breath, then spoke, "Tildi Chon. Any chance they're bluffing?"

The finger snapped out again. "Georgia, you know them better than most."

The chunky blond man got to his feet, looked around at the expectant faces. His own face was stolidly grim. "Georgia Myers," he said. "No. Not this time. For one thing, they've already hit a camp south of here, got that from one of our friends in the city. For another, same friend says they're just about ready to put up new spy satellites."

"Any chance we could ride it out?"

"Always a chance. Most of us beat the odds getting here. You know that. Almost no chance if we stay together. Have to scatter, groups of two or three, no more."

Tildi Chon nodded and sat down, shifting her square body with an uneasy ease, settling with her hands clasped in her lap, her face calm.

"You next, Arve."

The pudgy little man wiped his hands down his sides. "Arve Wahls," he said in an uncertain tenor. "Something not for me, but anyone who needs to know and don't like to ask. What happens to anyone wanting to surrender? Who can't take the pounding any more?"

One of the rescued prisoners, the history professor, jumped to his feet. "Don't," he burst out. He smoothed a long handsome hand over a rebellious cowlick, looked around, made a graceful gesture of apology. "Simon Zagouris. Sorry. New here."

"Samuel Braddock, professor. From what I hear, you're one to know well as any what would happen. Finish what you got to say and keep it short."

Zagouris looked down at his hands, then took a few steps out from the others and turned to face them. "If you're lucky, you'll be shot." He waited for the shocked murmurs to die, then went on. "Look at me. Tenured professor, fat cat in a fat seat, doing what I enjoyed, no worries about eating or rent, fighting off a bit of back-stabbing, office politics, nothing serious. When they leaned on me, told me what I had to teach and how I had to teach it, I sputtered a bit, they leaned harder, I caved in. But they didn't trust me even then. My classes had watchers with tape recorders. My lectures had to be cleared through someone in the Chancellor's office. And a blackshirt truth squad searched my office, my house, clearing out anything they thought subversive or immoral. My books . . ." His mouth snapped shut as he fought to control his anger and distress. "Came back again and again. Stealing whatever they fancied, daring me to say boo. Time and time again I was called in to listen to some airhead rant. I remind you, I didn't fight them, I didn't do more than protest very mildly at the beginning. Kept my mouth shut after, did what I was told like a good boy. And still they kept after me, never trusting me a minute, just looking for an excuse to haul me in for interrogation. And when they pulled me in, my god, you wouldn't believe the shit they tried on me. Until you have to listen to them, you can't imagine the stupidity of those men. Twice I was taken out of the University and held in a room somewhere—I don't have the faintest idea where it was—just put there and left, not knowing what was going to happen. I started looking about me for some way to fight them that wouldn't get me killed. I say that for my self-respect, but Im not going to talk about it more than that. The ones that questioned me never got near anything that was really happening, it was what was in my head that bothered them. This last time, though, it wasn't questions and a few slaps, it was cattle prods and purges, and wanting to know about friends of mine, what they were doing, where they were. Again I remind you, I didn't challenge them, I didn't reject their claims on me or work against them, not in the beginning. If any of you think about surrendering, consider how much more they've got against you. Say they use you for propaganda to get other holdouts to come in, let you live awhile. As soon as you're beginning to feel safe, they come to your house and question you, then they take you away and question you. They'll question you about things so crazy you can't believe they're serious, until you start thinking there has to be something more behind what's happening. But there's nothing there. They'll come back at you again and again until you're crazy or dead. No matter what happens here, I'm not going back alive." He returned to where he'd been sitting, settled himself, waiting with a calm that didn't extend to his hands, long fingers nervously tapping at his thighs.

Braddock pushed his glasses up. "Right," he said. "Connelly."

"Francis Connelly. Anóike just busted me out of an introg. What Zagouris said ain't the half of it. But he's got the right idea. Go back down as a corpse or not at all."

Half a dozen tried to speak at once. Braddock came back onto his feet. "Siddown and shaddup," he yelled at them. Into the ensuing quiet he said, "You talk, Tom. Rest of you keep still and listen or I'll have Ombele sort you out." He flashed one of his sudden grins at another of the council, a man three times as wide as he was, half a head taller; even standing still the muscles visible in arms and neck were defined and shining like polished walnut in the shifting light.

He chuckled, his laughter as rich and dark as the rest of

him. "Yeah," he said. "Papa Sammy's muscle." The assembly laughed with him but there was no more disorder. "Like the man said, Prioc, you're up next."

"Tom Prioc. We can't stay here. Can't go down either. Seems to me there's three choices left. We can do like Georgia says and scatter. We do that, I see most of us starving or getting picked up one by one and put in the labor camps they've set up down south, or some of us, the ones without families, we can keep moving, living outta garbage cans, picking up shitwork now and then from scum too greedy to pay the legal wage. We die and don't get nothing to show for it. Me, I want the bastards to know I was here before they wipe me." He folded his arms, nodded his head, his wispy brown hair blowing out from his face. "Or we head north tonight with as much as we can haul, split up in small groups so we can run round the roadblocks and copter traps they'll have waiting for us. Cross the border how we can. The Condies'll try shoving us back, don't want our trouble, they got troubles enough with the death squads coming across to hunt down what they call enemies of the UD. Won't be that easy, getting in and getting set up. Have to watch out for Condie feds, but we can stay together, that's worth something." He chuckled, looked about the crowd, eyes lingering on a face here and there. "That's one hard border to close. Me and some of you, we did our bit in trade across it. Tempts me. I know those mountains and the trails." He paused, rubbed at his nose. "But I'd kinda like to take me out a copter or two. Georgia and his bunch, they got us a good supply of rockets and launchers. There'll be gunships, but a single man's a hard target when he knows how to be. Third choice. I'd really like to take me out a copter." He sat.

Braddock's long finger flicked to a comfortably round middle-aged woman with short blond hair and a peeling nose. "Cordelia Gudon. Tom's just about set it out. I can't see anything else, maybe some of you can. All I got to say, whatever the rest of us do, the kids gotta get out." She sat.

"Blue."

"Blue Fir Alendayo. I know the trails and the border

well as Tom. Same reason. I say we go as soft as we can far as we can, shoot our way through if we have to, probably will, get the lot of us over the border, then those who want to come back and make as much hell as we can for these. . . ." She paused, searching for a word that would adequately characterize their foes, gave it up and went on. "Well, they can." She sat, bounced up immediately, eyes shining. "And anyone who wants to stay now and shoot him a copter or two, why not." She sat again.

The meeting went on its orderly way. Doubters and grumblers, quibblers and fussers, minor spats and a couple of yelling matches. Hern watched them, fascinated by a kind of governing he'd never seen before, even in the few taromate convocations he'd looked in on. He took his eyes away when the meeting was winding toward some sort of consensus. "Coyote," he called.

The scruffy little man came out of nowhere, his eyes darting from the image in the Mirror to Hern to Serroi, back to the Mirror. "Yes?" he said, pointed ears spreading out from his head, pointed nose twitching.

"I want those. If they're willing. Those people, their weapons and transport."

"Willing? What willing? You want them, I bring them through."

"No point, if they won't fight. Are you going to bring them through here or can you transfer them directly to the Biserica?"

"Will I, not can I, Dom. Will I? Yes. No. Maybe. You go there." His ears went flat against his head, then his grin was back, mockery and anticipation mixed in it. He giggled. "Hern the happy salesman. Death and glory, you tell 'em. They buy you or they don't. Come through where I want if they buy. Not Biserica. Maybe Southport. I think about it."

Serroi straightened. "Ser Coyote."

Coyote rocked on his heels, his head tilted, long narrow eyes filled with a sly laughter that she didn't particularly like. "Little green person."

"If they refuse, then Hern chooses again because your debt isn't paid."

Coyote squirmed, went fuzzy around the edges as if he vibrated between shapes, then he wilted, even his stiff gray hair. He sighed. "Yesss."

"That being so," she said more calmly than she felt, "put us through."

# POET-WARRIOR

Julia set about the reams of paperwork, the miles of red tape that should eventually land her in the public ward of some hospital and pay her surgeon's fees.

You know the route, you've helped a thousand others along it. Faces pass before you, good people, petty tyrants, both sorts overworked until anything extra is an irritation not to be borne, both sorts harried by their superiors and the local politicians who found attacking them a cheap window to public favor. You're unemployed? Haven't you tried to get work? What do you mean too old? At forty-seven? They say no one's hiring untrained forty-seven-year-old women? You say you're a writer. What books? Oh, those. You own nothing? Not even a car? Estimated income for the year. Oh, really, you expect me to believe that? I've seen your name, you're won prizes. Or—hi, Jule, haven't seen you for years, what you been doing? Oh, god, I'm sorry. Cancer? All that high life catching up with you, no I'm just joking, I know it isn't funny. I hate to tell you what funding's like this year. Look, let me send you over to Gerda. And don't be such a stranger after this. On and on. Keep your temper. They're really trying to help you, most of them, if they get snappish it's because they hate having to tell you they can't do anything. Answer patiently. Show the doctor's report. Explain you couldn't afford insurance, you can't afford anything, you're just getting by. Say over and over what you've said before as you're shunted from person to person, watch them hunt about for cracks to ease you through. Be patient. Experience should tell you that you can outwit the system if you keep at it. Try to wash off the stain of failure that is ground deeper and deeper into you. And try to forget the fear that is ground deeper and deeper into you as the days pass. You know the lumps are growing. You can't even feel them yet, but you know they're there, you have nightmares about them. Treacherous flesh feeding on flesh.

Yet more aggravation. The landlords raise the rents to pay for a sort of sentry box they've built into the side of the foyer, equipped with bulletproof glass, a speaker system and controls for the automatic bolts on the inner and outer foyer doors and the steel grill outside. An armed guard sits in the box day and night, no strangers are allowed in without prior notice. The landlords also save money by doing no repairs no matter how much the tenants complain. And as the chaos increases in Julia's flesh, the disruption increases in society around her. There are food riots and job riots. In the suburbs, vigilante groups are beginning to patrol the streets armed with rifles and shotguns. There are a number of accidents, spooked patrols shoot some night-shifters going home, but are merely told to be more careful. Police are jumpy, shoot to kill at the slightest provocation, even imagined provocation. At first there is some outcry against this, but the protesters are drowned in a roar of outrage from those in power. The powerless everywhere begin to organize to protect themselves since no one else seems willing to. No one can stand alone in the world that is coming into being here.

Except Julia. Stubbornly alone she plods through the increasingly resistant bureaucracy. More and more of the people she has worked with are being fired or laid off or are walking away from impossible conditions; funding is decreasing rapidly as the fist of power squeezes tighter about the powerless. It is becoming a question of whether she can break through the last of the barriers before the forces eating at the system devour it completely. She is growing more and more afraid, but bolsters herself by ignoring everything but the present moment. The economy is staggering. More and more are out of work, thrown out of homes, apartments, housing projects, more and more live in the streets until they are driven from the city. Tension builds by day, by night. Prices for food are shooting upward as supply systems begin to break down. Underground markets dealing in food and medicines begin to appear. Hijacking of produce and meat trucks becomes commonplace, organized by the people running the illegal markets, by bands of the homeless and unemployed desperate to feed their families. The UD overgovernment organizes convoys protected by the national guard. It is clumsy and inefficient but food fills the shelves again. Prices go up some more. The first minister of Domain Pacifica declares martial law. The constitution is suspended for the duration of the emergency. The homeless, the jobless, the rebellious are arrested and sent to labor camps. The city begins to quiet, the streets empty at night, night shifters are rarer and generally go home in groups. Knots of angry folk begin to form in the mountains, people driven from the city by the labor laws, local vigilantes or GLAM enforcers—bands of men generally in their twenties and fanatically loyal to GLAM principles. Because these men wear black semi-uniforms on their outings, they're given the name blackshirts by those likely to be their victims.

Julia gets her novel manuscript back without comment; the next day a letter comes requesting the return of the advance. She immediately withdraws the last of her money from her savings account, leaves just enough in her checking account to cover current bills, writes the publishers that she is taking their request under advisement, wishing she could tell them they could whistle for their money. She sighs over the royalties they'd withhold, but with the courts in their present mood, there isn't much she can do but be glad for once that these are reduced to a trickle, since most of the books are vanishing from stores and libraries into the fires of the righteous. She cannot understand what is so offensive about her books. There's a bit of sex, but nothing really raunchy—it wasn't necessary—some misery, for after all she is writing mostly about the poor, about the odd characters she'd grown up with. She likes her people, even the most flawed and evil of them, writing of them with sympathy and understanding of the forces that shaped them. She grows depressed when she thinks about them vanishing in black smoke, can only hope that moderation and intelligence will make themselves felt before the country tears apart.

She sleeps badly; things are closing in about her. She has enough money to keep her going another few months if prices don't rise too drastically, or the city itself doesn't shut down. By then she should be in a hospital somewhere. She has stopped watching the news or reading newspapers, notices events only when they impact directly on her life. . . .

Until the day she comes home worn out, sick, beginning finally to admit she could fail, dispiritedly wondering if she could somehow pry the money out of Hrald.

She pressed the bellbutton, stood with weary impatience while the guard looked her over. She was too tired to feel any more anger at the obstacle between her and the bath she wanted so much, even though the water would be cold and she'd have to heat pots of it on the stove, feeling absurdly like the pioneer women who helped settle this region more than five centuries before. When she was still writing, she rather enjoyed the process, working on her novel while the water heated, the tub was filled, pot by slow pot. How good it was going to feel, sliding into water almost too hot to bear, hot soapy water spreading over her body, a last pot set aside to wash her hair. The locks buzzed and she pushed inside.

As she trudged up the stairs to the fourth floor, she ignored the irritating echoes, the ugly smears on the walls, the dead smell in the air. These were once the firestairs, meant for emergency use only. The metal steps were worn and dangerously slippery especially during the hot rains of summer when the walls oozed moisture and drips fell six floors, bouncing off the steps and spattering on the heads of those that had to use them. She plodded up and around, cursing the landlords who wouldn't fix her heater though the law said they were responsible for it. And she couldn't bring in an outside repairman without permission and she couldn't get permission because they wouldn't answer her calls or her letters, leaving her more than half convinced they wanted her out of there. If she wanted hot water, she could move.

Halfway up she stopped, laughed, seeing as silly the gloom she was indulging, knowing she'd almost regret getting the heater fixed. Once she was inside her apartment, she'd relax into the pleasures of anticipation. The making of her bath was one of the many small rituals she found herself adopting lately, rituals that gave a kind of surety and continuity to her life as things around her degenerated into chaos. She straightened her shoulders, chuckled when a single warm drop of water bounced off her nose, then started up again. It wasn't that late, not even two yet. Three of the people she had to see left word they'd be out of town until the end of the week. She glanced at her watch, nodded. She could start looking through her manuscripts and her notebooks, seeing if there was something that could be salvaged, something she could get to her foreign publishers that might bring her in a little money. She knew what those messages meant; one of them was from an old acquaintance who liked her well enough to be uncomfortable about giving her a bad answer; she suspected he'd seized the opportunity to send a nonverbal message he knew she'd understand. She stepped onto the fourth floor landing, shoved at the press-bar with her hip, nudged the door open and started down the hall.

She dealt automatically with the three locks, pushed the door open, kicked her shoes off, dropped her purse on a small table and swung around.

And stopped, her heart thudding.

Five men stood at the far end of the room watching her.

Young men. Not boys. Mid to late twenties. Short clipped hair. Clean shaven. Black shirts. Button-down collars. Neat black ties. Tailored black trousers. Black boots, trouser cuffs falling with clean precision exactly at the instep. Black leather gloves, supple as second skins. They looked like dress-up spy dolls, vaguely plastic, with less expression than any doll.

"Who are you?" She was pleased her voice was steady though the question was stupid, she knew well enough what they were, who didn't matter.

"Julia Dukstra?"

Anger began to outshine fear. "Get the hell out of here," she said. "You have no right. This is my home." She scowled, remembering the locks she'd had to open, silently cursed the landlords—who else could get them past the guard and hand them whatever keys they wanted? She started for the phone. "I don't care who you are, get out of here. I'm calling the police." One of the plastic dolls stepped in front of the phone. She wheeled, started for the door. A second blackshirt got there before her. She swung back around to face the one who'd spoken. "What is this?"

"Julia Dukstra?" he repeated. He had a high, light tenor that rose to a squeak at times. He didn't wait for her to answer but went into what was obviously a set speech. "There are those who corrupt the morals of all who touch them; there are those who spread filth and corruption everywhere, who mean to destroy goodness and innocence in women and children, who advocate adultery and unnatural acts, who incite the poor to rebellion instead of blessing God for letting them be born into the United Domains where hard work and steady faith will reward them with all they need or want. There are those who are intent on destroying this nation which is the greatest on God's green earth. These purveyors of filth must be warned and if they persist in their treachery they must be punished. . . ." He went on speaking with the spontaneity of a tape recorder. I bet he says that to all us purveyors of filth, she thought and wanted to giggle. They were so solemn, so ridiculous. . . . Good god, what a tin ear he's got, him or whoever wrote that spiel.

But as the man went on, the stench of violence grew thicker and heavier in the room, as if this pack of wolves smelled her growing terror and grew excited by the smell.

". . . must be disciplined, taught to fear the wrath of the

Lord, the anger of the righteous man. Your filth will no longer be permitted to pollute the minds of the young and the weak in spirit. Temptation will be removed from them." He stepped aside and pointed.

One of her bedsheets was spread out in the corner of the room, the mint green one with the teastain at one end. On it was heaped most of her books, the ones she'd written, the others she bought for reference and pleasure, books she'd kept because they meant something to her. Beside the tumbled towers of the books, all her manuscripts, the old ones, her copies, the novel and story just returned, both copies, her notebooks. Fifteen years work. They were going to wipe it out. They were going to take all that away. Her books, her manuscripts, her bedsheet. Take them away and burn them. "No," she said. "No." She started for the pile.

The blackshirt caught hold of her arm, jerked her around. Without stopping to think, she slapped him, hard.

He slapped her back, swung her around and threw her at the blackshirt beside him.

Who punched her in the stomach, slapped her, laughed in her face and threw her to the next man.

Violence was a conflagration in the room. Around and around, slapping her, punching her, not too hard, not hard enough to spoil her, around the circle then around again. They began tearing her clothes off, calling her all the names men had dreamed up to get back at women who made them feel weak and uncertain, the vomit of fear and hate and rage. She tried to break away, got to the bathroom, couldn't get the door shut in time, tried to get into the hall, but they pulled her away; she kicked at them, hit out, clawed at them, sobbing with the futility of it and the anger at herself for letting them see her cry, struggling on and on, fighting them with every ounce of strength in her, even after they got her on the floor, twisting and writhing, biting and stuggling until one of them cursed and kicked her in the head.

When she opened her eyes, they were gone—leaving the

door open behind them, a last expression of their contempt. She stood up, moaned as her head throbbed; she touched the knot and wondered if she had a concussion. At least she wasn't seeing double. She stared at the door for what seemed an eternity, the locks intact, their promise of security a lie now, must have always been a lie. She wanted to die. Filthy, soiled, never clean again, oh god. Then rage swept through her, she ground her teeth together, swayed back and forth, then stopped that as she felt the grind of bone against bone, a stabbing pain that shut off her breathing. Broken rib. At least one. Slowly, carefully, she got to her feet. The room swam in front of her. She crashed back onto her knees, moaned with pain, fought off the dizziness. She crawled to a chair and used it to pull herself back onto her feet, stood holding the chair's back until the room was steady about her. Moving like a sick old woman, she scuffed to the door, pushed it shut and fumbled the chain into place, then stood with her back pressed against the door, looking vaguely about the room. I can't stay here, she thought. Not alone. Not tonight.

The books were gone, the manuscripts. "Choke on the smoke," she said and pushed away from the door. She shuffled to the bathroom, stood looking at the tub. A hot bath. No chance of that now. She would not have strength enough to haul the pot from the stove. Clutching at a tap handle, bending with exaggerated care, she fumbled the plug in place. A cold bath was better than nothing, she had to scrub away the leavings of those wolves. She started the water running, stood there listening to the soothing splash and tried to think. She looked at her watch. Three. Out over an hour. She stripped the watch off and laid it on the sink, looked into the tub. There were several inches of water in it. She stepped over the side, clutched at the tap handles and lowered herself slowly into the water, the cold sending a shock up through her. She sat quietly for a while, watching a red mist move out into the water from between her legs. One thing about cold water, it wouldn't make her bleed more than she already had. She pumped some soap from a soap bottle and began scrubbing at

herself, her final admission to herself that she wasn't going
to the police. In the best of worlds it would be difficult
talking about what had happened and this was far from the
best of worlds. Besides, stories were common enough among
the folk she'd been with recently about how the police
always turned a blind eye to what the blackshirts did. I've
been drifting in a dream too long, she thought, too involved in my own troubles. Suddenly dizzy, she pressed
her head back over the rim of the large old tub. After a
minute she realized she was crying, salt tears sliding off
her cheeks into hair. Irritated, she pulled herself up again,
splashed water onto her face, then used the towel rack to
lever herself onto her feet.

Dizzy again with the effort it took to get out of the tub,
she began drying herself, dabbing very cautiously at her
body with the clean bathtowel she'd hung there that morning. It would have been easier on her if she hadn't fought
so hard, but she wasn't sorry she'd refused to give in. It
seemed to her if she gave up in any way, if she stopped
trying, she would die. Which was funny in its macabre
way because she was dying, or would be dying if she
didn't somehow finance the operation. She looked at the
towel. Still bleeding. Shit. She slipped the watch back
onto her wrist, went into the kitchen, found a clean
dishtowel, then into the bedroom where she found a pair of
safety pins. She pinned the folded towel into her under-
pants. Holding onto the back of a chair, she stepped into
the pants, grunting as the movements shifted the cracked
rib and pulled at sore muscles. She had to stop several
times because of the pain, but she wouldn't give up. You
can always find a way to do what you have to do, she told
herself. You only get lax and lazy when there's someone
around to do for you.

Moving with patient care, she got dressed, flat sandals, a
skirt and blouse because a woman in pants was unnecessary provocation these days. She stood holding onto the
chair back for a short while, gathering her strength, then
went into the living room, her mouth set in a grim line,
her eyes half closed. She reached for the phone, intending

to call Jim, let him know she was coming and why, pulled her hand back, knowing with sudden dreadful certainty that she was marked now, typhoid Mary for all her friends and anyone who might help her. The phone might not be tapped or bugged or whatever they were calling it these days, but she was in no mood for taking chances. Money, she thought, I'll need money. For a panic-filled moment she wondered if they'd found her stash, but they hadn't been looking for money and they hadn't torn the place apart. She went slowly into the bedroom, a wry smile for her shambling progress, tortoise, old, old tortoise, slow and steady wins the race. We'll beat you yet, you shitbags. That was a favorite word of the old woman she'd sat next to one whole afternoon a couple weeks ago. Good word for them, expressive. She stretched up, grunting with pain, unscrewed the end of the curtain rod, thrust her fingers inside. And went limp with relief as she touched the rolled up bills. She took enough to pay for a cab, tried not to think about how fast the stash was dwindling.

She phoned for a cab, not caring about listeners, arranged for him to pick her up in a half-hour, promising to be waiting outside—not that she wanted to, but drivers wouldn't leave their armored enclosures for anything. She eased herself onto the edge of a chair, wondering if she could make it down the stairs without passing out. She looked at her watch. Quarter to four. Time to start down, might take a while. She got slowly to her feet, pushed the purse's strap over her shoulder and shuffled across to the door, stood looking at the locks, wanting to laugh, wanting to cry. She did neither, just pulled the door shut, twisted the key in the landlord's flimsy lock and didn't bother with the others.

She started down the hall, moving a little easier with each step; going somewhere seemed to loosen her up and ease the pain, so that could manage the stairs.

The door to the apartment nearest the stairs was open partway. She started past it, stopped when she heard a low sound filled with pain. She wanted to go on, to ignore that moan, but she knew only too well what that open door meant. I won't give in, she thought; I won't let them make me a stone. She reached into her purse, got her dark glasses, put them on to cover the swelling around her eyes, and went into the room.

He was on his knees beside the sprawled body of his lover, the boy who'd come to help her some months before, who'd grinned at her after that if they chanced to meet on the stairs, who'd helped her tote her packages up the stairs. His friend's head was turned so his profile was crisp against the dark blue of the rug, his head tilted at an impossible angle against his shoulder. He looked as if some giant had picked him up, snapped his neck and thrown him carelessly aside. The youth, whose name she still didn't know, was crying very quietly, rocking forward and back, his arms closed tight over his chest, his mouth swollen, bleeding, his nose swollen, perhaps broken.

"Hello," she said. It seemed absurd, but what else could she say?

The boy jerked around, somehow propelled himself away from her and onto his feet, reminding her of a wild cat she'd seen late one night when she was supposed to be in bed but couldn't sleep because the moon was so bright it made her want things she couldn't name. She'd come on the cat while it was tearing at a rabbit's carcass. It had leaped up like the boy, put distance between them, then waited to see what she would do, unwilling to abandon the rabbit unless it had to.

The boy's face changed when he recognized her and saw her injuries. "They got you too?" His voice was mushy, lisping, his arms up tight against his ribs again, an automatic movement dictated by pain.

"Little over an hour ago." She walked slowly to the man's body, stood looking down at it, then lifted her head and looked at the boy. "What are you going to do?"

He turned his head, with a farouche look, but he said nothing.

She glanced at her watch. The cab wouldn't wait, she had to get downstairs. She dug into her purse, brought out her spare keys, held them out, said, "Look, I don't know you, nor you me, and I've got no right to tell you what to do and maybe you already know what to do, but I suggest you get the hell out of here. Leave your friend. You can't do anything for him now. Those shitbags who did this, they'll call the police on you. This isn't a time when you could get anything like a fair trial. You probably wouldn't even survive long enough to have a trial." She jangled her keys. "Take these. If you want, you can go to ground a little while in my apartment. Think things out. Be out of the way if the police do come. I'll be back . . . um . . . in a couple of hours probably, going to see my doctor." She smiled, winced as the cut in her lip pulled. "Look, I've got to go. Make up your mind."

He gazed at her a moment longer. "You sure you want to do this? Could make trouble for you. More trouble."

"Hnh! More trouble than I got already? You notice they had keys? The police come down on me, you won't make more hassle for me. I've got a feeling. . . ." She touched her ribs then her cut lip. "I wouldn't last longer than you." He gaped at her. "Purveyor of filth," she said. "I'm a writer." She looked at her watch. "Last time—you want the keys or not. I'm going."

His face went drawn and bleak, gaining ten years in that moment, and he came to her, taking the keys. "Thanks. Mind if I pack some things and shift them over?"

She started for the door. "Whatever you want. Better keep it light, but you know better than I do how much you can shift and keep easy on your feet. And remember the guard downstairs; you'll have to get past him."

She heard a soft clearing of his throat, smiled a little and went out to tackle the stairs.

The sun was brilliant, the sky cloudless. She blinked as she stepped outside. She'd known it was still early, she'd looked at her watch again and again, yet the brightness and calm of the afternoon startled her. The street was empty. Perhaps the blackshirts hadn't called the police about the dead man, perhaps they were expecting the boy to do himself in by trying to rid himself of the body, perhaps they were just making sure of alibis before they acted.

The cab was a few minutes late, giving her time to catch her breath. The boxy blue vehicle stopped in the middle of the street. The driver thumbed a button and the passenger door hummed open, then he sat drumming his fingers on the steering wheel as she walked slowly across and with some difficulty climbed into the back.

"Where to?" The driver's voice, tinny and harsh, crackled through the cheap speaker.

She opened her mouth, shut it again. As bad as phoning. She ran her tongue over her lips, tasted the slight saltiness of blood. The cut had opened when she was talking to the boy. She tried to think. "Evenger building," She said finally.

"Right."

As the cab ground off, she pressed her hand hard against her mouth as some of the strain left her. She was on her way to help at last. Evenger building was across the square from the Medical Center where Dr. James Alexander Norris had his office. Her friend, her doctor. He'd spent time and patience on her, filling in and signing the interminable forms that the office snowed on her and had looked into private charities for her. This was the end of all that struggle. She probably shouldn't be going to see him now, but she had no real choice. She pushed the dark glasses back up her nose. I'd better phone from the Evenger, she thought. Let him know what to expect. She sighed. Let him decide if he wants to see me.

She lowered herself into the chair as the nurse went briskly out. Her head was swimming; she felt nauseated and worn to a thread.

A hand touched her shoulder. "Julia?"

She lifted her head. For a moment she couldn't speak, then she grunted with pain as the cracked rib shifted and bruised muscles protested. She reached up, pulled off the dark glasses.

He came round in front of her, a slight dark man, grave now, his usual quick nervous smile suppressed, his dark eyes troubled. He leaned closer, his fingers gentle on the swellings under her eyes. "Blackshirts did this?"

"That and a lot more. Five of them. They came for my books and manuscripts. I made the mistake of slapping one of them." She spoke wearily, dropped her head against the back of the chair, closed her eyes. "They raped me. Anything that's started I want stopped. Off the pill. You know. No lover. Me over forty. You warned me. God, I couldn't stand . . . couldn't stand it. Pregnant by one of those. . . . those neanderthals." She sighed, opened her eyes. "Jim, I'm poison. Guilt by association. That's the way their minds work, those lumps of gristle they call minds. I'm afraid I've already made trouble for you. Your name on all those papers. . . ."

"Let's get you on the table." He took her hand and helped her to stand. "Technically the nurse should be here but I thought you'd rather not. How long ago did all this happen?"

"You're right as usual." She grunted as she eased onto the slick white paper. "I got home a little before two. By the way, I didn't tell you. One of them kicked me in the head and I was out until just about three. No double vision but one hell of a throb."

His hands moved quickly over her, producing assorted grunts, gasps and groans that he listened to with a combination of detached interest and anxiety. "And how are you feeling right now?"

"Sore." She tried to laugh but couldn't. "Angry. Frightened. But you don't want to hear that. Nauseated. But not to the point of having to vomit. Kind of sick all over. There was some dizziness but that hasn't come back for a while now, aaah-unh! One of the boots must've got me there. Most of all tired. So tired, it takes all I have to move, you know, like trying to run against water."

"Mmm. X-ray first, then some more tests. I've got things set up so they'll take you now, no questions."

"I . . . I can't pay for them."

"Don't worry about that, Julia. Forget about everything and let me take care of you."

When tests and treatment were done, he walked with her down to the basement carpark, meaning to take her home before he went out to the safer suburbs and the family he kept resolutely separate from his practice. They walked down the gritty oily metal ramp, their footsteps booming and scraping, the sounds broken into incoherence, echoing and re-echoing until there seemed an army marching heavy-footed down into the cavernous basement. He dipped his head close to hers. "I can't live with what's happening here, Julia," he said. "Police and others have been at me for weeks to open my records. I won't do that, burn them first. I've been making arrangements to go north. There's a medical group in Caledron willing to take me in." He hesitated. She felt his uncertainty, felt the resolution grow in him. "You can't stay here. Come up with us."

She glanced at him, surprised yet not surprised after all. She appreciated the invitation all the more because of the reluctance with which it was given. It wasn't easy for him, he'd be a lot happier if she refused, but the offer was genuine. In a lot of ways he was a very nice man. A nice man with a sweet bitch for a wife who owned his baffled loyalty. He'd stopped loving her years ago but to this day wouldn't admit to himself that he didn't even like her. Julia didn't know the woman but some years back when she'd met Jim over the tangled lives of several of his charity patients, she'd heard more than she wanted about her. He was going through a phase where he was unable to stop talking about her whenever he could find a receptive ear. Her name was Elaine. She was a slim dark woman with a natural elegance and much charm when she chose to exercise it. He never spoke of intimate things, that was a matter of taste for him, bad taste to take such things outside the home, but she gathered there was a wall between him and his wife he couldn't penetrate. Because he was wholly uninterested in anything beyond the diseases and disabilities in the bodies he examined, yet had a sensitivity to nuance he couldn't quite suppress, Elaine had him in a ferment of misery and guilt which she seemed to take a certain satisfaction in creating. Julia had sufficient good sense not to tell him what his wife was doing to him, sufficient perception to see that being shut off from nine-tenths of his life had driven her to this, and not enough sense to avoid comforting him as much as she could. While they worked out the tangles of the cases, they worked themselves into a brief affair. He clung to Julia with an urgency that troubled her; she wasn't in love with him, or so she thought, but she liked him very well indeed. And she was grateful for the need that brought him to her. The casework was getting to her more and more, eroding the hope and humanity out of her, sucking her dry of all feeling but a generalized impatience with the self-defeated souls she was trying to help. Even the ones with the capacity to break out of the morass had so many defeats ahead of them, so many leeches battening on them, that after a while they ran out of energy, they simply had no strength left to climb over the next barrier that folly, greed and prejudice raised before them. In those last days before she quit, it was a kind of race to see if she could manage to leave before she was fired. She began working as her clients' advocate rather than as an impersonal conduit for services; she bent the rules more and more savagely as they (the anonymous gray *they* in offices she never visited, never wanted to visit) threw the worst cases at her, then reprimands for sidestepping regulations. She tended the chinks in the system and did her best to help her people through them; she brought her work home with her. She couldn't write. She began to feel brittle, dry, as if the least blow would shatter her to powder. She lost her laughter and the thing she'd never thought to lose, her rush of delight in the sudden beauty of small things. Somehow, by loving her and needing her, Jim breathed life back into her. Only a handful of meetings, yet they triggered in her a healing flow that she couldn't tell him about because he would never understand the only words she could find to express what had happened to her. She did manage, by tact and indirection, to give him ways of dealing with his wife and earned his profound gratitude by easing the sex out of their relationship as soon as she realized how unhappy and uneasy he was about what they were doing; he had no idea how to stop without hurting her and he was unwilling to hurt her. Though the change was rather more painful for her than she'd expected, nonetheless she was happy enough with the affectionate committed friendship they'd shared afterward. She owed him something else too, a debt she hoped he'd never discover. He and his troubles with his wife had formed the basis of the one novel she'd come close to getting on the best seller list, the novel that had won a fairly prestigious award, that had brought her enough money to quit the job, enough recognition to make her next two novels sell almost as well and to get the first into paperback.

She reached over, touched his face with reminiscent tenderness, shook her head. "They wouldn't let me out, Jim. They need their objects of scorn. Though I thank you for the offer."

"What are you going to do?"

"I don't know. Go somewhere. Fight them somehow. As long as I can."

He ran a hand through fine, thinning hair. "Suicide, Julia. And it's unnecessary."

"By whose terms?" She shrugged, the tape around her ribs tugging at her. "These days there's only one solution to the problems of poverty. Can't make it? Too bad. Go curl up and die, preferably at the city dump so no time or money has to be wasted carting you away. I'd rather make them shoot me. At least that's over fast. And no, I won't kill myself. I don't think I could, anyway that's giving in to them. I'll never give in to them."

"You oughtn't to be alone, Julia." He looked at her, worried. "I don't like the way you're talking. "It's not. . . ."

"Not healthy? I know. The times are out of joint, my friend, and there's nothing I can do to set them right. Did I tell you? No, I'm sure not. Publisher rejected my last book, wants his advance back. No, don't worry about me, I won't be alone. A boy from down the hall is there waiting for me. My little band of brothers visited him after they left me. Broke his friend's neck. An excess of zeal, no doubt. Kicked him about too, but seems a corpse made them nervous so they were a trifle half-hearted in the beating. He can still move." She got into the car as he held the door open for her, sat with her head against the rest, her eyes closed. When she felt the seat shift, heard the other door close, she said, "Don't mind me, Jim. Gloom and doom's all I have in me right now. I'll be back to my usual bounce and glow given a night's rest. I'm just tired. That's all. Just tired."

Suicide. She brooded on that during the struggle up the stairs. The lumps had started showing up on x-ray plates though she still couldn't feel them. Bigger but operable. She did have a bit of hope again. If she could get across the border and up to Caledron, if she could manage to get some sort of papers, Jim had promised to ease her into a hospital there. Money. It was going to take a lot of money. If I have to rob a bank, she thought and grinned into the turgid light about the stairs. She leaned for a moment on the rail and rested, then started up again. It might take something like that. Been honest all my life, she thought. Proud of it. She sighed. I'm going to make a lousy criminal. Have to use my connections. She giggled, caught her breath as she clung to the rail. A drop of water plonked on her head, another hit her shoulder. Oh hell. She started on again. Scattered among the beaten-down, the frantic, the wistfully hopeful, the ignorant, greedy, despairing, lazy, energetic, damaged and ambitious mixture that made up her files were a few whose sons, husbands, boyfriends or girlfriends she'd met on home visits when they'd learned to trust her enough to show up—burglars, pimps, whores, conmen and women, a bankrobber or two and a charming forger who took an artist's pride in his work. He'd be useful if he was still out of prison—or out again, as the case might be. And there was old Magic Man. He knew everything about everybody. If he hadn't been rounded up and shoved into a labor camp. Probably hadn't, he looked too decrepit to do anything but breathe. He loved ripe apricots; she always took him some, even when she couldn't afford it, she enjoyed so much watching him enjoy them. Sometimes he helped her with her books; more often than not she just went to hear his stories. He had a thousand stories of places he'd been, things he'd done and he never told them the same twice. He'd worked for her father a couple summers, helping with the haying, milking the cows, disappeared as quietly as he'd come until he'd showed up one day on her client list. He hadn't forgotten her, recognized the girl in the woman without any prompting, talked to her a lot about her father after that, something she'd been needing for a long time. Thinking about him she forgot about her body and went round and round the stairs until she almost blundered past her floor. She stopped, put out her hand to the wall to steady herself, a little dizzy with her exertions and her sudden return to the unpleasant here and now. She pushed the bar in, grunting as the effort caught her in muscles that were getting stiffer and more painful as the hours passed. The door thumped to behind her as she started down the hall, the sound making her jump, reminding her just how nervous she really was. The hall was empty. The worn drugget was full of holes and so filthy she couldn't see what color it was, couldn't remember either. I stopped noticing things, she thought. When I stopped being a writer. She looked at her watch. Almost eight. Weariness descended on her. She stood, resting against the wall a moment, then made off toward her apartment.

The one lock was engaged as she'd left it, but when she pushed on the door, it caught. For an instant she didn't realize what was wrong, just stood there staring at the door that wouldn't open, then she saw that the chain was on. And remembered—the boy from down the hall.

"Just a minute." It was a whisper from inside. The door pushed almost closed, she heard the greased slide of metal against metal, then the door was open, though the boy was canny enough to stand behind it so no one outside could see him. She shuffled in, irritated that the boy was there because she didn't have the energy to cope with company, to bestir herself and put on her company face. She dropped onto the couch with a sigh and a groan, pulled off the dark glasses that had begun to be too small to conceal the bruises round her eyes.

The boy stood hesitantly in the middle of the small shabby room, then went out into the kitchen. He came back almost immediately with a tray. Her teapot and a cup of tea poured out. He set the tray on the couch beside her and stepped back. "There wasn't any coffee so I figured you wouldn't want that, but I don't know if you use sugar or lemon or milk or what. If you're like Hank . . . was . . . you drink it straight. You use loose tea like him and there wasn't any of the other things." He looked down at his hands. "I hope you don't mind. I've made a casserole out of the chicken in your refrigerator. Something I could reheat without ruining it." He knew he was chattering but he looked as uneasy as she felt.

She smiled, took up the cup, sipped at the hot liquid, holding each mouthful a second then letting it flood down her throat. The heat spread through her, washing away some of her tension and uncertainty. She sighed, held the cup with both hands curled about it. "Feels marvelous," she said and watched the boy relax even though she winced at the phoniness she heard in her voice. "And I'm half-starved." That was true, she hadn't had anything to eat since breakfast. "Smells good." At least that was real, the truth of her sudden enjoyment firm in her voice. She sniffed again and smiled.

"It should be done in another fifteen minutes." He moved to a straight-backed chair next to the phone. The lamp beside him, picking out fine lines about his eyes and mouth. *He's older than I thought, maybe even late twenties.* He looked gravely at her. "You were right," he said. "Police came about a half hour after you left, took him away, started pounding on doors. Most everybody was out—working, I suppose, so they didn't get many answers."

"Half hour. Long enough for the blackshirts to fix up

their respectable alibis." She poured more tea, gulped at it. "I didn't see anyone hanging about." She lifted the cup and held it against her cheek, her eyes closed. "But I wasn't in any shape to notice much."

His long mobile mouth curled up in an ugly grin. "If one pervert kills another," he said in the round mellifluous tones of a TV preacher, "that is God's judgment on them for their evil, sinful ways, God's way to protect the righteous from their corruption." His face looked drawn and miserable, the effect exaggerated by the light shining down on him.

"What are you going to do? Do you have family you can get back to?"

That painful travesty of a smile again. "I grew up in a small town a few hundred miles east and south of here. If they've got a local branch of the blackshirts, my dad's more likely than not the head man."

"Ah. Sorry."

"Been living with it more than long enough to be used to it. He kicked me out when I was sixteen. That's a while back."

She sat up, sore still all over. "I forgot. They were in here. The blackshirts."

"Uh-huh." This time he showed his teeth in the familiar broad grin. "I swept the place. Not to worry. They left a passive bug in the phone. No imagination. It's down the garbage chute. That's all."

"You're sure?"

"Uh-huh. Been playing with gadgets, games, computers long as I can remember. I'm good, if I can brag a bit. And I work in this hobby shop that's more than half a comp-security source, so I keep up. Besides, you know from what you said, the kind of shit I get rained on me, so I like to keep my nose sharp. And it's not like these batbrains are government, not yet anyway; they get their stuff from shops like Dettingers."

She refilled her cup, sat back holding it, the warmth in her middle spreading outward, loosening up stiffness, making the soreness more bearable. "I'm not used to all this ducking and swerving."

"Better get used." He shrugged. "There was a time." He lifted his head, sniffed. "I better check. You want to eat in here or in the kitchen, or what?"

"Kitchen," she said. "Give me a hand."

She looked down at her plate. "You could make a living at this, young Michael."

He shook his head. "Hank was a lot better, but he taught me a few useful tricks. What about you? You going to stay here or what?"

"Not here. I'm going to see about getting myself across the border. Pain's no turn-on for me—that I can swear to—and those vultures will be around when they get their nerve back." She arranged the fork and knife in neat diagonals across the plate. "Besides, I'm going broke too fast." She watched as he put what was left of the casserole in a small bowl and topped it with foil, then began filling the kettle with water. She was amused as she watched him run cold water in the sink and frown at it, then set the pots and plates in it. He was so much more domesticated than she'd ever been.

He looked over his shoulder. "You don't have any hot water. Cold baths all the time?"

"No. Just lots of hauling."

"Stinking landlords. Won't fix it or let you?"

"Not a hope." She rubbed at her eyes. "I tried." She put her hands flat on the table and stared at them. "Happens I need a mastectomy in the next few months and I haven't a hope of money for that either which worries me a trifle more than a niggling little inconvenience like a hot water heater that won't heat water. Sorry, didn't mean to dump that on you, it's just . . . hell."

"Hey, Julia, no sweat, hey. I thought I had problems." He tried to smile but his mouth quivered helplessly before he could control it and he turned hastily away, began scrubbing hard at one of the plates.

"Forget it," she said briskly. Her parents had died within six months of each other not long after she married Hrald. She remembered how her mother kept looking about her for that six months, almost as if she expected to see the old man walking in or standing about, then breaking down when she realized he was gone; it was the same now, Michael suddenly remembering that his lover was dead. "Look," she said. "You have to get out of here sometime. Try going out any window and you'll have alarms going off, the police here before you could sneeze. Well, you know that." She watched the taut slim back, muscles bunching and shifting about under the skin-tight tee-shirt as he used the scrubber on the casserole dish; he said nothing, making no response to her words. "Garbage truck isn't due till the end of the week, so the chute's out. You'll have to get past the guard and he knows you." She chuckled. "I wrote a thriller once, so I've got the patter down and can pull a plot together with the best." He looked over his shoulder at her as he rinsed the dish, a slight but genuine smile denting his cheek. He said nothing, just started on the frying pan. She chuckled again, feeling infinitely better for no reason she could think of. "There's a gaggle of secretaries on the second floor who usually leave in a bunch, seven-thirty most mornings. I've seen them several times since I gave up being a nightowl and sleeping through the mornings. So—you're small-boned and about my height, a little shorter maybe but not enough to hurt. I've got clothes left over from the days of my servitude. And a rather nice wig I haven't worn since . . . well, never mind that. Shoes could be a problem, but if you've got a pair of boots, they might do. What you can't carry out in a shoulderbag, I could smuggle out if you'll give me somewhere to send it. If our landlords keep on form, I'll be getting an eviction notice before the week is over. That will give me excuse enough for taking boxes out. No need to leave your things for the vultures to inherit. Me, I'd take the paint off the walls if I could." She looked around, sighed again. "Dammit, Michael, I earned this place. I've lived here ten years, It's been home."

He made an attractive woman in the blond wig that one of her more absurd miscalculations had bought for her, a spare pair of dark glasses, a close shave and makeup. Add to that a long brown skirt, a loose russet blouse, a wide soft black belt to match the soft black leather of his boots, black leather gloves of his own. She shuddered when she saw those. A black leather shoulderbag. Some basic instruction in sitting, standing and walking.

She followed him down, though he wanted her to keep well away in case he was stopped, afraid that she'd be connected with him and pulled into his danger. He didn't stop arguing with her until he stepped into the hall, then he sighed and started away toward the stairs. He had a swimmer's sleek body, a resurgent vitality powering the tiger-walk that looked female enough to pass. In many ways he was far more graceful than she'd ever been even when she had the energy and transient charm of youth. Watching him vanish into the stairwell, she felt an odd combination of chagrin, nostalgia and amusement as she started after him.

She went slowly down the steps, listening for the brisk clatter of his bootheels on the metal treads. The tape around her torso was beginning to itch. She was sweating too much. Below her, young women were talking, their words too distorted by the echoes to make sense. A burst of laughter. The hiss and clank of the exit door. The boots still clattering. She groaned. Catch up closer, Michael, closer so you'll seem to be one of them, closer so he won't look too hard at you. She turned the last corner and saw the flicker of the full brown skirt as he went out. She closed her eyes, held tight to the rail, then took one step down, another. . . .

He was already out on the street and sauntering away when she came through the grill and passed onto the sidewalk. She glanced after him, making the look as casual as she could. He wasn't hurrying and he'd forgotten what she'd told him about carrying his hips. Maybe I should have stuffed his feet into heels, she thought. She sighed and went the other way, heading for a breakfast she was really beginning to want.

\*　　　\*　　　\*

She sat at her writing table, the typewriter pushed to one side, the credit cards and ident cards in neat lines before her. Five different idents, a scratched worn image that might be her likeness on each of them, three credit cards for each ident. She looked at them without moving; sighed. Once she started there was no turning back. Bash the Kite following with the van, Julia into the store because her face wasn't known. It will be, after this, she thought. Can't be helped. Hit the stores quick. Know what you want. Don't hurry when you're inside but don't waste time either. Large stores, you can touch several departments. As long as you got good numbers and names no one's going to question you. Quit before you think you should. That's important. Bash's rules. She smiled when she thought of the round-faced brown man who could vanish in a crowd of two. With a half-angry sweep of her hands, she collected the cards in a heap before her. "I hate this," she said aloud; the words fell dead and meaningless into the silence.

That silence began to oppress her. She took the five leather folders from the wire basket and began fitting the idents and the credit cards into the slots inside the folders, working slowly and neatly though she wanted to throw them in anyhow and get them out of sight. She rose from the table, put her hand on the phone, took it away, swore softly, went into the bedroom, got her coat, some change for the public phone, bills for the cab, her teargas cylinder and the keys. It was foolish to the point of insanity to be going out now, but she couldn't stay here any longer, not tonight.

She went down the stairs too fast, had to catch the siderail to keep from plunging headfirst, but didn't modify her reckless flight until her hand touched the pressbar of the ground floor exitdoor, pausing to consider the situation before pressing the button for the outer doors to be opened.

"Ma'am," the speaker said suddenly.

"What?" She turned, startled. The guard was looking at her oddly, she thought. She was frightened, but kept her face quiet.

"It's after nine, Ma'am. Don't leave much time. The curfew, remember. Or maybe you didn't hear. You get back after twelve, I hafta report you."

It was a minute before she could speak. "Thank you," she said. "If I'm not back before then I will be staying with friends."

"Just so you remember, Ma'am. Don't want no fuss."

"No," she said. "Better no fuss." She went out the door a bit surprised that he'd bothered and cheered by the unexpected touch of caring.

She swung into the all-nite drugstore, saw the new sign, crudely lettered, CLOSE AT TWELVE, sighed and edged her way through the cluttered aisles to the public phone at the back of the store.

"Simon? Julia. Look, I need to talk. You free tonight?"

"Jule." A hesitation, then a heartiness nothing like his usual dry tones. "Why not. Come over. But . . . um . . . be discreet, will you? Always a lot of attention on a bachelor professor." He hung up before she could respond.

She wondered if it was worth the trouble. If she went now, she'd have to spend the night there. Irritated and miserable, but unable to stay alone this particular night, she dropped a coin in the phone and called a cab.

She left the cab at the edge of the faculty housing and walked briskly through the open gate, half expecting a guard to step out of the shadows and stop her. Not yet. But she could see the time coming. She walked along the curving street with its snug neat houses, neatly clipped lawns, strains of music drifting into the perfumed night air. Lilacs bloomed in some front yards, roses in others, a spindly jacaranda dropped purple petals that looked black in the sodium light and lay like drops of ink on grass and sidewalk. I'm too old to relish paranoia, she thought. Passwords and eavesdroppers, bugs in the phone, bugs in the mattress, censorship and thought police in the end, I suppose. She looked around. How absurd in this serenity, this remnant of a saner age.

There were cars dotted here and there along the streets as she wound her way deeper into the maze of curves, most with men sitting in them. One or two smoking cigarettes, all with small earphones and wires coiling away from them. Well, that's it, she thought. The sickness is here too, my mistake. She recollected the phonecall and nodded. Nothing strange about the way he spoke, not now.

When she reached Simon's house, she went round to the side door, and knocked there, hoping that this was what he meant, a gesture toward propriety meant more to mislead the watchers than any attempt to hide her presence from them. Watchers and listeners. He had to be at least a little frightened by the listeners like fleas infesting the streets.

The door opened before she had time to bring her hand down. Simon pulled her inside into a passionate embrace that made her grind her teeth as her not-quite-healed rib protested with a stabbing ache like cold air on a sore tooth. His hand went down her back, cupped a buttock, then reached out and pulled the door shut. "Hope the bastard got an eyeful," he said with the dry burr more akin to his usual tones than the prissy caution over the phone. "What the hell, Jule, you look like something you find stretched out on a freeway."

"So kind of you to notice. I need a drink, Simon."

He led her through the kitchen and into the living room. "What's it been? Six months? I tried calling a couple times but you were either not in or not answering your phone." He slid open the door to the liquor cabinet. "Gin or what?"

"Gin'll do," she said absently, staring around her with blank dismay. Vast holes gaped on the shelves that covered the walls. "You've had. . . ." Her eyes swept over the phone sitting with silent innocence on the table beside the TV and his sleek, expensive entertainment center. She swallowed and stopped talking. Passive receptor, pick up a whisper and pass it out over the phone line. Michael's voice calm and competent. The one they use, loud noises scramble it like an egg so if you can't stomp it or flush it, turn the radio on. "I see you've still got your records. I'm down tonight, feel like hearing the Bolero loud. Would your neighbors howl?" Paranoia, she thought. Do the futile little tricks, jump through hoops for the bastards.

He brought her the drink, the ice cubes clinking, his bare feet whispering over the plush of the rug, the intractable cowlick a pewter gray comma in the lamplight. "What. . . ." he began, but went quiet as she laid her finger across her lips. "Let them complain. Not that they will."

Once the driving rhythms of the music were filling the room, she relaxed a little. Simon settled on the couch beside her. "What's all that about?"

"You've had visitors." She waved a hand at the bookshelves. "They leave droppings behind." In quick spare language she told him about the visit of the blackshirts, about the dead man down the hall, about the bug in her phone, about the men sitting in the cars outside. "We don't know how to deal with a police state, our kind," she finished. "We can't take it quite seriously. I've got a cracked rib, my books are being burned, my publishers won't touch me any longer, that's real, all of it, but when I hear them talking on the TV, when I stand in the middle of my own living room and listen to that vulture rant, I just can't believe in him or any of them. This kind of thing belongs in a bad thriller, don't you think?" She looked around at the plundered room, shook her head. When did they clean out your books?"

"A month ago."

"How bad is it getting? Are they burning professors yet?"

"Not funny, Jule. The apes are in charge of the men. No. That's insulting apes." He looked at the phone, passed his hand over his hair, ruffling the cowlick further. "I've been told I have to revise my texts. Correct them, if you will. Some of the things I said happened didn't, at least in the new official version of history."

"Ah. I always thought some of ours envied some of theirs their control over what gets printed or put out on the air." She laughed unhappily, raised her glass. "Here's to one world. Their bastards and ours, brothers under the skin."

He made a grumpy throat-clearing sound, half a protest, half a reluctant agreement, flicked a fingernail against his glass, watched the pale liquid shiver. "I'm too comfortable, Jule. I'm going to do what they tell me and try to ride this thing out. You're right, it's absurd. People will see that, they have to. This country, we're too stubborn, too . . . well, I don't know . . . too sane I think, to let this go on much longer. We wobble from one side of the center to the other, but the wobble always straightens and makes most people just a little wiser than before. History and time, Julia, they're on our side; when this is over they're going to need people like you and me to write it down and put it in perspective."

She watched him with a familiar detached interest, her writer's eye. In spite of his optimistic tone he was uneasy with his position, felt diminished by it but hadn't the energy or will to drive himself the way he knew he ought to go. This was a man struggling with his ideals—no, struggling with his will to surrender those ideals, or if not surrender, set them on the shelf for the moment because they are inconvenient. At this moment, he seemed collapsed rather than convoluted, his humor banished by the inner and outer pressures that were combining to drive him toward those extremes he both feared and despised. She got up, changed the record and came back, the melting ice still musical in the remnants of her drink.

"Maybe you're right," she said. "Time. I've come to the end of my time, there's none left, no time nohow." She held the glass against her face and thought dispiritedly about her own disintegration, here she was analyzing the poor man down to his back teeth, judging him, when she couldn't keep her own mouth shut, had to dump her own worries on him, worries that were none of his concern, nothing he should have to deal with. The drink was mostly melted ice and tasted foul, the ice clicked against her teeth and made her shiver.

"Jule, I get the feeling you're telling me something but I don't hear it."

"Just getting maudlin, Simon my love. I came to say good-bye. I'm broke. Flat. Giving up my honest ways and starting on a life of crime. Tomorrow morning, as a matter of fact. Going to work a credit card swindle with the help of an old acquaintance and when I've got money enough, I'm going to buy me a smuggler and head for the north countree."

"Jule, you shouldn't be telling me all that. What if I. . . ."

"Sold me? Poor Simon. They're going to push you too far one of these days, my dear, and where'll your comfort be then? If they do, go see the Magic Man, he'll put you onto something to save your soul. Before I go, remind me to tell you how to find him."

He took her hand, his own was trembling a little, sweaty and hot. "Look Jule, if you need money. . . ."

"No. No. Let me do this my own way. I'm poison, Simon. Guilt by contagion, you know what that is." She sat up, laughed aloud. "If you could see your face, poor dear. Ah well, it's all material for the next book. I think I'll try another thriller. Once I'm in another country. Mind putting me up for the night? Damn curfew complicates things. I don't want anyone asking me questions right now, might prove a bit embarrassing with five different idents in my purse." She gave him a rueful grin. "I know, my love, but I couldn't leave them home, god knows who gets in my place when I'm not there. I'm rather off men right now, so the couch will do. I feel like a leech, but things were coming out the walls at me. That's enough about me. More than enough. What are the peabrains getting after now? Who they planning to banish from the lists of history?"

# THE PRIESTESS

The sun was clear of the horizon, a watery pale circle covered with haze, when she slid wearily off the macai, slapped him on the rump and sent him off to wander back to the tar. She stumbled on cold-numbed feet along behind Cymbank's houss and stores, empty gardens and empty corrals, to the deserted silent grove behind the Maiden Shrine. She was giddy with fatigue and the need for sleep that pulled more heavily on her than the bucket or the overloaded satchel. She forced herself on; it couldn't be long before the Agli or his minions came after her. She was breathing through her mouth, sucking in great gulps of air, shuddering with the cold, the heavy white robe sodden past her knees, slapping against her legs, making it increasingly difficult to walk.

But she went on, step by slow step, vaguely rejoicing in the difficulty and discomfort. *She* said it would be hard enough and it seemed that was so. The hitching posts were black fingers thrusting up through the snow. She passed them, circled round to the side of the living quarters and found the door. She pulled at the latch. The door wouldn't move. She turned her back on it, set the bucket down, shrugged the satchel and the quiltroll off her shoulder. Then she got down on her knees and began scraping the snow away from the door with bare hands that were soon numb and blue and beginning to bleed. She worked without stopping or paying attention to the pain, worked until she had cleared a fan of stone before the door. Then she forced herself up and stood on trembling legs before it, for a moment unable to move, no strength left to pull it open and go inside.

Scent of herbs and flowers.

Warmth spread through her. She stepped away from the door. It swung open before she could reach for the latch again. She lifted the bucket and the satchel and the quiltroll and stumbled inside.

It was dark and no warmer in there, but wood was stacked on the foyer hearth. She laid a small fire and turned aside, meaning to get the firestriker from the satchel.

Scent of herbs and flowers.

The fire was burning before she completed the turn. She froze, straightened and looked around.

To her left were the public rooms of the sanctuary, to her right the living quarters of the Keeper. She got to her feet, bent her weary body, caught up her burdens and shuffled toward the right-hand door. She set her hand on it, marking it with a bloody handprint though she didn't know that till later. It opened before her and she went inside.

The room inside was sparely furnished: a worktable, a backless chair pushed under it, a cobwebbed bedstead in one corner with a dusty pad on the rope webbing that crossed and recrossed the space between the posts and sideboards. There was a window over the bed, the glass rounds intact in their binding strips of lead; no light came through them as the window had been boarded over outside. As Nilis stood gazing dully at the glass, she heard a creaking, then a clatter, then dull thumps as the boards fell away and light came in, painting bright rounds of color on the wall and floor, ruby and garnet, emerald and aquamarine, topaz and citrine. She smiled, tears coming into her eyes at the unexpected beauty. She put her burdens on the worktable, hung her cloak on a peg, turned to the fireplace built in the inner wall. Wood was laid on the firedogs, ready for lighting; a wrought-iron basket held more wood for replenishing the fire when it burned low. She took the striker from the bucket and a paring knife and knelt on the stone hearth, her knees fitting into hollows worn there by generations of shrine keepers. She cut slivers of dry wood from one of the split logs, got the pile of splinters burning and eventually had herself a slowly brightening fire. She stood, pulled her forearm across her face, shoved the hair out of her eyes, warmth beginning to glow within her, the smells of spring blowing round her with the sharp clean scent of the burning wood. For the first time in many passages, she bowed her head and sang the praises of the Maiden, the words coming back as clear as they'd been when she learned them as a child.

With some reluctance, she left the warmth of the bedroom and went back into the small foyer. She pulled the outer door shut, slid the bar through its hooks, stood a moment enjoying the quiet and the dark, the flickering red light from the fire, then she went back into the bedroom, crossed it and moved through a doorless arch into the small narrow kitchen.

The end walls were mostly doors, two at each end. There was a heavy table, a backless chair, several porcelain sinks with drains leading outside into a ditch that went past the hitching posts into the grove behind the shrine, a bronze pump whose long curved lever looked frozen in place, whose lip had a dry smear of algae grown there and died in place since the Keeper had been taken away. Above the sink, there was a row of small windows, boarded up, the boards shutting out the light except for a few stray beams that came lancing in, lighting up the dust motes that danced thick in the air. Again, as she stood watching, the boards dropped away and rounds of jewel colors played over and about her.

She smiled, opened one of the nearer doors. A storage place, a few bowls and pans left, a glass or two, milky with dust, some lumps that weren't immediately identifiable. The door beside it opened on another shallow closet—brooms, the straws worn to a slant and curling on the ends; another bucket, its staves separating at the corners, dried out, needing a good soak and the bands tightened; a large crock half full of harsh lye soap women made in the fall at the winter cull from rendered fats and potash, taking turns to stir the mess with long-handled paddles, trying to avoid the coiling fumes of the mixture, adding the potash by handfuls, watched over by an aged soapmaker who knew just when she should stop that and wash the soap out with brine. Hard stinking work, a whole week of it each fall, but well worth the time and effort—a year of clean for a week of stench. The Keeper worked with the tie-women, stirring and rendering and boiling and reboiling, earning her portion of what was produced. The women didn't ask it of her, they would have given her the soap as gift, but they felt happier with her there blessing their work by being part of it. Nilis wrinkled her nose. It wasn't something she looked forward to, in fact she'd kept well away from the soap grounds as had most of her family, but she looked down at the soap now and knew she'd keep the Keeper's tradition. The soap ladle had a leather loop tied through a hole in the handle and hung on a peg beside the crock. There was a tangle of dusty rags, some worn bits of pumice stone and a few other odds and ends useful for cleaning small bits.

She crossed to the far side of the kitchen. The first room there held split logs packed in from floor to ceiling, filling the whole of the space. Depending on how deep the room was it could be enough to last till spring, Maiden grant there'd be a spring. She shut that door, opened the next. A pantry of sorts. A flour barrel that proved to be half full when she took the lid off. A few crocks of preserved vegetables she was a little doubtful about but not enough to throw them out; they'd stretch her supplies a few days longer. A root bin, half full of several sorts of tubers, rather withered and wrinkled but mostly still edible. The vandals for some reason seemed to have left the Keeper's quarters intact when they'd vented their spite on the sacred rooms.

She went back into the bedroom for the satchel and the bucket, hauled them into the kitchen, piled them on the table. She dusted off the shelves in the storage closet, sneezing now and then, eyes watering, then emptied the satchel of the kitchen things, the food and utensils she'd brought with her and set them on the shelves, item by item, sighing at the meagerness of her supplies. In a few days she'd have to do something about food, but that could wait. She set the clothing and other things on the table to be put away later, except for the sleeping smock. She shook it out and carried it into the other room, hung it on a peg beside her cloak, untied her sandals and stepped out of them, dragged the wet cold robe over her head, hung it on one of the pegs, pulled on the smock. Taking the the quiltroll from the worktable, she pulled off the cords without trying to untie the knots. She could deal with them later when she wasn't so tired. She spread the quilts on the bed, not bothering with the dust. That was something else for later. The fire was already warming the room, turning it into a bare but cheerful play of light and shadow, of color and coziness. And the warmth was multiplying her weariness until she was almost asleep on her feet. She added some more wood to the fire, then stumbled blindly to the bed, stretched out, pulled the second quilt over her and was asleep before she murmured more than the first words of the sleep blessing.

When she woke, the fire was out but warmth lingered in the room. She sat up, the rope webbing sagging under her, the mattress pad rustling. She expected pain and stiffness but felt neither. She touched her shoulder, the one that should have been bruised and painful. She felt nothing, pulled loose the neckstring, pushed aside the heavy cloth, looked at her shoulder. It was smooth, firm and pale, no sign of bruising, not even a reddening or depression in the skin. She jabbed her thumb into the muscle. Nothing. She smiled.

The light coming in the uncovered window was so dim it barely woke the colors in the glass. She got up off the bed and went to look at the robe; it was still damp about the hem and streaked with mud. She thought of washing it, then shook her head. Too much work to do, might as well finish cleaning the Keeper's quarters, the sanctuary and the schoolroom. I can wash both of us when that's done, my robe and me.

She put on the robe, tied the cord and bloused the top over it until the the damp hem was hiked almost to her knees. She went into the bare foyer. The fire there was long out but a remnant of warmth lingered in the stone. She took down the bar and tried to open the door. It wouldn't budge. She set her shoulder against the planks and shoved. It scraped reluctantly open just enough to let her put her head out.

The snow was smooth and new in the narrow court. It must have snowed while she slept, covering her traces. If they're looking for me now, luck to them. She rubbed at her nose, giggled, a little lightheaded with hunger and the long sleep. New flakes were beginning to dust down, settling onto her hair and eyelashes. It was cold and still out there, a stillness so thick she could feel and smell it. She pulled the door shut, slipped the bar back and went into the kitchen.

She worked the pump handle until her arms were shaking, but brought nothing up. She drew the back of her hand across her sweaty face, closed her eyes and tried to remember what the ties had done to start a pump. Priming, she thought suddenly, water to fetch water.

A melted pot of snow later and the icy flow from the shrine well was gushing out to fill her bucket, then one of the pots. There was a bread oven in one corner and a brick hearth raised about waist high with an open grate and a grill over a firebox. She put some sticks of wood on the hearth, carved off some curls from the chunk of resinwood and put them in the box and snapped the firelighter. A few sparks, a few puffs and the curls were crackling. She added sticks of wood, watched until they caught, added a few more, then set the pot of water to boil. All too aware of the hollow in her middle, she cut a slice from the loaf, smeared a spoonful of jam on the bread and set it aside, cut a hunk of cheese, put it beside the bread, dropped a pinch of cha in a mug. While the water heated, she went briskly through the bedroom, into the foyer and opened the left-hand door.

For a long, numinous moment, she stood with her hand on the latch, looking into the dark room, feeling as if she was only now entering into her tenure as Keeper.

She wandered through the sacred rooms—the Maiden Chamber, the vestiary, the vessel room, scowling at the disfiguring smears of black paint everywhere, floor, walls, ceiling, at the broken vessels, the dried scum of oil and unguents, the books that were tatters and black ash, the tapestries turned to rags and thread, half burned. There were deep scratches everywhere and other muck as if the hate and rage in the Followers who did the damage wouldn't leave anything alone, wanted to pull down the walls and soil what they couldn't destroy. The worst of the damage was lost to the shadows but she saw enough to disturb and discourage her. So much to do. She shook off her malaise and went back to the kitchen.

After washing down bread, jam and cheese with cha almost too hot to drink, her dejection vanishing as her hunger abated, she went rummaging for something to hold the candles she'd found in the pantry. The gloom was thickening outside and in as the day grew later and the snow fell harder. The quiet was gone, the wind screeching past the windows, an eerie lonesome sound she hated. As she poked into the corners and crannies of the kitchen, the fire hissing and popping in the firehole, she was nervous for a while out of old habit, then was startled by the realization that she rather liked the wind's howl. It was as if the wind wrapped her in its arms and protected her from everything that would harm her. She rubbed at her cheek, shook her head and went back to her search, relaxed and easy in a way she couldn't define or comprehend. She located several wooden candlesticks and a glass candlelamp with a tarnished silver reflecter behind it. She carried it out and set it on the kitchen table. After she wiped the reflector with a soft cloth, buffed it as clean as she could, she rinsed off the glass, polished away dust, spider webs and insect droppings, then she pushed one of her candles onto the base and lit it at the firehole, let it burn a moment before she set the chimney back over it. It put out a soft yellow glow that pushed back the shadows and gave a golden life to the kitchen that warmed her heart as well as her body.

She took the lamp into the bedroom where she laid a new fire and used the sparker to get it started. The ash was beginning to build up beneath the dogs. She should have cleared it away before starting a new fire, but the room was growing too chill for comfort. Tomorrow morning, she told herself. I'll clear the grate tomorrow morning. She watched the fire start to glow and snap and thought about going to bed, getting an early start on the cleaning in the morning, but she wasn't sleepy and there was such a lot of work to do.

She went back in the kitchen, scooped up a dollop of soap and dumped it into the bucket, following that with the last of the hot water, set another pot to heat for later, tucked one of the worn brooms under her arm, picked up the bucket and the lamp and went around through the bedroom, the foyer, stood a moment in the vestiary wondering where to start, then went through into the great chamber, the Maiden Chamber.

She set the lamp against the wall under the window. Floor first, she thought. An icy draft coiled round her ankles. No. Fire first.

When the fire began to crackle and add its light to the candle lamp's, she stood in the center of the room and looked around at the sorry desolation where once there'd been dignity and beauty. She went to her knees, knelt without moving, sick with memory and with the sudden realization that the anger she was feeling now at the vandals was only another face of the anger that had driven her to turn against her own blood. Forgive yourself, *She* said. It's easier to forgive them. She sighed and opened her eyes, got stiffly to her feet.

Humming the chants she could remember so she wouldn't remember more troubling things, she began sweeping up the debris that cluttered the floor, leaves, fragments of stone, bottle shards, the ruins of the tapestries, a year's worth of dust and dead bugs.

She fetched the rags and pumice stones she'd forgotten and began cleaning the floor, slopping soapy water onto the tiles, using rags to wash away old urine and feces, the clotted dust, not trying to deal yet with the paint. Handspan by handspan she removed the filth from the mosaic tiles, changing the water several times before she finished. Then, with pumice and scraper she attacked the thick paint, the smears and splatters, the glyphs of obscene words, humming to herself as she worked, the humming just a pleasure now, no longer a barrier to thought. She wasn't angry any longer. She was too busy to be angry, attacking a tiny patch of floor at a time, trying not to harm the glaze on the tiles, in no hurry at all, happy when she got a single tile cleaned off, contented at spending hours, days, perhaps a full passage on a task she'd have screamed at a while before. She took little note of the passing of time until the growing chill and darkness in the room reminded her that there were other things she had to do and many days to finish the work.

She sat on her heels and stretched, working her back and shoulders, wriggling her fingers. The fire was a faint red glow nearly smothered in gray ash. The candle was a stub hardly a finger-width high. It was totally dark outside, the colored rounds of window glass turned to different shades of black. She looked at the cleaned tiles with satisfaction, their bright colors winking at her in the dying light. She'd cleared off a space as long and as wide as she was tall. Setting the worn pumice stone against the wall, the scraper beside it, she got to her feet, plucking at the skirt of her robe which was damp and heavy against her legs.

Taking the lamp and firestriker with her, she left the Maiden Chamber. The foyer was an icebox, but the bedroom was toasty warm though the fire had burned low. She put on a few sticks of wood, waited until they caught, added more wood and left a cheerful crackle behind as she went into the kitchen. After blowing the coals to life in the firebox, she set water to heat for cha, cut several slices of bread, laid thin slices from the posser haunch on them, topped the whole with slivers of cheese, set these concoctions on the bricks to melt, washed the dust off one of the Keeper's plates and put a new candle in the lamp. When the cheese had melted into the bread and meat and the water was boiling, she assembled her meal, sat at the kitchen table, almost purring with contentment, sang the blessings and began her solitary supper.

When she woke, early the next morning, her lye-burnt, abraded hands had healed as her bruises and chilblains had before. She sang the praises of the Maiden, made a hasty breakfast and went back to work on the Maiden Chamber.

The days that followed were much the same. Hard monotonous physical labor all day, meager monotonous meals morning and night. By the end of the first tenday the cheese was a pile of wax and cloth rinds, the jam was getting low, the posser haunch was close to the bone and she was eating water-flour cakes baked on the bricks, the withered tubers with the rotted spots cut away and slow-baked all day at the hearth of her bedroom fire. At night she slept hard and dreamlessly. When she wasn't scrubbing, she struggled to reconstruct from memory what she knew of the Keeper Songs and the Order of the Year. How little she did know troubled her at times but mostly she was too busy to fuss.

By the end of that tenday the Great Clean was all but finished. All the sacred rooms were in order and shining with her efforts. But the unguent vessels and oil vessels were broken, the oils and unguents missing; the tapestries were destroyed, the formal robes of the Keeper were gone. The Maiden Chamber was bare. The face carved into the Eastwall was so plowed with gouges and battered it gave her a pain in her heart to look at it, but on the eleventh day she did just that. She stood in the middle of the room, hands on hips, and gazed at the ruined face. "Could I?"

Scent of herbs and flowers.

"Oh, you think so, mmmm? Then I'd better try." She went up to the stone, touched the face, ran her fingers over the few unmarred bits, trying to get the feel of the stone into her hands. "At least I can smooth this out so it isn't quite so dreadful a scar and I can learn something about the tools and the stone while I'm at it. After that, well, we'll see."

She left the room, frowning and walking slowly, trying to remember what tools she'd seen stacked up on shelves at the far end of the pantry. A mallet she was sure of, an axe, but that wouldn't be much help until she needed firewood, chisels? She stepped into the foyer, pulled the door shut behind her.

A heavy knock on the outer door caught her in mid-stride. She stared at it open-mouthed, shocked and frightened. A second knock. She stood with her hands crossed above her breasts, her arms pressing hard against her torso. In a way she'd forgotten that there was a world outside the Shrine. All her life, as long as she could remember, she'd been surrounded by people. Surrounded by family and ties and bitter with loneliness. From the moment she'd crossed the threshold here, she'd been utterly alone and for the first time was not lonely at all. She felt a flash of resentment at the person who was shattering this calming, comforting solitude, recognized the feeling and shoved desperately at it. She didn't *want* to feel like that anymore, she was furious at herself for entertaining the feeling. She was falling apart, falling back into the tense, angry, resentful Nilis she was trying to escape. Escape? There was none. Forgive yourself. Forgive myself. Forgive. Forgive. No new starts, no changes, the same soul. Live with it. Forgive yourself for being who and what you are. It was a litany, a prayer. The thudding of her heart slowed, her hands unclenched, her breathing slowed, steadied. She looked down at herself, smiled tremulously, tugged the filthy hem down so it hid her dirty bare feet. Walking on the sides of her feet, toes curled up from the icy flags, she crossed the room, took the bar down and shoved the door open.

It moved more easily than she'd expected and she stumbled farther out than she'd intended, putting one bare foot into the snowbank. She jerked back, rubbed her freezing foot against the back of her calf, stood one-legged, holding the edge of the door, looking around.

There was no one in sight, though a trampled track led around behind the sanctuary. *I didn't fuss that long*, she thought, *they must have raced away*. She switched feet, rubbed the other along her calf. "Maiden bless," she called. The wind's howl was the only answer. She frowned at the track. It led behind the door. She pulled the door toward her and looked around it.

A bulging rep-cloth bag; two bowls with folded clothes covering what lay inside, a tall covered crock, a lumpy bag. Hopping from foot to freezing foot, she carried these leavings inside, pulled the door shut, dropped the bar in place, then started transferring the goods to the kitchen.

When she had the whole load on the kitchen table, she unfolded the cloth laid on top of one of the bowls. It was another robe, a clean robe. She touched it, smiled, dropped it onto a chair. The bowl held a dozen eggs, a small cheese, a chunk of butter wrapped in tazur husks. The second bowl was covered by a pair of soft clean dish-towels; it held two roasted oadats and two cleaned and dressed but uncooked carcasses. The small lumpy bag held a sac filled with salt, several packets of dried herbs and spices and a small bottle of slayt-flower essence, some woman's cherished luxury, a gift almost worth more than the food in the things it spoke to Nilis. The crock held fresh milk. The rep sack held tubers, dried vegetables, dried fruit, a packet of cillix whose white grains poured like hail through her fingers. Her unknown benefactors had risked a lot to bring this. Briefly she wondered how they knew anyone was in the shrine, then she saw the glass in the kitchen windows glittering with the light of the late afternoon sun and laughed at herself. She'd been pro-claiming her presence since the first fire she'd lit. It didn't matter. She wasn't here to hide. A sign, *She* said. A sign of a *Presence*. A sign that had to be seen to fulfill its purpose.

She put the supplies away in the pantry and on the shelves of the closet, then went back to the Maiden Chamber with the tools she'd started to fetch. She built up the fire, stood before it a moment, warming her feet. I'm going to have to contrive a bath of some sort, she thought. Now that I'm apt to have visitors. I wonder what the other Keepers did. She hadn't yet found anything like a laundry tub, but she hadn't been searching that hard and there was a lot of junk piled at the back of the pantry under a heavy film of spiderwebs, dust and mold. She turned her back to the fire and stood gazing at the broken face. First thing is cutting that off and leveling the stone inside the circle. Plenty of stone left in the wall, enough to work with. The face will just be set deeper in, that's all. She shivered with a sudden exaltation. A paradigm. The Maiden driven deeper than before into the life of the mijloc. She put her hands over her face for a few shuddering breaths, then pulled them away, laughing. How easy it was, after all, this shift from nothing to nothing to everything. Maiden before was fête and chant. Nothing. Soäreh was sourness and spite, triumph quickly burned out. Nothing. Now. Oh now. . . .

Dragging the kitchen chair up to the wall, she stood on the broad seat, set chisel and mallet to work cutting away the remnants of the old face, learning the feel and cleavage of the stone as she did so, working very carefully, perhaps too cautiously, removing the stone with a stone's patience, feeling a growing satisfaction as her hands slowly but surely acquired the skills she'd need to recarve the face.

All her life she'd drawn things, creating embroidery designs for her mother and sisters, for anybody who asked, though she was too nervous and impatient to complete any but the simplest patterns for herself. She hated weaving and sewing and the household arts that took up so much of any woman's time; that was one of the reasons she resented Tuli—the girl continuously contrived to escape the limitations of women's work and slip away from a large part of their world's censure for such escapades. It wasn't fair. Jealousy she refused to acknowledge had made her scold and pick at her sister because she herself lacked strength of will or imagination to make her own escape from a life that stifled her almost beyond enduring. Behind her passivity lay a profound ignorance. She didn't know what she wanted, she didn't know any other sort of life. The Biserica loomed more as threat than sanctuary. The thought of thousands of girls like Tuli was enough to make it no place she wanted to be, for it seemed to her that all the meien who came by and stayed with them were only older versions of Tuli. Even if they weren't, that was how she saw them. She chipped patiently at the stone, her hands learning its essence, feeling more and more the angles of cut, the amount of force required to chip away various amounts of stone. And her mind drifted along roads taken too many times before, all the hurts, the bitterness, the long struggle she fought against herself, the sense she had of being locked within her skin, of living in the wrong place, in the wrong way. When all the wrongness was taken away, how easy it was to step outside herself, how easy it was to be easy with herself. And how hard it had been once—and might be again, she thought suddenly—how hard to want and want all those things people said you ought to want—a home, a husband, piles of woven cloth, embroidered linens, children, a pantry stocked and overflowing with jams and jellies, smoked meats, cheeses and all the rest of it, suitably humble and happy tie-families—how terrible it was to hunger for what no effort of your own could achieve, the things that came as gifts or not at all, things like charm and a happy nature.

Behind her the fire burned low and began to die. The light coming through the windows dimmed, turned red, then gray. When she finally noticed the darkness and the ache in her arms, she rested her forehead against the stone and felt all the weight of her weariness come suddenly down on her.

Scent of herbs and flowers. A brief flush of energy.

She stepped down from the chair, laid the mallet and chisel on the floor beside it, and stood rubbing at her shoulders as she peered through the growing dark at what she'd done. Almost all the face was gone and the background was an odd pocking as if some hard-beaked passar had been banging at it. She yawned. As she moved to pick up the candlelamp she hadn't bothered lighting, the fatigue was pushed away, but she was surprised by a hunger that bit deeper into her than the chisel had into the stone. She glanced at the fire, thought of banking it to preserve the coals, but didn't feel like making the effort. She could think only of that roast oadat waiting for her, of the chewy golden rounds of dried chays, the cheese and fresh bread and hot cha to wash it all down. She hefted the chair and took it with her to the kitchen.

She ate and ate until she was ashamed of her greed, ate until there was no possibility of forcing down another bite. Heavy with food, aching with weariness, half asleep, she stretched out in the chair, her back against the wall, her buttocks caught at the edge of the seat, her legs spread a little, stretched out straight before her, giving her a good view of the filthy skirts of the robe and her equally filthy feet, the dirt ground into flesh that looked like pinkish gray dough. She wiggled her toes, sighed. "Bath," she said, tasting the word and nodding her head. "Tired or not, I want a bath."

She set water to boil, took the lamp into the pantry and rummaged through the pile at the back, finding a big wooden tub under a heap of broken odds and ends. It needed soaking, might leak some, but it would do well enough for tonight. She took it into the bedroom, set it before the fire. Then she built up the fire until it threatened to leap into the room, knelt a moment on the hearth, sweating, letting the heat soothe some of the soreness in her arms and shoulders.

By the light of that fire, she scrubbed at the heavy robe, scrubbed until her hands were blistered and abraded, the lye soap like fire on them, but she got most of the dirt out of the coarse material and dumped it into the scrub bucket. She took the sleeping smock down from its peg and sloshed it in the soapy water left over from the robe; its stains came from her unwashed body and the warm soapy water dealt easily with those. She dumped the sodden smock on top the robe, took them both into the kitchen and upended the bucket over a sink full of cold water, sloshed them about a bit, let the water out, pumped more in and left them to soak while she washed herself.

She carried more buckets of hot water to the tub, poured them into the soapy residue until she could almost not bear the heat, added a little cold, then squatted in the tub to scrub at herself. When she finished, she dried herself, then scooped the dirty water from the tub, bucket by bucket until it was light enough for her to manage, hauled it into the kitchen and emptied the rest down the drain. She finished rinsing out the clothing, then used an old rag to wash the soap off herself. More hot water, in the sink this time, laced with cold. She washed her hair, sighing for the mild, scented shampoo her father bought from traveling peddlers, but at least she was clean.

She wiped herself as dry as she could, squeezed excess water out of her hair, then stood a moment breathing deeply, surrounded by the warmth and smells of the kitchen, the burning wood, soap, bread, roast oadat, cheese, chays, damp stone and others too faint and blended to identify. Then she forced herself to move, hung the smock and the robe on drying racks from the pantry, set up on either side of the bedroom fire. She stretched out on the bed, the ropes squealing under her weight, the mattress rustling. She lay a moment on both quilts, staring up at the ceiling and seeing for the first time the mosaic of wood chips, an image of the mijloc being held in the arms of the Maiden, constructed from a dozen different natural wood shades, a subtle image that only developed out of the woodchips as she stared at them. She sighed with pleasure, closed her eyes, murmured the night chant and began drifting off. After a moment, she eased the top quilt from under her and pulled it up to her chin, then fell into sleep as if someone had clubbed her.

The mallet tucked under her arm, the chisel held point out, handle pressed against her thumb, she was moving both sets of fingers carefully across the cut-away stone, searching for any spikes of stone that had escaped her, this fitful fussing a last attempt to convince herself she ought to postpone the re-carving of the face. She felt uncertain and rather frightened. She touched and touched the stone, the smooth roughness under her fingers slowly seducing her into beginning, the stone calling to her to give it shape.

She faced the stone, holding mallet and chisel, breathing lightly, quickly, searching for the courage to begin.

"Nilis." Her brother's voice, angry and afraid.

She turned with slow deliberation and stepped down from the chair. "Dris," she said. She ignored the Agli scowling behind the boy. She felt his eyes on her, hot angry eyes, but all fear had fled somehow, she felt serene.

The Agli closed his hand tight over the boy's shoulder. He said nothing, but Dris's face went pale and stiff. Nilis was sorry to see that but knew there was little she could do about it. Dris's tongue traveled across his bottom lip. "Nilis Gradindaughter," he said, his voice breaking on the words as if he were older and in the throes of puberty. "Sister, your place is in Gradintar. Gradintar needs a mistress to see to the women's work. The Great Whore is finished in the mijloc. I am Tarom. I order you to come home. You must obey me. Or . . . or be cursed." His tongue moved once again along his lip, his hands were closed into fists, his eyes shone as if he were going to cry at any moment. "You got to come back, Nilis, I NEED you. Please. . . ." He broke off, wincing as the Agli's fingers dug into his shoulder. The frightened child vanished as Dris's face went blank. "Disobey," he said dully, "and the curse of Soäreh will land on your head." He changed again. "Come on, Nilis, huh?" Little brother now too scared to play his role. "Nilis, please, I don't want to curse you." His face contorted as he struggled not to cry.

"Ah, Drishha-mi," she murmured. She set the mallet and chisel on the floor and settled herself on the chair. "Do what you must, but don't worry about it. I can't go back with you. Gradintar isn't my home anymore. You're still my brother, dearest, you're always welcome here whenever you are free to come. Curse me if you must." She found herself laughing, a low warm chuckle that utterly surprised her, so much so that she lost track of what she was saying. She blinked, hesitated, finished, "I won't take any notice of it."

A soft hissing from the Agli. She ignored it, a little afraid now, but not as afraid as she'd expected to be. And glad her robe was clean and fresh, her hair and body were clean and fresh. It gave her a confidence she felt she could trust more than the mysterious sureness she felt in herself, a sureness that was a gift of the Maiden and because of this might vanish as inexplicably as it had come.

Dris's face twisted again. She could see the silent pressure the Agli was putting on him, a pressure he was trying to put on her now. She sat quietly as the boy began stammering out his lesson, watching him and listening with sadness and a little impatience.

128 · JO CLAYTON

"O thou follower of vileness," Dris shrilled at her. "Thou whore and betrayer. Thou apostate. May thy nights be given to torment, the demons of the lower worlds torment thee in body and mind. May thy days be given to torment, desires that fill thee and whimper in thee; and may no man be tempted to fulfill thee. May worms dwell within thee and eat at thee until thou art rotten and oozing with rot, until thou are corruption itself. May all this be done to thee unless thou renounce the Hag, renounce this rebellion against thy proper role, against those created to be thy guides and protectors. Renounce the Hag and return to thy proper place, Nilis Gradindaughter." Dris finished his memorized speech, gave a little sigh of relief that he'd got it right. She read in his eyes horror at what he was saying and at the same time a certain satisfaction at his daring to talk like that to her.

The Agli was looking smug. She saw in him what she'd never seen before. He hated and feared women. All women, but especially those he couldn't dominate or control. They were alien creatures who nonetheless could wake feelings in him he was helpless to resist. It was strange to see so clearly, having looked into her own real face, strange and painful because it meant she no longer had the option of pursuing her own goals without fully understanding the pain and distress her acts caused those around her; yet there were things she had to do, so she must take on her shoulders the responsibility for that pain. And with that came the first real understanding of what *She* had meant when *She* said the task was hard enough. Not the physical labor, that was easy. Forgive yourself. Yes. She saw the greed and fear and uncertainty and unlovely triumph and need and silly sad stupid blindness in the man standing before her and a part of her—the part that was sustained by the Maiden's Gift—understood and loved all these unlovely things while the other part of her was angry at Dris and the Agli for disturbing her serenity, for blocking off the thing she felt burgeoning in her, angry at the Agli for driving that baby into pronouncing that curse, a little afraid, but not much, of the curse itself. And even as she sat musing over these things, considering her answer, that other part of her cleared into laughter, laughter that bubbled through her and out of her before she could stop it. She saw the Agli's face pinch together and laughed yet more, but stopped laughing when she saw it troubled Dris too much.

"You did well, Drishha brother," she said. "You learned your lesson well. Clever boy. Not to worry, though, you've done no harm." She turned to the Agli, all desire to laugh draining from her. Words came to her. *She* spoke through her. "Agli, you act on the assumption that yours will win this encounter and you will not be called to account for the damage you do to those in your care. But I tell you this, you will be called to account for all the hate and all the destruction and all the upheaval you and yours have visited upon the people of the mijloc and the children of the mijloc. I look on you and see that you are sure of your power, sure of your victory, sure that you possess the only truth there is and must win because of this. And I say to you that you should think well what you are doing. If you cannot even shift an unfledged Keeper from her shrine, how will yours shift *me* from where I dwell?" Nilis blinked but added nothing of her own to what had spoken through her. She sat with her hands folded in her lap, waiting for what must come next.

The Agli's face twisted, went hot and red. He pushed Dris roughly aside, not meaning the roughness but in too much haste to do otherwise. Muttering a warding rite, he grabbed at her arm, meaning to jerk her off the chair and drag her out the door. With a shriek that echoed eerily about the room, he wrenched his hand away as if her flesh had seared his. Staring at her, he began backing toward the door, Dris forgotten, everything forgotten except the pain in his withered hand and arm.

"Your body lives," she said and could not be sure who spoke. "All things that live lie in the Maiden's hand and reach." There was a touch too much satisfaction for her comfort in those words, she hoped it wasn't dredged up out of her but put that aside for later thought and sat watching him.

He continued to back away, crouched and sidling sideways like a crab, his dark eyes bulging and madder than anything she'd seen before.

"Remember, Oh man, you will be called to account for what you do."

He turned and ran, vanishing in a step, black robe fluttering about his heels.

Dris stood forlorn and afraid in the middle of the room, trying not to cry, his world crumbled about him.

"Drishha," she said, putting all the patience and gentleness she could find within herself into the words she spoke. "Go home, little brother. Do the best you can to be a good boy so Father will be proud of you when he comes home." She watched the contradictory emotions play across his half-formed face. He wouldn't like giving up his autonomy, his power, his sense of bigness, but he did love Tesc and Annic and Tuli and Teras and missed them very much, especially in the middle of the night; she knew that well enough, having tried to comfort him more than once when his loneliness grew too much for him. Now he'd have no one at all except an Agli he'd just seen humiliated. And he knew, without being able to put it in words or even images, that the Agli would be angry at him for being a witness to that humiliation and would punish him for it even though he hadn't wanted to be there, had whined and wheedled and tried his best to be left behind. It wasn't fair, it wasn't right, but that was the way with adults sometimes, they made you do things and when the things went wrong blamed you for doing them and there was no use calling on *right* or *fair*. "I hate you," he shouted at Nilis, then burst into tears and ran out of the room.

She sat there for some time, too tired to move, too tired even to think, just sat there, hands folded in her lap, staring at the open empty door.

After a while she thought about the door being open, about the gate to the court of columns being off its hinges. Anyone can walk in on me any time. She twisted her hands together and her mind ran on wheels as she tried to think of a way to bar the door; the hooks had been torn from the wall when the rest of the damage was done; the bar had vanished. Then she remembered the Agli's face as he touched her, as he tore his hand away. This is *Her* place, she'll protect it, protect me. She rubbed at her thighs. But the first Agli, mine, the clown doll—he got the other Keeper out and no one's seen her since. *She* didn't protect her. She was afraid again—and found herself on her feet, glaring across the room. Then she thought, I'll wedge the bedroom door so I'll be able to sleep without starting awake at every sound in the night. If anyone tries to break in, that will give me warning enough to put on a robe and comb my hair. She smiled. Face the world clothed and neat.

Nervous, she wandered through the sacred rooms, looking about, remembering the place as it once was—and would be again if she had any say. She lingered in the meditation room, a small cubicle, bare and cold now. Tapestries worked by tardaughters and Keepers in warm, bright wools used to hang from the walls, scenes from the chants, lively with flower and beast. The flags had been covered with rush matting, thick and resilient, woven in the Cymbank pattern, complicated but beautiful. Her memory added the faded gold of the dried rushes, catching the light and changing hue as the pattern of the weave changed direction, as the sun changed position outside the small round window set with clear though wavery glass. Scented berrywax candles had filled the room with tart green sweetness. Like village girls and tie-girls, she'd made vigil here when her menses started and here crossed the line from girl to maid. Here she might have made her marriage vigil too, that was a dream as empty now as then, though for other reasons. Looking at the room with remembering eyes she acknowledged her love of it as it was, sighed for the familiar beauty now ashes enriching the earth of the grove.

She drifted back to the Maiden Chamber, stood looking at the oval emptiness, remembering with a clarity almost painful the face of *Her* she'd seen in the tower. She closed her eyes and began exploring her own face with her fingers, trying to feel how eye was set beneath the brow, how cheek was flat and curved at once, how it made a sudden turn on a line slanting down from the outer corner of her eye past the corner of her mouth. She explored the complex curves of nose and mouth, touched herself and tried to visualize what touch told her about plane and curve and distance and groped toward a slow comprehension of the bites she was going to make in the stone.

She picked up the mallet and chisel, balanced them uncertainly in deeply uncertain hands, then got heavily up on the chair seat. She stared at the stone, then ran the fingers of the hand holding the chisel back and forth across the hollow she'd smoothed as best she could. She was afraid. She couldn't do it. She'd only make a mess of it like the mess she'd made of her life. She tried to fix in her mind the face she remembered. For a shaky moment she remembered nothing, not even her own face. Then the image came back, strong as the feel of the stone under her fingers. She set the chisel against the stone; trembling until she didn't know if she could control it, she lifted the mallet. Steadying into a kind of desperation, she struck the first blow.

The light was gone and she was trembling with fatigue when she surfaced. She felt dizzy and uncertain as if every movement had to be made slo-ow-ly, slo-ow-ly, or she would shatter. She shivered. The Maiden Chamber was very cold, the fire was gray ash, the last tints of red had left the little bit of light coming through the tinted glass rounds. She stepped very carefully down from the chair, her hand pressed hard against the wall to give her some sense of balance. She sat heavily, staring down at the mallet and chisel in her lap. After a moment she uncramped her fingers, wincing as the chisel rang musically against the tiles of the mosaic. It was no way to treat tools but she couldn't think much now, just react. After a minute, she gathered herself and grunted up onto her feet and went slowly back into her living quarters.

*     *     *

Morning light poured with lively vigor through the stained-glass window, the lead strips holding the glass rounds painting a lacy tracery on the stone. She knelt by the fireplace and scraped the ashes into one of the gift bowls then laid wood across the dogs and used the striker to start a new fire. It was very early and very cold in the room, her breath bloomed before her and took a long time to fade. The cold struck up from the mosaic floor, up through her knees, her thighs, her soft and quivering insides. Without looking at what she'd done the past day, she went back into the kitchen for hot cha then shoved her feet in the old slippers she'd brought with her, entirely disreputable but warm.

Cha mug clasped between her hands, she went back to the Maiden Chamber, walking with her eyes fixed determinedly on the floor until she stood before the chair, then she forced herself to look up.

Five hours of hard cautious work, much of it done blindly, trusting the feel in her fingers and what the stone told her hands as its vibrations came up the chisel at her. Five hours' work gazed back at her. The face she'd seen in the tower, blocked into the stone, carved simply but with great power, all the fussy little touches melded into strong simple lines. A woman's face with an inhuman beauty, slightly smiling. It wasn't finished, there was a need here and there to take away a jarring bit of roughness, the hair to be shaped out of the rough mass she'd left for that, the last polishing and oiling to bring out the grain and beauty of the stone. She looked at what she'd done and almost burst with joy. Gulping at the cha, she tried to calm herself but could not. She strode away from the face, paced back and forth across the room taking large mouthfuls of the cha until there was no more left, set the mug down, scooped up the chisel, impatient to get started on the finishing.

But when she looked at the battered blunt end of the chisel, she swore and nearly threw it at the wall. She tried to pull herself together. She was shaking, driven, but she forced herself to calm enough to set the chisel on the chair and walk away from it, going out of the room to fetch the hone from the pantry.

She sat on the floor in front of the fire, her robe hiked up to mid-thigh, and began the tedious process of repointing the chisel, working slowly and carefully, not stopping until she had perfection greater than she started with, knowing she must have the discipline this took or any touch she gave the face would be the start of ruin; slowly she began to take pleasure in the stroking of the stone across the metal. Stone over the steel, caressing it, wearing it away. Stroke and stroke and stroke, touches of loving care. As she worked, she sang softly a Maiden Chant, the calm on the face she'd carved growing within her.

Late in the afternoon, when she was putting the last touches on the flaring waves of hair framing the serene face like ripples of running water, she heard the tramp of boots, the clatter of metal against metal. Another visitation. She sighed, put her tools on the floor, then seated herself on the chair, knees together, robe pulled decorously down to hide her scruffy slippers. Her hands folded, she waited, tense and frightened though she hoped she didn't show it.

The Decsel marched in, his men following and fanning into an arc on either side of him as if she were some unpredictable and thus very dangerous beast. She waited until he stopped in the middle of the room, his face uninterested, indifferent. She'd never seen that face change much, not when he'd taken her mother and sisters and Teras to the House of Repentance, not when he'd overseen the cleansing of Gradintar of all Maiden symbols, not when he'd handled the culling of the ties or read the proclamation of Floarin declaring Tesc Gradin anathema and outlaw. He obeyed his orders punctiliously and scamped on nothing, finding his pride in doing well whatever he attempted though she'd never thought him especially devoted to Soäreh.

"Nilis Gradindaughter," he said.

"Nilis Keeper," she said. "She has left the tar and severed her connections with Gradintar and Gradinblood."

"Nilis Gradindaughter. The Agli Brell and the Center of Cymbank demand you leave this place and return to the House of Gradintar. If you fail to heed this most serious demand we are required to remove you by force and confine you in the House of Repentance." His speech finished, the formal words gabbled with as little expression as if he were calling the roll at payday, he stood at ease in his leather and metal, a big blocky man, worn and scarred and so closed in the limits of his profession that he was inaccessible to her or anything outside it, or so she thought as she listened to him speak.

When he finished, she answered him with as much formality. "No, I will not come." This was ritual, not conversation.

The Decsel accepted her words, nodded his bony head as if this were a thing he'd expected, as if he were used to this sort of lack of reason from those who did not have his clearly drawn map of possible actions. He took a step toward her, a look of astonishment on his leathery face, a clown's gape almost, ludicrous almost, in contrast with the strength and hard-worn look of the rest of him. He shifted back a little, felt at the air in front of him with large knuckled hands. It was as if he swept them over a sheet of glass. He backed off farther, sent one of his men forward with a brief quick turn of his hand. The guard charged at Nilis, rebounded from the barrier, hitting it hard enough to knock himself off his feet. Another sharp-edged, economical gesture. The man unclipped his sword, saluted his decsel, dropped into a crouch and drove the sword's point against the barrier with all the strength of his body. There was no sound but the point struck the barrier and went skating up it as if he'd jammed it against a slightly curved wall of greased glass. The guard stumbled and would have fallen, but the decsel caught the shoulderstrap of his leather cuirasse, dragged him onto his feet and shoved him back at the rest of the men.

Long spatulate thumb pressed against his lips, fisted fingers tight beneath his chin, the decsel stood contemplating her. He dropped his hand. "There is no way we can reach you, Nilis Keeper?"

"I don't know. I suspect not." She was as astonished as he was by the events just past.

He gazed at her a moment longer, his face as impassive as before, then he raised his hand in an abrupt, unexpected salute, wheeled and strode out. His men saluted her, each in his turn, and followed him out.

When the rhythmic stumping of their feet had died away, she began shaking. Her mouth flooded with bile. She swallowed, swallowed again, pushed herself onto her feet, hitched up the robe so it didn't drag along the floor or trip her. She started shaking again, not from reaction or cold (an icy blast was pouring through the open door), but from a sudden consuming anger. She stared up at the face, unable to speak for a moment, then she gathered herself. "Why?" she shouted at the face. "Why?" she repeated more calmly. "Why let me go through all. . . . Why let me betray. . . ." She stumbled over the word, but bitterly acknowledged the justice of it. "Betray my own blood. If you can do that," she waved a hand behind her, sketching out the wall that had protected her, "if you can come to me and show me what you did, if you can chase off the Agli and the guards, why why why is all this necessary, this death and misery, the battle that's coming, more death, more useless, wasteful. . . . Why? You could have stopped it. Why did you let it happen?"

There was no answer. The face in the stone was a stone face, the chisel marks still harsh on the planes and curves of it. She quieted, the futility of what she was doing like a lump of ice in her stomach. Her own hands had shaped the face. Shaped it well. An intense satisfaction warmed her, smothered for the moment the other emotions. It was good, that carving. She knew it. And knew then, above and beyond whatever being Keeper required of her, she'd found her proper work. With a little laugh, a rueful grimace, she pushed sweaty strands of fine brown hair off her thin face, then went to fix herself some lunch.

For the rest of the afternoon, she puttered about, unable to settle at anything. Her first joy, her contentment—these were shattered. Her relationship with *Her* of the tower was so much more limited than she'd hoped; like everything else she touched, this too crumbled away and left nothing. For the first time she realized just how much she'd been hoping for . . . for love . . . for a felt love, and instead of that she was a tool in the hands of *Her*, as much as the chisel was a tool in her own hands.

The old poisons came seeping into her blood again, the anger, frustration, resentment, envy, self-hate, rancor, outrage. She recognized them all, old friends they were, they'd sung her to sleep many a night. Now and then she felt herself welcoming them, cursing the forces that had driven her from the comfortable sense of righteousness that had spread through her and sustained her in the first days of Soäreh's ascendancy. At the same time she couldn't avoid seeing the ugliness of what she'd been and of what she'd helped to create. Anything was better than that, even the desolation that filled her when she thought of the years ahead of her, the unending empty years.

Late in the afternoon she went back into the Maiden Chamber and stood looking at the carving. The lowering sun painted new shadows on *Her* face and it seemed to Nilis that *She* looked at her and smiled, but she soon dismissed that as more dreaming. She gazed at the face a long time, then looked down at her hands. The quiet came back into her, her own quiet. The years might be long, but they wouldn't be empty. She had a lot to do, a lot to learn. It wasn't what she'd hoped, but it was a lot more than nothing.

As the days turned on the spindle, offerings began to appear beneath the Face. More robes. Sandals. Food. Candles. Flasks of scented oil. A beautiful Book of Hours, something someone had saved at great risk from Soäreh's Purge. Reed mats. Bedding. Tapestry canvas. Packets of colored wools. Wool needles. And what delighted her most because it answered her greatest need, another book saved from the Purge—The Order of the Year that named the passages and the fêtes, the meditations and the rites proper to each fête.

In the evenings she sat in the kitchen sipping cha and studying the Order. Her days she began to organize about the Hours of Praise. She needed the order this ritual gave to her life, especially since the long drive to clean the shrine had come to an end. Between the chants and meditation she did what she could in the Court of Columns, but it was too cold to stay out long. She scraped at the paint she could reach, what was under the snow would have to wait for spring. When she couldn't stay out any longer, she sat in the Maiden Chamber and worked over the tapestry canvas, sketching the design she wanted, then beginning to fill in the areas with the wools, no longer impatient and fretting, working until she was tired of it, moving into the kitchen and trying again to bake a successful loaf of bread, spending some time in the schoolroom, cleaning out the thick layer of muck and rotting leaves, the drifts of snow. The door was off its hinges, thrown into the room. She struggled with that, got it outside, managed to rehang it, though it dragged against the floor and had to be lifted and muscled about before the latch would catch. She put the room in order, piled the broken furniture neatly after looking it over to see if she could somehow repair it. She shut the door and left that too for the coming of spring.

A girl came one night. For her bridal vigil. She smiled shyly at Nilis, then went into the room, still bare except for a maiden face and the mats on the floor, lit a candle she'd brought with her and settled herself comfortably crosslegged on the mats. Much later, when Nilis came to bring her a cup of cha, the girl had a happy dreamy look on her face. Nilis left, wrestled a little with envy, then went to sleep, content with herself and what was happening.

On the last day of the Decadra Passage the Decsel marched into the Maiden Chamber, his belongings in a shoulder roll, a large sack of food under one arm. He set the sack down, drew his sword and laid it at Nilis's feet. "I wish to serve *Her*," he said.

He took the schoolroom as his quarters, rehung the door, cleared out the old furniture, cobbled a bed for himself and turned the bare room into a comfortable place, being experienced at doing for himself, neat-handed, and skillful at all sorts of work. He took over the work in the Court of Columns, scraping the paint from the columns and Maiden faces, digging the snow and debris from the choked fountain, clearing the paint from that. He worried over what he could do with the painted pavement until Nilis told him she could paint it again once he'd got the smears off.

They worked alone, saw each other seldom, sometimes shared meals, sometimes a day or two would pass before they met again, settled into a peace with each other that never completely left them.

Shimar began. The Cymbankers grew bolder. Girls and maids came for vigils, young men trickled in for meditation and for their own vigils. A furtive group came into the Maiden Chamber for a minor rite, the Ciderblessing, defying the Agli and the new Decsel. Villagers, ties and even tarfamilies came more openly as each day passed. There were more floggings, more folk dragged to the House of Repentance, more muttering against Floarin because of this, more folk coming to the Shrine. And Nilis began preparing for the Turnfest, her first major fête as Keeper.

# THE MAGIC CHILD

Rane, on Sel-ma-Carth: Nearly fifty years back the governing elders of Sel-ma-Carth hired a stone-working norit to punch new drains through the granite not far below the soil the city was built on; the old drains had been adequate for the old city, but they'd just finished a new wall enclosing a much greater area. (A chuckle and a quick aside to Tuli: You've never lived in a city, Moth. Drains may make dull conversation but they're more important than bread for health and comfort. And this does have a point to it besides general information, so get that look off your face and listen.) The city sits at the meeting of two rivers. The intake of the sewer is upstream and just enough uphill to ensure a strong flow to carry away the refuse and sewage. By the way, you don't want to drink out of the river for some distance below the city. The old drains were abandoned and more or less forgotten. Even the cuts in the wall are forgotten. That's how we're going to get into the city. Don't make faces, Moth, the stink's dried by now. Maiden bless the Followers with boils on their butts. Tuli, Sel-ma-Carth never closed its gates, you could ride in and out as you pleased whenever you pleased and no one cared or was afraid you'd do him something. That's all changed now. If we showed up at the gates, they'd shove us into the nearest House of Repentance. Maybe I ought to leave you outside. I have to see someone, find out the state of things inside the walls, no need for you to walk into that mess. Oh, all right, come if you want. Be glad of your company.

At sundown on the sixth day of riding they topped a slight rise and 'saw Sel-ma-Carth, its gate towers losing their caps in the low clouds, a walled city nestling in the foothills where the Vachhorns met the Bones (a barren stony range of mountains rich in iron, gold, silver, opal, jade, a thousand other gemstones), at the border between the mijloc and the pehiiri uplands. The mines made the city rich, but were only one of its assets. It also sat on the main caravan route joining the east coast with the west.

Carthise were contentious and untrustworthy, automatically joining to cheat outsiders though they were scrupulously honest with their own. It was said of them you could leave a pile of gold in a street, come back a year later and find it where you left it. It was said of them that they took more pleasure in putting over a sharp deal for a copper uncset than they would in an honest deal that netted them thousands. It was said of them a man could come and live among them for fifty years and die a stranger and an outsider and his son after him, but his grandson would be Carthise.

They were the finest stonemasons and sculptors known, hired away from their city for years at a time, they were famous artisans and metalsmiths, gem cutters and polishers. One family had a secret of making a very fine steel, tough and springy, taking an edge that could split a hair lengthwise. The family made few swords but those were always named blades and famous—and exorbitantly expensive. The Biserica bought knives from them, as did the Sleykynin, until a daughter of the House eloped to the Biserica before she was married to a cousin she despised, bringing the family secret with her. Carthise were leather-workers, weavers, dyers, merchants, thieves and smugglers. But no woodworkers. The hills close by were brown and barren and wood brought premium prices. A well-shaped wooden bowl could fetch a higher price than a silver goblet.

"Hern always had a twisty struggle collecting the city-tithe," Rane said. "Once he even had to threaten to close the Mouth and turn the trade caravans north to the Kuzepo Pass before they discovered they had the money after all."

"Then they're not going to take very well to Floarin's ordering them about or to the Aglis."

"That's the trouble, Moth. No one's got in or out recently enough to say what it's like in there. Even Hal didn't know much. However. . . ." She started away from the road into the low hills. When they were hidden from the watchtowers, she went on. "However, I think you're probably right."

When the shifting colors of the dying day touched the low rolling hillocks of snow on snow, they rode across a rising wind that blew short streamers of snow from the tops of the hillocks, snow that sang against them, stinging faces and hands and crawling into any crevice available. Tuli glanced back and was pleased to see the greater part of their trace blown over. By morning the broken trail would be built back into a uniform blanket. That was one problem about spying after a snowstorm, a blind idiot could follow where you'd been. She stared thoughtfully at the bobbing head of her macai. Three days, no wind at all.

But the moment wind was needed to kick snow into their backtrail—she laughed at herself for imagining things.

Rane wound through the hillocks moving gradually behind the city, then left the city behind and started up into the hills toward the pehiiri uplands.

A smallish hut stood backed into the steep slope of a hillside, its stone beautifully dressed, the posts and lintel of the doorway delicately carved with vine and leaf. To one side was a stone corral with the eaves of a stable also dug into the slope visible over the top. The whole neat little steading was hidden in a thick stand of stunted trees, canthas still heavy with nuts, spikulim and a solitary zubyadin, its thorns glittering like glass.

Rane stopped her macai in the center of the small cleared space before the door. She waited without dismounting or saying anything until the door opened and a large chini stood there, broad-shouldered, blunt-muzzled, ears like triangles of jet above a russet head, a black mask about dark amber eyes, alert but not yet ready to attack.

Tuli dipped into a pocket, found a stone and settled it into the pouch of her sling. She might not have time at the chini's first charge to whirl the sling, but she trusted Rane to hold the beast off long enough to let her get set.

"Ajjin Turriy," Rane yelled, her deep voice singing the words over the whine of the wind. "Friends call."

The beast withdrew into the room and a broad squat old woman appeared in the doorway a moment later, not smiling but not sour either. She wore a heavy jacket and enough skirts to make her wide as the door. "Who is you said?"

"Rane."

"Ah." She stepped back. "Be welcome, friend."

Rane turned to Tuli. "Wait," she said. She dismounted, tramped through the snow to the doorway, and stood outlined by light as the dog had been. Whatever she said, the wind carried away her words before they reached Tuli. After a few moments, Rane nodded briskly, came wading back to the macain. She mounted and rode toward the corral.

Tuli slipped the stone and sling back in her pocket, feeling foolish and a bit angry. She was as tired and hungry as the macain were and too irritable to want to ask the questions whirling through her head. And she knew if she made any fuss Rane would leave her behind, was more than half inclined to do so anyway.

With Tuli silently helping her Rane stripped the macain, spread straw in two of the smallish stalls, put out the last of the grain. The gear and the packs they piled in a corner of the stable. Rane took two pairs of snowshoes from those pegged up on one wall. "We can't take the beasts into the city," she said. "We'll have to walk back."

"We aren't staying here?"

"Not tonight. Ever used snowshoes?"

Tuli nodded.

"Good." She handed one set to Tuli and knelt to lace the crude webbed ovals onto her low-heeled riding boots with the fur linings that Hal had provided.

To take her mind off the ache in her legs and the empty ache in her belly, Tuli hurried up and got closer to Rane. "Why couldn't we take the macain into Sel-ma-Carth?"

Rane slowed her swinging stride a little, held up a gloved finger. "One," she said. "The grain levy hit them extra hard. There are no riding beasts of any sort left in the city." She held up another finger. "Two. Ever tried to be inconspicuous on a beast that big and noisy?" Another finger. "Three. They wouldn't fit through the old sewer outfall."

Tuli was silent after that, concentrating on maintaining the looping lope that kept her from kicking herself in her ankle or falling on her face. Rane's long legs seemed tireless, eating up the distance smoothly. Tuli took two strides to her one and still had trouble keeping up. She began gulping air in through her mouth until both mouth and lungs were burning.

She stumbled, the front of the shoe catching against a hummock. Rane caught her, clucked her tongue. "You're sweating."

Tuli panted, unable to speak for the moment.

"You should have said something."

"Huh?"

"It's cold, Moth."

"I . . . uh . . . noticed . . . uh. . . ." She began breathing more easily. The black spots that swam like watersprites before her eyes were drifting off. Her head still ached, her legs still shook, but she could talk again.

"Damn," Rane said. The city was partially visible—the tops of some buildings, the gate towers. The wind blew snow streamers about them, the ice particles scowering their faces. With a shiver, Rane said, "We can't stay here. But don't play the fool again, Moth. If I go too fast, yell. Sweat will chill you worse than just about anything. Chill you, kill you. Don't forget. Let's go."

The remainder of the trip to the city walls was a cold, dark struggle, a nightmare Tuli knew she'd never quite forget. Rane was grim and steel-hard, with a harsh patience that grated against Tuli, but prodded her into going on. Once again Rane circled away from the Gate, then angled toward the place where the bulge of the wall blocked the view of the Gate tower.

There was a low arched opening in the wall over a ditch that might have been a dry creekbed, just a hint of the arch showing over the glowing white snow. Rane unlashed her snowshoes, tucked them under her arm, went cautiously down the bank. At her touch, or so it seemed to Tuli, the grate that covered the opening swung inward, a whisper of metallic rattle, a gentle scraping as it shoved aside a smallish drift of snow. Rane stooped and disappeared inside, legs first, head ducking down and vanishing.

Tuli followed. Inside the low tunnel she saw Rane's snowshoes leaning against the bricks, their shapes picked out by the starlight reflecting off the snow. She set her snowshoes beside them, pushed the grate back in place, and stood, the top of her knitted cap just brushing against the bricks at the center of the arch. About a half a body-length in, the damp smelly darkness was so thick she couldn't see a thing.

Rane's voice came back to her. "Make sure the latch has caught."

Tuli turned, shook the grate. "It's caught."

"Come on, then."

After a few turns it was almost warm in the abandoned sewer. The round topped hole moved in what felt like a gentle arc, though it was hard to tell direction down here. After what seemed a small eternity she bumped into Rane, stepped hastily back with a muttered apology. A whisper came to her. "Wait." She waited, heard a soft scraping and saw a smallish square of pale gray light bloom in the brick roof of the tunnel. She heard the rasp of Rane's breathing, saw her body wriggle up through the opening, heard soft shufflings and some dull hollow thumps. A moment later Rane's head came back through the opening, absurdly reversed. "Come."

Tuli pulled herself up. When she was on her feet again, she was standing in a closet hardly large enough to contain the two of them.

"Don't talk," Rane whispered. "And follow close." She hauled on a lever. Pressed up against her Tuli could feel her tension. The wall moved finally, with a squeal of rusted metal that was shockingly loud in the hush. Rane cursed under her breath. Tuli heard the staccato hisses, but couldn't make out the words. She grinned into the darkness. Though her father would be profoundly shocked, maybe Rane too, she had a very good notion of what the words were and what they meant, having listened on her night rambles to tie-men working with the stock when they didn't know she was around. Rane eased through the narrow opening. Tuli slid out after her.

They emerged into an empty stable, her nose as well as her eyes testifying to its long disuse, the floor swept clean, not a wisp of straw, the stalls empty; there wasn't a nubble of grain about nor any water in the trough.

As Tuli was inspecting the stable, Rane was pushing the hidden door shut and having trouble with the latch. It wasn't catching. Finally, with a snort of disgust, she stepped back and slammed the flat heel of her boot on the outside of the door just above the latch, hissed with satisfaction as it stayed shut.

Tuli chuckled.

Rane shook her head. "Imp," she murmured, then she touched Tuli's arm, led her to a door beside one of the stalls. "I haven't had to use this way before," she said. She wasn't whispering, but kept her voice so soft Tuli could barely hear what she said. "Nor has anyone else, from the look of it." She stopped before the door, frowned at Tuli. "In those bulky clothes you'll pass easy enough for a boy, Moth, but keep your mouth shut or you'll have us neck down in soup. We'll be going to the third floor of this building. No problem about who we are until I knock on a door, then it's yes or no, the knocking and the name are enough to sink me if something's wrong. You keep back by the stairhead. Roveda Gesda is the name of the man we're going to see. If I call him Gesda, you can come and join us, but if I call him Roveda, you go and go fast, get the macain and go back to the Biserica, tell them what we've learned so far and tell them our friend in Sel-ma-Carth has gone sour. That's so much more important than anything you could do for me that there is no comparison I can make." She reached out and touched Tuli's cheek, very briefly, a curiously restrained gesture of affection. "I mean it, Moth. Do you understand?"

Reluctantly Tuli nodded.

They went up a flight of stairs, down a long and echoing hall, up the flight at the far end of the hall, back down another hall, up a third flight. The building seemed empty, the doors to the living spaces so firmly shut they might have been rusted in place; the air in the halls and in the enclosed stairways between them was stale and had a secretive smell to it, a reflection more of Tuli's state of mind than any effect of nature. The third floor. Tuli waited behind a partially opened door while Rane walked alone down this corridor and knocked at another.

After a tense moment the door opened, swung out. Impossible to see who or what stood there, impossible to guess whether it was good fortune or bad for them. Rane spoke. Tuli saw her lips move, but the words came down the hall as muffled broken sounds, nothing more. Rane canted her head to one side, a habit she had when listening. She spoke again, more loudly. "Gesda, I've got a young friend with me." Tuli heard the key name, pushed the door open and stepped into the hall. Rane saw her hesitate, grinned and beckoned to her.

Roveda Gesda was a wiry little man, smaller than Tuli, his age indeterminate. His wrinkled face was constantly in motion, his eyes restless, seldom looking directly at the person he was speaking to, his mouth was never still, the wrinkles about it shifting in a play of light and shadow. A face impossible to read. It seemed never the same for two consecutive moments. His hands, small even for him, were always touching things, lifting small objects, caressing them, setting them down. Sometimes the objects seemed to flicker, vanish momentarily, appearing again as he set them down.

Tuli settled herself on a cushion by Rane's feet and endured the sly assessment of the little man's glittering black eyes. She said nothing, only listened as Rane questioned him about the conditions in the city.

"Grain especially, but all food is controlled by the Aglis of each district and the garrison settled on us. We got to line up each day at distribution points and some . . ." the tip of his tongue flickered out, flicked from corner to corner of his wide mobile mouth, "some pinch-head fool of a Follower measures out our day's rations." He snorted. "Stand in line for hours. And we got to pay for the privilege. No handouts. Fifteen tersets a day. You don't got the coin or its equivalent in metal, too bad. Unless you wearing Follower black and stick a token from the right Agli under the airhead's nose."

"Carthise put up with that?"

"What can we do? Supplies was low anyway." He glared down at his hands. "What with storms and Floarin sending half the Guard, Malenx himself heading 'em, to strip the city and the tars north of here—grain, fruit, hauhaus, you name it, she scooped it up. Needs meat for her army, she does. Once a tenday we get meat now, soon enough won't have any. Stinkin' Followers butchered all the macain and oadats and even pets, anything that ate manfood or could make manfood. Smoked it or salted it down. Sent a lot out in the tithe wagons. With the snow now that will stop but folk won't be able to get out and hunt in the hills, a pain in the butt even getting out to fish and having to give half what you catch as a thank offering. What I mean, this city's lower'n a snake's navel." After a minute his wrinkles shifted and he looked fraudulently wise and sincerely sly. "Some ha' been getting out, those that know how. Awhile back we had us a nice little underground market going. Snow shut down on that some, but some a the miner families are out there trapping vachhai and karhursin; better we pay them than those foreigners and sucking twits. Tell you something too, not a day passes but some Follower he goes floating out face down in shit. Even the aglis, they beginning to twitch and look over their shoulders. Trying to keep a tight hand on us, they are, but I tell you, Rane good friend, the tighter they squeeze the slippier we get." He grinned, his eyes almost disappearing in webs of wrinkles, then he shook his head, suddenly sobered. "Folk getting restless. I can feel the pressure building. Going to be an explosion one a these days and blood in the streets. One thing you say about Hern, you pay your tithes, keep quiet, he let you go your way and don't wring you dry. Where is he, you know? What's he doing? He weren't much but he keep the lice off our backs. Rumor says no Sesshel Fair come spring. That happen, this city burns."

He shifted around in his chair, sat with his elbow on the chairarm, his hand masking his mouth. "Always been folk here who want to stick fingers in other folks' lives, tell 'em how to think, how to talk, tell 'em how to hold mouth, wiggle little finger, you know; they the ones that got the say now, and by-damn do they say." He shifted again. "What's the Biserica doing? Do we get any kind a help? Say a few meien to kick out the Guards. Maybe a few swords and crossbows. The Followers, they aren't much as fighters, no better armed than we used to be. Course we had to turn in our arms. 'Nother damn edict. I wouldn't say there aren't a few little knives and you name it cached here and there, owners forgetting the hell out of 'em. Still, some bows and a good supply of bolts wouldn't hurt. Wouldn't have to get them inside the walls, me and my friends could see to that.

"Got five norits in the Citadel, they sticking noses everywhere. Maiden knows what they looking for, how much they see. One thing, they caught Naum peddling black-market meat. Whipped him bloody in the market square, took him to the House of Repentance. Lot of folk smirking like they something, watching all that. Well, he not easy to be around, but they don't need to enjoy it that much. I ain't seen him since. Me, I been lucky, you might say." He fidgeted nervously, one foot tapping at the reed mat on the floor, the shallow animal eyes turning and turning as if he sought the cobwebs of Nor longsight in the corners of the room. "It's hoping they won't sniff you out."

Rane shifted in her chair, her leg rubbing against Tuli's arm. Tuli glanced up but could read nothing in the ex-meie's face. "Any chance of that?" Rane held up a hand, pinched thumb and forefinger together, then widened the gap between them, raised an eyebrow.

Fingers smoothing along his thigh, Gesda shrugged. "Don't know how their longsight works. Can't judge the odds they light on us. Here. Now."

"A lottery?"

"Might say."

"The artisans' guilds?"

"Disbanded. Plotting and stirring up trouble, the ponti-fex, he say. Head Agli here, what he calls himself. Me, I'm a silversmith. We don't think we disbanded, not at all. No. Followers like lice in guild halls but we keep the signs and the rules, we do. Friend of mine, Munah the weaver, he . . . hmmm . . . had some doings with me last passage. From things he say, weavers same as silversmiths. Guilds be here before the Heslins, yeah, even before the Biserica, ain't no pinchhead twit going to break 'em. They went secret before, can be secret again."

"Followers in the guild halls, how bad is that? Do they report on you to the Aglim?"

Tuli listened to the voices droning on and on. The raspy, husky whisper of Gesda, the quicker, flatter voice of Rane with its questions like fingers probing the wounds in Sel-ma-Carth. Talk and talk, that was all this adventure was. That and riding cold and hungry from camp to camp. Especially hungry. She stopped listening, leaned against the chair and dozed off, the voices still droning in her ears.

Some time later Rane shook her awake. Gesda was nowhere in sight and Rane had a rep-sack filled with food that plumped its sides and made the muscles in her neck go stringy as she slid the strap onto her shoulder. Tuli blinked, then got stiffly to her feet. "We going? What time is it?"

"Late." Rane crossed the room to the door. "Shake yourself together, Moth." She put her hand on the latch, hesitated. "You have your sling with you?"

Tuli rubbed at her eyes, wiggled her shoulders and arms. "Yah," she said. "And some stones." She pushed her hand into her jacket pocket, pulled out the sling. "Didn't know what might be waiting for us."

"Good. Keep it handy. Let me go first. You keep a turn behind me on the stairs, watch me down the halls. Hear?"

Tuli nodded. As Rane opened the door and stepped out, she found a good pebble, pinched it into the pocket of the sling. She peered past the edge of the door. Rane was vanishing into the stairwell. Tuli went down the hall, head turning, eyes wide, nervous as a lappet on a bright night.

At the foot of the stairs she opened the second-floor door a crack and looked out. Rane was moving quickly along the hall, her feet silent on the flags in spite of the burden she carried.

A door opened. A black-robed figure stepped into the hall in front of Rane. "Stand quiet, meie." There was taut triumph in the soft harsh voice. "Or I'll fry your ears."

Tuli hugged the wall, hardly breathing as she gathered

herself. She caught the sling thongs with her right hand, held the stone pinched in the leather pocket with her left, wishing as she did so that she knew how to throw a knife. The sling took long seconds to get up to speed and though she was accurate to her own satisfaction, there was that gap between attack and delivery that seemed like a chasm to her in that moment. She used her elbow to ease the door open farther, moving it slowly until she could slip through the crack.

"Not meie, Norit." Rane's voice was cool and scornful as she swung the sack off her shoulder and dropped it by her foot. Tuli crept farther along the hallway, willing Rane to move a little, just a little and give her a shot.

"Spy then," the norit said. "What difference does the word make? Come here, woman." The last word was a curse in his mouth.

Tuli started the sling whirring, round and round over her head, her eyes fixed on the bit of black she could see past Rane's arm. Come on, Rane, move! Damn damn damn. "Rane," she yelled, hearing her voice as a breaking squeak.

Rane dropped as if they'd rehearsed the move. With a swift measuring of distance and direction, a sharp explosion of breath, Tuli loosed the stone.

Rane rose and lunged at the norit. As he flung himself down and back, the stone striking and rebounding from the wall above him, Rane was on him, taking him out with a snake strike of her bladed hand to his throat. Then he was writhing on the cold stone, mouth opening and closing without a sound as he fought to breathe, fought to scream, then he was dead. When he went limp, Rane was up on her feet, sack in hand, thrusting her head into the living space he'd come from. She vanished inside, came out without the sack and hurried back to the norit.

Breathing hard, almost dizzy with the sudden release from tension, Tuli ran down the hall. Rane dropped to her knees by the nor's body. She looked around. "Thanks, Moth." She began going through the man's clothing, snapped a chain that circled his neck and pulled out a bit of polished, silver-backed crystal, a small mirror no larger than a macai's eye. She threw it onto the flags, surged onto her feet and brought her boot heel down hard on it, grunting with satisfaction as she ground it to powder. Then she was down again, starting to reach for the fragments. She drew her hand back. "Moth."

"Huh?"

"Get his knife. Cut me a square of cloth from his robe big enough to hold this. Hurry," she said, her voice whisper-soft.

When Tuli handed her the cloth and the knife, she scraped the fragments onto the cloth without touching them, tied the corners into knots over them, still being careful not to touch them with her flesh. With a sigh of relief she dumped the small bundle on the nor's chest. "Help me carry him."

"Where?"

"In there." She pointed to the half-open door. "No one lives there."

After they laid him on the floor of the small bare room, Rane put her hand on Tuli's shoulder. "Would you mind staying here with him a minute? I've got to warn Gesda."

Tuli swallowed, then nodded, unable to speak.

"I won't be a minute." She hurried out.

Tuli wandered over to the shuttered window. Little light crept in between the boards. Unable to stop herself she glanced over her shoulder at the body, thought she saw it move. She blinked, looked away, looked quickly back at him. He had moved. His head was turned toward her now, white-ringed dead eyes staring at her. Tuli gulped, backed slowly to the door. Her shaking hands caught hold of the latch but she scolded herself into leaving the door shut and watching the corpse, ready to keep it from crawling out the room and betraying them. Her first shock of terror draining off, she began to be interested, feeling a bit smug. Anyone else would still be running, but not me, she thought, not realizing that a lot of her calm was due to her gift for seeing into shadow, nothing for her imagination to take hold of and run with; she'd automatically shifted into her nightsight, that sharp black and white vision that gave her details as clearly as any fine etching.

The body humped, the arms thumped clumsily over the uneven flags, the booted feet lurched about without direction or effect. She frowned. That weird, ragdoll twitching reminded her of something. "Yah. I see." It was just as the Agli had moved when her father and Teras had hung his naked painted body like a clowndoll in front of Soäreh's nest in Cymbank, just as he twitched when Teras jerked on the rope around his chest. "Gahh," she whispered. "Creepy." The mirror fragments on the corpse's chest, they were doing that; the other norits, they were calling him. Maiden only knew how long before they came hunting. She started to sweat.

The latch moved under her hand. She yelped and jumped away, relaxed when she saw it was Rane. "Look," she whispered, "they're calling him."

Rane frowned, flinched nervously when the body humped again, slapped a dead hand down near her foot. "Shayl!"

"What are we going to do?"

Rane skipped away as the hand started flopping about almost as if it felt for her ankles. She looked vaguely around. "Moth," she whispered, "see if you can find a drain."

"Huh? Oh." Tuli looked about, saw a ragged drape, pushed it aside and went through the arch into the room beyond. Nothing there. Not even any furniture. A familiar smell, though, the stink of old urine. Another curtained arch, narrower than the first. Small closet with assorted holes in the floor, several worn blocks raised above the tiles, a ragged old bucket pushed under a spigot like the tap on a cider barrel. She turned the handle, jumped as a gush of rusty water spattered down, half of it missing the bucket. "Hey," she murmured, "what city folk get up to." When the bucket was filled, she managed to shut off the flow. Grinning and very proud of herself, she raced back to Rane. "Through here," she said.

Rane carried the bundle with thumb and forefinger, holding it as far as she could from her body. She dropped it down the largest hole and Tuli dumped the bucket full of water after it. She filled the bucket and dumped it again. "That enough?"

"Should be." Rane straightened her shoulders. "That'll be on its way downriver before the other norits can get a fix on it, if what I'm told is accurate." She spoke in her normal tones but Tuli could see the beads of sweat still popping out on her brow. "If we leave that body here, everyone in the building will suffer for it. We've got to move it."

Tuli followed her back to the first room. "Where?"

Rane glared down at the body, put her toe into its side and shifted it slightly; Tuli watched, very glad the pseudo-life had gone out of it when they got rid of the mirror fragments. "Out of here. Somewhere. Damn. I'm not thinking." She ran her fingers through her stiff blonde hair until it resembled a haystack caught in a windstorm. "Have to get him completely out of the city and far enough away or they'll animate him. No way to burn him. I'm afraid I jammed the panel we came through. Umm. There's another entrance to the old sewerway a few streets down. Maiden bless, I hope we don't have to take to the streets carrying a corpse. Keep your fingers crossed, Tuli; pray I can get the panel open. Let's haul him down to the stable first, then we'll see. Get his legs." She stooped, heaved the sack onto her shoulder, got a grip on his and lifted.

Rane pushed and pried about with the norit's knife, kicked it again, but the panel stayed stubbornly shut. She came back to the body and scowled at Tuli. With hands that shook a little, she dug into Tuli's jacket pocket, pulled the knitted helmet out and dragged it down over Tuli's head. Then she took a long time gettimg the stray locks tucked under the ribbing. She stepped back and sighed. "Moth, it's dark out there." She nodded at the windows rimed over with ice. "Might be snowing some, norits snooping, Followers, Maiden knows what you'll find out there. I'd rather do this myself, but your eyes are made for the job, and you'll stand out less. Take a look at the street.

I'll stand back-up this time. See if anyone's about, see if it stays clear. Anything looks funny, get back fast. You hear?"

Tuli raised her brows but said nothing. With a challenging grin and a flirt of her hand at Rane's warning growl, she went out.

The big heavy door opened more easily than she expected and she almost fell down the front steps. Of course it's cleared, she thought. Don't be an idiot like Nilis. The norit came through, didn't he? Pull yourself together, girl, and act like you know what you're doing. She put her hands in her pockets and looked around as casually as she could.

The streets had been cleared of snow sometime during the day. The clouds hung low overhead and a few flakes were drifting down, caught for a moment in the fan of light coming from the hall behind her, enough snow to speckle the dark wet stone with points of ephemeral white, promise of a heavier fall to come. She waited there for several minutes, oppressed by the cold and the silence. There was no one about as far as she could see; not even her nightsight could find what wasn't there. If there was danger, it was hidden behind the gloomy façades fronting the narrow street. *I could use Teras's gong,* she thought. *Maiden bless, I wish he was here.* She looked around again and went back in.

Rane was waiting just inside the front door, tense and alert; she relaxed as soon as she saw Tuli, but shook her head when Tuli started to speak. When they were back in the stable beside that cumbersome body, she said, "Any vermin about?"

"None that I saw." Tuli shrugged. "Late, cold, wet, starting to snow again, who else but us'd be idiots enough to leave a warm bed?"

"Good enough. Get his feet."

Tuli went shuffling along, panting under the growing weight of the dead norit's legs. She would have sworn that they'd gained a dozen pounds since they'd started. Conscious always of what they carried, she tensed at every corner and that tired her more. The cold crept into the toes of her boots and stabbed needles into her feet; the flakes blown against her face and down her neck melted and trickled into the crevices of her body, the icy water burning like fire. The wind was a squealing blast, sometimes battering at her, sometimes circling round her like a sniffing sicamar when the buildings protected them from its full force. She wondered why the streets were clear of snow, then remembered her own wretched time in the Cymbank House of Repentance where they tried to wear her spirit away by making her scrub and rescrub a section of hallway (until she threw the dirty water over the matron in charge after she'd made disparaging remarks about her mother). She grinned at the memory and felt a bit better. She decided the Followers didn't seem to have much imagination; they probably worked those they wanted to punish in some lesser way than flogging, making them dig up and carry off the snow. She could see herds of sullen folk tromping through the streets filling barrows of the soggy white stuff and wheeling them out in an endless line to dump them in the river. Or somewhere. After a minute, she grinned again as she thought of the Carthise having enough of this endless and futile labor, turning on the Followers and dumping them instead of snow into the river, but the cold sucked away that brief glow and she was stumbling along, miserable again.

-Her feet slipped and nearly went out from under her if she didn't set them down carefully; once the stiffening legs she held saved her from crashing. The snow was coming down faster; Rane was little more than a shadow before her. Tuli felt herself a shade, a being without substance, a conductor of the lower levels of Shayl, ferrying unblessed dead to their torment. She walked grimly on, half-blinded, concentrating most of her will on feet she could no longer feel. Then Rane turned into a narrow alley between two large buildings, solidly black, melting into the black of the strengthening storm. The sudden cessation of the wind's howl, the withdrawal of its numbing pressure, made her footsteps boom in her ears and her face burn as if the skin was ready to peel off the bone. She started shaking, fought to control it, but could not; it was all she could do to keep her hold on the corpse's legs.

Rane halted, shrugged off the sack, dropped the corpse's shoulders, dragging the legs from Tuli's grip, pulling her onto her knees. While the ex-meie knelt before a small heavy door and started work on the lock, Tuli crouched beside her listening to the faint clicks of the lockpicks. She wiped carefully at her nose, pulled off one of her gloves and used the knitted liner to wipe the wet from her face and neck, still shivering.

Rane stood, waved at the black gape. "Get in," she said. "Ramp going down. Don't fall off it."

"What about him?"

"Never mind him. Here." She pressed a firestriker into Tuli's hand. "See if you can get a lamp lit."

"Lamp?"

"On the wall by the door at the far end."

The lamplight was a soft, rich amber, but there was only a fingerwidth of oil left in the reservoir. Tuli suspected they were lucky to find that much since this subterranean chamber looked as bare and deserted as the stables where they'd first come in. She watched Rane roll the corpse down the ramp, leave it sprawled at the bottom, dumping the sack beside it. Her nose was red and beginning to peel a little, her face was windburnt and strained. She came over to Tuli, cupped a hand under her chin and lifted her face to the light. "You're a mess."

Tuli moved her head away. "You're not much better. I'm all right."

Rane frowned at her. "I've got no business dragging you into this. Hal was right." She pulled off her cap and shook the snow from it. "If I had the least sense in my head, I'd have sent you back the night we left."

"I wouldn't have gone," Tuli said flatly.

"Dragged you then."

Tuli glared at her. "I won't melt," she said. "Or blow away. I've seen winter before."

"From a well-provisioned house with fires on every floor." Rane touched her nose absently, quick little dabs, her eyes unfocused as if she was unaware of what she was doing. Then she shrugged. 'It's done."

"Yah. What is this place?"

"Warehouse, part of a merchant's home complex. Usually isn't this empty, but I took a chance it would be. Not much trade the past few months." She went quickly to the wall that fronted the street and began feeling along it. Tuli got to her feet and started walking about. It was appreciably warmer in this long narrow cellar, but the air had a used-up stale smell. She waved her arms about, wiggled her fingers, did a few twisting bends. Sitting down had been a mistake, she'd known it as soon as she was down, could feel her muscles seizing up as the minutes passed. She watched Rane fumbling about the wall, cursing under her breath as she sought the trigger that would let them back into the ancient dry sewerway.

Then Rane hissed with triumph and tore the panel open. She came striding back, thrust her arm through the strap of the sack, blew Tuli along before her to the corpse and swept on to haul his shoulders up and wait impatiently for Tuli to lift the feet.

Crawling on hands and knees they dragged the body through the long dark hole. In an odd way, Tuli found it easier hauling him where she couldn't see him, not even with her special sight. Now there was only the stiff feel of wooden flesh wrapped in heavy wool. She could pretend it was something else she was helping to drag over the bricks. She had no idea where they were going, but plenty of confidence in Rane. Owl-eyes, Rane had called her once. Only a few months ago? So much had happened since, it seemed like several lifetimes. Moth, Rane called her now. She liked that, she liked the image, great-eyed winged creature swooping through the night, she liked the affection she heard in the way Rane said it.

There was no light at-all down here. Never in her life had she been in blackness so complete. She began tasting and sniffing at the thick black around her. Blacker than an agli's heart, blacker than Nilis' soul had to be. Black. Raven, ebony, obsidian, jet, sable, sooty, swart, pitchy.

In the blackness, sounds: scuffle of hands, knees, feet, sliding whisper of the norit's black wool robe over the bricks, pounding of blood in ears, assorted rubbings of surface against surface, the rasp of breathings.

In the blackness, smells: wet wool and stone, wet leather, ancient dust, sour-sweet taint of something recently dead, not the corpse they pulled behind them, smell of cold over all like paint, the dead smell of the cold.

Then she saw bricks a short distance ahead. Then she saw Rane's hand and side. The light crept up to them, shining back at them off the snow. They crawled around a bend and she could see the crossbars of the grating and the spray of snow drifted through them.

Rane dropped the nor's arm and crawled up to the opening. She fished in her boot for the lockpick, reached a long arm through the grating and began working on the lock. Some fumbling and grimaces later, she got to her feet, stood hunched over, brushed off her knees and tugged at the grating. It squealed and hung up on the small drift but she jerked at it, muscling it a little farther open. She frowned at the opening, twisted half-around to look at the corpse. "I suppose we can kick him through."

"Well, he's getting a bit stiff."

Rane leaned back, reached out, tapped Tuli on her nose. "That's a norit for you; anything to make life difficult."

After some awkward maneuvering, they got the body through the opening. Tuli shivered as the long sweep of the wind slammed into her as soon as she stepped out from the wall. Above the whine of the wind she could hear the tumble of the river close by, so close it startled her. She stomped freezing feet in the snow as Rane tugged the grating back into place and snapped the latch.

The river was not yet frozen over, though plates of ice were forming along the banks, breaking off and sweeping away with the hurrying water. Rane and Tuli swung the body back and forth, then launched it into an arc out over the broad expanse of icy black snow-melt. It splashed down, sank, resurfaced; for a short while a stiff arm appeared and disappeared, the body rolling over and over as the current sucked it away.

Rane plucked at Tuli's sleeve, leaned down to shout in her face. "Hook onto my belt. We'll pick up the snowshoes and get back to the macain."

"What about Gesda?"

"He can take care of himself."

"Tell me about him."

Rane chuckled, "Later, Moth. When I don't have to yell every word." She took Tuli's gloved hand, hooked it over her jacket's belt and started plowing forward through the deepening snow, the sack that Gesda had given her bumping rhythmically with the shift of her shoulders.

The stone hut was cold and stuffy at once, the windows shuttered, the heavy door shut tight. Inside, it smelled of old woman and chini in equal proportions (though the big black chini Tuli had seen before gave no sign of her presence) as if generations of both species had in some way oozed into the walls and stayed there to haunt the place with their odors. There were cured hides on the walls to break the drafts that somehow found their way through the thick stone walls and the tightly fitted shutters and the door. More hides were scattered about the floor, pelts piled on pelts so that walking across the room was an exercise in caution and balance. The old woman sat crosslegged before the fire, her face a pattern of black and red, glitters of eyeball from the drooping slits in the smudges about her eyes. Her hands were square and strong like her face, wrinkled like her face, the palms broad, the fingers so short they looked deformed, more like an animal's paws than human hands. Tuli watched her and felt the last of the chill, physical and mental, begin to seep out of her. She glanced at Rane and saw something of the same relaxation in the ex-meie's face. "Tell me about Roveda Gesda."

Rane sighed. "He calls himself a silversmith, but he'd starve if he had to live by it. He's a thief and smuggler and, well call him an organizer. He's got connections in Oras with the man we're going to see there, with a number of caravan masters and certain merchants on the east coast. He and some others like him give us a lot of information from all over the world." She yawned, twisted her head about. "Shayl, I'm tired. Hal's part of the net, so are the others we'll be talking to." She smiled at Tuli. "Maybe you'll be a part of it one day." She turned to the old woman. "Read for us if you will, Ajjin."

The old woman flicked a hand at the fire. The pinch of herbs she tossed on the coals flared up, blue and green, a pungent, pleasant smell floating out into the room, trails of misty smoke drifting out to hover about them. The old woman breathed deeply three times then three times more. Her hands moved on her thighs, fingers curling to touch her thumbs. Her lips, dark, almost black, trembled, stilled, trembled again. "A changer's moon is on us," she said, her voice at once soft and harsh. "The land is stirring, a strange folk come with strange ways. What was will be lost in what will be. Follower and Keeper both will fade. Changer's moon. . . ."

The words echoed in Tuli's head. Moon. Moon. Moon. Moon. Passages of change. Change. Clang-clang, chimes ringing, the world, the word, the clapper ting-tant-tang. War. War. Warooo. A howl. Churn the land. Waroo, oohwar, wrooo. Waroo. Churn the land. Destroy. Destruction. Death, rot, death and rot, the old gone, the new born from ashes, ashes and pain. Changer's moon. New newborn thing . . . thing what will  what will  what will come? Who knows what it is, misborn or wellborn, mis or well?

The red light shifted across the black of the wood, forming into shaplier blobs, melting into anonymity, forming again. Each time closer to the shape of something—as if something agonized to be born out of the fire. Tuli watched that struggle with a growing tension and anxiety. Now and again, for relief as much as anything else, she shifted her gaze to Rane. Who sat silent, exhaustion registered in the map of faint lines etched across her pale skin, too tired to move, too comfortable with the warmth on her face to go to the sleep she needed, too tired to see the thing that was happening before her eyes. Tuli swung her head and stared at the old woman.

Ajjin was brooding over the fire. Whether she too saw nothing or saw the beast trotting about the coals, Tuli couldn't tell. Beast. Small and sleek, as long as the distance between her elbow and the tip of her longest finger, translucent body with a sort of spun glass fur, red and gold. The beast leaped from the fire and went trotting about the room, pushing its nose against things, small black nose that twitched with an amazing energy in spite of the stuffy chill of the room. The old one sat staring at the coals, silent now, but Tuli thought she looked inward, not out. Her lips moved, the black hole of her mouth changed shape like a visual echo of the rhythm of the silent chant.

Gradually the walls around the room turned to mist, melted away entirely. At first Tuli was only peripherally aware of this, then suddenly—yet at the time so smoothly she felt no shock or surprise—she wasn't in the room at all. Somehow she floated above the mijloc, could see the whole of it, see it from many directions at once, moving points of view. It was as if she was in a great round dance, fleeting from point to point, round and round the mijloc—and others danced with her, wraiths of folk she knew, wraiths of folk she'd never seen before, dancing the round dance of Primaver. She was euphoric, then later as the dance went on and on under the dance of the moons, through moonshadow and moon glow, across the snow-stifled land, she was afraid and not afraid, the others lifting her, cradling her, singing soundless songs to her that she sang back to them; they sang together to the land slipping away below them, they sang to the life of the land, calling to it, comforting it, rousing it and the life it bore to slip the chains laid on it, to burst free of all but the round of life itself, the round dance of birth and death and rebirth.

The snow boiled and bubbled, white fire spitting out,

birthing out animal shapes, more animals like the fireborn in the old woman's hut. The animal shapes, eyes glowing ambergold, ruby gold, sungold, dance the round dance, exuberant, elegant, elegiac, mute voices chanting soundless song, the earth replying with sonorous bell notes to the touches of the dancing feet.

One by one, as the spiral of the dance tightened, the animal shapes dropped away; the ghost dancers dropped away with them and sank into the land to wait. Yes, wait. That was the feel. A tension, an explosion of terrible patience. They were waiting. . . .

Tuli blinked, dazed, wet her lips, stared at the dying fire, moved her shoulders, surprised at the ache in them, and looked down to see the fireborn curled like a bit of shaped light in her lap. She moved again, her legs had gone to sleep and the biting aches and nips of twitching muscles made themselves known, moved without thinking of the beast lying in the hollow of her lap. It made no sound when she jarred it, but adjusted quietly to the new hollows it filled, lifted the pointed head and gazed at her from alert and eerily knowing gold-amber eyes.

"What are you?" she said.

"What?" Rane looked up. She scrubbed her hands hard across her face, straightened out her legs, drew her knees up again. "Time we were for bed." She got to her feet, moving more laboriously than usual, stumbling as a foot caught on one of the layered pelts, catching herself with one hand pressed to the stone wall close beside her.

Tuli reached down to touch the shadow beast. For an instant only she felt a sort of resistance, then her hand passed through it to rest on her thigh. She jerked the hand up with a sharp exclamation, startled and rather frightened. The beast's eyes seemed to twinkle at her, its mouth opened in a cat-grin. She felt a chuckle bubble in her blood, its laughter injected into her veins. She scratched delicately behind a glassy ear and laughed again, her own laughter this time.

Rane blinked at her. "You're overtired, Moth, getting silly."

"Not me," Tuli said. She started prodding very carefully at the red-black outline. "Ajjin, what is this? Do you know?" It cocked its head, sharp ears pricking, and grinned that curling grin at her and she grinned back, feeling giddy and very happy. It was warm and heavy and alive, no matter if her hand slipped into it like a finger poking through the skin on hot milk.

The old woman stirred. She looked at Tuli's lap and smiled. "Soredak," she said, her husky voice soft and filled with wonder. "In your tongue, a fireborn. A channel of power."

Rane frowned. "What are you talking about?"

Ajjin chuckled, but she said nothing more, only shook her head.

Rane thrust impatient fingers through her straw thatch. "We have to leave early," she said. "With the norit vanishing like that, they're like a wasps' nest stirred up. If the weather's right for them, they'll have a dozen traxim up, the other norits, I mean. Ajjin, Gesda's provisions should hold you till your son gets back from the hunt. Have you messages we can carry for you? Or is there aught else we can do for you? Favor for favor, my friend. To keep the balance."

Tuli enjoyed the feel of the warm softness of the beast on her thighs and began to accept that Rane could not see it, would not believe it was there even if told of it. The ex-meie was excluded from almost all of what had happened here. She felt a sadness that this was so, and a touch of pity that the woman she admired so much must for some reason be excluded from this wonder. She looked down at the beast. "Ildas," she whispered to it. "I'm going to call you Ildas." She smoothed her hand over the curve of its side and back, slanted a glance at Ajjin, met her eyes and knew suddenly that there were going to be very few who could see her new companion and that his presence was part of the changes to come. Changer's moon. She turned round to Rane and knew that their time together was coming to an end. She'd expected to cling to Rane long after this probe was finished, she knew that now, and knew also there was no hope of this, that she and Ildas would move in another direction to other goals that did not include Rane.

Ajjin rocked gently on her haunches. "Ah-huh, ah-huh," she said, not the guttural double grunt of assent everybody used, but more like the drumbeats that opened a dance. "Oras," she said. "Debrahn the midwife. My son's wife's elda-cousin. The feeling comes that Debrahn has troubles."

"We won't be there soon." Rane sounded more than a little dubious. "It's a tenday of hard riding if we were to go straight there from here, and we won't do that, we can't do that. It'll be a passage at least before we get to Oras. At least, Ajjin."

Ajjin nodded. "There is no pressing, only an uneasiness. Debrahn lives in the hanguol rookery. Not a place of power."

"To say the least. Well, if she's kept her head down. . . ."

"There are calls she must answer."

"Healwoman?"

"The training but not the name. She was one who left before the time was complete. Mother died and father called her home."

"But she still keeps the covenants?"

"For her, that is not a matter of choice."

"Then she won't be willing to leave with us."

"There will be something for you, so I feel."

"What we can, we will."

Ajjin smiled. "For you as her there is no choice."

"Except to win the battle coming and hope such as she can stay alive."

"You will have help. Hern comes."

"You saw that?"

"Last night I looked for my son and found Hern. He brings strangers to the mijloc. Fighters with ways that clash with ours and weapons of great power; they carry with them the seeds of the change—it is they, not the Nearga Nor, that bring the end to us—I who walk on four legs and two, the child your friend who has magic of another sort. Our time is passing, not yours, Rane; you'll find them much like you and fit well with them."

"You're full of portents and prophecies tonight, old friend, and I don't understand a word of them."

"You never did, that's why you'll fit so well into the new age, good friend. The magic fades, it fades, ah well— get you to your beds, both of you before sleep takes you here."

They rode in silence over the white fields, a gray sky lowering over them, fat, oily clouds thick with snow that dropped a sprinkling of flakes on them and kept the traxim from spying on them. They followed the river a while until it began pushing them too far east, then risked riding onto a bridge road; a ford was far too risky in this cold and the watches at the bridges far more apt to be huddled over mulled cider and a warm fire than keeping an eye out for fools trying to travel in such weather.

The bridge was unsteady, moving to the push of the water in a way that so frightened the macain they wouldn't budge from the bank. Ildas leaped down from Tuli's thigh where he'd been perched with confident serenity since the ride began and ran a weave across the rickety structure, battered into a dangerous state by the violent storms of the Gather and the Scatter. Hern had kept norits employed to see that the bridges and the roads were maintained, but Floarin had other priorities. It was one more wrong to mark against her. But after Ildas had spun his invisible web, the span steadied and the stones knit together more firmly, their macain relaxed and crossed the bridge at an easy lope.

Rane lifted an eyebrow at Tuli, but said nothing.

The tar hedgerows began not far from the river, restricting their movement to the twisty country lanes, piled high now with snowdrifts—and more snow promised from the clouds overhead although they seemed reluctant to let down their burden and the fall held off day after day as they angled toward Oras, spending most nights either camped out of the wind in the thick groves that dotted the landscape or creeping into empty outbuildings of the winter-settled tars whenever they were reasonably sure of being unobserved. They visited a tar here and there, Rane collecting reports from men or women whose anger lay like slumbering geysers under a very thin skin of control. The farther north they got, the more depressing the tars were, the tie villages were more than half empty, always children crying somewhere, signs of hunger everywhere even among the more prosperous villagers in the scattered small settlements dotted among the tars. Rane grew tense and brittle, scolding Tuli about her delusion—which is what she called Ildas—telling her it wasn't healthy to carry the tricks of her imagination so far. She could not see, feel or hear Ildas and was deeply troubled by Tuli's persistence in playing with him, talking to and about him. But Tuli watched the little creature jig about, listened to him sing his soundless tunes, laughed as he ran on threads of air, turned serious when he mimed the presence ahead of traxim or patrols out on sweeps from the villages, guards and Followers after food thieves and vagrants. For three tendays they traveled across the mijloc without serious trouble, only the niggling little things, the cold, the meager unsatisfying meals, the depression from constant reminders of the misery of the mijlockers, the floggings they'd watched in villages, the hunger in men's faces, the pinched look of the children. Twice more Rane left Tuli in empty outbuildings, hidden with the macain and instructions to wait for no more than three hours then get away fast and quiet if Rane had not returned. No noncombatants in this war, Rane told Hal while Tuli listened not understanding. She did now. She was Rane's insurance. She was able to take care of herself so Rane wouldn't have to worry about her and she wasn't more urgently needed elsewhere, so she was available as back-up. Rane liked her well enough, that she was sure of, didn't have to fret about. But the ex-meie didn't really want companionship, despite all her assertions to the contrary; if she hadn't needed backup she'd never have brought Tuli with her no matter how much she liked her. Tuli found these thoughts cold comfort, cold like everything else these days, but comfort nonetheless, and she settled down to prove her competence and deserve the trust Rane was showing in her.

At the first of those tars Rane took her inside the House and they slept in relative comfort that night, with full bellies and a fire in the room, at the second Rane came back looking grimmer than ever. Without saying anything, she took her macai's reins and led him outside, walked beside him, alert and on edge, not relaxing until they were almost an hour away from the tar. Tuli asked no questions, walked beside her, keeping up as best she could. Finally Rane stopped and swung into the saddle. She waited until Tuli was up also, then said, "Norit." She kneed her mount into a walk. "Sniffing about. Not really suspicious but looking to catch anything that stuck its head up. Keletty only had a moment to warn me there were noses in her household and tell me about the norit. Nothing else she could do. Mozzen was doing his catechism for the Agli who was nervous as he was with the norit listening in. Catch this." She tossed a greasy packet to Tuli. "Some bread and dripping, a bit of cheese, that's all she could spare."

Tuli looked down at the packet. She was too tired to be hungry. She smiled down at Ildas, a blob of warmth cradled against her belly. "Think you could hang onto this for me?"

The fireborn grinned his cat-grin, held up his forepaws; she tucked the packet down between those tiny black hands, smiled again as Ildas curled round it. Melt my cheese, she thought. Nice. She looked up to see Rane scowling at her. "I'm too tired to eat," she said.

"Take care, Tuli, don't lose the food, it cost Keletty something, giving it to us."

"Don't worry, I won't."

They rode another hour, slipped into a broken-down herdsman's hut, gave the macain some stolen grain and sat down for a quick cold meal. Tuli's wasn't cold. The bread was steaming, the cheese melted all through it. She looked up to see Rane staring. "The fireborn who's only my imagination," she said, grinning in spite of her fatigue. "He's got a hot little body."

Rane shook her head. "Or you're more talented than you think. Ajjin called you a magic child and, by damn, I think she's right." She stretched, groaned. "We'll ride by night from now on. Could use the rest, both of us. I'll take first watch. You crawl into your blankets and get some sleep. Barring accidents, we'll spend the day here. Couple of nights' ride to Appentar. Lembo Appen's a man who likes his meals so at least the food should be good."

The signal came when she was about to lead the macain out of the half-collapsed hut in the grove's center—long and breathy, the wail of a hunting kanka, one, then two, then one. But Ildas was as twitchy as the fire he was born from, darting about as if blown by a wind that didn't exist except for him. The silent gray trees stood like old bones about her, not a rustle or a creak out of them, the snow shone an eerie gray-white in the pulsing moonlight as Thedom and the Dancers rode gibbous through the breaks in the clouds. She frowned at Ildas, looked over her shoulder at the macain. Working with furious speed so Rane wouldn't be worried, she stripped the gear off the beasts, all but the halters, led them back inside and tied them where they could reach the snow if they needed water, dumped before each of them a small pile of grain. Ildas was too upset; even if Rane thought it was safe, Tuli wanted to take no chances. The fireborn ran before her, nervous and excited; he came back to circle so closely about her feet she was sure she was going to trip over him. She started to scold him, then saw that he was kicking up the snow and hiding all trace of her passage so she pressed her lips together and endured that along with the soundless yaps that were making her head hurt. She wasn't feeling very well anyway, hadn't been sleeping well for several days, her menses were due, she was overtired, underfed and ready to snarl at the least thing. He sensed that finally and went quiet as she reached the edge of the grove.

Rane was waiting in the shadow of a hedgerow. When she saw Tuli without the macain, she said nothing, only turned into the narrow curving lane, shortening her stride as she led Tuli along it toward the gates of a small tar, then over the wall of the House's private garden.

Two girls like enough to be twins met them at the garden door. One had a small candlelamp muted by a darkglass, a child's nightlight, used, Tuli supposed, to shield the girls from discovery. Eyes glistening with an excitement that Tuli found excessive, they spoke in whispering rushes Rane seemed to understand. Tuli didn't feel like puzzling out what was said, so she didn't bother listening. With furtive stealth, the girls took Rane and Tuli up into the attics, showed them into a cozy secret room with a small fire burning ready there, a table set with plates and cups, two bedrolls ready on straw pallets.

The fireborn didn't like it at all; he ran his worry patterns over the walls and ceiling, but ran them in silence so at least Tuli's headache didn't worsen. She wanted to talk to Rane but those idiot girls wouldn't leave them alone; while one was downstairs fetching the meal and gathering supplies for them to take when they left, the other stayed in the room, making conversation and asking questions. Tuli didn't like the feel of this whole business, even without Ildas's fidgets, but she wouldn't say anything because if the girls were honest they were putting themselves in some danger so she couldn't be actively rude. Rane was nervous too, but anyone who didn't know her well would never guess it. The ex-meie was being very smooth and diplomatic, talking easily with the girl, answering her questions with apparent expansiveness and no hesitation, but Tuli noted with some surprise and a growing admiration just how little she was telling the girl. And she began to realize how much of that girl's artless chatter was made up of questions, innocent until you added them together; if she'd got the answers she'd wanted, she'd have had a detailed account of their travels across the Cimpia Plain.

The other girl came up the stairs with a heavily laden

tray that gave out remarkably enticing smells. A fresh crusty loaf, still hot from the oven, one probably meant for the workers' breakfast. A pot of jam, two bowls of savory soup thick with cillix and chunks of oadat. A pot of spiced cha filled the room with its fragrance. Tuli sniffed and was willing to forgive the girls all their unfortunate dramatizing and nosiness. She looked about for Ildas. He was curled into a ball, sulking in one of the corners of the fireplace. She left him there and joined Rane at the table. The girls finally left them alone.

Eyes warily on that door, Tuli swallowed a mouthful of soup, whispered, "Do you know them?"

"Yes." More loudly, "Looks like the weather's breaking."

The door was eased open and a girl was back with a crock of hot water. She smiled shyly, put it down and scurried out.

"Makes riding a bit sticky," Tuli said. She spooned up more soup, glared at the door. "Don't like them popping in and out like that," she whispered. "Ildas is upset a lot. You sure you know them?" She nodded at the door, took a hefty gulp of the cha.

"Knew their father better." Rane wrinkled her nose at Tuli, shook her head. "We'll know better in the morning," she said more loudly.

"If it's snowing, we'd better find a place to hole up." Lowering her voice, Tuli went on, "Well, where is *he*?"

"Visiting a neighbor, his daughters said."

All through the meal one or the other of the girls was bringing something or popping her head in to see if they wanted anything. After the first whispered exchanges Rane and Tuli kept to safe subjects like speculations about when the snow would start. The food was good, the cha was hot and strong, the heat in the room enough to tranquilize an angry sicamar. By the time she emptied her cup for the last time Tuli could hardly keep her eyes open. She knew she should get out of the chair and go lie down on the pallet but she didn't feel like moving. She didn't even know if she could move; the longer she sat, the more pervasive her lassitude grew.

A harsh croak, a rattle of dishes, a table leg jolting against hers. She found enough energy to turn her head.

Rane was struggling to get onto her feet, the tendons in her neck standing out like cables. Her pale blue eyes were white-ringed, her lip bleeding where she'd bitten it. She shoved clumsily at the table, pushing it over with a re-bounding crash that nonetheless sounded muted and dis-tant to Tuli. Rane managed to stagger a few steps, then her legs collapsed under her. She struggled to crawl through the mess of broken china and food toward the door. Tuli watched, vaguely puzzled, then the meaning of it seeped through the fog in her head. Drugged. They'd been drugged. This was a trap. That was what Ildas had been yammering about outside. Fools to come into this, fools to eat the food, drink that cha, must have been in the cha, the spicing would cover whatever else had been added. She tried pushing up, fell out of the chair, made a few tentative movements of her arms and legs to crawl after Rane, but before she could get anywhere or concentrate her forces, she plunged deep into a warm fuzzy blackness.

Tuli wakes alone in a small and noisome room. There is a patch of half-dried vomit in one corner, the stones are slimy with stale urine and other liquids, beetles skitter about on floor and walls, whirr into flight whenever she moves, one is crawling on her leg. She is naked and cold, lying on a splintery wooden bench scarcely wider than she is. Her head throbs. There is blood on her thighs. Along with everything else, her period has come down. She feels bloated and miserable. Usually she doesn't even notice it except for the rags she uses to catch the blood and has to wash out herself, maybe the drug was affecting that too. She wants to vomit but won't let herself, vaguely aware that the food she'd eaten will eventually give her strength, and she knows she's going to need strength in the days to come. She is no longer just a rebellious child to these folk. Not like before. She is Tesc's daughter, though she can hope they don't know that. At least they shouldn't know that. But there is Rane, she is Rane's companion. When she thinks about Rane, bile floods her mouth. She swallows and swallows but it does no good, she spits it out onto the floor and forces herself to lie still, her knees drawn up to comfort her stomach. Ildas nestles against her; his warmth helps. Rane. Maybe she's already dead. She might have made them kill her.

Tuli dozes awhile, wakes with a worse headache, forces herself to think. *Got to get out of here. Get Rane out if she's still alive, but get out anyway whatever has happened to Rane. She's counting on me to get word back to the Biserica about how things are on the Plain. I should have listened more. Maiden bless, why didn't I listen? Never mind that, Tuli, think. How do you get out of here? How do you survive without telling them anything until you can get out of here?* After a moment's blankness, she adds grimly, *how do I kill myself if I can't get out?*

She forces herself to sit up, crosses her legs so she doesn't have to put her feet down on the filthy floor. She is cold enough to shiver now and then. Again Ildas helps, warming away the chill of the stone. The shutters on the single small window are winter-sealed; the air is stuffy and stinking but the icy winds are kept out and the sense of smell tires rapidly so the stench is bearable. She keeps her eyes traveling about the room, deeply uncomfortable with her nudity, growing more stubbornly angry as the morning drags past. No one comes. There is no water. No food. Though she doesn't know if she could force anything down in that noisome filth. Ildas paces the walls then comes and curls up in her lap.

Early in the afternoon they come for her.

The air in the dim round room is heavy with the smoke of the drugged incense, the sweet familiar smell she remembers from the night she and Teras sneaked round the old Granary and heard Nilis betraying their father. It makes her wary. She tries to ignore the way her nakedness makes her feel, the helplessness, the vulnerability, the absurd urge to chatter about anything, everything, so that they will look at her face and not at her body, those men staring at her, their eyes, those leering, ugly eyes. Then

Ildas curls about her shoulders, a circle of warmth and comfort and she is able to relax a little, to let the heat of her anger burn away the worst of the shame and wretchedness. She lifts her head, meets the Agli's eyes, sees the speculation in them and knows she's made a mistake. She should have come in sobbing hysterically, flinging herself about like the child she wants to seem. Maybe rage will do instead. She crosses her arm over her too-tender breasts and glares at the Agli, at the acolytes waiting with him, snatches her arm from the guard's hand, letting rage take possession of her, the old rage that carried her out of herself—funny how she couldn't invoke it now when she needed it yet once it came so easily she frightened herself. Faking that rage and calling on all the arrogance she hadn't known she possessed, the fire of the fireborn running through her, energizing her, she curses the two acolytes and the Agli, curses the guards silent behind her, demands to be given her clothes (lets her voice break here, only half-pretense). And as they watch, doing nothing, the rage turns real. Before they can stop her, she flies at the Agli, fingers clawed, feels a strong satisfaction when she feels his skin tearing under her nails, sees the lines of blood blooming on his skin. Caught by surprise, the guards and the acolytes take a second to pull her off the Agli. She will pay for this, she knows, even through the red haze of rage and fierce joy, the payment will be high, but it is a distraction and will put off her questioning. She doesn't exactly think this out, it leaps whole into her head. She struggles with the guards, kicking, scratching, trying to bite until one of them loses his temper and uses his fist on her.

Shock. Pain. Blackness.

When she wakes it is an indefinite time later. She is in the same round room, but her hands are bound behind her, her ankles are in irons with a short chain between them. There is no one in the room with her. She still feels some satisfaction. She has forced them to put off their questions. But she regrets the leg irons, they are going to make escape difficult. Have to find Rane, she thinks. Her picklocks would take care of the irons. If she is alive, if she has her boots.

Ildas is titupping about, sniffing at things. He lifts a leg and urinates liquid fire into the incense bowl, flashing its contents to sterile ash. He knocks over the charcoal brazier, plays in the coals, drawing their heat into himself. Almost immediately the air around Tuli begins to clear. She realizes after a bit how dulled her reactions have been, how sluggish her body has been feeling. The drugs and fumes from the charcoal have been poisoning her, softening her up for the Agli. She snarls with fury, wrenches at the rope, but it is too strong, the knots too well tied. Ildas comes over to her, curls himself onto her shoulders; she can feel his heat flowing through her, burning those poisons out of her. She laughs and croons to him, telling him what a beautiful creature he is, what a wonder. He preens, nuzzles at her face with his pointed nose, his laughter sings in her. Then he stiffens, his head comes up and the laughter turns to a hostile growling.

The Agli is returning.

Because she is warned, he finds her hunched over in a miserable lump, apparently drugged to the back teeth, dull and apathetic. The acolytes straighten her up, force her onto the hard bench, then go about cleaning up the mess she and Ildas have made of the room. When she dares sneak a look at the Agli, she almost betrays herself by a snigger of delight at the sight of his face, three raw furrows down one side of it, two more on the other side. Hope they poison you, she thinks, then understands she must banish that sort of thing from her mind, or the triumph and spite in her will seep through and spoil the picture she wants to present. There is a tie-girl in the Mountain Haven that she despises, even more than that creepy sneery Delpha. Susu Kernovna Deh. Who as far as Tuli can see has no redeeming virtues, who is sullen and stupid, who would rather pout than eat, who is lazy, giggly, spiteful and fawning. You hit her and she licks your feet and doesn't even try to bite your toes. Why she isn't one of the more avid Followers Tuli cannot understand, she seems made to be a follower. Susu is the image she wants to project, figuring she is such a nothing the Agli will get disgusted and toss Tuli-Susu out. She begins fitting herself into the role, looking out the corner of her eyes at the Agli, keeping her shoulders slumped, holding her knees together with a proper primness that seems to her only to emphasize her nakedness. She hates that, but thinks it is how Susu would act.

The acolytes settle themselves at the Agli's feet. He sits in a high-backed elaborately carved chair. It is raised higher than an ordinary chair, his feet rest on a small round stool. The acolytes kneel like black bookends on either side of the stool, what light there is—from the flickering wall-lamps and the high window slits—shining off their shaved and oiled pates.

The Agli speaks. He has a deep musical voice that he keeps soft and caressing. Not yet time for torment, it was the hour of seduction. "Who are you, child?"

She licks her lips, opens her eyes wide, looks at him, looks quickly away, hangs her head. "Susu Kernovna Deh."

The Agli taps fingers impatiently on the chair arm, raises a brow. She wants to laugh, but forces herself to pout instead. Briefly she wonders why the drugged smoke which is again billowing up from the brazier does not affect the agli and the acolytes, then dismisses that as unimportant. After all, an Agli is a norid and can most likely do such small bits of magic as keeping the air clear about himself and whomever he wants to protect. After a minute, he speaks again. "You are not tie, child. Who are you?"

"Susu. I'm Susu Kernovna Deh."

"Mmm. Who is your father?"

"Balbo Deh. He says."

"And what does that mean?"

"Hansit Kern took me into his house and had me taught." She makes herself smile a prim, soapy little smile. "Many say it is he and not Balbo who fathered me, that I've got a look of his oldest girl." She lets a touch of boasting enter her voice.

The Agli settles into the chair. "What is your tar?"

"Kerntar. It's out on the edge of the plain, near the pehiiri uplands." She shrugs. "I don't know exactly. It's a long way from here." More discontent in her voice. "Eldest daughter threw me out, Soäreh wither her miserable. . . ." She sneaks another sly look at the Agli, lets him catch her at it, looks away in confusion and fear. She is tempted to elaborate on her tale, but has just sense enough not to. Ildas on her lap is warm and supporting, and more important, he is keeping her head and body clear of the drugs from the smoke—especially her head, giving her strength and energy to maintain her efforts at deception. She can't afford to become too complacent, though, there is always Rane who knows nothing about this story or about the names, nothing about the original Susu. Rane, if she says anything at all, if she is still alive, will tell an entirely different story. Tuli chews on her lip, her unease not wholly pretended.

"Who is the woman?"

"Woman?"

"Who is the woman?"

"Oh her. Just some wandering player. Well, you couldn't expect me to travel about alone. She was going to take me to a cousin in Oras. Stupid Delanni paid her to. I didn't want to leave the tar, don't blame me for it. But when he got sick, Kern I mean, Delanni took over running things and I was the first thing she run off."

"Who is the woman?"

"Look, I told you, aren't you listening? Player or something. You want her name? Ask her. I forget, I mean, who cares what's the name of someone like that."

"What were you doing at Appentar?"

"Me? I wasn't doing nothing. Eating, getting out of the cold. What do you think I was doing? Watching those two snippy twits sucking up to her." She puts a world of venom in the last word.

On and on it goes—simple questions repeated over and over, questions that fold back on themselves, trying to trap her. She clings to Susu with a faint spark of hope growing in her when the questions change nearly imperceptibly until they are centering on Rane. On and on, until she is mumbling and drifting in a haze in spite of Ilda's efforts, a haze that is far too real for her comfort. She no longer knows exactly what she is saying, can only hide herself in the persona of Susu, answering as best she can in Susu's voice and Susu's life.

The questions are thrown more quickly at her, they blur in her mind until none of them make sense. After a while she just stops answering them and drifts into herself, no longer trusting mind and body, drawing in until she is closed up in a tight knot, no ends left out for them to pull. Again Ildas helps her, running round and round her, spinning threads from himself, weaving her into a cocoon of warmth and darkness that no one but her could break through. She lets herself fall away, protected, into her cocoon and fades back into darkness.

She comes out of the haze and confusion back in the cold and stinking cell, stretched out on the plank bed, Ildas a warm spot on her ribs. She sits up. Her hands are untied. It seems odd to notice that so belatedly, but that nonetheless is the order of things. She looks at her legs, grimaces at the crusts of blood on her thighs. What a luxury a hot bath could be. When we get out of this, she thinks, when we get to Oras, I'm going to live in a bathtub. The irons are off her legs. She smiles, flushed with a sudden optimism. It looks like Susu has won the day for her, like the Agli isn't taking her seriously any more, Maiden be blessed. She rubs at her ankles where the irons had been, then at her wrists. "Ildas," she says, drawing the word out as she thinks. "Ildas, go see if you can find Rane. Let me know if she's here. Please?"

The fireborn scampers uneasily around the room; he doesn't want to leave her, but he recognizes her urgency. After some vacillation, he melts through the door. For some time after he vanishes, she can still feel his grumbling like a shiver in her bones; it makes her teeth ache and she is annoyed with the little beast, but finally has to smile.

They come for her again before he returns. Because she can feel the drugs in the smoke sapping her will, she withdraws into herself, says nothing, answers nothing, tries to not-hear them, doing the best she can to show a degree of sullen petulance, clinging desperately to Susu to help her withstand the drugs and the hammering of the persistent questions. The questions are thrown at her by acolyte and Agli alike, taking turns, coming at her from the right, from the left, from the throne chair, beating at her: who are you/ why are you here/ what are you doing/ who is your father/ where is your tar/ why are you spying/ what do you hope to find/ tell us about the outlaws in the mountains/ where are they/ who are they/ what are they going to hit next/ where are you going from here/ who is the woman with you/ she's a meie isn't she/ who is she/ what is she doing/ what information have you gathered/ are you lovers/ is she planning to assassinate the regent Floarin or the son/ who are you going to see in Oras/ who have you seen so far/ who are the spies and traitors in our fabric/ tell us the names/ where have you been/ tell us the name. . . .

And on and on and on. Sometimes prurient questions of what activities passed between Tuli and Rane, a spate of these coming unexpectedly in the middle of the other hammering questions, almost startling her out of her silence. But she tightens her grip and fights the deadening pull of the drugs. She finds her mouth loosening to babble and catches herself again and again and begins to fear she will give in. The drug is making her sick, her concentration breaks more and more frequently. Her will is eroding all the faster as her fear grows, as her sense of helplessness grows. She opens further and further from reality like the spiral dance when she found Ildas, but spiraling out this time, not in, out and out and out until nothing seems to matter, until she is sick of herself, sick of them, sick of Rane and the mijloc and everything that has happened and is going to happen, until she is at the point when nothing matters anymore.

For a while she knows nothing that is happening, drifts in and out of grayness, repulsive, stinking grayness, only dimly aware of herself as self, clinging only to one idea and not sure what she knows. Silence. Say nothing. Whatever happens, don't answer, don't even listen, say nothing, nothing, nothing. . . .

Warmth nudges against her hip, crawls into her lap; the haze begins warming out of her, the room firms around her again. She is sitting hunched over, staring sullenly at her dirty feet, at the rough stone floor, the muscles of her face hurting, her head throbbing dully. She stares resolutely at the floor, wanting to know if she'd let the Agli cozen her into answering his questions while she was in that floating state, wanting to know if Ildas had found Rane, frantic because she can think of no way to ask him without betraying herself to them. THEM. The word writes itself with major glyphs on the air above her feet. She can see them wavering over her toes. Ildas nudges her and the word pops like soapbubbles, even with the same tiny noise a soapbubble makes when it pops. She nearly giggles, then reverts to a sullen scowl. She sneaks a look about her. The acolytes are gone somewhere but the Agli is still in his throne chair, frowning at her. Sometime in her haze the questions have stopped. That frightens her a little, she doesn't know why he stopped. Does he have all he wants or is he momentarily baffled by her silence. If he starts going at her again, at least that will mean she hasn't done anything too awful. Her feet begin to itch, her knees burn. She has to move. But she doesn't. Even moving her foot seems like a breaking down. Ildas coos to her, his silent chortles vibrating in her head. He is acting very chirpy. She tries to take comfort in that. Rane has to be about somewhere. Alive.

The silence is thick in the room. She can feel the Agli trying to push his will at her. She wishes he would say something, anything. She wishes she could move, could scratch the thousand itches that are tormenting her, wishes she were out of here, anywhere but here, even back at Gradintar with Nilis carping at her, no, mustn't think of

Gradintar, I might say something I don't want to. No. Think of Susu. Susu Kernovna Deh of Kerntar out by the pehiiri uplands. She sneaks a glance at the path of the lightbeam coming in one of the high slit windows, and nearly betrays herself. It hasn't been long, only a half hour of unknowing, if the slide of the light on the far wall meant anything. A half hour since she could remember questions coming at her. It feels an age. Her mouth is so dry she doubts she could speak even if she wanted to.

"What is your name?" The Agli speaks with unchanged patience.

Then the acolytes are back. One brings her a battered tankard filled with warm beer mixed with something else she can just taste over the musty staleness of the liquid. She drinks it avidly enough, though the taste makes her queasy. He takes the tankard away when she is finished and jerks her onto her feet, giving an exclamation of disgust when he sees the bloodstain she leaves behind on the wood. So give me some water to wash in, she thinks, and bring me my pants and rags. He handles her as if she is a bag full of slime after that, holding her at arm's length. She could jerk away from him any time, but what is the point, where could she go? He holds her arm up and the other acolyte uses a bit of rope to tie her wrist to a ring set in the stone. When they have dealt with the other arm, she stands with her face pressed against the stone, unable to put her heels down. She flinches inwardly at the thought of the pain to come, expecting it to come any moment from a whip or something similar. But nothing happens. Behind her she can hear dragging sounds, something metal pulled across the flags, footsteps, quick and busy about the room, some heavy breathiing, more clangs, a rattle, the snap of a firestriker, some breathy cursing, a little crackling, then an increasing feel of heat fans across her back. The charcoal brazier, she thinks, what. . . . She wrenches her mind to thoughts of the ordeal ahead and tries to decide how she will handle it. If she follows her instincts, she will grit her teeth and not make a sound, not give the creatures the satisfaction of hearing her cry out. Besides, once she starts yelping she isn't too sure she can stop. Or she can still keep in Susu's skin, though they don't seem to be believing her too much. Trouble is, Susu would never be on this kind of cross-country trek, even if what she said was true and she was kicked out of her tar by a jealous half-sister. She would have whined and balked and made such a nuisance of herself any guide and guard no matter how well paid would have pushed her into a river two days out of the tar. Or at least dumped her somewhere and taken off. And there is Rane. If they know anything about her at all, they know she'd be the least likely person to take on such a task. The holes in her story get bigger by the moment as she strains upward, her nose pressed against the stone.

"What is your name, girl?" The Agli's voice comes with a deadly patience.

"Susu Kernovna Deh," she says and whimpers.

"I think we'll leave that lie now, girl," he says. "Have you ever seen a branding?"

Tuli's whimper is all too real. Maiden bless, he's going to burn me. She presses her face against the stone so she won't cry out. *All right*, she thinks, *we leave Susu now. My mouth is shut and it's going to stay that way. I hope. Help me, help me, let me say nothing, if I scream, so be it, but help me say nothing.*

"Heating the irons takes a while, so you have a little free space, girl. Think about branding, think about the irons, smell them. Hot irons have a distinctive odor like nothing else in the world. I could hurry the heating if I wanted, girl, but I don't think that's necessary. We have all the time in the world. There'll be another smell in the room soon enough, so savor the irons while they're heating. Think of all the places we are going to use them on you, girl, think of your tendermost places. We'll save your face for the last. It's that disfiguring that breaks the stubbornest woman, and you're not a woman, are you, child. It isn't you we want, think of that. We want what the meie knows. Oh yes, we know her well enough here. Rane." He chuckles at the start she can't help. "So foolish with your silly little story; I imagine you thought you were clever, so clever to fool us. We'll break you first, child, then her. She's a stubborn one, she'll last a long time. Make it easier on her, girl. Tell us what you've seen and heard. Name us the traitors who've been supplying you with food and information. Then maybe we'll just put you to work until the war is over. Find you a husband then and let you live out your life in peace. I won't promise the same for the meie, you wouldn't believe me if I did. But she can have an easier death. Think about the irons, child. As long as they're still heating you're safe from them. You've got a little while to wait. Use it." The soft coaxing voice dies away and she hears his footsteps retreating from her, leaving the room, leaving her to her thoughts.

Maiden! What a. . . . I can't. . . . Shayl, how can I face. . . . whip's bad enough. . . . my face. . . . I can't. . . .

She must and she knows it. Get it over with, she thinks, clamps her tongue in her teeth so she won't cry out, the anticipation almost worse than the burning, but it won't be once the burning starts, she knows that too. The silence behind her stretches on and on, an eternity. She starts shaking. She is going to tell, she knows it, tears gather in her eyes and run down her face. *I can't . . . I can't.* . . . Her bladder gives way and hot liquid runs down her thighs, splatters on the floor. She goes rigid with shame, then she is shaking again, moaning. She tries to dredge up anger but can think of nothing but the irons burning her. . . .

The Agli's voice comes genially behind her. "What is your name, girl?"

She wants to tell him, she is going to tell him but she sees Rane's face Hal's face Her father's face Teras Sanani and her silly oadats. . . . And she cannot do it. Cannot. But she has to tell, what else can she do? What does it mean anyway, it is just postponing for a little what must happen anyway, they are bound to be taken, all of them, Hal and Gesda and the angry taroms and her father and Teras, and all of them. But there is something in her that will not let her do what logic tells her to do. She bites on her tongue till blood comes and says nothing.

The Agli makes a soft clucking sound of gentle disapproval. Tuli is almost startled into giggling, it is so like the sound old Auntee Cook makes when she catches her or Teras in the jam pots. Tears run down her face. Blood is salty on her tongue.

One of the acolytes—she thinks it is the one who curled his lip at her menstrual blood—brings the hot iron. He holds it close to her buttocks. She cringes away from the heat, tries to press into the stone. He sniggers, puts the iron between her legs and brings it up hard.

For just an instant the pain is something she can't realize, it is so greatly beyond anything she has experienced or even expected, she cannot breathe, cannot make a sound, can only sob, a high whining sound like an animal cry—then the pain is gone, the heat is gone, and all she feels is an uncomfortable pressure and a gentle warmth throughout the whole of her body. And she hears Ildas's angry chitter in her head.

The ropes burn off her hands, though no fire touches her skin. The warmth flows out of her. The acolyte behind her shrieks, the pressure drops away from her. The Agli screams in an agony equal to hers a moment before. She turns.

He writhes on the floor and as she watches, flashes to a twisted blackened mummy. The acolytes burn with him. The three of them are suddenly and utterly dead. The smell of roasted meat is nauseating in the room. She walks from the wall, stops by the hideous corpse of the Agli. "You said there'd be another smell in this room, but you didn't know you'd provide it. If I told you anything, it has vanished into your present silence." She touches the body with her toe. It is hard and brittle and stirs with a small crackling sound that wrenches at her stomach.

Hand pressed hard over her mouth she runs from the room.

She looked down at Ildas prancing beside her, smiled at his complacent strut, the glowing whiskers sleek and content. "Take me to Rane."

They wound through the dark and twisty halls of the Center, dodging an occasional guard or flitting female form. It seemed absurdly easy to Tuli, like dreaming of walking naked and unobserved through crowds of strangers. And there did seem to be very few folk of any sort about. *Maybe Floarin's taken them all to Oras,* she thought. Near the back she came to a row of cells like the one she'd waked in but too far on the side for hers. There was a drowsy guard leaning half asleep against one of the barred doors. Tuli chewed her lip. She didn't even have her sling, she didn't have anything. Except Ildas, and she didn't exactly have him, he did his own will and hers only when the two wills coincided or he felt like doing her a favor. He looked like a beast, he acted like a beast most times, she called him a beast when she thought about him, but she knew it was not the right word, he had more mind than any beast, more will, more . . . something. She knelt in shadow and touched him, drew her hand along the smooth curve of his back. "Will you help me, companion and friend?" she whispered.

The fireborn wriggled under her hand, then was away, a flash of light streaking along the worn stone flags, then a rope of light coiling like a hot snake up and up, around and around the man who wasn't aware of anything happening until the rope whipped round his neck and pulled itself tight. He clawed at the nothing that was strangling him, tried to cry out, could not, staggered about, finally collapsed to the floor. The light rope held an instant longer, than unwound and was Ildas again, sitting on his hind legs, preening his long whiskers, more satisfaction in his pose, reeking with self-approval.

Chuckling, Tuli came walking down the hall. She scratched him behind his ears, felt his head move against her palm, felt his chitter echoing in her head. "Yes, sweeting, you did good." She straightened, unbarred the door.

Rane was stretched out on a plank cot like the one Tuli'd waked on. She sat up when she saw Tuli, her eyes opening wide, the irons clashing on legs and arms. She was naked and there were bruises and a few small cuts on her body. She looked strained and unhappy, but otherwise not too badly off.

Tuli looked at the irons, then looked uncertainly about the cell as if she expected to find help in the filthy stones.

"The guard," Rane said. "He has the keys on his belt."

Tuli came back with the keys a second later. She took the wrist irons off first. "You have any idea where they put our clothes?" She bent over the leg irons, scowling as the key creaked slowly over in the stiff lock. The irons finally fell away with a slinky clanking. Rane worked her ankles, rubbed at them. "No, but I know how to find out." She swung off the cot and went out to squat beside the guard. She touched the charred circles about his neck, pressed her fingers under the angle of his jaw. "Good. He's still alive, just out cold."

Tuli smiled, felt a distant relief. "There's enough dead already."

"The Agli?"

"And the acolytes."

"How soon before someone finds them?"

"Can't say." She rubbed at the nape of her neck. "A while, I expect. They were getting ready to use hot irons on me, wouldn't want to be interrupted at their pleasures."

Rane shivered; once again she touched the blackened rings about the guard's neck. "How did you do this?"

"I didn't. It was Ildas." Tuli's mouth twitched into a brief, mirthless smile. "The fireborn you say doesn't exist."

"Seems I was wrong." Rane wrapped her hands about the straps of the guard's cuirasse and surged onto her feet. "Help me get him inside."

They dragged the guard into the room, fitted the irons on his wrists and ankles. He was a smallish man so they could just close the cuffs, though Rane wasn't worried too much about his comfort. She used his knife to slash the tail off his tunic and a second strip long enough to tie around his head. She dropped these on his chest and stood looking down at him; without turning her head she said, "Shut the door, Moth, this could get noisy."

The guard was beginning to wake, shifting his head

about, moaning a little as he began to feel the pain in his neck. Rane set the knife at his throat, the point pricking one of the charred rings. "Where did you put our clothes," she said softly. "No, don't try yelling, you won't get a sound out, I promise you. I'd prefer leaving you alive, man, but that's your choice. Where did you put our clothes?"

He blinked up at her, his neck moved under the knife point; he gave a small cry as it cut deeper into the burned flesh. "Storeroom," he gasped out.

"Where is it?"

"Go down hall. . . ." he cleared his throat, "first turn, go left, three doors down. Everything there."

"Good." She snatched up the hacked off bits of cloth, held them out to Tuli. "Gag him. You," she shifted the knife point a little, drawing a grunt from him, "open your mouth."

With Ildas scampering ahead of them, they loped down the long corridor, made the turn and dived into the storeroom.

Their clothing was thrown in a heap in the corner; no one had bothered going through them, Tuli's sling and stones were still in her pocket and Rane's boots had kept their secrets intact. Instead of dressing, Tuli started poking about the storeroom, seeking anything she could use as a pad. Now that the worst fears were behind her, along with all urgencies but the final urgency of escape, the little niggling irritations had taken over. She wanted water desperately, even more desperately than clothes to cover herself.

Rane's hand came down on her shoulder, making her start. "What is it, Moth?"

Tuli blushed scarlet. "Menses," she muttered. "I got to wash."

"That all? All right. Wait here, I'll see what I can find."

The ex-meie came back a short time later with a pitcher of water and a pair of clean towels. "Hurry it, Moth. No one around right now, but Maiden knows when the guard's due for changing." Tactfully, she turned away and began looking through the things on the shelves, taking a tunic here, a pair of trousers, two black dresses, exclaiming as she came across her own knife, her grace knife whose hilt she'd carved and fitted to her hand a long time ago. Tuli scrubbed at herself, sighed with relief as she washed away the crusted blood and found that where the iron had burned her there was no sign of burning. She looked down at Ildas and smiled tightly. *Should stop being surprised at what you can do*, she thought. He seemed to hear what she was thinking and rubbed his head against her leg. She tore a strip off the towel, folded it and pinned it into her trousers with a pair of rusty pins she found thrust into a crack between a shelf and one of its uprights. It was uncomfortable and was going to make riding a messy misery but it was better than nothing. She climbed into her clothes and felt much more like herself when she stamped her feet into her boots. "Ready," she said.

"Good. Help me with this." Rane was whipping a bit of cord about the bundle of clothing and other things she'd taken from the shelves. "Maiden bless, I wish I dared hunt out their food stores, but we'd better get away." She straightened. "Set your Ildas to scouting for us, Moth. Toward the back. That's best, I think. I wouldn't mind a bit of snow either."

"What about mounts? Can we hit the stables? It's some distance to Appentar. I put out grain for our macain and there's snow for water, but they're tied, Rane. We can't leave them like that."

"Yah, I know. We'll see when we get out. Tuli, if there are guards in the stable, we head out on foot. No argument please."

"No argument." She bent and scooped up Ildas. "Stables will be coldern'n these halls. You notice we haven't seen more'n two or three guards even in here. I think most of them, they're sitting around a barrel of hot cider and a nice crackling fire." She rubbed Ildas under his pointed chin, smiled as his contented song vibrated in her. "Ildas is used to scouting, he found you for me. He'll let me know if there's anyone coming at us." She scratched a last time,

set him down and watched him pop through the door.
"He's off."

Rane shook her head. "If I hadn't seen that guard's
throat," she murmured.

Ildas' head came through the door; he sang emptiness to
Tuli. She laughed and said, "Right. We come." To Rane,
she said, "All clear."

"Let's go then."

As they loped through the maze of corridors at the back
of Center, Tuli mused over the difference in the guards as
they moved closer to Oras. Down by Sadnaji most of them
seemed as committed as the Followers. But here they were
a rag-tag lot, as if Floarin had dumped all her misfits and
doubtfuls close to Oras where they couldn't make trouble
for her, where their slackness would mean little since the
shadow of Oras weighed heavy on the Plain here in the
north. For the past tenday, the patrols she'd seen out in
the snow and cold were mostly Followers with a guard or
two but no more. The ones here were probably drunk and
comfortable and not about to take much notice of what
was going on around them unless there was someone to
prod them to it. Thanks to Ildas the Agli was beyond
prodding anyone. She looked at the narrow back swaying
ahead of her and smiled. And it'll be snowing, she thought,
betchya anything. A nice dusty snow to powder in our
tracks.

She smiled again as they eased through the narrow door
and stepped into the stableyard. The yard was deserted
and dark and a feathery mist of snow was drifting onto the
trampled earth.

They reclaimed their own mounts and discarded those
taken from the Center stables—poor beasts, bad-tempered
and sluggish. Their own macain were uncomfortable and
complaining in low hoots but Ildas soon had them snuf-
fling happily at the grain, wrapping himself like living
wire about them, warming the chill out of them. Another
scoop of grain apiece, some melted water, and they were
ready to go on; Rane and Tuli stripped the gear off the sad

specimens from Center and turned them loose, hoping they weren't too stupid to smell out the nearest food and shelter.

"What about those two twits?" Tuli scowled into the snow toward Appentar. "They'll do the same to anyone that shows up."

"You'll see." Rane swung into the saddle and rode toward the edge of the grove, Tuli following, Ildas perched on the saddle in front of her.

At the gate of the tar the ex-meie dismounted and used her grace knife to cut an inconspicuous mark in the gatepost, then she was in the saddle again riding swiftly away. It was some time before she slowed and let Tuli move up to ride beside her. "That was a warn-off mark," she said. "Players, tinkers and peddlers have a series of marks they use to leave messages for each other. The warn-off says keep away, there's trouble waiting for you here. Anyone on the run who knows Lembo and doesn't know the signs will have to take his chances. Or hers. Lembo. . . ." She shrugged. "I don't know about him. Maybe he was away like his daughters said and we just came at the wrong time. Maybe he's dead. Maybe he's turned. It doesn't matter that much right now, we've got more important things to get busy on."

"What next?"

"Oras. Fast and straight as we can. One good come out of this, we've got grain enough to keep the macain going on long marches." She reached back and patted the fat sack tied behind the saddle.

Tuli nodded. "At least there's that." They'd been sparing in what they'd taken from tars, but there was no such moderation required when they were taking from the Agli.

They rode north and west and soon passed beyond the edge of the plain into down country, a region of low rocky hills. There were occasional flurries of snow; when it wasn't snowing, the clouds hung low and mornings were often obscured by swirling fog. Roofed stone circles alongside small huts swam at them out of that fog as they wound among the hills. Now and then, a young boy with a chunky, broad-browed chini pressed into his leg stood in the hut's doorway and watched them ride past. Sometimes the boy would lift a hand to salute them, more often he watched, silent and unmoving. The stone circles were filled with huddled linadyx, some of them wandering out into rambling pole corrals to chew on wads of hay and scratch down to the winter grass below the snow, their corkscrew fleeces smudges of black and gray and yellow-white against the blue-white of snow. Every fifth circle was empty.

Tuli waved back to one of the boys, then kicked her macain into a slightly faster lope until she was riding beside Rane. "How they going to feed those beasts if it keeps snowing?"

"You saw the empty circles."

"Yeah. So?"

"The Kulaan have winter steads in the riverbottom. Women and children work the fields there in the summer while the men and older boys are in the downs with the linas; come first snowfall they start bringing the herds down." She wiped at her thin face, scowled at the slick of condensed fog on her palm. "I'd rather it was snowing instead of this infernal drip. Other years all the flocks would be down by now."

Tuli shivered as she heard a distant barking and the high coughing whine of one of the small mountain sicamars. It seemed to come from all over, impossible to tell the direction of sounds in this fog. She thrust a gloved hand in her jacket pocket and closed clumsy fingers about the sling. "So. Why not this year?" Her voice sounded thin and lost and she shivered again.

Rane rubbed at her chin. "Well, the Kulaan treat their linas like members of the family. They don't kill them for meat ever, even if their own children are starving; when they're so old they can't get around any more and don't produce fleeces, they're very gently smothered and burned on a funeral pyre and the ashes are collected and kept till spring, then scattered over the Downs with drum and song and dance, whole clans going to celebrate the passing of their friends. You can see how they'd feel when Floarin sent her tithe gatherers to the winter steads and claimed whole herds of linas to feed her army. Those that hadn't brought the linas down yet are waiting until the army leaves Oras, hoping the beasts won't starve or freeze before then. Kalaan might put on Follower black for policy's sake, but even before the raids there'd be few convinced among them. Now, there's no question of that. Floarin has made herself an enemy for her back when she marches south. They're a dour, proud people, the Kulaan, they don't forget injuries and they never leave them unpunished."

"Are we going to stay at a stead?"

Rane shook her head. "I have acquaintances among them, but I wouldn't be welcome now. Besides, there's no point in it. Yael-mri knows all she needs to about their state of mind." Again she passed her hand across her face. "Shayl, how I'd love to be dry. Just a little, even an hour."

As the day oozed toward its end, Rane angled more directly westward until they were riding almost directly into the veiled red blob of the setting sun. Tuli began to feel a strain in her thighs and back, realizing after a while that they were riding downslope considerably more often than up, leaving the hills and aiming for the Bottomland. When she asked, Rane nodded. "We're due to hit the river about a day's ride east of Oras."

"Why not closer?"

"Traxim. The army. Floarin's norits. Any one's a good enough excuse to stay far away from the place." She slanted a tired grin at Tuli. "And that's our chance, Moth. Who would figure we'd be so crazy as to sneak into the jaws of a sicamar?"

The punishing ride went on and on, three days, five, seven. The grain sacks were almost empty and the macain were almost at the end of their strength. On the eighth day the snowfall stopped. On the ninth day they were making their way through the thickly timbered bottomlands, able to hear the sigh of the river they couldn't yet see, a sort of pervasive brushing that got lost among the creaks and cracks of the denuded trees. They rode through trees stripped bare of leaves, silent, brown-gray-black forms harsh against the blanket of snow. Here and there the snow was marked by the calligraphy of wild oadats, lappets and other small rodents, chorainin and limbagiax and other predators small enough to run on the crust. They saw nothing alive, not even kankas sitting like wrinkled brown balloons in the empty trees.

Near the river, the ground under the trees was a thorny tangle, a mix of saplings, many split open by the sudden cold, suckerlings, hornvines like coils of black wire stark against the white of the snow. Rane got as close to the river as she could, rode west along it for some time. About mid-afternoon, she called a halt. "Give the macain some grain, Moth." She slid from the saddle, worked her fingers, tugged her cap down farther over her ears. "I'm going to climb me a tree, have to check on some landmarks before it gets dark."

She went up an aged brellim with an agility that surprised Tuli. While Tuli flattened a sack on the snow and dumped a meager ration of grain on it, Rane sat in a high fork, her head turning as she scanned the river and the bank across from her. After about a dozen minutes she swung out of the fork and came dropping down the trunk, landing beside Tuli with a soft grunt as her boots punched through the snow.

"Find what you want?"

"Uh-huh." Rane moved to her macai, stroked her gloved hand down over the beast's shoulder, watched him lick his rough tongue over the sacking, searching for the last bits of grain.

"Well?"

Rane looked round at her, laughed. "A place to sleep and leave the macain while we're in Oras."

"A kual stead?"

"No, none of them this close to Oras. Bakuur. Charcoal burners. This time of the year they usually have a camp not too far from here."

Tuli retrieved the sacking and began rolling it into a tight cylinder. "You seem to know everyone."

"I've been drifting about the mijloc for a lot of years, doing this and that for the Biserica." She watched as Tuli tied the sacking to the saddle. "Never had a real ward after the first time, Merralis and I." She swung into the saddle, waited for Tuli to mount. "Getting a little old for all this rambling though." She started her macai walking. "Biserica's going to be needing someone familiar with the round, might be you if you choose that way, Moth."

Tuli looked at her, startled. "Me?"

Rane smiled at her again, wearily, affectionately. "Who better?"

The camp was set up inside a palisade of poles pushed into the ground long enough to have taken root and sprouted new branches, branches that wove together in a complicated bramble along the top of the fence. The poles were set about the length of a forearm apart with hornvine woven through the uprights, hornvine rooted and alive with withered black fruits dangling like tiny jetballs from the fruiting nodes, the thorns long and shiny and threatening enough to keep out the most persistent predator. Inside this formidable living wall more poles had been pushed into the soil, set in parallel lines and their tops bent together to form the arched ribs that supported sewn hides; five of these structures were spread around a stone firecircle like the spokes of a wheel.

The Bakuur were a small dark shy people. They welcomed Rane and Tuli with chuckling cordiality, a spate of words in a language Rane understood but Tuli found as incomprehensible as the murmur of wind through leaves. They stabled the macain with their eseks in one of the longhouses, set out straw and grain for them with a lavishness that oppressed Tuli; she felt she was somehow going to have to repay the favor and at the moment she didn't see how.

Later, after a meal of baked fish, fried tubers and a hot, pungent drink cooked up in kettles that produced a mild euphoria in Tuli, Rane took out her flute and began playing. They were in one of the longhouses seated before a smoking fire, all the Bakuur crowded in around them to listen to the music. After a short while Ildas leapt off Tuli's lap and went to dance on the fire, weaving in and out of threads of smoke, dancing joy on threads of air. Tuli watched dreamily, the drink working in her, opening her out until she felt one with the one the Bakuur had become, men, women and children alike. One. Breathing together, swaying together with the dance of the fireborn, with the music of Rane's flute. A while after that a slender woman neither young nor old, with bracelets, anklets and necklace of elaborately carved wooden beads came up out of the Bakuur meld to dance her counterpoint to the fire and the fireborn, twisting and swaying without moving her feet, curving flowing movements of arms, hands, body, that painted on the air the things the music was saying to her and her people. Tuli felt warm and alive and welcomed as a part of a whole far greater than the mere sum of its units. Gradually she relaxed until she drifted into a sleep, a deep sleep filled with bright flitting dreams that left her with a sense of joyful acceptance though she remembered none of them when she woke sometime after midnight.

Her boots were off, blankets were tucked about her. The longhouse was empty except for three ancient Bakuur, two men and one woman, sitting with Rane beside the dying fire, talking in low voices. She heard a little of it, snatches of tales about the state of feeling in Oras. They spoke in concrete terms, no abstract summaries like those Hal and Gesda and some of the angry taroms had given Rane: *Toma Hlasa cursed a guard and was dragged off; the jofem Katyan complained of the taxes, eyes darting about to see she was unheard, and bought only two uncsets of charcoal where once she'd have bought ten; a hungry-looking man whom they didn't know tried to steal from them and almost killed Chio'ni before Per'no and Das' ka drove him off.* As far as they could see, there was no unity anywhere, man against man, each bent on preserving his own life and possessions, no *zo'hava'ta*. . . .

Tuli blinked. They were speaking in the rippling murmuring Bakuur tongue, something she only realized when she came up hard against that word *zo'hava'ta* that on its surface meant life-tie, but that carried on its back wide-ranging implications that permeated all of Bakuur life, the bond that tied mother to child, tied all Bakuur to the trees they burned for their living, bound friend and enemy against all that was non-Bakuur, bound present generations to the dead and to the as-yet unborn, that affected everything every Bakru did from the first breath he drew until he was returned as ash to the breast of the Mother. Ildas, she thought, he danced the words into me. She reached down to the warm spot curled against her side and storked her hand along the curve of his back, smiled at the coo vibrating in her head, then settled to listen carefully to what was being said, mindful of the resolution she'd made at the Center when she knew she might have to take word back without Rane.

An hour before dawn the Bakuur hustled about harnessing eseks in teams of four to a pair of wattle-sided carts. Rane handed Tuli a large, coarsely woven sack. "Get into this, Moth," she said. "We're going into Oras as sacks of charcoal."

Tuli looked at Rane and giggled. The ex-meie raised an eyebrow but said nothing. She climbed into one of the carts and began easing her long body into a sack.

Tuli hopped into the other cart, stepped into her sack and pulled it up around her, then crouched in one corner while the Bakuur piled bags of charcoal around her. They were light enough that they didn't overburden her, but drifts of char-dust came filtering through her sack, getting into eyes, nose, mouth, every crevice of her body. Even after both carts were loaded, the Bakuur seemed to take forever to get started, each of those going with the carts taking elaborate leave over and over with every other Bakru not going on the expedition to Oras. Finally though, the carts creaked forward and passed from the palisade into the snow under the trees. The eseks labored and brayed their discontent; a Bakru walked beside each of the leaders singing to him, clucking to him, urging him on. Other Bakuur followed behind and put their shoulders to the wheels and the backs of the carts whenever they threatened to get stuck, all of them laughing and talking in that murmurous language that sounded much like a summer wind among the leaves. The three-toed feet of the eseks crunched down through the trust, the carts lurched and complained, the beautifully carved wheels squealed and groaned, the trees around them creaked to the light wind and above Tuli the charcoal sticks chunked together, rattled dully and showered more dust on her. And through it all the Bakuur went on their leisurely way, in no hurry at all, content to proceed as circumstances allowed.

It was still dark out when they left the trees and started up the rolling hills to the high plateau where Oras sat. The road wound up and up, curving back on itself when the slope was too steep, straightening out now and then, almost flat, only to pitch upward after the eseks managed to catch their breath. The extra weight of Rane and Tuli made things more difficult for the shaggy little beasts, but the Bakuur coped with more laughter, a lot of shoving and joking; the tough little eseks dug their claws in and the carts lumbered on. By the time they reached the flat again, Tuli felt a lightening in the dark, saw bits of red-tinted light coming through the coarse weave of her sack.

The Bakuur circled wide about the army encampment. Tuli could hear noises from the herds of riding and draft stock, and sentries calling to one another, but it was all very distant and placid and she couldn't get excited by any of it. She was sneaking into a city that was the heart of the enemy's territory and what she mainly felt was discomfort. The commonplace presence of the Bakuur wove such a protection about her, she almost fell asleep.

The sounds from the army dropped behind, the cart tilted up, then the wheels hummed smoothly over the resilient pavement of the Highroad. She waited for the challenge of the guards at the gate, but the carts went on without a pause, the sound of the wheels changing as they moved from the Highroad onto the rougher cobbles of the city street. The gates were already open. If there were guards, they were so accustomed to the coming and going of the charcoal sellers that they didn't bother challenging them. The carts wound on and on until she was so tense she felt like exploding, when were they going to get out? how? where? what was going on? Not that she was afraid or anything like that, she just wanted to get out of that damn sack. Only the soothing coo of Ildas in her head kept her crouched in her corner.

The cart turned and turned again, winding deeper and deeper into the back streets of Oras, then shuddered to a stop. Tuli lay still forcing herself to wait, forcing herself to trust the Bakuur and let them release her when they were ready.

She heard the backgates being taken off, felt the sacks of charcoal being swiftly unloaded. When she pushed the sack down, small hands fluttered about her, helped her up, urged her out of the cart. They were in the deep shadow at the far end of a blind alley, the carts and the shadow hiding them from anyone passing the alley's mouth. While she worked her arms and legs, did a few deep bends, following Rane's example, the Bakuur were piling the sacks back in the carts, working swiftly but taking moments to grin broadly at Tuli and Rane, savoring their part in this tricking of Floarin and her guards. Before Tuli managed to get all the kinks out of her limbs, the Bakuur were clucking the eseks into motion, heading out of the alley.

"Where they going?" she whispered.

"Market. Middle of the city." Rane's voice was harsh, abrupt.

Tuli was thirsty, there was char-dust packed in her nose, clogging her throat, more than anything she wanted a glass of water, but she looked at Rane's taut face, streaked like hers with black dust, and kept her peace. Rane leaned against one of the building walls and waited until the squealing of the cart wheels had died to a faint scratching, then she went to the mouth of the alley and looked into the street.

There was no snow falling. The streets were cleared

here as they'd been in Sel-ma-Carth. Dawnlight was reddening the roofs high over them. Rane beckoned and began moving along the street at a fast walk; Tuli had to trot
to keep up with her. With Ildas scampering before them,
they wound swiftly deeper into Oras, through narrow
alleys that smelled of rotten fish and urine and cheap wine,
over all that the indescribable but pervasive stench of
poverty. The gloom was thick in these winding ways in
between houses that leaned together and seemed too rotten
and worn to stand on their own. Rane never hesitated as
she turned from one noisome street into another, stepping
over ragged bodies of sleeping men and a few women, or
loping around the piles where they'd huddled together
against the cold in the meager shelter of a doorway. In
some places they were thick on the ground as paving
stones, gaunt, groaning men, sleep coming as sparely to
them as the scraps they ate. Hunger and destitution in the
city seemed more devastating than in the country, perhaps
because there the hungry and the failures were more scattered and hidden from view and because it was easier to
get food of a sort and shelter of a sort in the groves and
outlying herders' huts.

They came to a rickety structure several stories high. It
was backed onto the great curtain wall and stretched out
its upper stories close to the building on either side as if
fearing a moment's weakness when it could stagger to one
side or the other and need help to keep standing—or so it
seemed to Tuli as Rane loped across the street and plunged
into a narrow alley along one side of the building.

The ex-meie stopped before a door with corroded hinges
and a covering of muck dried on it so thick it seemed the
door hadn't been opened in years. She reached into a hole
in the wall beside the door, groped about a minute, then
jerked hard on some invisible cord. She pulled her hand
out, stepped back and waited, the tension draining from
her lanky form, the weariness suddenly increasing as if
she'd suddenly gone slack.

A moment later the door swung open, slowly, carefully,
but with no suggestion of furtiveness. Doesn't want to

disturb the camouflage, Tuli thought. The smallish man who stood in the doorway scowled at her, then turned to Rane. "You bleeding-heart meien, always shoving children on me; well, get in before the traxim fly and spot you."

# IV

## THE JUMP

## POET-WARRIOR/KINGFISHER

### 1

Julia lay groggy with pain and drugs, trying to convince herself she should ask Grenier to give her enough to kill her in the next shot. Trouble was, she couldn't yet bring herself to give up so very finally. I am the distilled essence of what this country used to mean, she thought, making phrases to take her mind off the pain. Unquenchably optimistic in the face of disaster, absurdly expecting something to come up and change everything if only I work hard enough and wait long enough. Logic says die and save the drugs, the care, the strength spent on me for those they can help. But I'm not logical about this. This dying. Say it, Julia. Dying. Not logical. Half of what I think is fantasy. She stirred restlessly and the young girl who sat reading in the bar of light coming through the tent's door put her book aside and come over to her.

"Time for another shot, Jule?"

Julia smiled at her. "No. Maybe a glass of water though?"

As the girl helped her sit up and drink from the glass, she heard an outburst from the meeting place loud enough to reach them through the trees and the heavy canvas of the tent. She sputtered, turned her head away. The girl set the glass aside and eased her back down on the pallet. "Lyn," she said. "Go find out what that's about. Please?"

Lyn looked dubiously at her.

Julia gathered herself, lifted a hand, touched the girl's arm. "What a hoo-haw. Lyn, if I have to lie here and listen to all that without knowing what's happening out there, my curiosity will drive me up the wall."

Lyn got slowly to her feet. "You be all right?"

"No better, not worse than I always am; what's to worry about, dear Lyn. Find out what's going on, then hurry back and tell me. I really do need to know." She sighed as the girl pushed out of the tent, listened to her light footsteps hurry away and fade into the shouts and uproar coming from the meeting. They've made up their minds what to do about the attack tomorrow, she thought. Reason enough to swallow the bitter pill. I'm declining into cliché at the end of my life. The noise that had startled her muted until nothing more came to her ears than the usual camp sounds. She lay back with her eyes closed, listening to the wind brushing through the trees, soothed by the sound, calmed enough to go back to the depressing considerations she'd been immersed in before the noise began. She had to make up her mind before the next shot, bring herself to do what she had to do. Whatever they decided, they could not take her with them, yet chances were they'd try. She couldn't bear to think of it any longer and deliberately turned away. Fantasy. I've never written a fantasy. I wonder if I could? Magic. I don't believe in it. I wish I could, but my optimism doesn't stretch that far. Magic healer, yes. I could bring him out of air and nothing, a shaman who would make this wrongness in me right. Then, since you've gone this far into never-never land, why not conjure a shaman who could magic the ills out of your poor damned doomed country? God, I wish I could believe in that enough to write it. She listened for a minute but could hear nothing except the usual noises. Come on, Lyn. Get back here and tell me what they've decided. Magic wand, she thought, wave it over the country and set things right. Set things right, that's a frightening thought. She shivered. That's what started this, one bunch of peabrains trying to make reality fit their idiot schemes. Anyway, who's wise enough to say what's right for anybody but himself. Herself. Not me. Only, let the killings stop, let people work out their own lives. Stop the slaughter of minds. Almost worse than bodies, what you're doing to the minds of good people. Magic wand. Magic want. She giggled. Magic chant. Give me a magic chant, a curse that would strike only those with rigid minds, those who think there's only one right way to do and be, give me a curse tailored to those types, give me that curse and I'd loose it over the world, I'd loose it laughing, no matter what misery it brought. Hunh! probably just as well I'm only dreaming. She sighed and tried to relax, tried to sink into the soughing of wind through the needles, the scattered bird cries, the distant chatter of a squirrel, all the wild sounds of the mountains. The smell of the pines crept into the tent, sharp, clean, the essence of greenness, of remembered mountains. Mountains. I ought to write an essay on mountains. She smiled into the dim brown-green twilight in the tent with its dusting of fine red dirt, dirt that smelled like the trees that grew out of it, dirt that smudged her fingers and the base of the glass. She rubbed her fingertips on the blanket. Her hands were bundles of sticks now, bones and skin with no flesh left. I used to have pretty hands. Forget that, no point in it. Mountains. I was born cradled between mountains. I have always had a hunger for blue mountains, a hunger like that, I suppose, that has called so many sorts of men to the sea and inspired bad poetry. Odd, isn't it, how some verse you know is only doggerel can reach down into blood and gut and stir them mightily. But the sea's a capricious and undiscriminating mistress; she calls everyone and welcomes them with equal eagerness and treachery. We who succumb to mountains have to share our love only with the few and the odd; our lover is harsh and demanding yet forgiving in her way; she punishes stupidity but welcomes back those willing to learn, she kills a few but most survive to return to her. I have come to die in my mountains, one last embrace, one last green breath of free air in this nation that has forgotten the meaning of freedom. . . . eh, Julia, you grow maudlin, this part of the essay would need extensive editing. . . . dumb, lying here, coaxing sentimental tears out of yourself. Enjoy your good cry, fool, and get back to the hard things . . . still . . . blue mountains . . . pine smell and bark dust. . . . better to die here if one has to die . . . Lyn, where are you? Oh god, it hurts . . . can't stand . . . have to . . . can't think . . . fantasy . . . bring me . . . my magic healer . . . let me escape . . . let me live. . . . She folded her wasted arms over her swollen belly, closed her hands about wrists like withered sticks and fought to endure the growing pain as the drug wore off. There was too much riding on the next shot, too much. She wasn't ready to face it, not yet.

Lyn came in like a burst of sunlight, her straight black hair spreading out from her face in a fan. She took a deep breath, calmed herself a little, blinked as her eyes adjusted to the sudden twilight. "Out of nowhere." Her high light voice went up to a breaking squeak. She cleared her throat, breathed in again. "Two people," she said, snapping her fingers. "Like that. Like they do in TV and movies, except this was real. A man, in clothes like you see in history books, Robin Hood, you know. With a sword. A real live sword, Jule. Short and kinda fat, but looks like he can handle himself good as Georgia if he wants to. But that's not the weirdest thing. There's a woman with him. Tiny bit, wouldn't come up to here." She indicated her collarbone. "She's got on this white thing, sort of a choir robe without sleeves. And she's green. Uh-huh. Green. Sort of a bright olive. And she's got orange eyes and dark red-brown hair. Sounds yukky, doesn't it, but she isn't, she's really kinda pretty in her weird way." Lyn smiled and settled herself on a pillow beside Julia. She leaned forward. "Like I said, one minute Sammy was telling Danno to sit down and shut up, he'd get his turn to talk, the next thing, there they were, the man and the woman, standing by him. Anyway, that's what Liz said. She said Ombele jumped the man and Georgia got his sword away, but the woman, she just told them not to be idiots and to behave themselves. Then the man started talking. He's come to give us a way out. A way we can stay together and not get killed. Well, not exactly giving it; he wants us to help him fight a war against some bunch of sorcerers. Sorcerers!" She giggled. "Would you believe it? Magic. They're asking him all sorts of questions now, what we gonna get out of it, who's he, you know, stuff like that. He's sounding good, Jule, but it's hold your nose and jump in the dark."

**2**

When Hern and Serrbi stepped through the Mirror, the gathered crowd surged onto its feet, the big brown bald man, Ombele, descended on Hern like an avalanche and had his arm twisted behind his back before Hern had a chance to catch his balance. The fighter band lunged through the crowd at him and stood guard while Georgia patted him down with quick efficiency and none-too-gentle hands, removed the sword and held it up, disbelief in his square face. He turned to Serroi and stopped, his jaw dropping. "Green?"

Serroi chuckled. "Green," she said. "Suppose you let my friend go and listen to what he has to say." She looked up at him, with a wry smile. In the mirror Georgia had seemed big enough but not enormous compared to the others, yet her head barely passed his belt buckle. These were a large people. Even the smallest of the adults would be at least a head taller than the tallest of the mijlockers; only the Stenda came close to watching them.

Georgia grinned down at her. "Feisty li'l bit," he said. He waved his fighters back, handed Hern his sword and went to squat in the front row of the gradually quieting crowd, balanced on his toes, ready to move swiftly if there was need.

Hern sheathed the sword and brushed at his sleeves, his eyes glittering, his long mouth clamped in a grim line. He wasn't used to being handled like a child and looked ready to skewer the next to try it, but even as she wondered if she should say something, the anger cleared from his face and his palace mask closed down over him. He swung around to face the council and Samuel Braddock who was polishing his glasses with a crumpled white handkerchief. "May I speak?"

Braddock slipped the glasses on. "Think you better." He climbed onto his stool to sit, resting long bony hands on long bony thighs.

Hern turned to the intently listening folk. "I am Hern Heslin, hereditary Domnor of Oras and the Cimpia Plain, a land on a world other than this. I've come to offer you a refuge from your enemies." As he paused, Serroi studied the faces before them, some interested, some skeptical, some hostile, some indifferent, all of them alert, following his words with an intensity that startled her. Talk well, Dom, she thought, they're going to need a lot of convincing. "I've been watching you," Hern said. "On my world there is a being who calls himself sometimes Coyote, sometimes Changer, with a Mirror that looks into other worlds. To pay off an old debt, he in effect gave me my choice of whatever I saw in his Mirror. I have watched you govening yourselves and I like what I've seen. I've watched your fighters in action, effective action with a minimum of force used and blood shed." He smiled. "I was much impressed." A blend of interest and alarm lit Georgia's faded blue eyes. "On my world we are engaged in a battle that is much like the one that engages you here. From what I heard, your government has been taken over by a group that is trying to control every aspect of your lives. So it is with my land. I need you. I have no gold to pay you, but I can offer you a refuge from those that pursue you and land to build a new country, raise your children, govern yourselves as you please. Fight for me, help me throw out those who want to tell my people how to act, what to think, who want to destroy an ancient seat of learning and refuge. In return, I will take all of you back through the Changer's Mirror, all of you, old and young, fit and sick, fighters and non-combatants alike. I will cede to you a stretch of land north of Oras, a territory empty of other folk and kept as a hunting preserve by my father and grandfather. The soil is fertile, it has an extensive seacoast and access to one of the major rivers of the land, a good part is forested, and there is abundant game." He made a small deprecating gesture. "Since I don't find much pleasure in hunting, they've been left undisturbed for a number of years. The size. . . .um . . . that's a difficulty." He rubbed a hand across his chin. "I would say the preserve is just about three times the area of that city where the armory was. You understand, I can only promise you that land if the Nearga Nor and Floarin's army are defeated, but no matter what happens some of you will survive and there is much open land on my world." He turned, made a slight bow to the council, then swung back to the others. "I stand ready to answer your questions."

A man got to his feet, scowling, a stocky dark man with long black hair braided into a single plait and tied off with a thin leather thong. "Havier Ryan," he said. "A lot of us don't think much of hereditary anythings. We got 'em and we close to dying of 'em." In spite of his stolid appearance, he radiated an immense anger tautly controlled, control that flattened his voice to a harsh monotone. "Fight for you, you say. All right, what's the chances? We don't mind a fight if something comes of it, or why the hell we here? Lost causes, that's something else. Might as well stay and tend to our own miseries as jump off into the back end of nowhere." He crossed his arms over his chest and stood waiting.

"Your weapons are far more lethal than ours, with a much greater range. My world fights with sword and bow, lance and sling. With those two-wheeled machines you have mobility and ten times the speed of anything my people know. You would be fighting beside several hundred meien, women trained to weapons who will give the last ounce of their strength to defend the Biserica, not least because they can look forward to a slow skinning over a hot fire if they're defeated. Also a few hundred irregulars, men and boys driven off their land, and some Stenda mountain folk who don't take well to being told what to think. You'd be fighting behind a great wall, defended from sorcerous attack by the most powerful concentration of life-magic in our world. Your numbers are few, but as I said, your range, power and mobility will more than make up for lack of numbers. There might be other allies joining us, but I've been away from the Biserica for some time and haven't seen the latest reports. As for the other side—I think we can count on having to face three or four thousand. Not all of those will be trained fighters, but enough of them to roll over my meien like a flood tide no matter how fiercely they fight. And there is the council of sorcerers, the Nearga Nor. Since they are the ones who started this mess, they're gathering in all the norits and norids they can lay hands on. Norids you don't have to worry much about since they're barely able to make a pebble hop. Norits are something else. Besides things like longsight and flying demons sent as spies and saboteurs, they can compress the air above you so that it falls on you like a stone, turn earth to bogs that suck you down, or open wide cracks under your feet, burn anything flammable you have on your body, including hair and nails, freeze the breath in your lungs, or snatch it away, freeze the blood in your veins. But they can't work their magic from a distance greater than ten or a dozen bodylengths and there are only a few hundred of them—and as long as the Shawar are untroubled, they can block everything the norits throw at us. The most powerful of the nor, the norissim, are very few, one active, the others reduced to shadow extensions of his will. But he'll be concentrating on the Shawar shield so won't be a direct threat as long as we can keep the army from breaking through the wall. With you there, we can stop them. A tough fight, but far from a lost cause."

"And what happens if we don't choose to come?"

"I go back through the mirror and look for another force to fight for me." He looked round at them. "And you pack up and start running."

### 3

Julia ran from the pain, ran into memory, fading from scene to scene, indirectly taking leave of the struggle that had brought her here, preparing herself for the final yielding.

A hand reached out and caught hers, a strong arm hoisted her into the back of the truck. As she stumbled into the darkness, the dim light from the overhead bulb touched momentarily the flat spare planes of a familiar face, Michael, dressed again in the skirt and blouse she'd given him. She settled herself beside him, her back braced against the steel side of the box. "Making this permanent?"

"This side of the line."

"They still looking?"

"When they feel like it."

The truck began filling up, people packing in around them, so they stopped talking and sat in growing discomfort until the smuggler had his load and the back doors were slammed shut and latched. Julia heard the rumble of the motor, grimaced as she caught a whiff of exhaust smoke; the truck started forward with a lurch that pushed her into the dim figure on her left.

The truck crept forward, waddled into the street, hesitated, then picked up speed along an empty street.

The hours passed too slowly. There was no talking, a grunt or two now and then, a cough, a sigh, scrapes as one of the fugitives shifted cramped limbs. There was a stink of fear and sweat, of hot metal and exhaust fumes. The uncomfortable jolting as the truck sped through twisting, potholed back roads became a kind of bastinado of the buttocks and heels, but the stale air had its anodyne for that, dulling her mind and senses, dropping her into a heavy doze.

Whoom-crump of a warning rocket. Bee buzzing of rotors, grinding of engines. Man's voice blatting from a bullhorn. You can't tell what he is saying, but you don't need to.

Truck bucking round, racing off the road into the woodlands, roar of motor, chatter of machine guns, bullets pinging off the sides of the truck, punching through, shrieks, groans, a woman keening in the murk, a man cursing. The truck lurching wildly, tossing them all together in a tangle of arms and legs. Screams. Moans. Banging and clawing at the doors, shrieking, howling, confusion, floundering, muddle. They are locked in a bounding, shuddering box with no way out.

Squeal and shriek of metal. The truck is tumbling over and over down a precipitous slope. Over and over. . . .

Bashing into a tree or a boulder and the back doors spring open and the fugitives spill out in a long trail of whimpers moans and silence. . . .

Bee-buzz of rotor blades, beams of blue-white light stabbing at them, pinning one after another, chatter of machine guns, shrieks. Then silence.

Julia crawls frantically into the brush, fiercely intent on getting away from the slaughter. On and on, brush tearing at her, clawing open her skin, shredding her clothes. Fall into a ravine, rolling over and over, out of control, rocks driving into her, bruising her to the bone, ripping open her flesh.

Slam against the bottom of the ravine, scramble some more on hands and knees, follow the ravine until it dribbles out, on and on, away and away, the noise diminishing, the lights and turmoil left behind.

Finally she collapses on her face, gasping and exhausted.

And a hand comes down on her shoulder, another catches her arms and holds her still.

She struggles. She is held firmly but gently and she cannot squirm away.

"We're friends. Quiet. Don't be afraid." A woman's voice murmuring in her ear. "Hush now. Be quiet and we'll help you up."

Julia coughs, croaks out, "Who. . . ."

Strong hands help her up, support her.

A man, blond and chunky, pale eyes almost colorless in the moonlight. A woman, tall and thin, dark gleaming skin, a broad glowing smile.

The man says, "You're the last, we've picked up the rest of the survivors, got them safe."

Julia swallows, tries a smile. "One called Michael dressed like a woman?"

The woman laughs. "Sure, hon. Who'dya think sent us after you?"

## 4

Several others surged to their feet as Havier Ryan sank to squat. Hern flicked a finger at the lanky brown woman with the wounded shoulder.

"Anoike Ley," she said crisply. "You say the greater part of your army is made up of women fighters. Explain, please."

Hern raised his brows. "You ask that?"

"It's better to get things clear."

Hern rubbed at his chin. "Hard to know just what to say. Mmm. Some five hundred years ago an ancestor of mine, Andellate Heslin, rid the mijloc of the feuding war-lords that kept it in constant turmoil, and made Oras his capital, built it up from a small fishing village perched on the cliffs above the Catifey estuary. He chose to reward certain women who had been of great service to him in this by giving them a diamond-shaped valley between the Vachhorn mountains and the coast of the Sinadeen." He smiled. "Not so generous a gift as you might think since he was giving them what they already held, but by making their possession official and backing it with his approval and his army he made life a lot easier for them. That was the beginning of the Biserica as we know it now. In the mijloc we serve the Spring aspect of *She* who has three faces, *She* who is the circle of birth and death and rebirth. The Maiden. The Biserica is the heart of that worship. But you'd better ask Serroi about the Biserica." He touched her shoulder, smiled at her, his face changing and softening. "My companion." He looked up, the palace-mask back in place. "Serroi was a fighting meie of the Biserica before her talent for healing bloomed in her. Don't let her size fool you. With a bow I have never seen her equal and I wouldn't be that sure of besting her with a sword given reasonably difficult footing. And she's better than most at using her head. You're good, Anoike Ley, the fighters with you, but I'd bet on Serroi to take you out, singly or in combination." He chuckled, drew one of the sprinty russet curls between thumb and forefinger. "Or I would have when she was meie. She's a healer now and that's a different thing." He stepped back. "Explain the meien, if you will."

Serroi made a face at him, turned. All those eyes. Waiting. She found it easier to ignore the others and concentrate on Anoike Ley. "The first thing I have to say to you is that the Biserica is a refuge for all girls and women who have nowhere else to go." She smiled. "I am a race of one, a misborn of the windrunners. By a complicated chance I escaped the fire that waited me, and by another set of chances the Biserica became my home, the only place where I found real welcome. First thing anyone sees of me is my skin; most stop there, but not the teachers and the sisters of the Biserica. Hern told you what's going to happen to all of us if the Biserica falls. . . ." She swallowed, looked over Anioke's head seeing nothing. "There are four types of women who come out from the Biserica. Every village on the Cimpia Plain has a Maiden shrine. Until recent times, every Maiden shrine had a Keeper who was trained by the Biserica. These women taught the children, served as midwives and mediators, advocates for those without hope or power; they presided over the seasonal fests and were involved in all aspects of life in the villages and on the tars. Healwomen are the wanderers, they go where they will, all over the world, drifting back to the Biserica when they feel the need, sending back reports of new herbs and new ways of being sick. They're trained in minor surgeries, herbcraft, treat both men and beasts. And a few of our artisans go out to earn the coin we need, metalsmiths, glass blowers, stone cutters, leather workers, weavers, potters and others, not many; most prefer to stay home and sell their goods not their services. And there are the meien. The weaponwomen. Some girls come to us with an interest in weapons; if they have the

necessary eye and hand coordination, the proper mindset
—by that I mean no love of hurting and killing—they are
given weapons training and taught the open-hand fighting.
Meien also earn coin for the Biserica. They are hired on
three-year stretches we call wards, sent out in pairs,
shieldmates, acting as guards for women's quarters, for
caravans, as escorts for the daughters of the rich and
powerful especially on their wedding journeys, as trainers—
that's enough to give you an idea. We don't fight wars,
except as defenders."

Anoike frowned. "Sounds like you had it pretty good,
helluva lot better than here. How come you in a bind
now?"

"Power. Groups wanting it. The Biserica is the one area
on our world the Nearga Nor can't touch. A prize that
mocks at their claims to power. The sons of the Flame
who follow Soäreh consider us anathema and want to
destroy us. Listen. *Woman is given to man for his comfort and
his use.* Biserica women are decidedly not available for such
use. *Cursed be he who forsakes the pattern/ Cursed be the man
who puts on women's ways/ Cursed be the woman who usurps the
role of man/ Withered will they be/ Root and branch they are
cursed/ Put the knife to the rotten roots/ Tear the rotten places
from the body/ Tear the rotten places from the land/ Blessed be
Soäreh the Pattern-giver.* That's one of the fuels that drives
Floarin, that and her ambition to rule. And that gives you
a good idea what's going to happen to the meien and the
others that do what the Followers consider men's work."

"Hunh, sounds familiar." She looked over her shoulder
at the others. "You want my vote, I say go. I'd like to get a
look at that Biserica." She sat.

## 5

Julia drifts.

Blocky building, floodlit, inside a double electric fence,
patrolled by guard-pairs with dogs running loose, scouting
ahead of them. Mobile antennas opened like flowers to the
stars.

A car painted official drab moves steadily, unhurriedly along the winding mountain road. It stops at the gate. A brief exchange. The gate swings open.

Watching with Anoike and the rest of the band, hidden on the hillside above the complex (with the rocket launcher and rifles in case of trouble) Julia follows them in her mind, closing her eyes because the waiting is making knots in her stomach. Present papers to the officer in charge. Wait. Papers passed (if they're passed). Escort to the control room. Night shift—only three monitors. Unless the schedule has changed since the press aide took her through when she was researching her thriller. That was before all this, when even a quasi-military operation like that below was eager for favorable publicity to ensure the continuation of its funding. It was amazing where a writer could get when Parliament was debating the budget. She opens her eyes a moment. They are already inside the building. Michael as driver, their expert on electronics. Georgia, career military until ordered to shoot into a peaceful though noisy march of protesters, handling atmosphere. Pandrashi, silent and muscular as aide and bodyguard and carrier of official papers in a neat though rather large leather briefcase. Inside the building. Marching with crisp, unhurried steps into the throat of the enemy.

She counts the seconds. Opens her eyes again. The car sits undisturbed. No alarm of any sort.

Control center. There by now. Escort darted and unconscious. Guard likewise. Nightshift tucked away in a storeroom, thumbs wired to big toes, gags in place. In the center of the main board a locked black box. Inside, six fat red buttons that trigger the destruct charges in the six armed spy satellites in orbit above the UD. Any attempt to pick the lock or break it sets off very noisy alarms and transmits a warning to the nearest base. But the guard has a key. If nothing has changed. Boasting of their efficiency, the press aide volunteered this bit. If there's ever need, if the country is invaded or one of the satellites is knocked from orbit, the Colonel doesn't have to be on the premises. He can phone instructions to the guard, give him the proper password and wait on the phone till the guard reports the destruct charge is activated.

She remembers the look of the box, sees Michael keying it open. No alarm. Sees him lift off the guard rings, press all six of the thick red buttons, then lock the box again and pocket the key. It's done by now.

The silence goes on and on, the tension in her rises until she feels like she's choking on her heart. Tranquil lovely night, cool but not cold, clear, frost-painted sky. Moon's not up yet, but the stars hang low and very bright.

Julia wants to scream.

The door opens. Three men come out. Michael. Georgia. Pandrashi. Michael opens the back door for Georgia. Pandrashi gets into the front without waiting on ceremony, a small mistake but there is no one about to notice. And no one to notice he is no longer carrying the briefcase.

The car backs smoothly, turns onto the exit road. Another leisurely exchange at the gate. It passes through and moves off the way it came.

Julia lets out the breath she has been holding unawares. Anoike makes a soft little sound like a squirrel's snort, all the satisfaction in the world packed into it.

The ten watchers get to their feet, stand a moment looking down at the placid complex, then they start away, moving at an easy lope through the scrubby trees.

When they are several miles away, the explosion reaches them as a soft crump and a shiver and a brief glow near the horizon.

## 6

Again the clamor to speak. Hern looked them over, chose the battered, drawn man who'd been one of the rescued prisoners.

"Francis Connolly," he said. "You don't look like a trusting man. What makes you think we won't decide to sit this one out once we're safe? And who's to say we don't use those weapons you're licking your lips over to boot you out and take over?"

Hern grinned at him. "Nearga Nor," he said.

Serroi watched him, amused. He clasped his hands behind him and stood with his feet apart, enjoying all this more than a little (though he didn't let it show to anyone who knew him less well than she). He'd been absorbing impressions from these people, doing that instinctively, now he was giving them truth, but feeding it to them in ways that more and more fitted with their expectations. She covered her smile with her hand, watched the loosening of the listeners, their tilt toward acceptance.

"Here's what I mean," he said. "Your supplies are limited. You don't know the world or the kind of life my people live. Fight alongside me, you use up your supplies and are no threat. Turn on me and join them, you'll get exactly what you deserve, abject slavery. Sit out the war and try to take over from the Nor, same thing. Your weapons mean nothing without the protection of the Shawar. The Nor will explode them in your hands."

"No resupply." Connolly eyed him skeptically. "You sure of that?"

"I see your machines and your weapons and I don't understand how they work; I doubt any of our blacksmiths, skilled as they are, could repair them or build more."

"Blacksmiths. Everything hand-made?"

"How else?"

"I see." He smiled. "Clever." He pushed at the lank reddish hair falling forward into his pale gaunt face. "Sam, rest of you. I say go. Nothing for us in the shithole this country's turning into." He sat.

Hern smiled, nodded to the square blond man. "Georgia Myers."

"You'll be in command?"

"Yes. With a staff of meien and your people. I know the land and the enemy." He raised a brow, grinned. "Believe me, Georgia Myers, I'm not going to waste you on futile charges or suicide forays, nor am I stupid enough to believe you'd waste yourselves in anything foolish."

"Good enough." He sat.

Hern looked over the folk who surged to their feet. "Professor . . . um . . . Zagouris?"

"You have been watching us. " He tucked his thumbs behind his belt, unconsciously falling into his casual lecturer's pose. "Being a historian, I take the long view. Say the battle is over. You've won. What happens then?"

"Maiden knows. Too much upheaval. Too many ties and taroms forced off the land. The Heslins out of Oras for the first time in five hundred years. People starving, angry, desperate. Outcasts back from the moutains. No Keepers in the Shrines." He spread his arms, smiled wearily. "I was born into a position I never wanted. For the past thirty years I've been courtier and mediator, wagging my tongue endlessly; I've been judge of last resort and overseer; I've lived with folk fawning on me while they wormed about to get their hands on gold or power. I'm tired. I want out." He looked at Serroi a moment, looked back to Zagouris. "I have a dream for the time when there's peace in the mijloc, the two of us on our wandering again, greeting old friends and making new ones. What I'm trying to say is if you're worried about putting a tyrant back in power after his people rose against him and kicked him out, forget it. I'm a lazy man and I want a simpler life." A small throwaway gesture with his sword hand. "But I'm Heslin and I've been Domnor since my sixteenth year. Until there's someone else to do it, I take care of my people."

"Mmmm. Right. Maybe you'd better tell us more about what your role is right now. I'm a bit hazy about that."

As Hern began the convoluted explanation of how he'd arrived where he was, Serroi strolled away to stand in the shadow of one of the conifers that surrounded the smallish grassy meadow, more comfortable at the sidelines, watching the faces of the listeners, interested in the response Hern was drawing from them. After a short while she saw a girl come from under the trees and walk purposefully to the man sitting at the end of the council row. There was a familiar tugging, something like a string tied about her liver; she blinked, surprised. Somehow she hadn't expected to suffer that healing urge away from her world. The girl bent close, whispered to the man. A little round man with a shock of yellow-white hair, his face went grim as the whispering continued. When the girl had finished, he patted her arm and got to his feet, scooped up a black satchel resting against a leg of his stool, and started after her. The string tightened until it was a pain beneath Serroi's ribs. She hurried after the man, caught up with him as he moved into the trees, put a hand on his forearm. His shirt had short sleeves and the stiff white hair on his arm felt like wire under her hand. "Let me come," she said. "I must."

His pale brown eyes were shrewd, his expression unhelpful, but he nodded. "If you must."

The girl looked over her shoulder, a desperate urgency in her gaze as if by rushing she could avert whatever it was that troubled her. The man plunged after her, a furious frustration in the drive of his walk, the set of his face.

Serroi followed a half step behind him, though she needed no guide to what waited. Then there was another tug at her, a tiny nip almost lost in the greater pain. She looked back and was not overly surprised to see the dark woman Anoike Ley following her. His bodyguard, she thought.

The woman inside the tent was groaning and twitching, too weak to move much or cry out louder. The man was kneeling beside her, touching her face; he started to take her pulse, swore under his breath, put the arm down across her body. "Wait outside, Lyn," he said. "Don't argue, child." He summoned up a smile. "Go to the meeting, we'll sit with Julia for a while."

Lyn hesitated, looked from Serroi to the man, to the dying woman, back at Serroi; after a moment she nodded and slipped out. Serroi gazed after her, startled. The healing gift was very strong in that child; the woman's sickness was churning in her, but she'd sensed Serroi's Gift and it calmed her a little. Serroi shivered, turned to scowl at the sick woman; the pull was becoming unbearable.

The man was flicking open the latches on the black bag;

when he finished, he didn't pull it open, but rested his hands on the smooth leather and looked up at her. "Damn them," he said, a violent whisper; his face went red and he snapped the satchel open, sat staring into it. "They knew she was sick, they knew she. . . ." He clamped his mouth shut, took out a small glass bottle with a milky fluid in it and a slightly bulging paper packet. "No sanitation, no life support . . . you're a healer, that man said. Magic. God I can't believe I'm saying this. All I can do for her here is try to block some of the pain. Can't even do that much longer. Not without killing her. It's obscene to be relieved she's let it go too long so she can't ask for a massive overdose. . . ."

Serroi stopped listening. She knelt beside the woman, touched her; the wrongness was knotted through most of her body, it fought her as she probed at it. She bowed her head, closed her eyes, let the strength of this alien world flow into and through her, clean and fresh, strong as the stone of its bones, the soil that was its flesh. An old and powerful world. And as it flowed into her and through her into the woman, she felt the wrongness breaking up and changing and being re-absorbed into the healthy flesh. She opened her eyes and smiled down at the woman, seeing only the glowing green glass of her hands and the healing body beneath them.

And when it was finished, she took her hands away, looked dreamily at them, sighed and dropped them on her thighs. The earth fire drained out of her, leaving her a little tired, but cleansed and invigorated, rather like a plunge into icemelt. She yawned, surprising herself, lifted a belated hand to cover the gape.

The man-healer looked up. "What did you do? She's not in pain." He touched the blanket over her stomach; the swelling was gone. "God, if what I think . . . I don't believe it. Everything I know, everything I believe, everything I learned in thirty years of practicing . . . only charlatans. . . ." He stopped babbling, took hold of the thin wrist, checking the pulse against his watch. "Strong and steady. Natural sleep, better leave her like that long as we can. What did you do?"

Serroi shook her head. "I don't know. Except that I provide a pathway for a strength that teaches the body to heal itself." The nip she'd noticed before was pricking hard at her. "I haven't much choice in this, you know. Where there's sickness or hurt, I must heal. Sometimes . . . well, never mind that. Now that it's begun here, you might as well call in the rest of the sick and wounded. Starting with your bodyguard."

"What?"

"Anoike Ley. She followed when I came with you."

"I didn't know."

Serroi chuckled. "I'm not angry. It was a good sensible move, tactfully handled. She reminds me a lot of a shieldmate I had once." She shook off the old pain that time and the hurry of events had reduced to a gentle melancholy. "Call her in."

"You're upsetting a lot of dearly held notions, little friend." He began taking items from the satchel, putting them on a tray. "By the way, my name is Louis Grenier. Doctor Grenier to the general, but Lou to my colleagues, colleague." He grinned at her, went round her to the door slit, thrust his head out. "Anoike, come in here, will you."

She came into the tent, wary, ready for anything. "How's Julia?"

"Hard to say. She's sleeping. Sit down. I want to look at that shoulder wound."

Anoike frowned. "Why? You saw it a couple hours ago when you changed the bandage."

"Now, Anoike, a big girl like you shouldn't be afraid of this friendly old doctor."

"Yeah sure, friendly old butcher more like." She kicked Lyn's cushion around, folded down and unbuttoned her shirt, letting him ease it off her wounded side.

"You know, Anoike, you've got what my down-home grandfather used to call the luck of the devil." He used a pair of blunt scissors to cut away the tape and gauze over the hole in her shoulder. "A fraction of an inch in any direction and there'd be a lot more damage." His hands very gentle, he cleaned the wound with a liquid he poured onto a bit of white fluff. Anoike grimaced at the sting. "Anoike's luck," he said. "You're making me a believer. Anyone else would have to spend the next weeks hurting and itching." He sat back on his heels. "It's a puncture wound, Serroi. That's your name, isn't it. I got it right? Good. A clean wound, very little laceration of the flesh. Except for what I did when I was looking for the bullet. Gone back three hundred years to the age of probe and forceps."

Serroi shifted to kneel beside him. The wound was a little thing, not to be taken lightly, but nothing to incapacitate the tigress before her. She looked down at her hands, felt earth fire gathering in her again. Reaching out, she flattened her hands on either side of the hole. The woman started to pull back.

"Don't move." Grenier's voice was calm but commanding. "Let Serroi work."

Serroi watched the flesh of her hands go translucent again, shining with the earthfire that sank deep into the woman's body and rebuilt the injured cells, layer by layer, until new skin closed over the wound and erased the last signs of it. She dropped her hands, moved back a little so the doctor could get a closer look.

"I see it and I still don't believe it. How's it feel Anoike?"

The woman probed at the spot with shaking fingers; she wiggled her shoulder, moved her arm. "Me either, Lou. Shit, it's like it didn't happen. Julia too?"

"I begin to think so." He reached out, touched Serroi's arm. "Are you tired? How do you feel?"

"A little drunk. This world of yours is like strong wine." She thrust her fingers through her hair, yawned again and didn't bother covering it. "Bring 'em all, Lou colleague." She giggled. "This doesn't exactly tire me."

"Ram," Anoike said. She shoved her arm back into her sleeve, did up the buttons and pushed the tail back into her trousers.

"Tell Dom Hern where I am, Anoike Ley," Serroi said quickly. "He worries and might decide to come looking for me."

"He don't look the worrying kind."

"About me he is."

"Come through whatever in his way?" She looked skeptical. "Little man, not so young anymore."

"Through or over."

"He don't look it."

"Lot of dead men thought that."

"He got him a two-ended tongue."

"He's giving you the truth."

"Truth he sees." Anoike shrugged, a quick lift and fall of her shoulders. "Wasn't talking 'bout truth. He a good politician."

"Politician?"

"Guess you never had no election campaigns." She grinned. "Hey Lou, I vote we go for sure. No politicians."

The doctor's chuckle was warm and filled with contentment. "Never be a world without politicians, Anoike. I suspect they just call them something else."

"Glass half-empty, hey, Doc?" She grinned effectionately at him. "Right . . . uh . . . Serroi. Message to Dom Hern, then Ram for here. Then what? Connolly, I think. He some messed up inside. You want I should round up everything down to mosquito bites, or just bad-off?"

Grenier frowned thoughtfully at Serroi, then nodded. "Stick with the bad-off until we see how much time we've got. Anoike, tell the council what's happening."

"Uh-huh." Anoike moved her shoulder again, grinned, then went through the slit with a quick energetic twist of her lean body.

"How long before Julia wakes?"

"I'm not sure." Serroi strolled over to him. She clasped her hands behind her head and stretched, feeling a deep pleasure in the pull of her muscles. "Don't worry, Lou. Her body's worked hard. Takes time to recover from that."

Anoike leaned through the door. "Want them in here?" She looked around. "Make it some crowded."

Serroi pushed the hair off her face. "Better outside

where we won't disturb Julia's sleep. What's happening at the meeting?"

"Prioc, he making a speech saying we wrong to run out on our country. Should stay and fight. Not many agreeing with him. Your man, he got him his army."

## 7

Julia woke to well-being and thought for a moment she'd died, but the familiar smells chased that idea off. The blackness around her was thick and still. She was alone. It felt very late, how late she had no way of knowing or even guessing. She felt a stab of fear, a flash of illogical anger. Illogical because she'd meant to tell them to leave her. Anger because they hadn't given her the chance to make the gesture. That anger like the death-illusion lasted only a few seconds. She sat up, clutched at the pallet as dizziness sent the dark wheeling. She took a deep breath, another. No pain. Weak as a wet noodle, but no pain. And she was hungry. Not just hungry, but ravenous. I could eat one of Angel's horses. What happened? Did I snatch my shaman out of dream? Nonsense. More likely the visitors did something. Some kind of drug. Miracle drug. That's the only kind of miracle that happens here. Where is everyone? She threw off the blanket, rolled onto her hands and knees and levered herself onto her feet. Lyn, she thought, I could use you now. After this new dizziness passed she pulled off the sweaty nightgown, dropped it on the blankets and stumbled to the end of the pallet, stopping when she kicked into the battered suitcase there. She lowered herself onto her knees, opened the case and began feeling around in it. Her fingers caught in a loop of leather, sandal strap, her old sandals, worn but more comfortable now than her boots would be. She lifted them out and set them beside her, poked about some more. Something folded. Heavy zipper, snap, double-sewed seams. A pair of jeans. Soft powdery dust lay deep in the folds, whispered from the worn denim when she shook the jeans out. A shirt folded under the jeans. She didn't bother looking farther, enough to cover herself, that's all she wanted. Getting onto her feet again showed her how weak she still was. All those weeks lying on her back, her muscles rotting. Stopping to rest every third breath, she got the jeans pulled up and zipped; they rode precariously on her withered hips, would have slid off but for the jut of her pelvic bones. She pulled the shirt on without bothering to unbutton it, rolled up the sleeves and let the tail hang, slipped into her sandals and wobbled to the door slit. Another stab of fear, hastily suppressed, then she laughed at herself and pushed through.

The moon was a feeble glow through the cloud fleece and the camouflage netting, but enough light came through to show her the disruption around her, shelter sides without their canvas tops, the edge of an empty corral—but over the noise of the wind she could hear a muted mutter of voices. She took a few steps and leaned against a tree, shaking with relief. She wasn't abandoned. After her heart slowed and her breathing settled, she started toward the sounds.

Lyn came rushing around a bushy young pine and nearly slammed into Julia. "Oh!" Her eyes lit and she grinned with delight. "Jule, you're up. You're looking lots better." She looked over her shoulder, looked quickly back. "Dr. Grenier wanted you to sleep as long as you could, but we're 'bout ready to jump and he said go wake you and bring you. Bring the blankets and your clothes, it's winter where we're going."

Julia laughed. "Going? Slow down, Lyn. You've lost me."

Lyn pulled her hand over her hair. "Don't you remember what I told you?"

Julia leaned against a tree and closed her eyes. "Umm. . . . a little. The man and the little green woman." She opened her eyes, stared into the darkness. "Offered . . . what? A refuge. Is that what you're talking about?"

"Uh-huh. You go on and find Dr. Grenier. I'll collect the blankets and things. Get him to find a place on a truck for you, if he hasn't already; you're not ready for a long march." She clasped her arms across her narrow chest as if she were holding herself down, muting the excitement that made her want to fly. "Henny and Bert, they're coming for the tent. We leaving nothing behind for the creeps." A frown. She reached out and touched Julia's arm. "You need a prop? I can go with you, come back later."

"I'm fine if I take it slow. Any chance of getting something to eat?"

Lyn drooped. "I doubt it. Everything's packed. Maybe Serroi saved you something; Jule, she healed everybody, not just you, Anoike's shoulder, Ram, even old Anya's rotten tooth, she puts her hands on you and they go transparent and shine and when she takes them away, well, that's it." She hesitated a minute longer, then with a wave of her hand she darted away.

Julia started shakily toward the meeting meadow. Before she reached it, Lyn trotted past her, blanket roll over her shoulder, suitcase bumping against her leg. She flashed Julia a grin and vanished into the darkness ahead. Julia kept moving along, stopping at a tree here, a tree there, catching her breath. After a while she started giggling softly. Magic healer. I did it. Missed one little detail though, *she* not he. Was right, after all. 'M dead and dreaming. Fantastic. Out of thin air. Don't believe it. Not quite moral, is it. Too easy. Magic, it's a cop-out, friends, you got to earn your salvation, slog along or it ain't worth it, it's smoke in the hand, squirting out the fingers if you try to hold it, the fish that got away. . . . She reached the edge of the clearing and stood gaping at the organized chaos before her.

Several military vehicles in the middle of the meadow, crammed to the canvas with cargo, motorcycles crowded around them. She recognized all but the largest, having been in on the raids that took them. More vans and a pair of pickups. Off to one side Angel and his band squatted beside a large horse herd. She looked up but couldn't make out any stars through the net. Must be getting close to morning, she thought. It was obvious that Georgia and Angel had taken their people out on raids to gather up as much as they could before the what did Lyn call it? the jump. Some folk were bustling about, though what they were doing she couldn't tell, some were sitting in groups, waiting, the adults with stuffed backpacks, the children with smaller loads. In spite of the crowding and the constant swirling movement, the meadow was surprisingly quiet, though there was an explosive excitement trapped beneath the net. Most faces were grave, some were sad. An old woman reached out and touched the trampled grass, stroked it as she would a cat or a dog, something loved.

Unnoticed in the shadows Julia began circling round the meadow, looking for the doctor, expecting to find him with the other council members somewhere near the uphill point of the meadow, the visitors with them. When her legs began to shake, she stopped and caught hold of a tree; even that gentle slope was almost too much for her. She hung on a minute, then eased herself to the ground. Some of the trembling passed off after a few minutes: she pulled herself together and opened her eyes.

Samuel Braddock came strolling around one of the trucks and stopped to chat with a knot of boys working up to a fight, driven to the point of exploding by the tension and excitement that seemed to build without release. He got them laughing with a few words and sent them off in different directions; he passed on to exchange a few words with a glum-looking man, left him relaxed, still not smiling but looking around with interest. Another group was struggling with an awkward roll of canvas, on the point of spitting at each other as they tried to get it on top of the load in the back of a pickup. He did little but say a few words, yet in a few minutes the roll was being roped into place and he was strolling on. She watched him, smiling. Last year, when she'd followed Georgia and Anoike to this place, she'd been surprised to find a prosperous small community hidden under the trees, a printing press powered by a water-wheel, gardens growing everywhere, schools outdoors under the trees and a thousand other small details that added up to a placidly working society that was also very effective at attacking the monster growing below. It'd taken her less than a day to understand who was responsible for the shape and continuation of the community. She pulled herself back onto her feet. *This isn't getting me fed.*

Three shadow shapes stood apart at the high edge of the meadow, watching the confusion, talking now and then, a few words only, Dr. Grenier, the alien woman and the man. They shifted position a bit and saw there was a fourth with them. A quick hand, a flash of stiff gray hair, a bit of leg. Not enough to recognize.

Lou Grenier saw her first. "Julia." He came toward her, his hands out. When he reached her, he gripped her upper arms, searched her face. "How are you?"

"Hungry."

A quiet chuckle. The little woman Serroi came up to them. "Here." She held out a packet. "I thought you might be hungry when you woke. A woman named Cordelia Gudon made some sandwiches for you in between rounding up a herd of children and getting them started collecting their possessions and fixing their packs. I'm afraid it's water if you're thirsty."

"Del. She would." She held the packet in both hands and gazed at Serroi across a chasm greater than the chasm between their two worlds, a chasm whose name was magic. She could begin to accept and perhaps comprehend it as a sort of alien technology with rules to its manipulation like those that governed the physical sciences here. Yet she was dimly aware that there was something more, something numinous and luminous and sorrowfully shut away from her that existed within the delicate porcelain figure before her. She opened her mouth, closed it again. Words were her profession but she was robbed of them here. Everything she thought to say seemed banal or impertinent. Since banality seemed the least offensive, she said, "Thank you for my life." She lifted the packet. "Twice."

A quick brushing gesture swept the words away. "If I could choose to heal and did, then I could accept your thanks, but no. You owe me nothing. The same would have happened were you my worst enemy and threatening what I hold most dear." She grinned suddenly, an impish, urchin's grin that banished magic and mystery and made Julia want to hug her. "I will take credit for the sandwiches."

Lou touched her arm. "And you'd better find a place to sit and eat. Before you keel over and Serroi has to work on you some more. No way to treat a work of art, you should know that, Jule." He was half-serious, half laboriously joking, missing what she was missing though he wasn't aware of it, yet something was provoking him into caricaturing himself. She patted his arm though he was making her more uncomfortable than Serroi had, started to turn away. The shifting of the others let her see the fourth person more clearly. "Magic Man, they chase you out too?"

He grinned at her, his pointed nose twitching as it always did when he was amused.

Serroi looked from him to her. "You know the Changer?"

"Since I was a little girl. He used to work on my father's farm."

Serroi looked amazed, then skeptical. "Work?"

"Uh-huh, helped with the planting, milked the cows, mowed, raked, ran the baler; we used to hoe weeds together and he'd tell me stories to make the rows pass faster . . . stories . . ." Her voice trailed off. "You called him Changer?"

"I know him as Coyote or Changer. He's the one who brought us here, Hern and me."

Magic Man winked at Julia. "Didn't I tell you that you'd be all right, Little Gem?"

She smiled at him, feeling the old warmth come flooding back when she heard his pet name for her, then blinked at the sudden thought that all this might be only his scheming to bring the healer to her. She dismissed that at once as obvious nonsense, but there was still this little niggling question that wouldn't go away.

Braddock came sauntering up the slope, a canteen dangling from one finger. "Julia," he said, smiling his startling, youthening smile. "Here. You might want something to wash those sandwiches down with. Anoike's saving you a place on one of the trucks. Better go find her, we're about ready to jump." He turned to Magic-Man-Coyote-Changer. "Anything special we need to do? If not, let's move."

# PRIESTESS

She wanders about the shrine unable to settle at anything. At first she thinks it is the residue of excitement from the Turnfete. It had been a subdued celebration, yet filled with joy and hope as it was meant to be. The Turn toward light and warmth. In the heart of winter a reminder of spring's promise. A promise too, that the winter will one day be gone from their hearts.

Mardian is working on the painted pavement. He has shoveled out the snow and is scraping away at the black paint, wholly content with this tedious occupation as she had been when she cleaned the interior. She watches him awhile. He should have looked absurd, big tough male on his knees like a tie scrub-maid, but there is nothing ridiculous about him. Nor anything particularly different from before. As a soldier he'd committed his whole being to his profession in exactly this way. He doesn't notice her. He wouldn't have noticed a raging hauhau bull unless it started trampling him.

She goes back into the shrine, mops the kitchen floor, rearranges the things on the closet shelves. She cleans the grates and carries out the ashes, lays new fires. It is cold in the shrine, but she and the decsel have agreed that they should conserve the wood. On still, sunny days like this they will not light the fires until late afternoon. She washes her hands, takes the canvas she is working on into the Maiden chamber and sits on a cushion before the Maiden Face.

There is peace for her in this room, coming from many sources, her pleasure in the work of her hands, the smell of the aromatic oil in the votive lamps Mardian has installed on either side of the Face, the memory of the times *She* had touched her here and, above all, the comforting silence that surrounds her in here. The needle dances in and out

of the canvas, drawing her after it, in and out; the slow
growth of the design slows her into a tranquility much like
Mardian's as he scrapes at the paint. After a while she
notices nothing but the growing of the pattern; she has
forgotten everything else. The hours pass. The images
take shape under her hands. The light dims until she is
squinting, then brightens but she notices neither event; the
chill in the room begins to warm away. A spark snaps out
of the fire. She starts, looks around.

Mardian is sitting beside her, waiting until she is ready
to notice him. He has lit the fire and fetched a pair of
candlelamps for her. She smiles at him.

He looks grave, uneasy—as if her itch has passed to
him. "Word has come . . ." He coughs, looks away.
"Floarin's army is moving south. The Guards are summoned to join it."

"All of them?"

"All but the Agli's bodyguard."

She drops the canvas. It lies in stiff folds over her knees.
There is a pain in her like a long needle through her heart.
She must do something, but for the moment she doesn't
know what. She looks down at the tapestry, the bright
colors flash at her without shape or meaning. Slowly,
automatically, she tucks the needle into the work, begins
folding the canvas.

A fleeting scent of herbs and flowers.

She sets the tapestry aside, reaches out to Mardian. He
takes her hand in his. Words come welling up in her: the
summoning chant that is usually just a formality, opening
each major fest. The words swell out of her, then out of
him, his deeper voice supporting and reinforcing hers.
They chant the words once—tentative, exploring. Twice—
reaching out and out, asking. A third time—a demand that
throbs out of them into earth and air.

Nilis falls silent, her throat raw with the force of that
last repetition; Mardian sits silent, waiting. She withdraws
her hand from his and gets clumsily to her feet. He stands
beside her, again waiting. He is angry and disturbed,
worse than she was earlier. She has an idea about what is
bothering him and feels a great sadness for him.

They come. One by one, in pairs, in groups they come, Cymbankers and ties in from the tars for one reason or another. They fill the room, silent, made uneasy by the power that had drawn them here.

The candlelamps at her feet cutting her out of the darkness, touching Mardian, the Maiden face over her head, Nilis stands waiting for the words to come. She knows they will come. She is the Maiden's tool for shaping this small bit of the Biserica's defense. The scent of herbs and flowers fills the room. And the words come. She sings them out into the room's waiting silence.

"Floarin's army marches."

A groan like a wind sweeping from man to woman to man:

"Floarin's army marches to raze the Biserica, to ravage stone from stone, to gut the servants of the Maiden."

A spreading silence broken suddenly by a woman's sob:

"What is there for you, here or anythwere, if the Biserica falls? What is there for your daughters or your sons? Flogging, starving, misery, nothing. That is what waits them if the Biserica falls. You know it, each of you has tasted it."

yes   yes   I have tasted it   The words fly from man to woman to man   yes   yes   I have tasted it

Mardian steps past Nilis, his face hard with the decision that will tear him from his deep contentment in this place. "I go south come morning, walking. Those who wish to join me should be in the Maiden Court at sunup with what food and weapons they can bring, be it sling or scythe. Those of you who know others of like mind, send word to them." He moves back into the shadows.

As quietly as they had come, the summoned leave, one by one, in pairs, in groups.

When the Maiden Chamber is empty again, Nilis puts her hand on Mardian's arm, wanting to comfort him, but not knowing how.

He starts when he feels the touch, looks at Nilis as if he is surprised to see her there, twists around to look up at the Face. "She gives and she takes away."

# THE MAGIC CHILD

They stood on the city wall with much of the rest of Oras, merchant and beggar alike, watching the army move out— Coperic, small and inconspicuous in his dusty black tunic, and trousers, Rane and Tuli in the black dresses Rane stole from the Center south of here, their hair hidden under stiff white kerchiefs Coperic had given them.

The snow cleared suddenly from the rocky plain where the army was camped and off the Highroad as far as Tuli could see, as if some great unseen hand had scraped the plain clear, then drawn its forefinger along the road. Tuli shivered but not from the cold morning air. She'd seen snatches of norit power and seen it overcome, had seen scattered examples of the effect of Floarin's acts, but it suddenly began to come clear to her what it was the Biserica faced, what it meant if the Biserica fell. No wonder Rane hadn't bothered playing adventure games with her.

A great dark blotch against the lighter earth, the army stirred and began unreeling onto the Highroad.

The Minarks, their knots of ribbon fluttering, came by first, mounted on spirited rambuts, the gems and bangles braided into the beasts' red manes glinting with each caracole, their red stripes gleaming like bands of copper, their short, slim horns sharp spikes of polished jet. Attendants rode before them, playing raucous music on curl horns. Attendants rode beside and behind them with embroidered silken banners whipping from the ends of long poles. The sun glittered on the gilt spikes of their elaborate armor. They were at once absurd and formidable. They cantered up the bank and onto the resilient black-topping, moving south totally unconcerned for what followed them.

Sleykynin began to pour up the slope onto the High-road. Riding in pairs and groups, no Minark display about these fighters, nor any sign of military discipline, they went south as casually as they might if it were just coincidence such a mighty mix of men went with them. They weren't soldiers and made no pretense of being soldiers. Deadly, sly, determined to survive at all costs. They were more usually employed as assassins or torturers, occasionally as harriers and threats; the only reason they were here in these numbers and under these constraints was their obsessive hatred of all meien. Coperic sucked at his teeth, his face grim as he counted the adversaries. Five hundred, and more to be picked up along the way. He'd known his estimate of their numbers was likely to be off, but hadn't suspected how far off it was. He could almost smell the malice and hatred as they rode past. He glanced at Rane, wondering what she was thinking.

They rode the finest macain Rane had ever seen, sleek, spirited beasts. That brought her a measure of comfort in her anger. There would be Stenda on the Biserica walls because of those beasts. Floarin must have sent men and norits to take them because all the gold in Oras wouldn't buy that many. It looked as if she'd depleted a dozen herds. Stenda would rather sell their sons than reduce their herds to a few culls and ancient sires.

Two norits rode beside the Sleykynin, ignoring them and being ignored.

A black mass of footsoldiers accompanied by more mounted norits shouting to one another, but as the departure went on and on, into the third hour, many of them fell heavily silent or gave up watching and made their way along the walls to the narrow stairflights and climbed back down to the streets, hurrying for their homes before the jackals came out. Tuli stroked Ildas and swallowed the lump in her throat. She glanced at Rane, saw the ex-meie's hands tightened on the stone until her knuckles shone white.

The river of men went on and on. The Highroad was clogged with men and riders as far as she could see, even at her height above the ground. Yet the blotch of the army on the plain seemed scarcely diminished. An hour passed. The sun was close to zenith and breakfast was a distant memory. Tuli was hungry but the thought of food made her feel sick.

A break.

Surrounded by mounted norits, the tithe wagons began rolling up onto the road three abreast, heaped high with barrels of meat and flour, sacks of grain and sacks of tubers, each wagon pulled by six sleek draft hauhaus, splendid beasts gathered from tars all over the Plain. Tuli watched over a score of the wagons rumble past and turn south and saw superimposed on them the faces of men, women and children gaunt with hunger, pinched with fear. Before she could control it, rage flashed through her, shaking her, blinding her, strangling her—she fought the rage with her last shreds of sanity, afraid of betraying them all, until she was sufficiently in control of herself to open her eyes. She wanted to see it all. She had to know the worst.

The wagons were so distant already she could barely hear the rumble of their wheels and while she'd been immersed in her struggle, another, smaller band of mercenary footsoldiers had mounted onto the road.

A break.

Floarin rode past in her traveling carriage, the canvas top folded back so her blonde hair shone bright gold in the glare of the nooning sun. The team of six rambuts that pulled the carriage were specially bred so their stripes were a rich gold rather than the ruddy copper of the more common kind. Tuli looked down on her and wished she dared whirl her sling. Floarin was at the edge of her range but she knew she could make the woman uncomfortable if nothing more. *Later*, she told herself, *I'll get my chance at you later*. She stared at the woman, fascinated by her awfulness. How could any human being cause so much suffering and not be touched by it? Impossible to see the expression of Floarin's face from this high up, but the set of her body spoke eloquently of her satisfaction and implied her expectation of defeating all opposition.

Mounted mercenaries rode, six abreast, onto the High-road. Like the Sleykynin, they rode Stenda macain, but their mounts were the smaller, more fractious racers.

Coperic heard the air hiss between Rane's teeth and remembered that she was Stenda. Knowing how Stenda felt about their racers, he put his hand on her arm, intending both to warn and comfort. Her head jerked around. He winced at the blind fury in her eyes. Then she forced a smile. "I owe you one, my friend," she murmured.

The long massive warwagons started onto the High-road, pulled by twelve of the draft hauhaus, piled high with war gear and the parts of siege engines. Mercenaries— miners, sappers and engineers—rode with their machines and mounted norits swarmed about the three lumbering monsters.

Another band of mounted mercenaries, lighter armed than the first mounted fighters, short bows, coils of weighted rope, grapples. And passare rode perches grafted onto their saddles, strange flyers Tuli had never seen before with bands of black and white fur; they swayed with the motion of the macain, preening their fur with long leathery beaks edged with rows of needle teeth.

"Moardats," Coperic breathed. Tuli started to ask about them, looked around at the Orasi standing beside them and changed her mind. He caught the small sound she made, raised a brow, but said, "Trained to attack eyes and throat. Claws usually have steel sheaths, sometimes dipped in poison when their handlers take them into a fight."

"Oh."

Nekaz Kole and his personal guard were the last off the field. It was early afternoon before he galloped slowly past and mounted the Highroad. Riding his gold rambut at an easy lope, he began moving up the side of his army, the sunlight glinting off his utilitarian helmet, his heavy gold cloak rippling behind him; he acknowledged salutes with easy waves of his hand.

Tuli gasped; Coperic swung around, followed her eyes. A flood of traxim came winging in from the sea. They spread out over the army, a web of flying eyes looking for anything that might mean trouble. He watched a a moment longer, then grunted and turned away, walking heavy-footed toward the nearest stairflight. Rane came out of her reverie and followed him. Tuli stared a moment longer at the soaring traxim, then, silent and unhappy, she started after the others.

Coperic paced back and forth across the dusty floor. Abruptly he turned to confront Rane who straddled a reversed chair, her arms crossed on its back, the black dress bunched up about her knees. "I got to open up. What you going to do?"

"That rather depends on the Intii, doesn't it?"

Coperic scowled. "He should've been in already. If norit come back with him from Sankoy. If."

"Lot of ifs."

"Yah." He glanced at Tuli who sat on the bed stroking Ildas and gazing vaguely at the wall across from her. "Yeah. I go and kick Yiros off his butt, get him to fix you something to eat. Mmm. Be a good idea to send Haqtar up with the tray; he been sniffing around trying to find out dirt about you two; he reports to the Agli on me. Still enough guards left to drop on me 'fore I'm ready to get out." Once again he looked from Tuli to Rane. "You keep the black on, be doing something female when he come in. That ought to take the gas outta him."

Rane passed her hand over her tangled hair, grimaced. "Been a long time since I spent so much time in a skirt."

He grinned at her, his eyes narrowing to slits, sinking into nests of wrinkles. With a chuckle he turned and went out.

Rane poked absently about the room, finally took up the old charcoal sack the Bakuur had dropped off at the tavern before they left the city. She dumped it out on the bed, rummaged through the odds and ends and found her small leather sewing kit. She set that aside and took up an old tunic. With a quick jerk of her hand, she ripped out a short length of the hem, tossed the tunic onto the bed beside Tuli. "Your camouflage."

Tuli blinked. "Huh? Oh." She tapped Ildas on his round behind. "Move over, bebé." She shook the tunic out, held it up. "Why'd you bother bringing this along? I'd say it was one giant patch except it's about a hundred." She tilted her head, put on a coaxing smile. "Thread my needle for me?"

"Hah!" Rane tossed her a reel of thread. "Watch it. There's a needle in there."

Tuli yelped, sucked at the base of her forefinger, took her hand away and sniffed when she saw the tiny bead of red. "Little late telling me." She pulled the needle loose from the reel, shook out a length of thread. "From the look of that thing a little blood would liven it up."

"Maybe," Rane said absently. She took one of the wobbly chairs, set it by the shuttered window, stepped back, eyed it, then set a stool beside the chair. With her own bit of sewing she settled herself in the chair, smoothed the wrinkled skirt down over her boots, straightened it as much as she could. She looked up. "Come over here, Moth. Proper young ladies don't sit on beds."

Tuli snorted but she wadded the ancient tunic about the reel, twitched the coverlet smooth, then she settled herself at Rane's knee. She threaded the needle without fuss. "At least some things go right." She began sewing the hem back in, taking small stitches to make the job last because she didn't want Rane thinking up something worse for her to do. "Mama would faint if she could see me now."

"Mmm."

Tuli lifted her head, looked round at Rane. The light seeping through the rotten shutters slid along the spare lines of the ex-meie's face, pitilessly aging her. Rane's hands lay still in her lap. Her mind was obviously elsewhere. Certainly she wasn't listening to Tuli. Tuli went back to the sewing, setting the small neat stitches her mother had tried to teach her, surprising herself with the pleasure she got out of the work. She thought about that for a while and decided the pleasure came partly from the realization that this wasn't the only thing she had to look forward to the rest of her life.

She glanced now and then at the door, expectation wearing into irritation as the minutes crept past. She was hungry and rapidly getting hungrier. "He doesn't get here soon, I'll eat him." She slanted a glance at Rane, sighed and went on sewing, finishing the ripped part. With a glare at the door she began double-sewing the rest of the hem. The minutes still crept. Rane was still brooding over whatever it was. Tuli lifted her head. "You're wondering what to do about me?"

"What?"

"It was all right up to now." Tuli cleared her throat, not sure she wanted to go on with this. Her stomach rumbled suddenly; she went red with embarrassment. That idiotic little sound sucked all the drama out of her, leaving only her curiosity and her pride in her ability to reason. "I was insurance," she said. "In case you got snagged. Now you figure you can move faster and safer without me, but you promised Da you'd take care of me, so you're trying to convince yourself I'll get along all right by myself. I will, you know; you don't have to worry about me."

Rane pulled her hand down over her face. When she took it away, her mouth was twisted into a wry half-smile. "Hard lessons," she said. "You've had to grow up too fast, Moth. You're right. Well, partly right. What I do depends on the Intii. If he's able to lend me his boat, we can scoot down the coast with no problems. If we have to run. . . . I don't want to speculate on what might be, Moth. It makes for sour stomachs."

Tuli nodded, frowned down at the hem without really seeing it. She was more than a little uncertain about what she wanted to do. The sight of the army had shaken her more than she wanted to admit to herself or anyone else. She couldn't see herself going to sit tamely behind the Biserica wall waiting for that army to roll over her, just one more mouth to feed, contributing little besides a pair of hands not particularly skilled, her greatest gifts wasted, her nightsight and Ildas. Well, if not wasted, certainly underused. She brooded over just where her responsibilities lay until there was a loud thumping on the door. With more eagerness than grace, Tuli dropped her sewing and went to open it.

Haqtar came stumping in with a two-handled tray. Grunting, he slammed the tray down on the table, his eyes sliding with sly malice from Tuli to Rane and back to Tuli. Tuli retreated to Rane, dropped her hand on the ex-meie's shoulder, the look in those bulging eyes, the greed in the doughy face frightening her. After a minute, though, he turned and shuffled out.

"Whew." Tuli shuddered. "What a. . . ."

Rane caught hold of her arm and squeezed. A warning. After he slammed the door there should have been the sound of his retreating footsteps, especially over those yielding groaning floorboards. There was only silence, which meant he had an ear pressed against the door. "Help me up, daughter," Rane said.

Swallowing a nervous giggle, Tuli said demurely, "Yes, mama."

Rane dragged the chair noisily to the table while Tuli fetched the stool and made a lot of fuss over getting her "mama" properly seated.

Rane made a face at her, then solemnly intoned, "Blessed be Soäreh for the food he has provided." There was a quaver in her voice that Tuli hoped the clothhead outside the door would take for age and not for a struggle against laughter. She managed to quaver the response. "Soäreh be blessed."

They ate in silence after that even when they heard the floorboards groan and creak under the lumbering feet of their spy.

The Intii Vann came with the dark; he sat in the taproom drinking and grousing with Coperic about the ingratitude of relatives, the miserable fishing, wives and their whims, saying nothing that would trigger any interest in enemy ears. Coperic served him and saw to it that his wine was heavily watered so he could give the impression of drunkenness without acquiring the real thing; the repeated refillings of his tankard also gave him all the excuse he needed for spending hours at that table. Sometime after midnight, he wobbled out, the key to the alley door in his pocket and with instructions to knock on Rane's door, then go on to Coperic's room and wait for him.

When enough time had passed after Vann's departure so the two things would not appear connected, Coperic shooed out the last drunks, locked up, watched Haqtar bumble off to his cellar room, waited until he was sure the man was shut into his den, then went wearily up the stairs and down the hall to his room.

Tuli was sitting on the bed stroking her invisible pet, Rane silent beside her. Vann was standing with his shoulders braced against a wall, arms crossed over his chest, his eyes fixed on the floor; he looked up when Coperic came in.

Coperic swung a chair about, sat in it. "What's the problem?"

Rane lifted a hand, let it fall. "He's been like that since we got here."

"Vann?"

The Intii began stroking his beard. " 'Tis not them. 'Tis I've a notion what you're wanting of me, and it can't be. 'Tis· I've been ordered to my village with a trax on my tail to make sure I go straight there." He nodded at Rane. "Knowing what that one has in her head is life-and-death for Biserica and maybe me and mine. 'Tis knowing too that the army has marched and we got Kapperim thick as lice on a a posser's back and a shaman like as not going to gut the bunch of us if we sneeze wrong."

Coperic nodded toward the other chair. "Sit, old friend. I been doing some thinking about that since last we met. I don't mind talking about them now they're out and not going back. I put a couple plants in the Plaz. Picked up an impression of the lock on the Guard Armory. 'S afternoon a bunch of us, we got in, cleared out what was left there. Not much, damn the bitch, but some bolts and a few crossbows, a bundle of lances and a good pile of knives. We keeping some, getting some ready for you to take."

Vann came away from the wall, his usual containment

vanished. He said nothing but threw himself into the chair; it creaked precariously and seemed about to come apart beneath him. He ignored that, drew a huge breath. "How?" A moment later he added, "The trax."

"Packing them in water casks and a flour barrel—with a bit of flour too, courtesy of the Plaz." He rubbed his nose, glanced at the time candle burning on its stand next to his bed. "Should be finished hauling the barrels soon. When you come in, I got word to Bella; she's going to leave men on the wharf, guards. You grab 'em, tell 'em to help you load the barrels. My folk and me, we figure the next couple days things going to be looser than before, agli keeping one eye looking south instead of both on us."

Vann stroked his beard. "Can't take the barrels through the village gate. Kappra shaman got a nose for edged steel." His hand smoothed repeatedly down the oiled plaits of his beard. The oil had gone a trifle rancid and the plaits were frayed, some of them coming undone, an outward sign of the disorder in mind and spirit. "Stinking Kapperim, got half the women 'n children shut up in my hall. Shaman's got it set to burn, we give him any trouble. Saw Vlam and Vessey." He glanced at Rane, smiled. "My sons," he said. "We figured to go after Kapperim barehanded. Save part anyway. Them outside the hall." He leaned forward, cupped large hands over his knees. "Cut more throats than we can choke with those knives you got, 'n half a chance we maybe can take out the shaman and stop the burning. We owe you, Coperic old friend."

Coperic grinned at him. "We talk about that a passage from now."

Rane broke in. "Be easier if you could catch the Kapperim asleep," she said. "Especially the shaman."

"That viper?" Vann ran his tongue over his teeth, his upper lip bulging under the bristly moustache. "Evelly, that's my wife, she tells Vlam he set wards that wake him if anyone even think too hard about him."

"Who cooks for the Kapperim?"

"Our women. But they make them taste everything before they eat." He scowled. "Children too; keep the women honest, they say."

"Seems to me a nice long sleep wouldn't hurt your women and children and your men could dump one meal."

"Drug the trash?"

"Right. There's a couple drugs I know could do it, probably lots I don't know, put them to sleep without hurting them so your women and children would be safe." She grinned. "I figure you and your men can do all the hurting the Kapperim are very likely to need."

The Intii's lips moved back and forth as if he were tasting the idea, then spread into a grin. "Yah." he said. Then he sobered. "Always that Maiden-cursed shaman. He suspect his dam if he weren't hatched."

"I ate a kind of fish stew in a fisher village once when I was a lot younger and tougher. Called tuz-zegel, if I remember. I see you follow me." Rane chuckled. "The inside of my mouth still remembers. You couldn't taste stinkweed through that. If you showed up with a collection of the right spices, a little present for your wife, wouldn't it be the most ordinary thing if she fixed up a batch of tuz-zegel for the whole village? You could warn the men you trust to dump theirs." Vann sighed and Rane chuckled again. "I suppose it's your favorite dish; well, a little sacrifice won't hurt." Vann snorted, his eyes gleaming, the sag in his spirit banished. Rane ran her hands through her hair. "First thing, get those spices; you give Coperic a list. I suspect he won't have too much trouble filling it. Next, what drug. I'm a long time out of my training, but there's a healwoman in the hanguol rookery."

Tuli's eyes opened wide. *Ajjin was right*, she thought. *Trust Rane to remember after all that's happened and fit it right in with her plans.*

"Healwoman? Never heard of any. Not there." Coperic scowled past her. "Healwoman, mmm, she'd disappear into the House of Repentance soon's an Agli got a sniff of her."

"This one hasn't got the name since she didn't finish the last bit of training. Debrahn the midwife."

"Oh, her. Yah, I know her."

"You can find her?"

"Rane."

"Yeah, I know. Silly question. She'd know about herbs, have a good mix tucked away somewhere. One of those sleepytime drugs I was thinking of, a lot of midwives use with difficult deliveries, doesn't hurt the baby, but puts the woman's head to sleep. There should be at least one woman ready to birth in your village."

"My middle daughter." He smoothed a forefinger along his moustache. "M' wife would have my ears for bringing a stranger in."

"Would the Kapperim know that?"

"Don't see how."

"Would your wife make a fuss?"

"Front of that trash? Never."

"Good enough. Ajjin Turriy asked me to coax Debrahn out of the rookery. This is a better excuse than most."

Coperic nodded. "Be a good idea for any lone female to get out of the rookery before it turns into a rat pit. I owe the Ajjin a favor or two myself. Give them a tenday in there'n they'll start cutting each other up for stew." He frowned at Rane. "Best I fetch her now. Morning might be too late."

Rane shook her head. "We."

Coperic raised a hand, pushed it away from him. "Bad enough for a man to be out this hour, if some Follower sees you. . . ."

"I'll get my other clothes. He'll see two men, that's all. Good thing I was never voluptuous." Rane chuckled. "What she knows of you, old friend, wouldn't persuade a rat into a granary."

Coperic grinned. "Hard to argue with you when you're right. Meet me in the taproom." He glanced at Tuli. "Alone." He turned to the Intii. "Write me up that list of spices, Vann. I'll put my people to scratching up what you need."

"Come on, Moth." Rane touched Tuli's shoulder. "You need sleep."

Back in their room, Tuli stripped off the hateful dress while Rane changed into her tunic and trousers. Neither spoke. Tuli crawled into the bed wondering how she could possibly sleep with so much to worry over.

Rane crossed the room and stood beside the bed. She slapped her swordbelt around her lean middle and buckled it as she looked down at Tuli. "Don't fret, Moth. With his knives Coperic could split a zuzz-fly on the wing and I'm not so bad with this." She tapped the hilt of the sword. "I'll wake you in good time; you won't miss the boat."

Tuli found she'd made up her mind without knowing it. "Rane. . . ."

"What is it?"

"I'm not going with you. You were right, you've got a better chance traveling alone. And I. . . ." She paused. "I don't want to be herded in with a bunch of giggling girls, you know that's what Da would do. I'm going to stay with Coperic if he'll have me. If not, well, Ildas and me, we'll go after the wagons, do as much hurt as we can, maybe tie up with Teras again. He 'n a bunch from the Haven are sure to be out against the army."

"I promised your father. . . ."

"This is more important. Me and Ildas, we can hurt 'em a lot more 'n a bunch of men who the norits will stomp on before they get close. You know that."

Rane sighed. "I'll talk to Coperic. Mind if I tell him about Ildas?"

"Course not."

Rane looked down at her. The silence became overcharged. Tuli felt tears gathering in her eyes. She wanted to turn her head away but she didn't. Rane bent over her, touched her cheek. "It's too bad you weren't a few years older," she said, her voice husky, uncertain. She bent lower, kissed Tuli lightly on the lips, straightened and went quickly out of the room.

Tuli lay still a moment, then she sniffed and scrubbed her hands across her eyes and sat up. "Sleep," she said to the empty room. "Maiden bless." She blew out the candle. wriggled back down under the covers, Ildas humming against her side, a spot of warmth that spread rapidly through her whole body. She yawned, worked her lips.

thought about wanting a glass of water but stayed where she was, too comfortable to move. "What do you think of that?" she asked Ildas. He crooned to her, his meaningless silent sounds soothing her jagged unreliable emotions, beating in her blood, singing her to sleep.

Ildas scampering before her, Tuli ran from tree to tree, meaning to get as close to the Highroad as she could, a task made easier because the Nor had swept a wide swath of land free of snow. The army was camped on the grassy slopes of the Earth's Teeth at the Well of the Blasted Narlim, but the Warwagons were sitting on the Highroad, sticking up there like wanja nuts on a harvest cake, a tempting target Tuli wasn't prepared to pass up. Coperic had made a half-hearted protest, then got down to planning her attack and his. He and his people were on the far side of the army, ready to hit the majilarni when she provided a diversion to take the attention of the norits off the army.

She only came across two sentries prowling through the grove, though there were quite a few traxim roosting in the upper branches. Ildas and nightsight were enough to keep her away from either. She fled through the grove like a ghost and crawled into the space beneath the desiccated air-roots of a dead spikul. While she looked over the ground ahead, Ildas trotted busily about the roots, spinning fine lines of light out of his substance, weaving them into a web of protection about her. When he was finished, he nosed against her, wriggled with pleasure when she rubbed her fingers behind his ears, then he trotted off. She settled to watch.

The bare ground between her and the last of the Warwagons was thick with norits. Some sat in close groups talking quietly, some were rolled into blankets, asleep, some had gone slightly apart and into themselves, meditating or searching about with their longsight, Tuli didn't know which but suspected the second and was very glad of Ildas's web. There were a few traxim still aloft but most were roosting in the trees or perched on the Warwagons;

they didn't seem to like night flying much. Tuli suspected from what she'd seen of them that their eyes weren't all that good in daytime, let alone night.

Ildas trotted toward the last of the huge wagons, circling unseen about sleeping forms, norits or the mercenaries that rode the wagon, about meditators and talkers, coming close to them, almost brushing against them, his leisurely progress a teasing, mocking dance. Then Tuli was part of that dance and it was a small piece of the Great Dance she'd wheeled in when Ildas came to her. She knew she was lying in dark and dirt, but she was also locked into the Dance; she laughed to herself; Ildas laughed with her, their joined laughter was the music of the Great Cycle of death and birth and death, the endings that were also and always beginnings.

Then Ildas was leaping onto the Warwagon, fastidiously avoiding the hunched forms of the sleeping traxim. He pottered about, pushing his nose into the load, searching out a place that suited him. The traxim stirred uneasily as if they felt a wind sneaking through their fur, but they didn't wake. Somewhere near the center of the wagon, Ildas lifted his leg and urinated a stream of fire into the load.

There is an oil distilled from the flesh of the vuurvis, a deep-sea fish the size of a small whale; the secret of preparing it belongs to the mercenaries of Ogogehia, it is their most fearsome weapon, used in clay melons that shatter and splatter fire. The burning oil clings to flesh, it can't be wiped away, water won't put it out, it can't be smothered. It keeps eating into the flesh until the last trace of the oil is consumed. Ildas had sniffed out barrels of that oil and used it as his target.

Flames exploded into the air five times a man's height and splashed outward much the same distance, landing on norit and mercenary alike; the sleepers writhed and rolled about on the ground, living torches that filled the night with screams of an agony beyond comprehension: those on their feet howled and ran until their hearts quit and they crashed to the ground, some of them into snow that did

nothing to put out the fire. Burning traxim leaped shrieking into the air, came spiraling down to crash among the
trees or into the army, spreading the chaos. The few that
escaped were those near the ends of the wagon that had
time to flip from this world into that place the Nor had
fetched them from. Most of the sleepers were dead or
dying. More than half the nearby norits had escaped though
they spent some minutes in frantic efforts to shield themselves from the flying oil. Tuli gaped at the damage Ildas
had done with one well-placed squirt.

He came prancing back, wriggled round her, bumped
against her, rolled onto his back so she could scratch his
belly. "You're a one soredak army, Didi," she whispered to
him. She continued to stroke him as she watched the
surviving norits go from body to body, cutting throats of
any who still lived. The noise diminished here by the
Highroad, but she heard screams and shouts and curses
drifting from the army, the protesting hoots of macain and
the high angry squeals of rambuts. *Coperic*, she thought.
*No, can't be. He and his folk must have been in and out already;
they wouldn't make that much noise. Should be getting out myself
before they start hunting.* She began inching backward out of
the shelter of the roots. Ildas walked beside her, snapping
the web of light back into himself. When she was clear of
the roots but still deep in shadow, she sat on her heels,
looking about. The traxim in the trees had whipped into
the air with the explosion of the Warwagon and hadn't yet
settled back to their roosts; any sentries close at hand had
rushed into the open, looking vainly for some way to help
the dying, or joining other men to roll the next Warwagon
farther from the fire and save that one from burning also.
Soon someone out there would start thinking instead of
reacting and send searchers into the trees to sniff out
whoever had set the fire. But not yet. She got to her feet
and fled through the trees, leaving the seething turmoil
behind, heading for the redezvous with Coperic. He was
probably there already, waiting with the others for her to
show up. She slowed and began to relax.

A norit stepped from behind a tree, hands raised and

filled with fire, eyes glaring, mouth opening in a long ululating scream that tore from his throat and assaulted her ears. He flung the fire at her.

Tuli swerved so sharply she had to scramble to keep on her feet; arms waving, kicking herself in the ankle, she plunged for the shelter of the nearest tree, a spindly brellim, knowing she couldn't reach it in time, suspecting its shelter was no shelter at all from the magic fire.

He screamed again, outrage in every hoarse syllable of those unintelligible words.

She looked back, saw Ildas leap between her and the fireballs, bat them down, the norit not seeing him but seeing his fire fail; she sucked in a breath to laugh her triumph—and crashed into the tree.

She was stunned for an instant, then got shakily to her feet. From the the corner of her eye she saw Ildas play with the fireballs, jump on them and eat them. The norit stared, open-mouthed, as his fire vanished, bite by bite. For the moment he'd forgotten her.

Tuli whipped around the still shivering tree and fled into the dark, her head clearing as she moved, her first panic settling into a mix of terror and rage. She ran furiously, twisting and turning through the trees. And Ildas kept the fireballs as well as the rest of the norit's magic away from her. But she couldn't outrun him and he was an adult male, so much stronger than her, he didn't need magic to deal with her; it was only his rigid mind-set that kept him stopping to use that magic. Not that she thought all that out; fragments of it came to her while she ran, coalescing into a sense of what was happening, adding pinches of hope and contempt to the mixture seething within her. She forced herself to slow a little and use her nightsight to plot her route, diving beneath low-hanging limbs, bounding over root tangles that were traps for unwary feet. Several times she heard him flounder and curse, felt a fleeting satisfaction that vanished into the chill realization that she couldn't get away from him no matter how hard she ran. Twice more he stopped and tried his magic on her, twice more Ildas slapped fireballs down, ate them and set himself between her and other manifestations of the norit's magic that made her hair and skin tingle but had no other effect on her.

Before she was ready, she was out of the trees, running into moonlight that nearly blinded her, through grass that whipped about her flying feet and threatened to trip her. She was getting tired, her legs were stone-heavy, the breath burned her mouth and throat, but she drove herself on. She could almost feel his hands reaching for her, his breath hot on her neck. He was so close, so desperately close. She zigged and zagged like a startled lappet, trying to get back into the thin fringe of woodland along the Highroad beyond the grove of Blasted Narlim camp.

His fingers scrabbled at her arm. With a small sobbing cry she flung herself around and away, cutting perilously close to him, trusting in the agility that had saved her so far. Again and again she managed a swerve, a dodge, a lunge at the last moment, avoiding the clutch of those long pale fingers; once she threw herself into a rolling fall past him and managed to bound onto her feet before he could bring himself around. That time she nearly made it to the trees, but in a straightaway run she was no match for him and she had to swerve again to escape him. As she had in the hallway in Sel-ma-Carth, she wanted fiercely and uselessly to know knife work, to have Coperic's skills in her hands and mind. It might have given her a chance, at least a chance. This chase had only one end, but she refused to think about that. While she had breath in her body, until her legs folded under her, she would fight him, she would struggle to get away. Ildas brushed against him, drained his strength, brushed against her, gifting her with that strength so she could keep on long after she should have dropped, exhausted. The image of the charred agli came to her. *Burn him,* she screamed silently at the fireborn, *burn him like you did the agli.* But the norit must have had stronger defenses than an agli; he and Ildas balanced each other. Neither could harm the other. And it seemed to her Ildas shrugged and told her in his wordless way that he was doing all he could.

The norit's fingers were lines of fire on her shoulder, but her tunic burned away from under them and she threw herself to one side, rolling up onto her feet and darting away. Ildas, she thought, ashing the cloth. Her legs were timber baulks, as weighty and stiff as the beams in the watchtower, her breath came in great gulps, she was beyond pain now, knew the end was near. Ildas brushed her leg, and fire jolted through her. Again the norit's hand closed on her, catching the cloth of her sleeve, again the cloth ashed as soon as he grasped it, but this time instead of rolling away from him, she dived past him only inches from his body, too soon and too fast for him to change his lunge. As he came around, his boot caught in the grass and he fell on his face. Hardly believing her luck, she forced her body into a sprint toward the trees.

And was forced to swerve away again; a straight run was impossible. He didn't quite touch her but she felt him like a torch at her back.

She heard a gasp, quickly hushed, a slithery thump, felt a coolness in the night about her as if a fire were suddenly smothered. She chanced a look over her shoulder, stumbled to a shaking stop; her legs folded beneath her and she went down on the grass with a silthery thump of her own.

Coperic knelt beside the body of the norit, wiping his knife on the black wool robe. He got to his feet and waited as Tuli wobbled onto her feet and stumbled over to him. Without asking questions or saying anything, he gave her his hand and led her toward the lane between the hedges, walking slowly, letting her catch her breath and gather her strength. Ildas trotted beside her for a few strides, then leaped onto her shoulder, draped himself about her neck, bleeding energy into her.

"I feel. Like a puppet. With its strings cut," she said.

"Takes some like that."

"Good thing you came."

"Got worried when you didn't show up, so I come looking."

"Lot of noise back there. After the fire started."

"Not us."

"Didn't think so. You see who?"

Stenda after the racing macain. Saw a boy going back into the mountains driving half a dozen of them in front of him, he'll make it, enough left still attacking to cover him. Probably other Stenda hitting for the mountains soon as they busted racers loose."

"Still going on."

"Tar-folk and outcasts trying to get off with a tithewagon. Won't make it, those that don't get killed'll have traxim and norits on their tails. Dead, all of 'em."

"No," she said. Not arguing with him, but trying to interpose that lack of belief between her twin and danger. "Teras," she said. "Could he be there?"

"Too far north. Saw some of 'em. Didn't see him."

"You wouldn't know him."

"Didn't see no one looks like you."

"Ah." Though they were fraternal twins she and Teras did look very much alike. Her knees gave way, but he hauled her up and supported her until she had herself together again. "Your folk?"

"Slit some throats, sliced some girths." He grinned. "Have to do some sewing before they can ride. Bella swears she got herself a shaman while he was gaping at the fire. Got out. All of us. Got loose easy with all the other stuff going on." He pushed through a flimsy place in the left-hand hedge, pulled her after him into the field. "Maiden give them luck, but most those others they dead. Too much noise, trying for too much."

"Won't be so easy for us next time."

"Do something different next time."

Tuli nodded. She was suddenly as tired in mind as she was in body. She yawned, leaned more heavily on him. "Gonna have to tie me in the saddle." She yawned again, blinked slowly at the riders waiting for them under the moonglow with its load of dangling moth cocoons. "Teach me 'bout knives."

"Tomorrow," he said. "Time enough."

"Yeah." She giggled. "Cut off a toe, I try anything tonight."

# POET-WARRIOR/KINGFISHER

## 1

"Liz."

The dark woman leaned out the driver's window of the old battered pickup. "Jule."

"Anoike sent me, said you could give me a lift."

Liz nodded. "Come round. I'll get the door. Handle's off outside." She pulled her head back in and a moment later Julia heard the loud ka-thunk of the latch, the squeal and clank of the opening door.

With the help of Liz's strong nervous hand, she was half-lifted, half-climbed up onto the seat. The cracked fausleather squeaked under her as she slid over, the stiff springs gave and bumped against her less than padded behind. She moved tentatively, seeking the least uncomfortable way of sitting; her knee bumped into something, knocked it into a slide toward Liz. Automatically she reached out and caught hold of it, realized that she held the hand-carved stock of Liz's favorite rifle, close at hand, ready for use.

Liz saw her consternation, smiled, leaned back. "Our new employer says we'll be jumping into hostile territory."

"I slept through a lot."

"Yup, sure did."

Julia unwrapped the sandwiches, her stomach cramping with hunger. She forced herself to eat slowly, chew the bread and meat instead of gulping down large chunks. Cold greasy venison tough as bootleather, on stale bread. Metal-tainted water from the canteen. But it was the most wonderful meal she'd had in years, definitely the most satisfying. She ate with an intensity greater than that of the greediest of children and knew it and laughed at herself and only just managed to stop herself from licking the paper. She brushed the crumbs from her hands and thighs, crumpled the paper, looked around, frowning.

Liz grinned at her, her black eyes squinted into shallow curves. "Out the window, Jule."

Julia looked at the wad of greasy paper. The thought of messing up a mountain with her leavings gave her a pain almost physical. She couldn't do it.

"Toss it, stupid," Liz snapped. "Garbage men coming by in the morning. Sanitizing these mountains down to stone."

Julia flinched, screwed the paper into a tighter ball, then pitched it out. Liz was right, what did a few scraps of paper matter now? She looked out the window at the vague shapes of the trees, dark columns in the darkness, heard the lazy sibilance of the wind through the branches, listened for that moment to that sound alone, hearing nothing else, wanting to hear nothing else. After a moment she shivered. "Don't they realize," she whispered, "don't they realize they might make a new Sahara here?"

Liz snorted, shocking Julia out of her trance. "Them?" She reached out, touched Julia's arm with an uncharacteristically gentle hand. "It won't all be gone," she said. She patted Julia's arm, drew back. "Prioc's staying, him and some others. With some mortars and rockets." She chuckled. "Making garbage out of the garbage men. Even you shouldn't worry about that sort of litter, Jule."

Julia passed a hand across her face. "Forty-plus years of conditioning, Liz." She looked down at the rifle, shook her head.

"Gloom and doom. Give you a few good feeds and something to keep you busy, you'll be humming along good as new."

"Liz?" Julia raised a brow. "This isn't like you."

"What isn't?"

"All this maternal . . . what? fussing."

"Just a bit of boredom." Liz fidgeted on the seat, tapped her fingers on the steering wheel. "I hate waiting." She ran dark eyes over Julia, frowned. "You want to drive or ride shotgun?"

"Drive."

Ombele's voice boomed out over the clearing. "Get ready."

"Jump coming," Liz said. "Start the motor, be ready to

roll when we're through. Supposed to be daylight on the other side."

A murmur and a sigh as if the mountain itself exhaled—those who were walking got to their feet and stood waiting. A yipping whoop—Angel sending a part of his band in two horns about the low end of the meadow. Rear guards. A ragged splutter, then a burring drone as the truck motors started up and settled to rough idling, waiting. A stuttering harsher roar from the motorcycles about the high end of the meadow. Foreguard. Jumping into hostile territory, Julia thought. Be ready. She put her hand on the knob of the shift lever and waited.

Liz sat with the rifle's barrel resting on the shaking metal of the door, pointing out the open window at the sky, the butt on her thigh so she could swing it up and aim with a minimum of time and effort, yet avoid accidentally shooting someone if the jump proved rougher than she expected. She was wire-taut, glittering with the excitement that took hold of her, kept her alert and deadly during times of threat. Often enough before now Julia wondered what had happened to her to leave her like this, but she never asked. No one asked questions; whatever people wanted known about themselves they volunteered; there was no point in anything else. Liz chuckled suddenly. "The Kry," she said. "That's what Dom Hern called them."

"What?"

"Desert tribes. The hostiles. Use firespears sometimes," he said. Dom Hern. Better hope we catch them squatting. Our load's mostly fuel."

"Yike." Julia grimaced at the dirty, cracked windshield. "Anoike didn't mention that little detail."

"Want out?"

"If I was sane I would." Julia sighed. "No."

"Then what's the fuss?"

"Right." Julia laughed. "What's the fuss? I was right the first time. I'm dead and this is dream."

Liz's chuckle mingled with hers, a macabre cheerfulness blending with her tension. "And I've been crazy for years, Jule, so enjoy."

Ombele's basso roar sounded again. "Hang on. Jump starting."

Like an oil smear birthing damp and gawdy rainbows out of rain and asphalt, a vast opalescent membrane appeared at the high end of the meadow and began sweeping toward them, eating everything it passed over. It touched the bumper, ate the engine. Julia sat stiffly, more terrified at that moment than she could remember ever having been even including when she had turned and seen the blackshirts waiting for her.

It passed through them, a cool breath, a leap from dark to light.

A brief chatter of automatic rifles, followed by quieter snaps from the hunting guns, the roar of motorcycles, the thud of hooves.

Lanky blue men, ragged and howling came running from house to house, burned-out shells of houses in this sea village backed up against crumbling chalk cliffs a dirty white in the cold brilliance of the winter sun. The Kry came swarming at them, spear-throwers filled and swept back. And they fell when the chattering began, as if some mighty scythe had swept across them. A single short spear came wobbling at them, but the distance was too great, the cast too much a desperation. She heard a whoop and saw Rudy Herrera, the youngest of Angel's collection, ride at the spear, knock it out of the air with a barrel of his rifle, then kick his mount into caprioles while he shook his rifle and taunted the Kry.

Georgia yelled at him and he came back, his round dark face split into a gap-toothed grin. Gap-toothed because a Dommer had taken exception to his curses and struggles when he and his family were evicted from land they'd worked for three hundred years, the parliament having condemned and taken the land from them after paying the pitiful sum they called just compensation. There was supposed to be a dam built there so that water would drown that land, but somehow it was never built and somehow the land ended up in the hands of the local seigneur, all of it. Just one of those things that happen to people. Rudy with a tooth knocked out, his parents in a workcamp somewhere. One of those things. Julia shifted into gear, ready to roll when the order came, wondering how that destructive rage in Angel and his band was going to be harnessed once the fighting was over. She thought a second. Maybe no problem at all. Will any of us be alive then?

"Southport," Liz said.

"This place? You're full of little nuggets today."

"Whatever you're full of, I wish you'd pull the plug."

"Sorry. Hunger speaking, I suppose."

"Sourbelly, uh-huh." Liz smoothed her hand along the rifle's stock, over and over as if she were petting a cat, while she gazed past Julia at what must once have been a prosperous, growing town. "Doesn't look that different from Broncton or Madero, does it."

"Form follows function," Julia said, pursing her lips and lifting her chin; then she grinned. "No phone lines. No electricity here. No plumbing."

"No flush toilets, no laid-on water, no hot baths without heating and hauling." Liz ran a hand through her short hair.

"Well, we've had the better part of a year to get used to that."

"Doesn't mean I ever learned to like it."

"Does mean we've got to get this bitty war over and let Trig get working with Norman on pipes and heaters, Ellie dreaming up some kind of generator; I suppose she brought along the parts of the one she and Thom built for us. And there's the press, they must have brought that along." She smiled blindly at the windshield, seeing nothing but a dream she hadn't known was in her, feeling a lift in her blood at the thought. "Me, I'd like to be my own printer and to perdition with all censors."

Liz said nothing, just continued to stroke the wood of the stock. After a moment's silence, she leaned forward, peered through the bug-splattered glass. "Here come our allies."

The jump had landed them on a flat, pebbly space

before a three-story wall that sat like a dam across a narrow break in the cliffs. Near the center of the wall there was a wide gate, its twin leaves made of heavy polished timbers that looked as tough and impenetrable as the stone of the wall. The two sides of the gate swung open and half a dozen riders came out, crossed the narrow open space, stopped in front of Dom Hern and the healer. All of them were women. They wore short-sleeved leather tunics and loose, knee-length trousers of leather; they carried bows and all had swords clipped onto heavy pocketed belts. Their mounts were vaguely lacertine, with smooth knubbly skin, spongy growths along thin necks, large, lustrous intelligent eyes, powerful legs and clawed feet. Julia watched the horses that Hern and his companion rode and was startled to see both beasts placidly accepting the strange creatures coming up on them. She glanced at Liz and saw she'd noticed the same thing.

"The healer," Liz said. "She's got a thing with animals."

"Magic." Julia sighed. "Helps."

"Yup. Curls my hair just thinking about it."

"I suppose we could treat it as just another kind of technology. What I know about motors you could write on a stamp, but I never had trouble driving a car."

"Right," Liz said absently, her gaze still fixed on the women. "And sorcerers die like anyone else if you put bullets through their brains."

## 2

The roar of the cycles was making the horses nervous. Serroi soothed her mount, watched Hern settle his. She didn't try to help; he wouldn't like that. He grinned at her, knowing exactly what she was thinking; he'd come a long, long way from that sheltered arrogant man who'd ridden on quest from the Biserica with her, perhaps in part because he'd shared dreams with her on the plateau and in the sharing had been reshaped—as she had been reshaped by him, though she hadn't given much thought to that part of the experience.

The membrane passed over them and they were in Southport, a burnt and desolate travesty of the busy, cheerful place she remembered. That's what the mijloc will be after this war, she thought. The waste, the horrible waste. And for what?

Kry came howling from among the burnt-out houses, set to hurl their spears, but Angel's band and the folk on the cycles lifted their weapons. There were loud rattles and a series of sharp snaps and the Kry went down, the charge was broken and those still on their feet began to run back for shelter. One of them got off his spear, but a boy rode out and knocked it down, taunting the Kry all the time.

It was quick, lasted a few seconds only, and was as precise as a healwoman's knife. She began to appreciate Hern's eye and that part in her shaped by him saw more clearly how he'd evaluated their possibilities from the meager evidence of the Mirror.

The Southgate swung open and a band of meien rode through, came across the scree toward them, familiar faces, all of them; she sighed, deeply pleased to see them all again. "Kindayh," she said.

"Serroi," Kindayh smiled, lifted her hand in a quiet, warm greeting, then turned to Hern. "Dom," she said. "Yael-mri got word of your coming and sent a message flyer telling us to be ready for you." She looked beyond him at the mob he'd brought through with him. "Though we aren't quite prepared for all that. Have to stretch, but we can manage, I think."

Hern glanced at the lowering sun, then faced Kindayh. "That's good to hear." A swift arc of his hand sketched the wall and the gate. "A cold night out here; should get them settled by sundown."

"Right. Follow us." She swept her arm in a wide arc, brought her macai around and started toward the open gate.

## 3

Ombele's voice came a third time, oddly diminished even in the taut silence that was broken only by the steady lapping of the ocean close behind them. "Going in," he boomed. "Ahead slow."

Julia eased up on the brake as the jeep just ahead of her with Braddock and the rest of the council in it began to roll forward. Around her the walking families started after it, moving faster than the pickup's creep. She could feel their excitement, their eagerness to get their first sight of what they'd be fighting for, then living with. She felt much of that herself. How many months . . . no, years. Yes, years since she'd felt that bright glow of anticipation. It wasn't just growing older that had diminished her, but the dusty gray everyday despair that spread over the whole country, darkening and thickening as the years passed. It was different here; she breathed that difference in with the clean bracing air and was exhilarated by it. She couldn't isolate reasons for this; there was no more hope here, no less violence, but there was a new smell to the place as if the world itself were somehow younger, as if the possibilities they'd exhausted on their homeworld were open here and multiplied. She drove past the gates and nosed into the dark hole that turned in a shallow curve putting the opening at the far end out of sight. The wall was thick, far thicker than she'd guessed, more than six times the length of the pickup. She twitched the lights on and breathed a bit more easily, then she was out and the walkers around her were letting out whoops of their own, especially the children, whoops that bounced back and forth between the ragged cliffs that towered over them, crumbling chalk with a toupee of scrub and scraggly grass. She squinted into the jumping side mirror and tried to estimate the size of the exit hole, wondering if the biggest truck was going to fit through it. Close thing, if it did. They might have to unpack the truck and haul the load through. Too bad to lose that transport. Too bad to lose anything here, no way of replacing it.

Liz leaned over, slapped the lights off. "Don't waste the juice. No rechargers here."

Julia glanced at Liz, was startled to see in the small dark woman no sign of the excitement bubbling in the folk outside or in her own blood. Liz was the same as she'd always been, wired in the face of danger, even a danger that seemed so remote and undefined as the one ahead of them. Julia wanted to say something, to ask Liz what she was thinking, but there was no invitation in the woman's face, so she only said, "Right." And started forward, creeping along a rutted excuse for a road toward the vee of brilliant cloudless blue ahead of them.

At the mouth of the deep ravine a stone keep loomed like a continuation of the cliffs, forcing the road, such as it was, too swing wide around its walls. The women stopped them on a rocky barren plain dotted with tufts of yellowed grass and scattered stones. The keep's outer gate was an opening just broad enough to let two of those lizardish beasts walk side by side and just high enough to clear their riders' heads. With Ombele and Braddock directing traffic they got the trucks lined up and parked, noses facing the road. The wind sweeping along the plain was like an ice bath and the little heat the sun provided seemed more illusion than reality. Some of the younger children were crying and Julia was shuddering so hard she almost couldn't walk by the time she followed Liz through the double-gated entrance tunnel into the court beyond.

Around the inside of the high thick walls, slate-roofed three-story buildings were backed against the stone. The lower floors were stables, open face forges, storage rooms, or housed other, less obvious functions. The second and third floors were living space if she remembered her history correctly. She saw two of the women leading the riding beasts inside the stable nearest the gate and a third showing Angel where he could put his horses. The folk around her were beginning to relax now that they were out of the wind. Though it wasn't warm in the court, the air no longer seemed to slice the meat off her bones. She stood by the well in the center of the paved court, feeling a little lost, wondering what to do, then Ombele came out of the square tower, Samuel Braddock beside him. He bent and

listened a moment to Braddock's murmur, then straightened and used his foghorn voice to get the attention of the
thronging mob, sending Georgia to set up a guard rota for
the trucks, a clutch of girls to fetch spare blankets and
food, a string of boys to haul water for cooking, then broke
the rest into groups, took one himself and sent the rest of
the council to get the others moving.

Julia leaned on the railing of the gallery and gazed down
into the Great Hall of the tower. It was a peaceful and
comfortable scene, the fires in the four enormous fireplaces
beginning to die down, the floor everywhere except near
the hearths and the narrow walkways covered with a thick
layer of straw, the younger children fed and tucked away
in blanket cocoons, already asleep, warm and safe. Adults
and older children were sitting in groups about tubs of
coffee and tea, comfortable themselves, some of them beginning to stir about, getting ready to take themselves to
bed, others talking quietly, tiredly, countentedly about the
extraordinary events of the day. Angel and his bunch were
out with their horses; they ate there, planned to spend the
night there. Near one of the hearths Dom Hern sat with
the council, talking quietly. Braddock, Ombele, Lou, Evalina
Hanks and Samsyra. Julia looked for the healer but couldn't
find her. Several of the women fighters were there also,
the—what was it?—meien. Meie singular, meien plural.
*One aspect of the magic in this place is definitely a blessing,* she
thought. *When we passed through the membrane we seem to have
acquired the local language. And what's better, we got it without
losing our own; there's so much you just can't say in mijlocker. I
suspect the children will grow up mixing both languages. Well,
English is a mongrel tongue anyway and the stronger for it.
Forty-six, that's not old, got a good thirty years left, thanks to the
little healer. Serroi. I know her name, why do I have trouble
calling her by that name? Afraid of her? Distancing her? Stop it,
Julia. Serroi.*

As if the silent repetition of her name had conjured her
out of shadows Serroi came toward her and stood beside
her looking down at the crowded, peaceful scene. "Plotting

and planning." She smiled at the council and Dom Hern. "Catching up on everything that's happened since we left."

"How bad is it going to be?" Julia felt impelled to ask though she didn't really want to know, she didn't want to spoil the mellow mood and the spring scent of hope that hovered about her.

"I don't know. Bad enough, I suppose."

"Shouldn't you be down there with them?"

"No. I don't belong there. Not now."

"The land is the same," Julia said. She drew her hand along the polished stone of the railing. "Granite is granite, it seems, wherever you find it."

"People, too—they seem much the same everywhere, if you disregard custom." Serroi spoke absently, frowning down at the eroding groups below—more and more of the refugees were heading for their blankets though they'd lost the greater part of the day by their jump—but Julia didn't think she really saw them. "How long did you know?" Serroi said after a moment's silence.

"That I would die?"

"Yes."

"A little more than a year." Julia paused to consider. "I knew about the cancer before that. Several months before that. But I wasn't thinking about dying then. Mostly, I was angry at fate or whatever landed this on me. And I was furious at the circumstances that blocked me from a cure. And at the same time I was still sure I could get around or over those blocks. Ever see anyone with boils? That was me, a walking boil." She chuckled, went silent as she remembered the night when Georgia and Anoike tracked her through the brush and brought her back to the few left alive out of all those packed into the body of the truck. Remembered her rage and despair when she discovered that the border was shut tight, would be for the next six months until the Dommers got the fence built. Once that was done, they'd relax a little and it would be possible to get across if you knew the mountains well enough. Six months. Too long for her. A little crazy from anger and frustration and fear, she left the band and joined a group that called themselves the Mad Bombers. "When I lost all hope of living," she said, "all I wanted to do was strike out at those who'd done it to me, stolen my hope, I mean." She'd exaggerated her age and fragility, was their respectable front. No one ever connected the quietly dressed, middle-aged lady with the bombs that blew night after night. Bridges, airports, banks, police stations, introg centers when they could locate them, corporate headquarters, fuel storage tanks, a refinery, a thousand other targets, doing their best to avoid taking lives—until the time came that made her sick when she remembered it, the bomb that didn't go off when it should, in the middle of the night when the warehouse was deserted, but twelve hours later. Noon. She was staying with an ex-client, a prostitute specializing in dominance who picked up quite a lot of information and passed it on without asking questions. The two women spent the afternoon watching the bodies being hauled away and the firemen exhausting themselves to contain the fire, even listened to the speeches of community leaders rounded up by the Dommers, all of them frothing with outrage. The only time Amalie showed the slightest animation was when she recognized one of her clients and in a detached voice listed some of his odder preferences. "Time came," Julia said, "when I got sick of the bangs and the blood. Anoike took me up to the settlement in the mountains and I went on supply raids with them for a while, long as I was strong enough, then I worked with Dort and Jenny, writing pamphlets, running the offset, coaxing paper and ink out of Georgia and Braddock. When you can keep busy, you don't think about much except what you're doing. The nights were bad sometimes, but Georgia and Anoike got me morphine, so I did sleep. When I couldn't get around anymore, well, that was a hard time, until I went back to writing, not on paper but in my head. I used to put off the shots as long as I could so I could keep the words clear. I spun essays out of air, wrote a novel in my head paragraph by paragraph, saying the words over and over until they were engraved in my mind. It never seemed important that I might not finish the book; as a matter of fact, I was determined to live until I did, sort of a measuring out of the hours, nor was it important that nobody was going to read it but me. Can you understand that? Never mind. It was my way of telling myself that my life had meaning and purpose even though my death was without either of those. What happened to me was only a throw of fate, useless, without meaning even to me. If I'd died in a fight or a raid. . . ." She shook her head. "And even the book was spoiled when that chopper came over spitting fire at my mountain. The day you showed up, I was trying to convince myself it would be better to ask Lou to give me an overdose." She sighed, looked down at her hands. "Good thing you did come. He'd have hated that."

"If there was a purpose to your dying, it would have been easier?"

"I think so." She smiled at Serroi. "Likely I'll get a chance to test that theory in the days ahead." She rubbed at her nose, tapped restlessly at the polished stone. "Grace under pressure," she said. "That was a fad of writers and leeches a couple hundred years ago—watch a hunter kill, and evaluate the heart of the beast by how long he struggled and how well he died, that kind of thing, I suppose you've escaped that here so far. No? You're right, then, Custom aside, the beast that walks on two feet is much the same everywhere. Are you a seer as well as a healer?"

"No. Why?"

"I get the feeling it's your death as well as mine we're discussing."

"Not death. Just something that terrifies me, yet I have to do it. I think I have to do it. I don't know." She hesitated, lifted eyes that shone like molten copper in the dim light, searched Julia's face, then turned away and gazed at the group sitting beside the fire, deeply involved in what looked like complicated negotiations. After a while she turned once again to Julia. "Are you too tired to stay up a while longer?"

"You know I'm not."

"It's a long story."

"We've got a whole night." Julia touched the healer's hand, drew her own back, excitement and eagerness blooming within her. She throttled them down, spoke as calmly as she could, "If I can help. . . ."

"If you don't mind listening to the story of my life."

"Mind?" Julia chuckled. "Serroi, you don't know what you're saying. If I were two years dead, I'd crawl out of my grave to listen."

# PRIESTESS

Nilis tried to sleep, but the bed poked her and pushed at her; there was no position that felt comfortable. After an hour of that tossing she got up and went into the kitchen to heat some milk, hoping that would ease the tension. She sat at the kitchen table, sipping at the milk, staring at the flame of the guttering candle end, wondering what this was about, afraid she knew.

She wandered through the cold dark rooms of the shrine, feeling lost and alienated from them all, though she knew every inch of the stone in the walls and the floor, had scraped her hands raw cleaning them. After a while she drifted back to the kitchen, lit a new candle from the end of the old, and went reluctantly into the Maiden Chamber. She set the candlelamp on the floor and stepped back. "I know what you want," she said. She drew a hand across her eyes, furious at herself for wanting to cry. "You promised me I'd have the time I needed. You promise me a life here and give me a passage. I won't. . . ." Her voice broke and the tears she was trying to restrain gushed out. She dropped to the floor and knelt, hugging herself, sobbing out the pain of her years.

She spent an hour there, alternately hitting out at the Face, refusing to listen to what *She* was saying, and grieving for all the possibilities she'd lose if she let herself hear the call. When the candle was half gone, she sighed—grief, anger, denial all exhausted. Wearily she carried the candle into the kitchen and began packing the satchel with towels and food and other things she thought she might need.

\*   \*   \*

For a few minutes she watched Mardian bringing order into the motley group assembled in the Court of Columns, then she walked from shadow and stopped beside him, satchel on one shoulder, quilt-roll on the other, her fur cloak swaying about cold bare ankles. She heard the mutter of comment from the Cymbankers and tar-folk, but ignored it, stopped his protest with a quickly raised hand. "She gives and She takes away." Mardian looked at her a moment, looked past her at the empty shrine, then nodded and went back to what he was doing.

They walked south and west across the Cimpia Plain, gathering more newKeepers, villagers and tar-folk as they went. All day they walked, silent except when they were chanting the praises of the Maiden, their voices drowned in the great rumble of the folk following them. Hallam joined them at Sadnaji, along with all his folk who found the courage to cast aside Follower Blacks and cast with it their fear. They climbed the steep slopes to the Biserica Pass and led their rag-tag band chanting Maiden Praises through the great Gates of the Northwall two days before Floarin's army reached the Pass.

# MAGIC CHILD

Tuli scratched at her nose, grinned at the place where her hand should be but wasn't. Ildas had spun a net of light-wire that sucked eyes around her and left her unseen. She was stretched out in dead grass beside Coperic, peering at the sleeping Minarks through some weeds and a hump of dead brush, there only because Ildas wouldn't work on anyone but her. On his far side two of his people lay in another patch of shadow, Bella and Biel, Sankoise, younger versions of old Hars, with thick, sleek caps of dark gold hair, tilted, blue-purple eyes, the pallor of those who seldom walk in daylight, clad in matte black tunics and trousers that melted into shadow like a part of the night. They were cousins, tough, clever, skilled and impenetrable to most everyone but Coperic, content to follow wherever he led them. They'd accepted her into the band without argument or overt hostility but with no warmth, tolerating her because Ildas made it easier for them to attack and kill norits. They hated the Nor with a cold relentless passion that made Tuli shiver whenever she saw evidence of it.

There was a disturbance on the far side of the army, some shouting, a flutter of traxim, fireballs from the norits; she trembled when she saw those, the memory too recent to be easy to bear. More bodies left lying. She swallowed, seeing before her the bodies of tar-folk and villagers and Stenda boys left behind as the army moved on, clustered about the campgrounds like the piles of garbage and ordure. Teras might have been there at any of the camps, one of the dead, but she'd never know it, not being foolish enough to leave hiding and go poking about among the corpses. She moved restlessly, willing the raiders to go away and let things settle into quiet again; she didn't dare move until then. She could hear curses from the Minarks, froze as a norit rode past, started breathing again as Ildas cooed to her and the norit moved on, having noticed nothing.

Time slid by, minute by dragging minute. Silence descended on the army, a silence broken by the nearly sub-audible hum of breathing and snores from thousands of sleepers, and the scattered creaks, clanks and rustles from those who stood watch. The minutes added to an hour, then another. She touched the leather pouch hanging between breasts whose slow swelling was beginning to be a nuisance, felt the hard knob of the ink bottle and the long thin pipe filled with dreamdust. Might as well be now, she thought. If it's going to be tonight. Dawn couldn't be that far away. She breathed a very faint whistle, reached out and touched Coperic's arm. "I'm off," she whispered.

He nodded but said nothing.

She began creeping forward, moving on her toes and elbows, supple as a snake. The Dom was down and any movements she woke in brush or weeds would be lost to darkness, but the less she left to chance, the less she might have to regret. Ildas paced beside her when he was able to control his excitement, capered in circles about her when it broke loose, leaped onto her back and rode her awhile, his needle claws digging into her skin and muscle through the thin cloth of her tunic.

She eased carefully past the sentries, began winding through the sleeping Minarks toward the one she intented to work on, the one who had the highest status among these violent, mad and excessively proud princes. He'd be somewhere in the middle of the ground the Minarks had taken for their own, the safest place. She found him by wiggling from one armor pile to the next until she recognized the gear her prize wore when he cantered along the Highroad, ribbons singing silk about him.

Lying flat beside him, not even breathing, she dug into the pouch and pulled out the blowpipe. She scratched away the wax seals and puffed the dust in a cloud that hovered a moment over his face, then settled into his open mouth, was drawn into his nose with each breath he took. He sneezed, started to wake, then went limp. After a moment he was snoring a little, taken by the effects of the drug.

She got up and bent over him, inkpot in one hand, short thick brush in the other, a grin on her face. She knew that black ink all too well. You couldn't wash it out of clothes and even skin was hard to clean; the spots it left faded to an ugly gray-green but stayed with you for at least a month. With careful neat strokes she painted a glyph on his cheek, another on his forehead and a third on his other cheek; together, they meant *I am a lazy useless slave.* She set the pot and brush down and eased the blanket off him, then slit open the white silk tunic he wore. Working with the same care, she painted glyphs for the worst obscenity she knew, and below it the words *Soäreh sucks* and below those she drew an arrow pointing to his genitals; those she painted lavishly black, swallowing giggles as she remembered what her father and Teras had done to the agli; it was that very memory that made her suggest performing a similar service for the Minarks. She studied her work with satisfaction, but it seemed unfinished. She drew fat tear-drops dripping down his thighs and weeping eyes on his rather knobby knees, then gave him sloppy black feet. She emptied the dregs in the ink bottle onto the fresh white doeskin tunic he planned to wear in the morning.

Once again she sat on her heels and contemplated her work, repressing all show of amusement. The Minark shivered. Gravely she pulled the blanket back over him and tucked it in with maternal care. Can't have you waking from the cold, little one. Rise in daylight and let everyone see your fine new decorations. She collected the pot and brush and the blowpipe, even the bits of wax. No use leaving anything for the norits to work on. Ildas nosed about and helped her gather all the fragments. On her heels again, she looked around, regretting Coperic's adamant stand. One was enough, he said and repeated his formula, get in, do the job, get out and away. The other Minarks were sleeping peacefully, the attendants not on duty sighed in their sleep from a familiar exhaustion, but didn't wake. The sentries stood unmoving—dead, though they didn't know it yet. She lowered herself and went snaking away. Chances were she could stand up and stroll over to Coperic, but she needed the practice and she wasn't that sure of how well the web would hold.

When she reached Coperic, she saw Bella and Biel come slithering back, gliding with a silence and grace she watched with utter envy, glad she'd done her practicing out of sight because it seemed to her she'd never equal the skills of that enigmatic pair and she'd rather like to. Time to get out of here, she thought. She gave her low breathy whistle to warn Coperic she was near, then touched his shoulder to let him know how near.

As before, he nodded. Without a word, he started creeping toward the shelter of the trees. With Bella and Biel she followed close behind.

# V

# THE BATTLE FOR THE BISERICA

## 1

They climbed to the top of the west gatetower, Dom Hern and Yael-mri, Georgia Myers and Anoike Ley, stood looking down at the army stretched out through the low hills humping up toward the Pass, gazed at movement and form half-hidden, half-seen through the glitter-haze of Nor magic. In a ragged line along the barren flat where the hills stopped, a row of norits stood staring at the wall, radiating a virulent hatred for the weapon women behind the merlons, for the Stenda, the tar-folk and villagers waiting with bows, spears or tending the fires under kettles of bubbling fat.

Hern nodded at the widely spaced dark figures. "Norits."

Georgia looked over the shorter man's shoulder. "They don't fancy y'all that much."

"They don't fancy anything that limits their power."

"Yeah. Knew a few like that back home."

Yael-mri stepped away from her slit. "Dom Georgia, domna Anoike, those men are the greatest danger we face." She looked down at long slim hands that shook a little until she shut them into fists. "It won't take them long before they find out how to deflect your missiles. Two days. If we're really blessed by fortune, three. We'd appreciate it if you'd concentrate on taking out as many of the norits as you can. However many you kill or wound, that many weakens them," she nodded at the slit, the army below, "more than a thousand men. But as soon as you notice that you can't seem to hit any more of them, forget it and use your weapons where they can do some good."

Georgia nodded, then moved to one of the broader slits in the tower's side, leaned out and looked along the wall, using the small dark forms of the defenders to help him estimate the width of the walkway behind the merlons, tried to determine how much shelter the stone uprights would give his people. Anoike joined him in the opening, her elbows poking hard into his back until he wriggled a little, tensed some muscles, and sent them sliding. She caught at his shoulders, chuckled softly. He ignored that and the pressure of her body against his, pointed to the walkway. "Wide enough, you think?"

"For a wall, it's some wide. Not no expressway. more like a back country two-laner, with them hot-pots for wide-assed road hogs, but yeah, I say Angel could ride it. If he keep his head down. Horse's head it might show, might not. Way he move, take a piece a luck for them suckers to get a shot at him, specially with bows."

"Move the delicate bod, woman, I'm coming out."

Chuckling again, she stepped away from him, stood in the center of the small square room, hands in pockets, casually hipshot, looking from Yael-mri's faintly disapproving face to the bland round countenance of Dom Hern. The glint in his eyes was familiar. She tried to look, conspicuously uninterested.

Georgia pulled his head in, rubbed the back of his fist across his chin. "We got a pretty wide front to keep an eye on. Seems to me the best thing would be posting snipers along the wall. They'd be spread thin. Need competition quality shooters here to take out your norits fast and economical. Lay my hand on fifteen maybe, counting Annie Lee here." He grinned at Anoike.

She snorted. "You payin for that, Redneck. Wait till we in the sack, I show you Annie Lee." She jerked her thumb toward the wall. "Split Angel's band, half on each side the gate, use teletalks to send 'em where they needed. How many teletalks you pick up at the armory? Got some spare batteries, I do hope. One a us up here with binocs, we could see the whole damn war. Like some crazy board game." She shook her head slowly. "Weird. Hey man, think a the wars you been hoppin around to where most the time no sucker got any idea what's happenin, especially some shithead general." She strolled over to one of the front slits and looked down. "We got us a cozy down-home war. Almost makes sense."

Hern's eyes moved from her rigid back to Georgia. "Teletalks?"

"Yeah. Since you're running this thing kinda short-handed, you could do with better communications than they got. We picked up a gross of 'em, Anoike, brand-new in the cartons, enough to tie everything into a good tight web. And batteries sealed in plastic so they should be all right unless Procurement's more rotten than usual. You know, this could be a bigger edge than rifles." He turned to Yael-mri. "What're you doing about rock-climbers?" When she continued to look blank, he moved a hand in an impatient gesture. "Sabotage teams flanking the walls. Going round through the mountains. Give me a cloudy night, some rope and a half-dozen of my folk and five'll get you a hundred, I get into the Biserica and make a dent in your Shawar. You're vulnerable there, Yael-mri, and it don't take magic to do it, just a bit of work and the motivation. Dom Hern here," he waved at Hern, "says you got something called Sleykyn assassins with one big hate for you meien. If they half like the contract killers we got back home, climbing's something they got a lot of practice in. Whoever's running that show," another wave toward the army, "he'd have to be rock from ear to ear not to think of that. And don't tell me you don't fight that way. He got 'em, he's gonna use 'em. Hate between you and Sleykyn goes back hundreds of years, the Dom says, so he gonna have no trouble getting volunteers for a suicide run. Up to you to keep it from paying off. You better have spotters watching both sides of the valley. We got spare binocs we can let you have if you want." He frowned. "No night-scopes, though, what we got we better keep on the wall." He looked from Hern to Yael-mri, shook his head. "Dumb. Me. You don't know what the hell I'm talking about. Teletalks, nightscopes, binoculars. I've seen enough here. Anoike?" She nodded. "Right. Let's get back down to the camp, I'll walk you through our gear."

Yael-mri passed a hand across the gray-streaked brown hair cut close to her finely shaped head. "War," she said. "I don't want to think about it and that keeps me half-blind." She started down the stairs walking beside Georgia. "We have some sensitives that aren't strong enough for Shawar. I'll work out relays and keep them scanning the cliffs."

Georgia chuckled. "Crystal balls?"

"Not exactly. Why?"

"No reason; this world is so much like mine I keep forgetting the ways it's different."

As she continued to circle down the stairs, hand sliding along the wall, Yael-mri shook her head. "You have to remember, Georgia Myers, you and all your folk. Remind your fighters to keep their weapons inside the wall. Shawar protection ends with the outer surface of the stone. Anything that pierces the shield, the Norim out there will catch hold of and turn for their own purposes." She was silent for another few steps, frowning. "The shield only keeps magic out, does nothing to stop anything material. The mercenary longbowmen have strong reputations for accuracy. You'd better watch yourselves." She went down and around, spoke again as they started down the last flight of stairs. "When they spot your shooters the norits will tell Nekaz Kole. The Ogogehians have something called vuurvis oil they use to spread fire that can't be put out. If your sharpshooters are easy to spot, they'll attract fireballs like lodestones."

They emerged into the chill morning, started toward the jeep that brought them from the Biserica.

"How soon's the attack going to start?" Georgia settled

himself in the seat behind the driver, watched Anoike swing up behind the wheel.

Yael-mri got awkwardly in and perched beside him, still uncomfortable around the machines. "Depends on what you mean by attack. The Nearga Nor are battering at the Shawar right now. Fierce—but we're holding for the moment. The army? I'd give them till noon to get settled in and start building the siege engines. And put some order in the camp. And the first attacks will be more probes than serious thrusts, testing our resolve and our defenses. They'll send meat against us, not their trained fighters." She raised her voice so she could be heard over the noise of the engine. "Dom, meat first, don't you think?"

He looked back, frowning, his attention plainly elsewhere. "Yes," he said. "Most likely. Though what I've heard about Nekaz Kole, he's tricky. Have to watch for changes." He stared past them a moment, then faced around, sinking into his thoughts.

## 2

Julia crouched beside the crenel, the teletalk by her knee, the head of her target clear in the scope, trying to ignore the noise of the battle going on around her, the hordes of black-clad men swarming at the wall, dying by hordes from the shafts and spears of the defenders and most horribly under the floods of the boiling fat. She drew fingers over the wood of the stock, briefly amused at having discovered such an unlikely talent so late in life. Something about her mix of eye and hand coordination made her one of the best shots Georgia had. She resettled the rifle and listened for the signal from Dom Hern; she had three possibilities in her range of vision, figured she could take out all of them before they reacted to what was happening.

The teletalk crackled. "Ready. Now."

Careful not to let the barrel broach the shield, she squeezed gently, rode the recoil, shot again, and again. Another idiot Nor rushing to see what was happening

Four. Then she began firing calmly, methodically, cleaning off the section of slope visible to her.

### 3

Tuli lay hidden above the road where first she'd looked down on the Biserica valley, burrowed into a thick stand of dead brush, Ildas nestling against her side. Coperic and the others were scattered about the slope around her; she didn't know exactly where, it didn't matter, there wasn't much they could do, the last days there'd never been much they could do. She watched the army flowing over the foothills, the disparate parts settling out of the mass like cream clotting into cheese, the norits lining up to glare at the wall and the answering shimmer of the Shawar shield.

And the demon chini trotted alertly along the ragged, shifting rear of the army, demon sicamars pacing silent and deadly in unnatural proximity to these their natural enemies, the red eyes of both sorts sweeping the slopes above them. Now and then, one of them, chini or sicamar, would dart upward, feet barely touching earth, dive behind scatters or rock or into clumps of brush. Sometimes there'd be a shriek, sometimes just a rattle of rock, sometimes shreds of movement more guessed at than seen, and the demon beast would go placidly back to his patrol.

Tuli watched grimly, knowing the next victim could be her or Coperic or anyone. Even Ildas was an uncertain ally. He was both repelled and terrified by them, would act against them only if she were under immediate and inescapable threat. She looked away from the demons. Smoke rose in lazy spirals from the fat-kettles dotted along the wall; she caught glimpses of figures through the embrasures, more dark spots moving about the distant Biserica; she could hear loud roaring sounds that bothered her with their strangeness, noted some things moving with a speed that startled her and convinced her she was watching phantoms, nothing real. She sighed and went back to looking for possible vulnerabilities in the army.

*     *     *

When the Minarks had waked after she'd painted the lordling, there was a mad flurry that almost spread to the units
of the army camped nearest to them, when they woke to
find sentries bypassed and sleepers among them with their
throats slashed. Coperic and the others watched with deep
satisfaction as the attendants standing watch were beaten
to death with the spiked ball at the end of the lance the
Minark lordling carried, the painted man howling and
grimacing as he tore the flesh from their bones; when he
was finished, he went into a frenzied dance that ended
when he sliced open his own throat and went over backward under a fountain of blood. An hour later all the
Minarks and their remaining attendants were packed and
riding away from the army; the lordling's body was rolled
in cloth and tied onto his rambut; the bodies of the attendants were left lying where they fell. Tuli was appalled by
the violence but at the same time delighted by the out-
come. Her single act had removed almost a hundred fighters from the army; she'd expected some result but not so
dramatic a success.

The next night there were too many norits about and
traxim flying low in search patterns over the ground about
the army; the band kept back, watched other groups of
attackers fall to the Nor-fire and the arrows of aroused and
angry soldiers. For two more days Coperic led them after
the army; they circled it at night, looking for opportunity
to inflict hurt without getting killed themselves, uselessly
killed like so many of the others trying to nibble at the
edges of the army. Coperic had some hope of the vigilance
abating because of the ease with which the raiders were
being slaughtered. Before that happened, the army came
even with the Kotsila Pass and the force from Sankoy
came down to join the larger force from Oras, bringing
another swarm of norits, black lice to infest the Plain. Four
of these were something more than the rest, clothed in
arrogance and power so complete they seemed—and probably were—on the verge of leaping the chasm from norit to
noris. They rode apart from the others, mounted on black
fire-eyed beasts, macain in shape but not in spirit. Clus

tered around them, pacing with a terrible sureness and an arrogance equal to their masters', came a pack of demon chini and sicamars. Tuli counted fifteen of the black beasts. Interrupting her thoughts with silent whimpers, Ildas cowered against her, sliding into cloth and flesh until he was nestling within her body. She tried to comfort him, but her efforts lacked conviction. Those beasts terrified her quite as much as they did him.

The demons took over the night-guard and after that the army slept in peace, even though the pinpricks from the raiders continued. Coperic kept his distance. Even Bella and Biel were subdued. On the third night after the demons came they got close as they could, perched in trees of a small grove, watching the demon beasts pacing about the great blotch of sleeping men covering the slopes. From where she crouched high in the arms of a denuded brellim, Tuli saw three Stenda boys evade the demon guards, creep into a small herd of macain, saw them cut out a mount for each, slide up onto them and set them leaping for the shelter of the hills. They got about a dozen strides before a single black form came after them and was on them, red eyes burning, red mouth open, teeth like curved black daggers dripping fire. Though the boys tried to fight, metal wouldn't cut the black flesh, blows wouldn't bruise it. A swipe of a forepaw opened one boy from neck to crotch, a crunch of the dagger teeth and a second boy lost his head, a third was torn to bits and shaken into a dozen pieces that sprayed about as if the body had exploded; the macain fell to casual blows that seemed easy as caresses. The beast began playing with the bodies, shaking them, clawing them apart, mixing macai flesh and Stenda, even tearing up the grass and dirt, until he got bored with that and stood in the middle of the havoc he'd created, staring at the trees, his head moving from side to side, his nostrils flaring, his ears pricking forward, his eyes searching the darkness under the trees. Tuli fought the panic that was spurring her into hopeless flight and froze against the tree, knowing the others scattered about were flooded with the same overwhelming terror and priming themselves for the desperate and probably futile struggle to come. Ildas keened in her head and she almost lost control of herself. The demon sicamar took a step forward, stopped and listened, came on again.

Ildas gave a wild despairing cry and left Tuli, but before she would react to that, he was a great quivering sail of fire, gossamer thin, reaching from the ground to the tree-tops, interposed between Coperic's band and the demon beast. She could see the black sicamar through the veil, saw him lose his alertness, saw him turn his head from side to side a last time, saw him shrug his shoulders, saw him go trotting off. The veil shifted with him, keeping itself between the demon and the band. Tuli felt the fireborn's terror and revulsion, dug her fingers into the bark, somehow sucked strength up through the tree and fed it into him until he hummed with it, his confidence burning brighter and brighter as the demon sicamar trot-ted off. A moment more and he snapped back into himself. He sat on the branch beside her, preening his sides and oozing satisfaction.

After that, Coperic, Tuli and the others kept following the army, unwilling to give up the hope of inflicting more damage on it, no matter how minor, but they stayed well away from it when the demons were loose. They could only follow and wait for the battle to engage the attention of the norits and their beasts so they could again fight for the life they'd known and wanted back again.

Cold knots in her stomach, Tuli watched the Followers swarm at a section of the Wall, watched them falling from the arrows and crossbow bolts raining on them, watched them press on, those behind climbing over the dead, tak-ing up the crude ladders the dead had carried and pressing on the wall, falling themselves under the scald of the boiling burning fat. Then, over the screams of the dying the shouts of the attackers, she heard a rapid crackling that kept up for some minutes, a strange sound that resembled nothing she'd heard before unless it was the popping of posser belly meat frying in its own fat. The norits began falling; they were far beyond the reach of bow or cross-bow, even beyond range of the catapults, but they fell; in seconds half of them were down, some screaming and flinging themselves about, some crumpled and silent. For several more seconds the norits milled about in utter confusion, more of them falling, dying, then they were running, diving into the reserves, diving behind rocks or clumps of brush, anything to get out of sight of the wall. She dug her fingers into the earth, hardly able to breathe, hope more painful than the despair that had haunted her the past days.

The crackling went on and on and the attack of the tie-conscripts faltered as the mysterious death scythed through them. A few moments later they too were retreating in disorder, flinging themselves in a panic after the panicking norits. Then all along the mountain slopes, as if that were the one key that unloosed them, Stenda and outcasts, tie-folk and tar-men, all those left after the slaughter on the Plain, they flung themselves on the backside of the army, fighting with scythes and pruning hooks, knives and staves and ancient pikes, anything they'd found that could inflict a wound.

For some minutes the confusion continued and the ill-armed, leaderless attackers gnawed deeper into the army, killing majilarni and tie-conscripts, Plaz guards and a few of the mercenaries, though these trained fighters quickly organized themselves into defensive knots and took out most of those that came at them. Sleykyn assassins slaughtered any who dared attack them. Then Nekaz Kile got busy, sending bands of mounted mercenaries rushing in both directions from the road, squads of three peeling off at each center of disturbance and fighting with a methodical deadliness that steadied whatever section of the army fought there, and turned the attack to rout. The near-noris Four horned their beasts into order and sent them against the attackers; though their numbers were few, not more than fifteen, their deadliness and the terror they breathed out sent everyone within a dozen body-lengths into desperate flight, flight that was seldom escape; they were too fast, those demon beasts, leaping along the mountainside fast as thought, with no sign of fatigue.

The attackers began to melt away, leaving a large percentage of their number dead on the slopes, pursued by the demon beasts that reveled in their slaughter, filling the mountains with chopped-off shrieks.

Tuli clung to her hiding place, hoping silence and stillness and ultimately Ildas would protect her better than flight. Now and then over the screams and rattles of the fleeing, she heard softer and far less shaped sounds, the others in Coperic's band slipping away; she sent her blessings after them but stayed where she was, watching what was happening below.

The commotion began to settle. Nekaz Kole rode back and forth along the line, his guard flying behind him, quelling confusion and reorganizing the shattered army, sending a delegation under a white flag to arrange for the collection of the dead and wounded, got the cooks working, preparing meals back in the hills under guard of the norits; the raiders still alive were almost cleared away; the demon beasts were trotting back to their masters, most of them, one or two still nosing out knots of attackers gone to ground when they saw the result of the flight of the rest.

Tuli froze. Two shadows were moving through the brush below her. She saw a clawed hand reaching, twisted and brown like ancient tree roots, clumps of yellow-white hair escaping from under a dark kerchief tied about the man's head, dark worn shirt baggy about a narrow body, slightly bowed legs in leather trousers, strong square feet in soft shapeless boots. A gnarled, tough old man moving with taut silence across the small cleared area, making no sound at all on the treacherous scree and bits of dead brush.

And behind him, one she knew almost as well as she knew herself, who for a while had been another self Teras. Hars and Teras, both still alive. She wanted to call to them. She wanted desperately to call to them, but she didn't. They were getting away clear, would soon enough be beyond the reach of the demon beasts, reined in as they were by the Four below. She watched Teras as long as she could see any bit of him, weak with the joy of finding him still alive, not one of the corpses abandoned by the side of the Highroad. She wanted to whoop and dance her joy but could not. It seemed intolerable that she had to lay still as the stone around her or betray both of them, but she managed it. All too soon, slow as he was moving, he was out of sight, creeping on up the mountain toward some rendezvous she knew nothing of, perhaps with more of the outcasts from Haven. She lay in an agony of stillness, her forehead on her crossed arms, breathing in the dry red dust of the mountain, grinning like a fool, weak as a new-hatched oadat.

Ildas nudged at her, nipped gently at her rib when he couldn't get her attention; as she started to move, he yipped a warning. Slowly and carefully she raised her head, trying not to gasp in dismay. A demon chini stood in the clear space below, sniffing at the scree where Hars and Teras had passed. As if he sensed her watching, he lifted his head and stared toward her. Helplessly she lay where she was, watching him take two steps on the spoor of Hars and Teras, then lift his head again and look toward her as if he weighed whether to take her first or continue after the raiders. Ildas trembled and wailed his terror, silent cries that tore along her spine and bounced about her head. The demon chini shook his black head as if his floppy ears hurt, then started up the slope toward her.

Not her, she realized suddenly. Two more chinin burst from the brush to her left and bounded down toward the demon, dark russet beasts with pointed black ears and black masks over blunt muzzles, amber eyes that shone like molten gold, a sturdy bitch and a slightly smaller male. Rushing to their death, Tuli thought. Again she had to change her mind. Shifting almost as fast as the demon, they dodged his first careless swipe, splitting to attack him on two sides, the male distracting him while the bitch threw her body solidly against him, knocking him off his feet. Then they switched roles. Dependent so long on his terrible strength, he didn't seem to learn but repeated his mistakes over and over, while the other two handled him almost at will, keeping him confused and ruining his timing. But the chini pair were tiring; gallant as their attack was, they could not hurt the thing, their own teeth and claws won no purchase in the slick hide while the demon seemed to draw strength in with the air he breathed. Tuli dug her fingers into the dirt and tried to think. Strength alone wasn't going to win this; the advantage belonged to the demon. Wits and knowledge—watching the chinin fight their impossible battle, she thought of Coperic and the band, all of them still alive in spite of the dangers they'd faced. Courage and strength wasn't enough, guile was needed also and was more important than the other two. Guile—she frowned at the two chinin moving round and round the demon, avoiding his rushes, pinning him to the clearing with his lust to kill them; he could have brushed by them easily enough, gone on and left them behind, but the will to escape was not in him. And time was short. She could see the strain in the gait of the chinin, fatigue in the slowing of their escapes. She tore eyes from the contest and stared at the sky, trying to think—and saw the faint spirals of smoke rising from the fires on the wall. Fire. Traxim on fire and screeching with the pain, traxim on fire and plunging dead into the army, traxim fleeing this world to escape the fire. Another sort of demon, but still a demon. She watched the sturdy young male knock the demon rolling and dart away, bleeding from his rump where the demon's claw had caught him. *Ildas*, she whispered, *remember the traxim, the burning demons*. He whined and wriggled, tried to deny he heard her, but quieted as she cupped a hand about his buttocks and held him close. *Burn that beast, you can do it, remember the burning traxim. Next time the chinin knock him down, burn him, while he's going down he won't be able to defend himself, he'll be depending on his iron skin and his iron strength, concentrating on getting his balance back. Burn him.* Without waiting for an answer, she scooped him up and thrust herself recklessly through the brush too excited to notice the pain from the gouging of broken branches. When she emerged, the chinin took advantage of the distraction she provided to knock the demon off his feet again. As he fell, she flung the fireborn at him.

Ildas flattened and whipped around him, a skin of fire over the black body. The demon howled and went end over end in a torment greater than any he'd inflicted on his own victims, a torment that somehow split him into two parts, the skin and skeleton of an ordinary though rather large chini and a black cloud that held for a moment the chini shape then melted like smoke into the air. Then Ildas was tumbling away from him, away from skin and bones smoldering with a sullen stench, more smoke than fire. The fireborn sat on his haunches grinning at the mess, but after a moment he went over to it, lifted a leg and urinated a stream of his own fire into it. With a sudden whoosh, the skin and bones seared to ash. The two chinin limped over to Tuli and stood panting beside her, giving small yips of pleasure while the demon died, a twinned howl of triumph at that last sudden flash of destruction. Ildas trotted back to Tuli, sleek with pride and complacency. When she opened her arms, he leaped into them and lay against her chest vibrating his triumph into her bones.

"Yes," she crooned to him. "You're a wonder and a warrior, my Didi." Stroking him still she looked at the two chinin, saw them watching, knew they saw Ildas as clearly as she did—all she needed to recognize the bitch. "I know you," she said. "One of you. Time we left here. Any ideas? Right." Weary and filled with wonder, she started trudging up the slope, following the chini bitch, the young male following her.

## 4

Their engineers hidden by heavy plank barriers, the Ogogehian catapults hurled roughly shaped stones at the wall, stone thudding against stone with a steady malevolence, hammering at the same spots day and night. But even the thinner merlons were holding. As far as Julia could tell, the pounding could go on forever with much the same result. Praise whatever gods there be, she thought, no explosives here. She grimaced. Not until we make them. As several shafts came humming through the slit, she dodged behind the merlon, then she knelt and began picking off as many of the Plaz Guards as she could find in the ranks of the black-clad men massing for another go at scaling the wall, then started on the front ranks of the attack force, shooting quickly but deliberately, piling up the dead. Behind her she heard the clatter of hooves. Angel slid off his mount the next embrasure over, his youths spreading out to other crenels, sinking onto their knees, starting to shoot as soon as they were balanced, sharing each of the embrasures with the meien as she shared hers with the ex-meie Rane. She closed off all thought and concentrated on her targets.

Norim and Plaz Guards drove the black tide forward in spite of the confusion and disruption she'd started in them; fighters and leaders alike were getting used to the rifles and no longer panicking at the first crackles as they had earlier. As the wave came on and reached bow range, she backed out of the embrasure and let Rane take over. The meie had a pair of crossbows loaded and ready, a bundle of quarrels she tossed to Julia. She fired, flipped the bow back to Julia, fired the second, exchanged that for the reloaded bow. Julia clawed the string back, dropped in a new bolt, caught the emptied bow and passed the other over, a steady automatic movement so familiar now she didn't have to think what she was doing.

Behind and below she heard the roaring of motorcycles. Someone wounded, she thought. The motorcycles were carrying the young trainee healwomen (Julia thought of them as medics) to the wounded as helicopters had done on her own world. Dom Hern in his tower dispatching reinforcements, then the medics. Up there with his binoculars and teletalk, running his little war with those alien instruments as if he'd been born to them. And right now, managing to hold off the hordes coming at him. Five hundred and a wall holding off thousands, five hundred kept intact by those healwomen and the exile doctors, Lou and what was her name? the surgeon they fished out of the introg. Doesn't matter. She switched bows with Rane, clawed back the bowstring, slapped in a new bolt, switched again. Defenders fell on either side. An arrow whispered past Rane's shoulder. Julia jerked away, felt the flutter of its passage, heard it crash against the low guardwall behind her. Rane ignored it, reached back for the bow Julia held, locked the aim and fired, flipped it back, took the loaded bow and fired. And so on and on. The medics bent over the wounded, stopped bloodflows, did a little rough surgery. If they could walk, the wounded were sent down the backramps; if they couldn't, they were carried down on stretchers, all of them were loaded into the back of a pickup and carried to the field hospital set up in a tent straddling the rutted road leading from the great gates to the main Biserica buildings where it would be equally accessible to both wings of the wall.

" 'Ware fat." The yell was loud and close.

Julia scrambled away from the embrasure, Rane tumbling to the other side. Two well-grown girls came up, the poles of the fatpot on their shoulders, a third used a clawed lever to tilt the bubbling stinking fat along the grotesquely elongated lip and out the embrasure, spilling the fat on the men below until the pot was empty. Screams and curses, groans and shouts rose to her with the stink of the oil, the sounds of men scrambling away. When the pot was empty the girls went trotting back to the big kettle for another load.

Rane leaped to her feet, sword out, and ran down the walkway.

Several ladders projected above the merlons and men were coming off them onto the walkway. Meien and other defenders ran at them from all around, but dropped to their knees as Angel and his youths leaped up and began shooting, cutting the men down as they stuck their heads up. Several Stenda men were using their longer reach to get at the ladders, but were driven back again and again by the clumsy thrusts of the invaders' pikes. Julia caught up her rifle, checked the clip, but stood where she was, watching with a frown as enough of the men got over in spite of Angel to make further shooting a danger to the defenders.

A lanky half-grown Stenda boy swung up on a merlon, ignoring the shafts aimed at him, and leaped from one to the next until he was close enough to use his lance on a ladder. He reversed it, swung it back and slammed the butt into that ladder, sending it sliding along the smooth stone face of the wall, knocking into the next ladder over, shoving that into the third that also slid away. As the ladders and the men on them tumbled away, he started a whooping dance where he was, a mountain boy with no fear of heights. Julia swore and dived into the embrasure, began sweeping the hills where the bulk of the army had found shelter, shooting at anyone who stuck his head up, intent on distracting longbowmen and everyone else out there until someone with a bit of sense could yank that young idiot off the wall.

A hand touched her shoulder. She sat back on her heels, cradled the rifle on her thighs, looked around. Rane, back from the mélée. "Did someone get that idiot down?"

"After he took a shaft in the shoulder."

"Teach him anything?"

"Doubt it." Rane chuckled. "Didn't stop grinning even when Dina was sawing at the shaft and pulling it out of him."

Julia shook her head. "Him and Angel's bunch. Seems that kids are the same wherever they grow up."

Rane chuckled again, and began wiping her sword carefully with a bit of soft leather.

Farther down the wall Angel was cursing as he cut an arrow from a horse's flank. There was a girl in healerwhite holding the beast's head and soothing it while he worked. Another horse was down, dead. Stenda men and mijlockers were using pikes and ropes to pry it up over the knee-high guardwall. More of the white-clad girl medics were helping the wounded down the ramp, a slightly older medic was kneeling beside one of the mijlockers, working on a wound in his leg. As the wounded were helped away, reinforcements came up to take their places. Five hundred against five thousand. But they were holding the wall, a precarious hold maintained by Hern's careful use of his fighters, by the quick medical treatment, by the tireless efforts of Serroi. They were holding, but Kole hadn't sent his trained fighters against them yet, he was using the conscripts to wear them down, use up their ammunition, tire them out, whittle away at their numbers. Julia got to her feet, unclipped the canteen from her belt, unscrewed the lid and took a drink. The tepid, metal-tainted water went down fast and easy, cut the dust in her throat and washed away some of the sourness that came into her mouth when she thought of all the killing. She used her rifle with skill and coolness, concentrating on doing it well while she was in the midst of the skirmishes, concentrating on swallowing her loathing for the whole business when it was over. She passed the canteen to Rane. "How close was this one?" She took the canteen back, clipped it onto her belt. "I was too busy to watch."

Rane waited until the motor roar from below died down a little. "Got more over the wall this time. You saw Hakel doing his dance. He got off lighter than he should but he stopped them." She scowled back along the wall. "My sister's son. He does something like that again and I twist his ear for him." Julia smiled to herself at the reluctant pride in Rane's voice. The ex-meie went on, "We have five prisoners, the rest that got over are dead. Our side, three dead, a dozen wounded, six of them bad, don't know if they can get them to Serroi in time, the rest, arms or legs or a scrape. Most of them ready to be back on the wall tomorrow, blessed be *She* for giving us Serroi."

Julia looked past her, saw two men lifting a boy and putting him on a stretcher; his head swung to one side and she saw his face, the gap-toothed, silent scream, as they lifted him. Rudy. She sighed, rubbed her hand across her face. Nothing new for him, his life was one bloody wound. She didn't know if he could remember any happy times, though there should have been some good moments when he was with his family and they were still working their land.

Liz touched Julia's shoulder. "Time's up, Julia. Catch a ride to the shelter and get something to eat." She squatted beside the crenel, her companion meie with her, Leeshan, a golden minark who looked too small-boned and fragile to fight. "We'll keep the nasties off you."

"Hah." Julia slung the rifle over her shoulder, glanced at the men and women hoisting the dead attackers into the crenels and shoving them off to fall at the base of the wall. "They should be quiet a while now."

Julia and Rane trudged down the nearest ramp and snagged a ride in the pickup ambulance. The day was bright and cold but there were banks of clouds in the west and a dampness in the air that promised rain and chilled her bones. Julia was grateful for the fur-lined boots Rane had found for her. Must have belonged to a Stenda because the mijlockers had chunky square feet that made hers look like rails. They were a healthy bunch for the feudal society they lived in. An eon ago when she was working with Simon, he'd got her interested in the middle ages where the lives of the peasants and the poor were best described as nasty, brutish and short, however it offended her writer's ear to use such an overworked set of words. Even the older tie-men seemed sturdy enough, no signs of malnutrition. They'd obviously worked hard all their lives; their hands and the way they stood and walked spoke eloquently of that, but they weren't beaten down or dullwitted. There was one old tie who claimed seventy years; he was alert and active, a gnarled root of a man ready for another seventy if he wasn't killed in this siege. From the little she'd seen of the way they lived, they had the Biserica, the healwomen and the teachings of the Keepers to thank for that, not only for their medical care but for the emphasis on cleanliness of body and house. And there was always the magic. Simon was fascinated by how that capriciously accessible power had shaped lives here, the subtle and not so subtle differences he was finding in a society with much the same social patterns and degree of technology as those medieval societies he knew so well; whenever he could, he hung around the Biserica library with its impressive collection of hand lettered books and scrolls. The printing press was going to be an eye-opener on this world. Julia grinned as she thought about the subversive role books had always played back home. That'll shake them up if nothing else does.

The pickup rattled to a stop, letting them off at the huge canvas shelter where most of the defenders not on the wall spent their time. Heat, laughter, cheerful voices, food smells hit her in the face and gave her a lift as they always did when she came here. Girls were everywhere, eating, serving, collecting plates, running errands, chattering, sitting in groups working not too hard on fletching arrows; Stenda girls, lanky and blonde; minarks, all shades of brown with tilted black eyes and brown hair ranging from fawn to chocolate; black girls from the Fenakel, green-scaled sea-girls, other types she couldn't name, not knowing the world well enough; but most of all there were the slim brown girls from the mijloc, dozens of them, ranging from twelve to sixteen, a little frightened at what was happening, but coping with it, the brightest and most spirited girls of the Plain, many of them here against the will of their kin. Not all nice and sweet. There were greedy girls, lazy girls, quarrelsome ones, arrogant ones, girls with the need to dominate all around them, sly girls and sneaks, yet with all their flaws even the worst of them were fiercely determined to defend the Biserica, sure with the simplicity and arrogance of youth that they were going to win. Julia found it exhilarating to step into that bubbling mix, though she knew the dream for what it was. She picked up a tray and followed Rane to one of the quieter corners.

Meat stew in a rich brown sauce; a mound of white cillix, a ricelike grain with a sweeter, nuttier flavor; a cup of steaming strong cha; a hunk of fresh bread torn from a round loaf. Julia ate with appreciation and dispatch, not talking until the edge was taken off her appetite. Finally she set the tray on the ground beside her and sat sipping at

the cha, a little sleepy with the weight of the food. She
turned to Rane. "What are you going to do when this is
over?"

Rane looked out over the noisy scene. The corner of her
wide mouth curled up. "I'm tired of rambling. Think I'll
move in with your folk if you all don't mind."

"Not here?"

"Too much of my life buried here."


## 5

The pounding continued. Day and night waves of men
rolled against the wall; the black-clad Follower-conscripts,
grim but clumsy and ill-trained; whooping Majilarni, gal-
loping in swift arcs at the wall, loosing their arrows in a
deadly rain; sullen Sankoise, fighting with half their minds
on the norits driving them at the wall. Each day there
were more dead among the defenders, more names engraved on the roll of the dead in the Watchhall: meien,
Stendas, mijlockers, exiles male and female—a slow attri-
tion, every wounded fighter salvaged if he or she reached
Serroi alive. The healer lived in a steady daze, touching,
touching, a green glass figurine, the earth fire constant in
her as long as she walked between the pallets of the
wounded. Girls died too, skewered by stray arrows shot
blind from behind rough walls hastily slapped together to
hide them from the seeking rifles. Girls dropped exhausted,
burned by the fat fires, wounded, their exuberance settling
to a sullen stubbornness. Twice during that tenday small
bands of Sleykynin came creeping down the cliffs, trying
to get down behind the Biserica so they could strike at the
Shawar. Each time the watching sensitives gave warning,
then guided a pickup with fighters packed into the open
back to the place where the Sleykynin were descending.
Pinned against the rough stone by a battery powered search-
light, the Sleykynin died, all of them, five the first time,
three the second.

The first night raid, the exile Ram saw the traxim
circling overhead and knew enough about them to know

they were transmitting images back to the norits. He hissed
and lifted his rifle, but meie Tebiz put her hand on his
arm. "No use," she said. "Don't waste time. Or ammunition."

Three nights later in a localized rainstorm that killed the
fires under the fat kettles, Majilarni came at the east end of
the wall, hurling their short lances into high arcs that came
whistling down among the defenders. Near the great gates
several squads of mercenaries came at a trot toward the
wall, linked rawhide shields turning the crossbow quarrels, further protected by a rain of shafts from the
longbowmen on the hills behind them, their companion
moardats flying at the embrasures between flights of arrows, slashing at the defenders with poisoned claws, diving at eyes and throat, distracting them, making it harder
than ever to stop the ladders from going into place until
once again exiles and meien combined, meien swords holding off the moardats while exile rifles opened large gaps on
the linked shields over the heads of the advancing mercenaries. At the same time a clot of Sleykynin were creeping
toward the west end of the wall and got unnoticed to its
base. They were swinging their grapples by the time Hern
spotted them with the nightscope and sent Angel and his
fighters racing along the wall to reinforce the thinned-out
defenders (half their number had gone rushing to fight by
the west tower). Flashlights flared, catching the Sleykynin
unprepared and awkwardly placed, the meien skewering
half of them, the other half dropping away and scurrying
back to the shelter of the hills.

The pickups rattled back and forth, carrying the wounded
to the field hospital, the motorcycles *whooroomed* back and
forth carrying the medics, while meien, Stenda, mijlockers
and exiles fought off the Sankoise who endured for a short
while then fled to huddle round their fires and curse the
meien and curse their masters and curse the rain, the cold,
the night. In the center of the wall the mercenaries got
their ladders up and came flooding onto the walkway and
the fighting was fierce, hand to hand on slippery stone, in
rain and dark, a muddy wet cold confusion of hacking and
grunts and screams and curses, until. . . .

Roar of motors, cut off suddenly, great white eyes of light suddenly unleashed, exiles pouring out of trucks, a sudden blatting of horns. The defenders drop to hands and knees and crawl away if they can do so without being slaughtered or drop flat, or retreat however they can. Seconds after that a chattering sound from big guns mounted on the backs of the trucks, louder and more menacing than the quiet sharp snaps of the rifles. And far deadlier, chopping the Ogogehians off their feet except for the few quick enough to guess what is coming and drop below the guardwall instants after the defenders drop. The rest coming up the ladders retreat quickly and pass in good order to the shelter of the hills. Then it is over. Seconds only. Half a dozen heartbeats, half a hundred men dead or dying, lying in bloody heaps in the fringes of the blinding white light.

A few of the defenders were clipped by the bullets, but none was seriously wounded. They drove the last mercenaries back over the walls and threw the dead down on them. Another fifteen minutes, and the wall was cleared.

While these attacks were holding the attention of Hern and the greater part of the Biserica defense, two more bands of Sleykynin were making their way down the rugged slopes on both sides of the wide waist of the valley, many stadia beyond the cliffs where the first attempts were made, gambling that Hern and Yael-mri would have committed all their forces to the wall and, even if they hadn't, that there was no way they could get fighters there in time to stop the infiltration. The sides of the valley at that point were almost as steep as at the cliffs, the going almost as treacherous, but the stone was broken, with bits of soil trapped in tiny terraces, scraggly brush and spears of prickly broom scattered about, clumps of dry grass, much more cover, certainly enough for these veteran assassins to come down without showing more than an occasional patch of dulled leather. They moved carefully and confidently, without noise as a matter of pride though there was no one but themselves to hear any sounds they made.

The sensitives smelled them out and warned Yael-mri.

After kicking a chair across the room and demanding where she was going to find fighters, she used the teletalk to round up some of the wounded who were still able to get about, pulled two pickups from the mercy runs and went to the arms dump to look over what she had while they armed themselves, two bands of six, a mixture drawn from all those helping to defend the Biserica. "The sense-web locates them about halfway down the valley," she said. "You've got to get them all. If any of them get past you . . . if they get to the Shawar. . . ." She looked at the battered weary fighters and sighed. Exile Pandrashi, muscle and sinew like polished stone showing through his torn shirt, a bandage on one arm, a still oozing scrape that went up the side of his square face. Young exile Rudy with a bloody scab on his knee visible through torn jeans, the top of one ear gone, but his eyes were bright with excitement and his gap-tooth grin cut his thin face in half. Meia Asche-helai, left shoulder heavily bandaged, hair still clotted with the blood of the man she killed; she was right-eyed and could use a crossbow in spite of her wound. Meie Jiddellin her shieldmate. Stenda boy Pormonno, a rag about one leg, another about his upper arm, cuddling a bundle of short javelins against his side. Sensitive Afonya Less, horror dark in her dark brown eyes, her mouth set in a stubborn line, lips pinched together so hard they were invisible. The sensitives hated these hunts, feeling every wound, all the hate and fear and rage in the men they tracked, dying every death, but they faced that torment without complaint because they knew what would happen if the Sleykynin got to the Shawar. Yael-mri made a mental note to see the Ammu Rin and have sleep drugs ready when the pickups returned. She turned to the second band.

Exile Liz Edelmann, no visible wound but a slightly mad look in her black eyes. (Yael-mri remembered after a moment that Serroi had just finished healing a sword cut

in her side that had nearly separated her into two parts.)
Ex-Plaz guard Mardian, one of those who'd showed up
just before the army poured through the pass; another of
Serroi's patients, an arrow through an artery, almost emptying him before the trainee healwoman could stop the
bleeding. Meie Vapro, meie Nurii, both minor wounds.
Nurii was limping but not in much pain from the scrape
on the side of her leg. Exile Ram, his dusky face com-
posed, his slight body relaxed, an anticipatory smile that
found no echo in his eyes, another of the just-healed,
Yael-mri didn't know how bad the wound had been, though
she did know it was the fifth time he'd needed Serroi's
touch. She looked away from him not quite sure she could
endure that kind of buffeting and return for more. We'll
all go more than a little odd before this insanity has finished with us. Shayl, I hate this, using them until they've
nothing left inside. She sucked in a breath. "You've got to
get them all," she repeated firmly. "There's no one else."
She scanned the faces and abandoned the rest of her speech;
they knew the urgency better than she did. "Maiden bless
you," she said. "And keep you from the beast."

Since the searchlights were tied up at the wall, Cordelia
Gudon (put in charge of stores because of her phenomenal
memory and her ability to organize on the run) hunted
them out some parachute flares and flare guns, scowled
with affectionate concern at them, then went rummaging
through boxes and brought out some grenades. "In case
you have to get close," she said. "I heard those Sleyks can
be real bastards."

After a drive down the valley that none of them wanted
to remember later, the pickups split and raced, shuddering
over the rough ground, to the places where the assassins
were coming down, catching them on the last slope still
about a hundred feet up and coming across bare stone.
When the flares went off, Pandrashi counted six in the
east-side band, Liz counted five in the west-side band. On
both sides of the valley the meien, exiles and others killed
three Sleykynin before their dazzled eyes cleared and they
scrambled for cover. When the flares died, the sensitives

uncurled from their pain-battered knots and went grimly along with the hunters as they tracked down the wounded and finished them off, a dangerous and ugly task. A wounded Sleykyn fighting for his life—or fighting to take as many with him as he can—is the deadliest beast in this world or any other. Rudy went past some low half-dead brush with a bit of shadow that seemed too meager to hide a chini pup, and died from a poison knife thrown with deadly accuracy, while Asche-helai came too close behind him to escape from the velater whip that wrapped around her neck, cutting it to the bone before Pandrashi put a single bullet through the Sleykyn's spine. Two dead in two seconds. The other Sleykynin fell to the guns without getting close enough to take anyone with them. On the west side, the last Sleykyn there spent his strength and will to reach the sensitive Magy Fa, killing her with his hands an instant before Liz blew his skull to bloody shards. She stood over him staring down at him until Ram touched her arm. "Five out of five," he said. He looked down at Magy Fa lying in a tangled embrace with her slayer. "No more nightmares. That's something anyway."

Liz drew her fingers absently along the rifle's stock. "Looks to me like we changed worlds without changing anything else."

Ram shrugged. "In this place, Doubter, we make a difference; where we were, we made none."

Liz made a small violent gesture, then strode off toward the pickup.

**6**

Gaunt and half-starved, Tuli prowled along the backside of the army, Ajjin and Allazo beside her running boldly in their four-foot forms. They had it down to a game now, a game they played with fierce pleasure, a game they always won because the demon beasts seemed unable to learn its rules. Coperic and the others of his band were scattered along the line of the army, preferring to stay as far from demons and norits as they could manage, whether they were ambushing stray soldiers or cutting out rambuts to butcher for their meals. The food they'd brought was gone, what game might roam here in ordinary times had retreated to safer, more silent slopes. Tuli and Coperic and the rest of the band lived off rambuts now, sharing them from time to time with the silent deadly Kulaan who'd come south to avenge their linas and who were going to continue their killing as long as they could crawl. Or with the remnants of the outcast bands, hungry ragged men and boys as feral as a pack of addichinin. Rambut meat was stringy and tough with little fat to flavor it, but it kept them going.

Most of the mijlockers were gone. After the first tenday half of them were dead and the rest were beginning to starve; they'd begun to melt away, leaving the dead behind to be buried hastily in the muck by work parties from the army. The futility of what they were doing and the lack of food sapped their will, so they went back to the deserted tars and empty villages to find what shelter and food they could and sit listlessly waiting for the war to end. Or they'd gone to the Havens to help fight off the Kapperim. As Hars and Teras must have done. Though she'd watched for them, she hadn't seen either of them again. What little news she'd picked up from the mijlockers sharing fire and half-raw meat with Coperic's band was not comforting. The Kapperim had gathered and were attacking all the outcast Havens, trying to wipe them out. Some nights she dreamed of her family and cried in her sleep because she wasn't with them. She fretted about not being with them, wondering what possible good she was doing here, helping Coperic flea and Bella flea and Biel flea and Ryml, Lehat, Karal, Sosai, Charda, Pyvin and Wohpa fleas take tiny bites from the flank of the monster that darkened the hillsides. But there was always the Game to take her mind off brooding and under the brooding there was the calm knowledge that she'd be doing far less if she was where her father could keep an eye on her.

She settled into the shade of some brush on a hillside above the section of wall where the Sankoise were. Coperic had been concentrating on the Majilarni and the Sankoise, pricking them into disaffection. During the first days of the siege when norits were falling like dying moths, Coperic and all of them had crept with near impunity among the skittish Sankoise, picking off one after another as they ran for cover. They were mostly town-bred men or sailors conscripted off Sankoise merchant ships. The wild country around them disturbed, even frightened, them. They were intensely superstitious; coming from a mage-ridden land, they saw omens in every turn of a leaf and the deaths, the throats cut, the men strangled, or left with skulls crushed, the rambuts lost, the equipment destroyed, all this worked on them until they began to settle into the mud like rotting logs. Kole was forced to call on his shrinking force of norits, leaving a good number of them with the Sankoise to weave alarum spells about the camps so the raids stopped and the men could sleep in such peace as they could find on the cold and uncomfortable slopes.

Tuli sat on her hillside watching them with considerable satisfaction as they wandered unhappily about, or knelt on blankets gambling or sought escape in sleep. The day was coming when even their centuries of conditioned nor-fear would no longer drive them to the wall. She lost her contentment when she looked toward the great Gate. Nekaz Kole was getting the walking towers built far faster than she liked. She scowled, got to her feet and went back to hunting demon beasts. That was a danger she could do something about.

## 7

A full day after the towers were completed, they sat on their rollers, three tapering fingers of wood pointed at the sky; early the next morning Ogogehians brought teams of massive draft hauhaus to them, six in each hitch. With hauhaus digging their split hooves into the mud and shoving with mighty shoulders against the harness, with norits riding beside each team to turn aside all missiles, the towers began to inch forward, rocking precariously even at that creeping pace, getting stuck repeatedly in the slush left behind by the attacking rain until one of the Four got impatient and pulled the water from the soil in a flash of steam and a mighty hissing. Slowly, inexorably, the towers moved toward the wall.

## 8

Hern dropped the binoculars, letting them hang about his neck, and swung around on his stool until he faced the others gathered in the small, square chamber at the top of the west gate tower. He filled a glass with water from the jug on the table beside him, drank thirstily, set the glass down, frowned at Yael-mri. "How many dead so far?"

Yael-mri looked at her hands. "One hundred seventeen meien, twelve healer trainees, eight girls, fifty-six Stenda, two hundred thirteen mijlockers, six exiles." She began kneading at the back of one hand with the fingers of the other. "Almost everyone on or near the wall has been wounded several times, some as many as six or seven, many of them would have died except for Serroi; any we get to her with a flicker of life left she heals." She rubbed her hands, staring past him out the windowslit at the pale blue of the sky. "She can't heal memory away. You know my meien, Hern, they're fighters, they go back on the wall, they have to, but the edge is getting worn off them. And they're sickened by the killing, the slaughter. They know the need, who better? but there comes a time when the spirit and the flesh rebel." She made a small cut-off gesture, said nothing more.

Hern scrubbed his hand across his face. "Supplies?"

Yael-mri pulled her brooding gaze off the empyrean blue. "Arrows are a problem. We're salvaging what we can from the shafts shot at us, but even with the girls working in shifts on fletching and pointing, we're expending more than we can replace. Doing better with the crossbow quarrels, they don't require as much time or skill. Fuel's no problem. We had time to get in a good supply of coal. The fat fires and the food fires won't die for lack of coal or wood. Food—with a good harvest and a year to prepare, we had time and used it. Even after the influx of all those extra girls we won't starve. Herbs, salves, other medicines, holding out fairly well. Serroi again. She makes medicines unnecessary in the more serious cases." She smiled wearily. "You know well enough our only shortage is of trained fighters. Kole can't starve us out, but he can whittle down our numbers until he can just walk over us."

Hern nodded. "Even with the Shawar intact. The wall's holding him right now. Georgia, Anoike, your folk and supplies?"

Georgia glanced at Anoike. With a flip of her hand she passed the answer to him. "As Yael-mri said, six of us are dead, three of my bunch, two from Angel's, a driver who caught an arrow in the throat; her bad luck, wrong place, wrong time. Five horses dead or wounded. Ammo about half gone, some grenades left, other stuff we haven't used yet. Grenier's drugs, he scraping bottom, but he didn't have no big supply to start." Georgia grinned. "If you want to see a happy man, a whole new pharmacopoeia to play with. Fuel for the trucks going to be a problem if this goes on much longer. Nona, she's a research chemist, and Bill, he used to build his own racing cars, they're working on some way of restructuring the engines to run on alcohol. Last report, they making good progress, thought they could experiment on one of the trucks when things get slow. That's about it." he looked at Anoike.

"You said it, Dom. The wall holding them."

"Right. But we've got a problem. The walking towers."

Anoike crossed her arms, wrinkled her nose. "Thought that why you got us up here. How long?"

"Sundown."

"Hunh." She poked her elbow into Georgia's ribs. "Maybe you ready now to use those rockets." Her hazel eyes filled with laughter, she turned back to Hern. "He a skrinch with them. I keep telling him Kole the thing holds them out there together. Pull him and they fall apart. But he sitting on those rockets like a broody hen on a clutch of eggs."

Georgia shook his head. "He keeps that Nor too close. I figure we got one good shot with the rockets; if we try for him and that Nor shifts them aside, then we've lost the chance to finesse some advantage from the others we got. Those towers, they're different. Take them out and have a hot try for Kole. We miss him this time, no sweat, we get the towers and maybe some more norits."

Yael-mri cleared her throat; when they looked at her, she said, "He's right. The Nor with Kole and three more out there are only a hair away from the challenge duels that could lift several of them into full power. Take no chances with that Four."

Hern rubbed at the back of his neck, feeling tired. He'd been tired for days. Sitting up here, separated from his fighters, chained to the binoculars and the teletalk, directing the battles like some botso master moving his pieces about a board. Watching men and women die when they rushed to follow his orders. He was angry, frustrated, tired, occasionally despairing. He missed Serroi terribly; more than once he was tempted to send for her just to talk a little, to get away from the unending strain, to touch again the warmth between them and feel human again, but he didn't give in to that need. Her presence down there meant lives saved and he needed those lives. There were times, especially late at night, when he was stretched out on the pallet in the corner, a meie at the window charged to wake him if she spotted any movement below, there were times when he felt like walking down the stairs and away from the wall, away from the fighting and the responsibilities oppressing him, but he knew also he was the one person who could order events without getting an argument or mutiny from every part of his motley force. He was as locked-in here as Serroi was with her healing. At his lowest moments he wondered if he would ever escape, if the mijloc would claim him for the last part of his life as it had for the first. No, he told himself. No. But he could feel them all leaning on him, depending on him, everyone behind the wall and out in the desolation Floarin had made of the Plain. And the exiles who were fighting so powerfully for him, they'd need him too, he was the only one who could see that they got the land and help he'd promised them. He couldn't walk away, that much of his father he had in him. Heslin, he said to himself in the dark—and it was both a groan and a curse.

He poured more water and drank, turned to Georgia. "Can you move your launchers into place without alerting the traxim?"

Georgia frowned. "They're not that big. Have to be some work on them, takes a few minutes to sight them in on the towers."

Anoike touched his arm. "The little pults the meien been using, they worth shit so far, but Kole he got to be expecting the Dom here to try anything he can. Make a lot of fuss getting them moved, I expecting Kole he don't notice us here and there fussin with the launchers."

Hern clicked his fingers against the glass, then nodded. "That should do it."

Yael-mri sighed. "There's more bad news, Dom. My sensitives say there are Sleykynin in the valley."

"I thought you'd blocked that."

"Apparently bands on both sides of the valley have been working round through the mountains toward the southern narrows. The ones we killed peeled off the main parties, testing us, I think. As far as I can tell, they came down beyond the sensitives' reach and have been creeping toward us the past two days." She sighed. "I hate to ask it, dom Hern, but I need hunting parties and guard shifts. I know we don't have the fighters. I know everyone's needed on the wall, but how much good will holding the wall do if the Sleykynin break the Shawar? How long would the wall stand then?" She looked at her hands again. When she spoke it was in a whisper as if she feared to hear what she was saying. "How much good even those will do, I don't know. I just don't know. Sleykynin are old hands at games we meien have never played.

The launchers were slipped onto the wall in the midst of the contrived confusion Anoike had suggested. The three launchers they had were trained upon the three towers, the rockets nested in them. Overhead the traxim whirled about, thick black flocks of demon spies, but they took no special notice of three small knots of purpose in the larger flow. In the tower Hern scanned the army; it was late afternoon, a heavily overcast day that spread a cold gray gloom over the plain outside the wall and the foothills beyond. He could find no trace of Nekaz Kole, but did locate his tent, its fine waterproof silk walls lit from within by lamps and perhaps a charcoal brazier to keep the army's master warm. He murmured into the teletalk, reporting his observations to Anoike, adding that he saw no point in waiting longer. He flicked to the second channel, glanced down at the scale etched into the stone of the slit, spoke again. "Kole's tent. Ten degrees west of second tower, estimate this point. Comment?" He listened. "Right. Ready. On three. One. Two. Three."

Diminishing hiss, exhaust clouds glowing in gray light. Rockets whispering from the launchers, exploding with no appreciable interval between launch and hit, so close are the towers, three blasts that open out the gloom with sound and glare. The exiles handling the launchers muscle them around, change their aim and shoot off a second flight about two heartbeats after the first.

Hern grunted with satisfaction as the towers flew into splinters, shifted his gaze to the tents as the next flight converged on them and struck, throwing fire, dirt and stone in a wide circle about the place where the tents had been, the stone and shards from the rocket casing slicing like knives through the surrounding Ogogehians, sending even those hardened mercenaries into a panic flight. He lifted the teletalk, spoke into it. "Go. Get whatever you can."

More of the rockets streaked out, their flights diverging from the center. Though Sankoise and Ogogehian and Majilarni fled the terrible things that flew at them with paralyzing swiftness and slew by hundreds, not one by one, only the lucky survived. The first flight hit among the Sankoise, slaying many, wounding more. The second sprayed through the orderly camps of the mercenaries, but the third flight veered suddenly upward, curled to the east and exploded some minutes later among the mountain tops, almost too far off to see or hear. Hern cursed fervently, spoke again into the teletalk. "Shut down. No use wasting more of those. That should hold them a while."

## 9

Nekaz Kole wasn't in his tent, but sitting at a shaman's fire in a Majilarni shaman's hutch dealing with a potential rebellion. The Majilarni were tired of this interminable siege that was getting them killed without any of the usual pleasures of war. Other times they could hear the moans of the wounded and the dying, could see the city behind the wall begin to suffer, other times they could race their rambuts around the walls and yell mocking things at the defenders, boast what they'd do to them when the city fell, howl with laughter at their stupidity when they tried sending out embassies to cut deals with the shaman and the elders, other times they could play with sorties and smugglers and savor the growing desperation behind the walls. Other times they could ride off more or less when they chose, loaded down with loot and slaves when the city finally capitulated. They could see no profit in this business. The wall was too thick, too high, too long, the defenders were too deadly with their shafts and those tiny pellets that dug right through you and maybe wounded your mount too, that sought you out impossibly far from the wall. That wasn't fair. You died and you didn't even get to call your curses on your killer because she was too far to hear you. And that was another thing. They were fighting women. Oh, they'd seen some men's faces now and then, but they knew what this place was: it was where they trained those abominations that played at being men. How could a man gain honor fighting women? The Majilarni fighters were turning ugly. The shaman was getting nervous. Clans had turned on their shamans before. If he was negligent about bringing them to game and

graze, or milking water into dry wells, or if he got them
beaten too badly in contests with enemy clans, if he led
them to defeat before the walled cities too often, then the
shaman got roasted over a slow fire, fed to the herd chini
and his apprentice set in his place. That is, if the apprentice stuck around long enough to get caught, in which case
he wasn't much of a shaman, and would soon follow his
master into chinin bellies. The shaman squatting across
the fire from Nekaz Kole knew the smell of revolt; he
cursed the day he'd let ambition trap him into this business. Though he feared the Nearga nor, he was on the
point of leading his folk away, to take them on raids up
through the mijloc and across Assurtilas in hopes that loot
and proper fighting would put them into a better mood.

The talk went on for a while more, but Kole wasn't a
man to dribble away his authority in futile argument. He
cut off the discussion and ducked out of the hutch; before
he could get to his mount, the rockets hit the walking
towers, then his tents, then started ravaging his army. The
Nor at his side cursed, then spoke a WORD that shivered
the air about him. The last of the flaming missiles curved
up and away, exploding somewhere among the mountain
tops behind them. Kole watched that, then scowled across
the slopes at the devastation where his tent had been.
Being that close to losing his life shook him, not because it
was a brush with death, but because even the Nor wouldn't
have saved him if they'd both been in that tent; there
wouldn't have been time for him to act. Chance had saved
him this time. Another time it might destroy him. He had
no control over that sort of event. Luck. The idea disturbed him. He strode to his gold rambut, swung into the
saddle and rode at a slow walk toward the heart of his
army to look over the damage to his veterans, the Nor
silent, riding a half-length behind him. There was one
aspect of the destruction he was quietly applauding. Floarin
was gone; he'd left her huddling over a fire after listening
for an hour to her querulous demands for information and
for quick action to end the war. She was puffed to ash now
or blown into shreds of charred flesh. He'd deferred to her

since she was provisioner and nominal paymaster, but he knew well enough where the real power lay. She'd developed into an irritant impossible to ignore, equally impossible to endure. And she'd started getting ideas about him, hovered around him as much as she could, constantly touching him, pressing against him, even trying to force her way into his tent. That she disgusted him and the thought of coupling with her turned his stomach he kept to himself. He evaded her during the day, put guards around his tent at night. In Ogogehia there are spiders that grow as broad as a man's hand, ghastly, hairy bags of ooze able to leap higher than a man's head and poisonous enough to make a strong man deathly sick. The females are the big ones, males are elusive, shy and smooth-skinned, dinner for the females once the mating is over. In his eyes Floarin was as disgusting as one of those spiders, feeding on her husband, feeding any male that got close enough for her to inject her poison. He smiled at the scattered embers of the tents and felt a strong relief flood through him, with the result that he silently promised those inside the wall as generous a settlement as he could wring out of the Nearga Nor. He watched the embers dying to black, heard the wounded groaning, and coveted those weapons. Where Hern had got hold of them was something he was going to be very interested in discovering. With them in his arsenal, well, there would be very little he couldn't have for the asking. Once this was over. He bent forward and patted the neck of his nervously sidling rambut. Time for Vuurvis. He swept his eyes along the wall, scowled at the gate towers. Start loading the melons tomorrow. Hit the walls first, then the towers, get rid of spotters, then burn through the gates. Once he got enough men inside the wall, it was over. He kneed the rambut into a faster walk. The majilarni were lost but he didn't need them. Vuurvis was enough.

## 10

Serroi straightened, rubbed at her back, smiled at the lined face of the woman who'd been something of a mother to her. Pria Mellit. She took her turn on the wall with the others, her strong wiry arms hurling the javelins with great accuracy; fed by her stable girls, she could get three or four of the short lances off in as many heartbeats, but that meant she stood for long stretches without much cover. The wound Serroi had just healed was Mellit's fifth serious hurt. She endured the pain without complaint and went quietly back to the wall when her turn came, handling the pain-memory far better than the younger meien. Serroi helped her sit up, clucked her tongue at the deep bruises about Mellit's eyes. "Get some rest, pria-mama," she said gently, knowing Mellit would ignore her this time as she had before.

Mellit got to her feet, straightened her torn clothing. "Not here, child. You'll need this pallet soon enough."

Serroi reached out to help her as she stumped toward the tent's door, but drew her hand back. Mellit would walk where she wanted on her own legs and when she could no longer do that, then she'd die. She wouldn't appreciate one of her girls, old or new, hastening her toward that time. Serroi watched her look about then move off with that ground-eating stride her Stenda legs gave her and she took a moment to appreciate the old woman's undiminishing strength, then she started to go back inside.

And froze, mouth open, eyes glazed. Pain. A pain so far beyond description it blanked her mind. Hern. In agony. With a low whining moan she stumbled around, stood staring at the burning tower. "Vuurvis," she said. She heard it echo in her head, a soft plaintive denying word, then she shook off her temporary paralysis and ran for the only motorcycle near the tent. The rider was dismounting, coming off his shift. She grabbed his arm, pointed. "Take me there. Hurry." Again the words echoed in her head. She wanted to scream at him, shake him, force him to move faster, but her words came out in a whisper. She hitched up her robe, swung a leg over the long narrow seat above the rear wheel and got herself set as the boy started the machine and roared toward the tower. Everything was

floating around her, she couldn't think with Hern's agony
burning in her. She felt the machine shimmy under her,
felt the jolts and vibrations as it raced over the rough
ground, felt the bunching and shifting of the boy's muscles
where she clutched at him. The tower came at her fast-
fast, yet the ride seemed to go on forever. More vuurvis hit
the tower; the heavy, greedy flames ran over the stone,
eating pits in it. There were screams and shouts and
crashes sounding all along the wall but she ignored those;
her entire being was focused on the burning tower.

## 11

The heat was intense, the smell indescribable. The little
healer was off the cycle before Wes got it stopped, running
toward the tower's door, toward the flames and smoke
coming from it. He let the machine fall and started after
her. She's hysterical, he thought, killing herself, nothing
she can do for him now, she can't bring back the dead. He
reached her before she dived into that mess of stinking
smoke, lunged and caught hold of her arm.

Pain ran like fire into his hand and his fingers jerked
open. He couldn't keep hold of her though he tried again.
She ran inside, flames licking at the loose robe she wore, at
the bounding curls that made her seem such a child until
you looked into her eyes. He backed away, coughing and
spitting, looked around. There was more than the tower to
worry about. Forgetting the food and rest he'd been looking forward to, he muscled his machine up and around and
started toward the hospital tent to pick up a medic and
supplies and begin doing something about the burned; he'd
heard enough stories about vuurvis and what it did to flesh
to be glad that his belly was empty and his body tired.

## 12

Serroi is burning with her own fire as she runs up the
squared spiral stairs. Her robe is burning off her, her hair
is on fire, but she feels none of that. Up and around and

up and around and all the time Hern is dying, dying alone, his stubborn generous spirit burning out of his body. She will not let that happen, she must not, must not, must not, the words echo with the patter of her bare feet on the hot stone, she does not notice that where she steps, where her fingers touch the wall, she leaves a mark on the stone and the fire is quenched there. Hern hangs on, refusing to die. Reaching and reaching, she draws power to herself as she runs, her breath sobbing in her ears, up and around and up and around.

The upper room is awash with flame, but again where she steps, the flame dies. She runs to the blackened hulk, kneels. The fire retreats from her, leaving a circle clear about Hern's body. She gathers her will and puts her hands on him.

The oil fights her and he fights her, maddened by the agony. She holds him down and pours all the power she has called into him. The Biserica means nothing to her now, Ser Noris means nothing to her, Hern is all, she will not quit until he is whole. She reaches out and seizes all power she can reach, draining the Shawar, draining the Norim, draining even Ser Noris, swallowing whole the fragments of the other norissim, the bits he'd left of them, all this she channels through her body and into Hern, into the blackened hulk that writhes on the stone and threatens to crush her with its uncontrolled flexings. The tower hums about her, turns grass green and translucent and the earth-fire, nor-fire, shawar-fire kills the vuurvis fire and reinforces the flickering glow of life in him, begins rebuilding the life as she stimulates the cells of his body to repair themselves, the dead charred flesh sloughing off, replaced by new, building from the bone out, cell by cell, nerve by nerve, layer on layer on layer of flesh all over his body until new skin spreads over him, but she doesn't stop there. Eyes closed, body swaying, her will holding her, she keeps his body working until lashes grow back, eyebrows, body hair; his head hair coils out and out, black and pewter as before, until it is long enough to curl about her wrist.

The pale gray eyes opened and looked up at her, knowing her.

And she knew what she'd done, how much harm she could have done, and she snatched the power yet more from the Nor, though she could feel Ser Noris contesting with her for it, snatched it loose from him and fed it as gently and apologetically as she could back to the laboring Shawar. She sat back on her heels, smiling down at him through a skim of tears, her lips trembling.

## 13

He opened his eyes and saw her. She glowed terrible and wonderful, a green glass figurine in the charred rags of a sleeveless white robe, then he saw only Serroi with tears in her eyes, weariness in her small elfin face. He smiled and caught her hands, held them between his a moment, then reached up, drew his hand down the side of her face, traced the clean-cut elegant curves of her mouth. "There's half a world we haven't seen."

"Yes," she said. She swayed; her eyelids fluttered; she fainted across his renewed body.

For a moment he was afraid, but the pulse in her throat beat strongly. He eased her off his chest and sat up. His clothes were burnt off him, he'd expected that, but he was startled to feel hair when he brushed his hand over his head. "Very thorough, love." He lifted her onto his lap and held her close, stroking his hand over the singed curls, then the gentle curve of her back. Through the windowslits he could hear muffled curses and screams and knew he'd have to get her down to help the others, but for a little while he was going to hold her and forget everything else.

In a few moments, though, his legs began cramping and the stone that had burned him was giving him chills in his bare buttocks while air through the window blew off ice. He shifted position, looked down to see her eyes open. "Cold as the slopes of Shayl," he said.

She smiled. "They never last, do they, our moments, I mean."

## 14

Julia tilted the stoneware cha pot over the clay mug and poured out the last trickle of lukewarm liquid. She set the pot back, sipped at the cha. "Getting low on ammo," she said. "Remind me to snag one of the cycles and call in for some."

"Um." Rane scowled at the fragment of sandwich she was holding, threw it in a long lazy arc away from the wall and sat staring at the rag tied round her calf though Julia didn't think she saw it.

They were sitting in the sun, a winter sun that did not give much heat, protected from the sweep of the wind by the jut of the nearest ramp. No one went to the eating tent these days; time and energy were both in short supply. They slept in the lower floors of the gate towers, on call for reinforcement whenever they were needed. They were all weary and worn down to simple endurance, men and women alike, falling into their blankets on straw gone musty with the damp, sleeping as if clubbed, rising with only the top layer of tiredness gone, the residue of each day's weariness added to the last and the next until it seemed they'd never be free of it. Julia thought back to the days when she was grubbing out an existence and trying to write, when she was exhausted and depressed, tired of trying to cope with the complexities of her life and the complexities of her nature and the impossibility of reconciling the two, yet when food and warmth and shelter and privacy were there to take as she needed, when her horizons stretched beyond the visible edges of the world; she thought back to those times and found them curiously hard to visualize as if they were something she'd written in a novel she'd never managed to finish. She marveled at the difference between the Julia who'd lived then and the Julia sitting with a rifle beside her waiting to be called back into battle. Her edges had narrower limits these days, they chopped off five minutes ahead and stretched out on either side as far as the people she could see and name. She knew them all now, the meien and her own exiles, the mijlockers and the Stenda, knew names and faces, knew how steady or flighty they were in the face of danger, knew them intimately and not at all, especially the folk of this world; the novelist wanted to know their histories, to know the forces that had shaped them into the people they were. What had their lives been like? Who were their friends, their lovers, their acquaintances, their enemies? What were their hopes and fears, their ordinary eccentricities, their communal natures? What stories could they tell about themselves and others? What were the old, old stories all families accumulate and hand down through the genera-tions? She knew nothing of that and she wanted to; she hungered to discover those things about them. But there was no time, you fought, you rested, you ate, you slept. Everything outside this time and this place was as remote for them as her past life was for her, for this reason and others they seldom spoke of anything but here and now.

There was a thump and a brittle crash above. Working the catapults again, Julia thought, then dropped the cup and sprang away from the wall as she felt a leap of heat, a drop of something that ate like acid into her thigh. She heard a scream that would echo in nightmare later, then a burning thing leaped out from the top of the wall. Rane thrust herself up and limped as fast as she could away from the wall. Julia took a few steps after her, then turned to stare at what lay huddled on the ground; it was charred out of its humanity, but the rifle clutched in a burning hand had enough of its shape left for Julia to recognize the carved stock. Liz. Her stomach churned and she looked away, desperately glad that Liz was beyond all help. A second later she brought her own rifle up and put a bullet in the skull of the burning thing. Rane came back and stood beside her. "All you could do," she said.

Julia looked right and left along the wall, saw half a dozen fires. "Oh god, how many more?"

Rane cupped her hands about her mouth and shouted at the chaos on the wall above them. "Vuurvis," she shrieked. "Don't let it touch you. If you don't know what it is, ask. Vuurvis. Don't try to put it out. If there's oil on you, don't touch it, you'll just spread it." She walked along the wall, repeating those words and warnings until she was too hoarse to continue. Others among the older meien took up the calls and began getting the burned fighters down the ramp to wait for the medics and trucks to carry them to the hospital tent.

Julia looked down at her thigh. The vuurvis drop was smaller than a pinhead, but the pain was growing. It was bearable, so she shrugged aside her worry and limped up the ramp behind limping Rane, began helping her to get the burn victims down to the ground. The first time she saw the heavy flame crawling over the flesh of a living woman, she started to try smothering it, but Rane snatched her hand away. "No good," she said. "All we can do is let it burn itself out. Or let the healwomen cut away the saturated flesh. Nothing helps, nothing will put out vuurvis, you'll just get it on you."

She carried the moaning meie down the ramp and laid her on the ground beside the rows of the others, called the medic, a girl named Dinafar, to put her out until the truck came. An eerie hush was settling over the wall, muting the screams of the burned, the grinding of motors coming toward her, stopping, coming on, stopping as the trucks east and west picked up the burned. The medics had arrived swiftly at each of the burn sites but the girls knew enough about vuurvis to know there was nothing they could do but help bring the injured down to wait for the trucks, gently putting the worst sufferers out by pressure on the carotids. Over all this was that straining silence that Julia thought was in her head until she looked along the wall.

The west tower was no longer burning, it throbbed with the clear green light of the healer. Dom Hern, she thought. "Dom Hern," she said aloud.

Rane grunted. "She wouldn't let him die." Lifting her head, she sniffed at the air. "She's draining us for him."

Julia shrugged, not understanding what Rane meant. She watched the tower glow, the light running in waves down the stone and into the ground, gasped as a thought seized hold of her. She caught the medic as she went past. "When the truck comes, take the burned to the tower and pack them in the lower floors."

Dinafar's eyes opened wide. Not understanding, she turned to Rane. "What . . .?"

Rane looked at the verdant glow, then at the groaning forms stretched out around her. "Do it, Dina. Get hold of the other trucks and tell them."

Dinafar pushed the hair out of her eyes, then her weary face lit with a hope she hadn't had before. She ran to the motorcycle that had fetched her from the hospital tent, spoke into the teletalk strapped to the handlebar, then trotted back up the ramp and worked with a greater urgency to get the last of the injured down.

Julia looked at her watch and was startled to see that less than a half hour had passed since the beginning of the attack. She looked down, looked away. There were five dead like Liz. Dead but their flesh still burning. Two of them with rifles. Exiles. Three of them clutching the burned remnants of crossbows. She couldn't recognize them, knew them only by figuring out who was missing among the wounded. She whispered the names to herself, a leave-taking of comrades, and tried unsuccessfully to ignore the pain in her thigh and the moans of the burned still alive. She turned her back on them and stared at the tower, grieving for both the dead and the living as she waited for the truck that might save the living.

## 15

Tuli lay on the hillside, mouthing all the curses she could recall, furious at herself for her complacent conviction that Ildas had destroyed all the vuurvis oil in that extravagant annihilation in their first raid. The fireborn snuggled against her and tried to comfort her. She stroked and soothed him but she was too angry and afraid to calm herself.

Coperic touched her arm. "Can you . . .?" He finished the question with a gesture toward the barrels where the

Ogogehians gingerly loaded oil into clay melons and plugged the holes in them with wax and wicks, working slowly and with great care to keep the heavy oil from touching any part of hand or face. Three high Nor were there to protect them, the fourth was Kole's constant shadow. The rest of the norits were clustered about the seven catapults spaced along the wall from cliff to cliff.

Tuli scowled at the barrels, shook her head. "Too much Nor, Ildas couldn't get near." She pulled the back of her hand across her face, felt the rasping of dry, chapped skin against dry skin. She almost couldn't smell Coperic anymore; she was about as ripe as were he and the others. He was gaunt and grimy, his hair lank and too long, the front parts sawn off with his knife to keep them out of his eyes. None of them had been out of their clothes for more than a passage, the only water available to them cost a day's trip along the road across the pass. She watched him, hoping the clever mind behind that unimpressive face would find a way to attack the vuurvis. His eyes were slitted, his mouth open a little, his hands were closed hard on a clump of grass.

"One spark," he whispered, so softly she almost didn't hear him. He was right, a spark was all that horrible stuff needed. But it looked impossible. The Nor wouldn't let fire get near those barrels, and they were sticking tight as fleas.

Bella stirred, turned her face toward them. She was worn too, was brown and dark as damp earth now, her cousin Biel was brown and dark; dirt and oil and sweat and soot had dulled the fine gold patina of their skin, had darkened the bright gold hair to the color of last year's leaves rotting back into the earth. "We can get close," Bella said. She chuckled. "Long as we try it down wind." She sobered. "They're focused on the wall. Look at them. Gloating, I'd say. And the Ogogehians are staying well away from the barrels, look how careful those men are to keep the fumes from blowing on them. And look there. And there." She began pointing out clumps of brush and cracks, working out a line of progress along the slopes that would take a careful crawler close to the hollow where the barrels were.

Coperic followed the darting finger. "Mm." He watched a mercenary ride his macai at a slow walk away from the barrels, holding a net sling of clay melons stiffly out from his side. One of the Nor left the barrels and rode beside him, shielding him from anything off the wall. "Nekaz Kole," he whispered.

Tuli took the words as the curse they were. "He don't miss much," she said.

The two Nor sitting on the knoll above the barrels suddenly pulled their macain around until they were facing the mountains, their eyes searching the slopes. Hastily Coperic and Tuli went flat, the others ducking down beside them, shoving their faces into the dirt. Tuli felt the Nor eyes pass over her like an itch in the back of her neck. She didn't move until Ildas cooed reassurance to her. She lifted her head, exploded out the dead air and sucked in a hard cold lungful of new. The others sat up and began breathing again. "Seems like they don't want folk watching them," Tuli said softly.

Coperic glanced through the screen of brush. "They calmed down now." He eased around and went snaking down the slope into the small socket eaten out of the mountainside where they usually slept. Little sunlight got through the brush, so it was chill as any icehouse. He squatted at one end and waited until the others had crowded in and settled themselves. "Had a thought," he said.

He let a moment pass, his eyes shut, his brows drawn together, fingers of one hand tapping on his bony knee. Shadow seeped into the wrinkles of his face and hands, carved heavy black lines into his flesh. The muscles of his face shifted just slightly, enough to turn his face into a changing web of light and dark around the strong jut of his nose. Watching him, Tuli measured the change in herself by the change she saw in him; as the days slid past, as tenday slid into tenday and the stadia dropped behind them, he had stripped away his sly bumbling tavern-host mannerisms, dropping one by one as they moved down the Highroad and settled above the army. Now he was a prowling predator, limited to a single aspect of himself, little left of the complex man she'd caught glimpses of in Oras. They were all narrowed by the hunger, the stress, the killing, the danger, with the softer sides of their natures put away for the duration of the war. Sometimes she wondered if she would ever see those times again, gentler times when she could laugh and smile and run the night fields, sometimes she wondered if she'd be able to slough the memories that even now gave her nightmares. She realized suddenly that tomorrow was her birthday. Hers and her brother's. Teras. Fifteen? How strange. She felt more like fifty.

Coperic opened his eyes. "Still a dozen of us," he said slowly. "So far. Could change." He went silent again, gazed over their heads at the dangling brush. "Comes to me, we could get down close, and when the first melons hit the wall and start burning, one, two, maybe three of us rush the barrels. Right then army, Nor, you name it, they going to be watching the wall too damn hard to be looking out for us. With some of us in ambush covering, one or two of us break through and fire the oil. If we move fast enough. In and out." He scanned their faces again. "Anyone wants to back off, feel free. Me, I think it's crazy, but could just maybe work. Roll the bones, come up live, come up dead, but make 'em pay." He reached inside his vest, slipped out one of his throwing knives, looked at it a moment, slipped it back. "I'm crazy as that bitch Floarin, but I'm going in close to cover. Who's gonna carry fire?"

Bella's smile was a feral grimace. "Who's not gonna? Anyone got an uncset? Odd man out's the fire fool."

Tuli snorted. "You're all crazy. Can't no one get close enough without those Nor spotting him, they don't have to see you, they smell you out, Pero, and I don't mean sweat stink. Me and Ajjin, we're the only ones can get close enough, I got Ildas, she got her own ways."

"Thought you said he can't get to the barrels."

"Well, he can't. But he can shield me up to the spellweb. It's like the Shawar shield, magic to keep out magic.

magic to warn, but if those Nor are distracted enough, I can sling a fireball through the web and still stay far enough away so I don't get my face burned off. And if I trip, there's still the Ajjin."

Coperic gazed at her a long time. She could feel him fighting against letting her go while his plotter's mind saw a dozen advantages in her plan and was working to polish aspects of it even as he resisted giving in to it. For all his acerbity and cynicism there were parts of him softer and more vulnerable than Sanani. He was fond of her, she knew that, and in a cranky way was as proud of her as if she'd been his own daughter. She'd been wary of men since Fayd, but felt nothing of that kind of thing in the way Coperic treated her. Somehow he was more important to her than anyone, even Teras. The closeness between her and Teras was over; Teras didn't have the least idea what she was now (and she suspected he wouldn't care if he did, he was so wrapped up in the importance of what he was doing), but Coperic knew her possibilities. That amoral and disreputable leader of thieves understood her in ways her father and even her mother never would. She saw him smile at her, a slow and reluctant smile that admitted his capitulation. "Charda, go see if you can find Ajjin. Tell her what we're thinking and find out if she's crazy as the rest of us."

Tuli parted the brush and stared as the wall began burning. Holding her breath she turned from the heavy greedy flames and glanced over the Ogogehians gathered about the barrels, then to the three Nor sitting their black demon macain, their backs to her, satisfaction in the lines of their bodies, tall, fit men clothed in power, the air shimmering about them. Gilded light she sensed rather than saw rayed out from them, weaving into a bright web that humped in a dome over the barrels and the men lounging beside them. Spun into her own web, she got to her knees, stuffed the weighted tinder in the pocket of her jacket and waited a few heartbeats longer, sneaking swift glances at the Nor, trying to judge the extent of their absorption.

The tower began to throb behind the vuurvis fire and the fire went out and the gray stone turned a glowing new-green, lovely as polished chrysoprase. The Nor went rigid, the web-barrier vanished. Tuli sucked in a breath, let Ildas lick the tinder into a small flame. Ajjin chini got to her feet and trotted to stand beside Tuli as she rose and began whirling the sling about her head. The throb from the tower deepened and reached out farther. The air stilled and turned thicker, almost like water. As she released the fireball, sending it shooting at the nearest barrel, the lightweb was suddenly sucked from about her, Ildas squeaked and vanished; the Nor turned dull as if they'd changed to stone. She was frozen an instant with shock and loss, then wheeled and raced away. She could hear the hoarse wild screams from the wall, the burned meien shrieking, and that prodded her into a panicky scramble to put solid earth between her and the vuurvis, her back crawling in anticipation of the heat flare.

It didn't come. She reached the top of a slope, looked over her shoulder, stumbled to a stop and turned.

The glowing tower drew her eyes first, but after a few ragged breaths she looked away. The barrel she'd hit was burning, but it was a low sullen fire, not a leaping conflagration as before. She didn't understand it; she scowled at the pitiful flames until the Ajjin bumped her legs, calling her back to where she was. She looked down. "Right." Brooding on the change in the Nor, she walked with slow deliberation back to the ambush where the rest of the band were waiting, ready to cover her retreat if that proved necessary. Wanting to confirm what she suspected, she looked back again. Nothing had changed, no one had moved, not the men tending the barrels, not the great Nor on top their grassy knoll. And the air maintained its thick resistance to movement. Excitement rising in her, she pushed through the brush.

"Shoot them," she said. "The Nor. Pero, they're kankas without gas, their magic is being sucked out of them by something, I don't know, but as long as that tower glows they can't do nothing. Get 'em."

"Biel, Ramo, Sosai, try it." As the three best archers in the band moved to get a cleaner shot at the Nor, Coperic rubbed his hand across his mouth. "Bella, you and the rest might's well take advantage a that." He nodded at the tower. "Cut us out a rambut. We down to bone on the last. After that, I think hit the Sankoise. They about ready to quit, shouldn't take much to bog them down and make them worthless."

Tuli watched as the quarrels whistled through the thick unnatural air and socked home in the black forms. For several heartbeats nothing happened, as if the shafts were illusion not real. Then the three crumpled stiffly, toppled off the demon macain, fell onto the curve of the low hill and lay like discarded idols on the limp, bleached grass.

Then the glow faded. There was a confusion of shouts and curses as the stupor wore off the army and Nekaz Kole discovered the death of the three Nor. The air came loose with a rush of ice-breath and whipped Tuli's hair about, crept down her tunic and slid around her ribs, ribs that had no flesh on them to keep out the cold. It whipped the fire high, flung it out to the other barrels, sending a blast of heat for several bodylengths on every side. Tuli shivered; in spite of that heat, she was icy with unassimiliated grief. Ildas was gone and he'd taken all warmth from her.

Coperic saw the grief she was fighting to deny. He laid his arm across her shoulders, squeezed gently. "What's wrong?"

"Ildas." Her voice cracked. She licked her lips. "He's gone."

"What happened?"

"It took him just as it took the Nor-magic. I don't know, maybe it . . . it swallowed him." She leaned against Coperic, felt his wiry strength leaking into her, comforting her. "Like there was something there in the tower I mean that was sucking power out of everything. . . ." Her voice trailed off; she wriggled around until her face was tucked into the hollow between his neck and shoulder; she clung to him, her eyes dry though she was shuddering as if she sobbed;

for a moment she thrust aside everything that had happened to her and let herself be a baby again, let him hold her and comfort her.

It couldn't last. She pulled away from him. She wasn't a baby and she couldn't sustain the illusion that she was. Wind buffeted at her, shouts and screams came more clearly, Biel and the others were back, grinning at the success of their efforts. The tower was dark, only a ghost of the jewel glow left in the stone. Elsewhere along the wall the oil still burned and the massive wooden gates were beginning to char. The fire at the barrels leaped high, a thrusting tongue of flame and smoke, geysering up and up, swaying, throwing out burning bits that kept everyone at a distance.

She watched it, weary and warming in the crook of Coperic's arm. She felt empty, no hatred, no triumph, no anger left to prod her. A soft warmth brushed her calf, a coo fluttered through her head. She looked down. "Didi," she whispered and bent forward a little, opening her arms, cooing her extravagant delight as Ildas leaped up and settled against her ribs. She straightened, stroking him into rapture, glanced up; her mouth dropped open, she pointed, gasped, "Look."

Immense undulating serpentine shapes floated above the Biserica valley, dragons made of bending glass with waves of color rippling across their transparent scales like silent music. Tuli's body throbbed to the beauty of those beings and the sinuous songs they were weaving. She held Ildas close, felt Coperic strong and steady behind her, watched the glass dragons invent their chorales and knew contentment so intense that every other emotion paled before it.

# 16

Hate coiled in a tainted mist through the army. The grinding sullen hate of the Sankoise that embraced the meien and the rest of the Biserica's defenders, the norits that drove them at the wall again and again, drove them to slaughter, hate for Nekaz Kole who jerked like a puppet at the twitching of the Nearga Nor and twitched the Sankoise in his turn, hate finally for all other Sankoise—and a cold unrelenting hate of the Nor for the meien, the beasts (all men and women of lesser powers were beasts to the norim) that were somehow reaching through the veil of Nor-power and killing them, stripping away their certainty of their invulnerability. It should not be happening. It had to be chance. It couldn't be skill. The beasts had no such skill. But, somehow, two-thirds of their number were dead. Doubt crept in and mixed with fear and as the holes gaped larger in their certainty, their hatred intensified, feeding on that doubt and fear the way vuurvis fire fed on flesh.

Where the Ogogehians were, the miasma stank more of anger than of fear, a spreading subterranean rage at Nekaz Kole for getting them into this morass. They were mercenaries and death was a built-in risk, but a dead man's wages were of no use to him. Because Nekaz Kole had been a prudent, capable and occasionally brilliant commander who'd bought them loot and glory with a minimum of casualties, they'd followed him with confidence, making scurrilous but affectionate jokes about his appetites and idiosyncrasies. He'd gone from success to success until he was a serious threat to the power back home of the older generals, but now he was losing men and reputation equally. If he went down here, he was dead, no matter how long he lived. Five hundred defeating five thousand. He knew only too well the sneers and contempt, the stink of failure that would follow him the rest of his days, corroding all he touched.

Nekaz Kole sat his rambut above the catapults still hurling vuurvis at the massive gates, lobbing some high so it splashed into the openway between the inner and outer gates. An easy victory, Floarin said. Lean on them a little and they'll cave. Easy money. He leaned forward, patted his rambut's neck, looked down the slope at his disaffected army. The Norim had echoed her words. An easy victory. Just the wall. Once you take that, it's over. They can't have more than five hundred or so meien, only women, some of them too old to be worth much. He discounted their assurances and listened to their numbers and succumbed to temptation. Even then he knew it was probably a mistake; experience had taught him long ago that luck's fair face concealed a poisoned barb; it had also taught him that his employers were generally ignorant and always concealed something no matter how forthright they seemed. Not for the first time he wondered what it was the Nor weren't telling him. He seldom asked for reasons when the covenants were signed, only for what result his employer desired. The reasons they hired him meant nothing to him and he'd early grown weary of listening to them justify themselves. The rhetoric bubbling out from Floarin and scarcely less abundantly from the Nor around her had been so familiar and so boring he hadn't bothered to listen, but spent the time planning the best ways of spending that gold, daydreaming instead of picking through the rubbish for clues to the barb that had to be there, luck's unlovely face. He shook off vain regrets; he'd signed the thing, there was no escaping from that; breaking the covenants would sink him more thoroughly than this miserably botched campaign. He scowled at the gates. The vuurvis was eating slowly into them, held back a little by those triply cursed witches, but only a little. He glanced at the gray blur that marked the position of the sun. Dawn would see the gates so weakened that a few stones lobbed at them would shatter them. Have to wait till the vuurvis burned out. It wasn't going to be neat or fancy, just pushing enough men through the gap to roll over that puny force inside. By tomorrow afternoon he was going to be in the Biserica's Heart. He thought briefly about what was going to happen to the women and girls when the Biserica fell, but shrugged off vague regrets; his men needed something to take the edge off their anger. He straightened his back and contemplated the mountains stretching beyond the east end of the wall. The last of the Sleykynin were somewhere in those and in the mountains on the west side of the valley, circling round to come on the Biserica from the rear—if they hadn't decided the whole operation was a loss and abandoned it. They were better at saving their skins than manning assaults, couldn't be beat if you wanted an enemy cut down, but in a head-on clash they were too undisciplined, too inclined to fight as individuals rather than melding into an effective team. Probably he could count on their fanatical hatred of the meien to bring them into the valley, but he wasn't going to depend on them. Any distraction they provided would be a help, though Hag only knew what Hern and Yael-mri were hoarding to use against him if he got past the wall—when he got past the wall. He watched the gates burning and smiled. There was no stopping him now. One way or another he was in.

He heard screes of alarm from the traxim and looked up. Immense glass dragons undulated above the valley. One of them coiled about a trax and began squeezing. The trax vanished like a punctured soap bubble. The remaining traxim fled. Kole ground his teeth together, raging at the chance that had robbed him of his ability to see what the defenders were doing. He glanced at the Nor beside him, his face carefully masked to hide the flare of loathing he felt for the sorcerers who'd sucked him into this debacle with their promises of powerful aid and who'd proved so feeble since. He forced himself to relax. "What are those? What do they mean?"

The Nor was staring at them and for a moment he didn't answer. When he did, he spoke slowly, searching for words to explain what he didn't understand. "They're . . . other. Magic, but nothing *She*. . . . or we. . . . no one can command them. Third force. Do what they want where. Won't touch us, we can't touch them. *She* called, they came. I don't know why." He cleared his throat. "Won't hurt, can't help. Us or the Biserica."

Nekaz Kole scowled at the dragons, suppressing anger and scorn. He couldn't afford to offend the Nor now that the last stage of the battle was being set, but he swore to steer wide of magic and religion the rest of his days. He dropped his eyes from the enigma that still bothered him and watched the flames biting deeper into the stubborn wood of the gates, feeling a small glow of satisfaction. Not long now.

## 17

Julia leaned against the cold, pitted stone of the tower wall, picking idly at the knot in the rag tied about her arm, working it loose. Any heat from the sun couldn't reach her through the gusty wind that smelled of ash and ice. The overflow of Serroi's power had healed everyone they shoved into the tower, had healed the scratch on her arm and the hole the vuurvis had etched into her thigh. The rooms behind her were empty now, the healed were clustering about the tables set up near the rutted road where excited girls were serving bowls of a rich, meaty soup, loaves of fresh-baked bread and cups of hot spiced cha. Now and then a gust of wind brought the aromas to her, reminding her that she was hungry, but she didn't move away from the wall. She was fit and whole again, even the cold she'd been starting had dried up with her wounds, but she was tired, a weariness of the will as much as of the body. She knew food and hot cha would chase much of that malaise away, temporarily at least, but she hadn't enough desire left in her to shift her feet.

She pulled the rag off her arm and looked at the skin. No scar but a paler patch not yet tanned to match the rest. A lot of those patches scattered about her hide since she'd come here. Not the sort of thing you expected to happen to a sedentary middle-aged writer from a post-industrial society. Smiling a little, she looked down at Rane.

The ex-meie was sitting with her back against the wall, knees drawn up, arms draped over them, staring out into nothing. She looked as tired, as dead, as Julia felt. Rane yawned, then sighed. A gust of wind lifted dust, dead leaves, other debris and slapped the load against her. She got to her feet, brushed at the folds of tunic and trousers, looked up, caught at Julia's arm. "Look."

Long sinuous shapes undulated over the valley, dragons of flexing glass, scales delicately etched on the transparent bodies, pastel colors flowing in waves along the serpentine forms, a silent song in color. No two of the dragonsongs were alike but each complemented the others like chords in a chorale. They drifted eerily into the wind, not with it, creatures not quite of this world. Julia's heart hurt with their extravagant beauty and their strangeness, a strangeness that brought suddenly home to her the realization that she stood on alien soil, something she'd almost forgotten because of the familiar feel of the dirt and weeds under her feet, the familiar look of the mountains around her, the human faces of the people here. She watched the dragons sing and felt a new homesickness for her own land and people, felt like an exile for the first time since she'd jumped through Magic Man's Mirror. She wondered what was happening back home and whether she'd run out on her responsibilities by coming here. Maybe Tom Prioc was right, maybe they owed their country the effort to redeem it. But as she continued to watch the dragons, she felt her regrets leaving her. I've half my life left. No use looking back.

One of the dragons slipped away from the rest and came drifting to earth a few meters out from the west tower, its delicately sculpted head rising high over Julia's. The dragon tilted its head and gazed down at her with large glowing golden eyes. Half mesmerized she drifted away from the tower, not noticing that Rane was coming with her. She expected to feel heat from it, but there was neither heat nor cold, only a faint spicy perfume that was pleasant and invigorating.

Rane's hand tightened again on her arm, dragging her from her dazed contemplation of the dragon's eyes.

Serroi and Hern had come from the tower. They were standing close together looking at the grounded dragon, the flow of emotion between them so intense Julia felt a touch of embarrassment at watching them.

Serroi moved a few steps away from Hern to stand beside the dragon, one hand on the smooth curve of its side. She smiled at Hern, that wide glowing grin Julia remembered with pleasure. Her voice came to them on a gust of wind. "You'd hate idleness, Dom," she said. "Keep busy and live long."

Rane whistled softly. "Maiden bless, Jule," she whispered. "She's going to him, going to face him at last."

Julia said nothing, remembering all too clearly the silent fear in Serroi that night in the Southwall Keep.

"Come on," Rane said as she started for the nearest table. "I need something to wet my throat. This is the end for us, one way or another."

The dragon rose with easy languorous grace into the sky, floating slowly toward the great rock face at the west end of the wall.

## 18

Hern got to his feet, looked down at himself and grinned. "Better fetch me a blanket, love." He patted the smooth curve of his belly. "If I were as slim and elegant as you, I wouldn't bother. But there's a bit too much Hern on view."

Serroi laughed and went away. He watched her go, for that moment content with himself and the world. He hadn't forgotten the war, but he was refusing to think about it. Like Serroi, he was taking a rest from the urgencies of the moment and the pressures of his responsibilities. Smiling, eyes half-closed, he listened to the soft scrape of her feet on the stone, heard the sounds fade. When these were gone, he moved cautiously across the ashy, pitted floor and looked out a windowslit, being careful not to touch the stone. He raised his brows at the fires leaping from the vuurvis barrels, at the black sprawl of the dead Nor. The raiders were still busy behind the army, Maiden bless them, and making their efforts count. He watched Nekaz Kole send messengers to stop the catapults along the wall, all but the two in the center that were pounding at the gate. His throat tightened as he remembered the burning and the pain and knew that even with Serroi at his side he couldn't face that again. Mind or body, neither could endure that , . . . that . . . he couldn't find a word for the experience; *pain*, *agony*, *torment*, they were all inadequate for the totality he remembered. He frowned at Nekaz Kole. Bad luck for us you weren't in your tent. He watched the catapults fling two more clay melons then crossed to the side slit that looked down on the gates, watching the skin of flame eating at them. Yael-mri had warned him about vuurvis, that the Shawar could slow its action but couldn't quench it. At the rate it was consuming the wood, it'd burn through sometime before dawn. And once the gates were down, the army would come flooding over them.

"Hern?"

He turned. Serroi held out a thin gray blanket. As he wrapped it about himself, he scanned her anxiously, not liking what he saw. The eyespot pulsed through the curls that fell forward over her brow, its green turned almost black. Her flesh glowed, very faintly but visibly in the dim light that filled the blackened room. It seemed to him that if he looked too hard at her she would melt away altogether, dissipating like fog on a warming day. He tied two corners over his shoulder so the blanket hung in folds about his body. "How many did the vuurvis get?"

"Three to five dead at each place the catapults hit." Seeing him almost trip over the dangling blanket, she handed him a short length of rope. "Better hitch up your skirts, Dom. I don't know how many were burned and lived. Julia had a brainstorm, packed all of them into the rooms below. Apparently there was a lot of overflow while I was pulling you back, love, seems I sucked in power from everywhere and this tower was pulsing like a mothsprite in heat. Everyone she got here walked out again a while ago, they're getting food now, which reminds me, my love, I'm hollow from head to toe." Her strained cheerfulness melted suddenly. She came into his arms, leaned against him, trembling. "So much pain." Her voice broke and she pressed her face into his shoulder, shaking as if with ague. "So much waste. Lives, time, materials. Gone. And for what? Nothing." She was afraid, more than that, terrified, and he knew what frightened her and he too was afraid.

"No," he said. His throat tensed; she was going back to Ser Noris. "No." He wanted to say more but he couldn't— no words, no voice, no way to fight against the necessity that gripped both of them. He held her until her shuddering eased.

Serroi sighed. "The waste won't stop until he's stopped."

"How?" It was a challenge, a demand that she justify throwing her life away. He was angry and afraid and wanted her to know it.

"I don't know," she said, shaking the hair off her brow. "I only know I have to face him and let what comes come."

"Serroi, I need you."

"I know. I wish. . . ." She didn't finish.

He could feel her withdrawing from him though she didn't move away. "Serroi. . . ."

"You didn't have to come back here, Dom."

He started to say it wasn't the same, but in the end only shook his head, then held her without words until the noises from outside grew so intrusive they could no longer ignore them. He let her go and hitched the blanket up, tied the rope about his middle. Serroi patted the charred rags of her robe into a semblance of order, held out her hand. "Well, come on."

They saw the glass dragons as soon as they stepped from the emptied tower. Hern put his arm about her and together they watched the dragonsong, working as one mind for a short time as they had on the plateau, sharing that remembered beauty, that remembered closeness.

Then one of the dragons separated from the others, flushed with waves of green and gold, and came curling down to land near the tower, huge and wonderful and more than a little frightening. Hern felt shock ripple through Serroi, echoing his shock of recognition and denial. She pulled away from him and began walking toward the dragon.

*No*, he thought, *not so soon. How can you go so easily, how can you go without a word?*

As if she'd heard that, she turned. He waited.

She looked at him a moment but said nothing, then walked on. When she reached the dragon, she put her hand on the cool flesh, flinched as it collapsed into something like steps, turned once more to face him. "You'd hate idleness, Dom," she said, her voice not quite steady. "Keep busy and live long."

He wanted to say something, but the only words that came to him were the empty banalities of idle chat. She smiled, that sudden joyous urchin's grin that had enchanted him from the moment he first saw it, though she wasn't smiling for him then. She climbed up to settle herself in the saddle the dragon shaped for her. Waves of iridescence shimmered along the serpentine body then the dragon drifted upward and began undulating toward the stone face rising a thousand feet above the wall.

## 19

Ser Noris waited.

Rciki janja looked down at large hands closed into fists about the pieces she planned to set on the board.

"Play," he said gruffly.

She opened her right hand. A small greenish figure dressed in charred white rags lay on her palm.

"No," he said. He reached to take the figure from her, drew back when a flash of pain shot through his withered hand.

Reiki smiled. "You said once *I'll teach the child; after that, try and take the woman.*" There was a patina of sweat on her lined face, but her eyes were calm. She was solid janja except for hints in those dark-water eyes. "Do you have her, my Noris?"

He made an impatient dismissing gesture. "Play."

She set the green figure on the board, straightened and opened her other hand. A dark-robed figure with chiseled pale features lay on her palm.

Ser Noris sucked in a breath, slapped at the hand but before he touched her was stopped by an intangible barrier. While he struggled to maintain his control, she set his simulacrum on the board beside the other figure. "This decides it all."

"The army. . . ."

"How long will the Ogogehians stay, with the paymaster gone?"

Again he brushed the question away and sat staring at the black-robed figure. He knew his power and did not doubt he would prevail; what chilled him were the implications woven about that figure. Until this moment he'd been games-master, not a pawn in the game. He lifted his head. "What am I?"

"In what game?"

He hesitated, looked at the finger-high black figure. "I am not less than you." He pronounced each word with great care, flatly.

"Which I?"

A brush of his hand, a hiss of disgust. "Don't play with me, janja."

"You withdraw?"

"No. You know what I'm saying."

"Say it."

"No."

Reiki smiled.

He looked down at the greenglass figure glowing on the board. "I shaped her." The janja made a sound. Without taking his eyes from the figure, he said, "We shaped her." He reached out, didn't quite touch the sculpted red curls. "We shaped her. . . ." His voice trailed into memory.

He reclined on black velvet before a crackling fire, lifted onto his elbow as Serroi hesitated in the doorway. Aware of her loneliness and uncertainty, he wanted to reassure her, but he was uneasy with her, he didn't know how to talk to her. After a few breaths he called to her, "Come here, Serroi." That was easy enough. She grinned suddenly and came rushing in, her confidence growing with each step she took. They talked quietly for a while, she full of eager questions, he responding to her warmth as he would to a fire on a cold day. After a while his hand dropped beside her head. He stroked her hair, began pulling soft curls through his fingers. The fire was no warmer than the quiet happiness between them.

* * *

"And she shaped me," he murmured, then was furious that he'd exposed a part of himself. He got to his feet and walked to the edge of the cliff where he stood looking down at the wall.

The war subsided for the moment. Nekaz Kole was waiting for the vuurvis to burn through the gates; there was a skeleton force of defenders keeping watch at the embrasures but most of them seemed to be gathered about long tables heavy with hot food and drink. Farther down the valley, Sleykynin were spread in a wide arc, creeping secretly toward the Shawar. Small bands of hunters hunted them and were hunted in their turn, a game of blindfold chess where the pieces were pointed weapons.

And over it all the enigmatic dragons wove their color songs.

One of the dragons sank gracefully to the earth inside the wall. Serroi came from the blackened tower with the man she'd fought him to save. Hern. He glared at the pudgy gray figure. If he'd had enough power after his attack on the Shawar, he would have expended it all on the obliteration of that man. He watched and suffered as he felt the intensity of shared emotion radiated from the pair. And cursed himself for thinking so long that the little man could be safely ignored. A year ago he could have squashed Hern easily. Even on the Changer's mountain he could have erased him from existence. But he didn't know then how deeply Hern had insinuated himself into Serroi's life, usurping what Ser Noris considered his. Rutting beast, he howled inside his head, his mouth clamped shut to keep that beastcry from the janja. Debauching her. . . . He choked off that interior rant, frightened by his loss of control. His withered hand twitched, the chalky fingers scraping across the fine black cloth of his robe, a loathesome reminder of the last time he'd let emotion rule him, that aborted confrontation with Serroi on the Changer's mountain.

The dragon came drifting up, moving toward him with undulant languorous grace, the tiny figure on its back almost as translucent as it was.

## 20

Serroi stepped from the dragon's side onto the granite. Lines were worn smooth where Ser Noris had paced the years away gazing down on what he could not possess, only destroy. She saw the janja sitting with massive silence beside a gameboard that was a sudden eruption of color in all the muted grays and browns of the mountainside. Acknowledging the old woman with a small, sketchy gesture, she turned to face Ser Noris.

He was thinner than she remembered, his face worn and tired. The ruby was gone; she missed that bit of flamboyance, a tiny weakness that made him somehow more human, more approachable; with it had gone most of the color and vigor in his face. His black eyes were opaque, he was arming himself against her. "Ser Noris," she said.

"Serroi."

"Is anything worth all that?" She indicated the valley, the wall, the army, and ended with a flick of the hand that included the Plain beyond the mountains. "All that death?" She hit the last word hard, brought her hand around as if she would touch him but dared not. "Or what it's done to you? Do you know how you've changed, my father, my teacher?" She seemed resigned to no answer. "The waste, teacher, the waste."

His face stony, he said, "Is a leaf wasted because it falls from a tree?"

"People aren't leaves."

He brushed that aside. "We can't talk. We don't speak the same language anymore."

"We never did." She'd forgotten how impervious he had always been, how little he'd listened to her, how cut off from every other source of life he was.

"Why are you here, daughter?"

"To stop you, father."

"How?"

The cold wind whipped at her face. "Hern asked me that."

"I don't want to hear about him." She heard the anger in

that wonderful seductive voice. She was so tired, so empty, that she felt disarmed before the struggle began. He smiled at her. "Come home, Serroi."

"No. . . ." She looked vaguely about, seeing nothing, feeling adrift. She stared helplessly at the janja, wondering if the old woman or the Dweller-within could—or would—help her. Reiki's face was an eroded stone mask, her eyes clouded. Nothing there for her. She looked back at Ser Noris, her eyes fixing on the chalky, twisted hand she'd touched. She remembered the sense of *wrongness* that had triggered her healing impulse, but the great inflow that had salvaged Hern and healed the rest of the vuurvis victims seemed to have destroyed that reflex. Or had temporarily exhausted it. *It was a mistake to come up here before I was rested.* She shut her eyes. The waste, the terrible waste—all to feed his hunger for control. She groped blindly with hands and mind for something anything. . . .

And power flowed into her, earthfire strong and warm and oddly gentle, lapping up and up, washing away weariness and despair. She was Biserica, she was valley, she was mountain and plain, she was mijloc. . . .

Sadnaji lay quiet, empty; the shrine was cleansed, filled with power, power that flowed into her when she touched it.

Sel-ma-Carth itched with unrest. Carthise were slipping into the shrine to clean it, but there was no Keeper chosen yet, the power there was smothered, leashed—until she touched it. Outside, hidden from the walls in an icy gulley, Roveda Gesda looked up from the vach carcass he was bargaining over, eyes opening wide, at the sudden eerie touch, then shrugged and went on bargaining.

She dipped into a score of village shrines scattered across the Cimpia Plain, taking from them. They were empty, but humming with a new song, filled with the presence of the Keepers though they were all down below in the valley with their folk, helping to defend the Biserica in any way they could.

The Kulaan mourned their linas and gathered in their winter halls to sing their burning hatred of Floarin and her works, sending south their prayers that the hands of their men be quick and strong in vengeance. She touched them and flinched away from that corrosive rage.

The Kulaan raiders unfolded the clothing they'd taken from the Ogogehians they'd harvested from the army. Each kual had marked and stalked a mercenary approximately his size and coloring and used a strangling cord to kill him so there'd be no blood on his clothing or leathers, no cuts in them. Now they dressed in those tunics, buckled on the war leathers, and practiced walking until they were satisfied that they looked enough like the Ogogehians to fool any observers. Then they left their concealment and began winding through the brush, a small band indistinguishable from any other mercenary squad, walking with calm purpose toward the hill where Nekaz Kole waited for the gates to burn through.

The fisher villages waited, cleansed of Kapperim (some very bloodily, losing half their own folk, or more, in the savage battle to reclaim their homes), the dead mourned, the Kapra corpses cast out to feed the fish. The Intii Vann stood on the spear-walk of his village, gazing down into the tapata, his beard fresh-braided, slick with fine oil, contentment softening the hardwood of his face. A chunky, gray-haired woman shifted impatiently about on the planks. She looked up, startled, as she felt the touch; her face altered, flat nose pushing out, ears lifting, pointing. With an effort of will she stopped the change and scowled down at a line of boats beached on the mud below them. "It's time I went back," she said.

Vann shook his head. "Oras will be a rat-pit, healwoman."

"Midwife."

He ignored the acerbity in her voice. "Wait. It be

time to move when we know who won there." He
jerked a long thumb south and east.

"My people need me. Who else gives a spit in a
rainstorm for them." She looked into the unyielding
face. "I could always walk."

"Snow shut the passes."

She set her back against the wall and glared south.
"You get busy and finish it," she told Serroi. "I got
work to do."

"What?"

"Not you, Intii. Her." That was all the explanation she would give though he questioned her several
times before the boats arrived from the south.

In their palisaded winter camps the Bakuur gathered, drank the hot and heady brews, melded being
to being, house to house, camp to camp, until the
river bottom throbbed with their song, the clicking
of the spirit sticks, the bumping of the drums, the
beat of the dance, the wordless chant that gathered
past and future, dead and unborn and all the living.
When she touched the meld, it gave her its zo'hava'ta,
gave without stint or question, a hot and heady flow
of joy and generosity and endless endurance.

And all through the mijloc the Others—creasta
shurin, shapechangers, wood sprites, the strangely
gifted who hid in human form among the unseeing
mijlockers—these gave what they could when she
touched them. The despised and dispossessed, the
poor and sick and deformed, beggar and thief and
those who turned a hand to whatever would keep
them alive, they felt her touch and melded with her,
giving without stint and without exception what she
asked of them.

She took a step toward Ser Noris.
"No." He lifted his good hand. "No closer."
"I'm going to stop you," she said.
"Serroi." He sounded desperate. "Don't make me de-
stroy you." His breathing was harsh, and he lost his glacial

beauty but gained a warmth and humanity that she found far harder to fight.

She trembled. "What can I do? Stop this. Please stop. There are so many . . . there's so much . . . you can't touch what's down there—" a curve of her hand encompassed the valley—"you can only destroy it. Where's the profit in that?" She paused. "Can't you understand? You don't need to destroy the Biserica. It doesn't threaten you."

"You're the one who doesn't understand. That—" he indicated the valley—"diminishes me because it denies me. I will not permit that."

Anguish ran in Serroi's veins. "All or nothing." She thrust her greenglass hands toward him. "Sick. It's sick." She took another step toward him.

He spoke a WORD and wind buffetted at her, threatened to sweep her off her feet. The glow about her brightened and the wind split about her; it couldn't touch her. She took another step.

He backed away, spoke another WORD. The stone cracked beneath her feet, a mouth opened to swallow her. She took a fourth step undisturbed, her bare feet treading air as easily as stone.

He began to circle around behind the janja, spoke a WORD. Fire hotter than vuurvis surged about her. And was quenched by her earthfire which was hotter still.

Reiki janja sat without moving, a carven figure, massive legs crossed, large shapely hands resting on her knees, fingers curled loosely about nothing, so still she seemed a part of the mountain, a boulder roughly shaped to human form.

The janja between them, he cried out, "Serroi, yield to me. You don't know. . . ."

"I know what will happen if I don't stop you."

"Serroi. . . ." He gave it up, spoke a PHRASE, gathering to himself all his power, taking his combat form, the smoky giant as tall as the cliff, the form she'd seen when she was a child and witnessed the challenge duel with the last of the Nor who came close to matching his power, the duel she barely survived, caught like a bug in the fringe of those deadly exchanges. She matched him, calling to herself the earthfire, the aggregate strength of the little ones, the waiting shrines, rising with him until she faced him as a figure of light shimmering against his darkness.

He spoke a WORD, his huge voice booming out over the land.

Her form shivered and went vague about the edges, but solidified immediately as she absorbed his power and added it to her own.

The battle changed to a stately pavanne among the mountain peaks, a dance on a crumbling floor, the land churned by the WORDS flung at Serroi and shunted aside. Fire fell into the valley, scorched an orchard and half a set of vines, burned one pasture clean. Air buffeted the watchers inside the wall and out, erratic winds that struck like hammers. The earth rumbled uneasily beneath their feet, its deep grumble rolling continually across the valley.

And the immense dance went on, Serroi advancing, the Nor retreating, circling, avoiding the touch of her fingers.

# 21

Julia watched the dragon until it curled away from the rock and rejoined the others. She took the cup Rane handed her, nodded at the rock. "What now?"

"Maiden knows. One thing sure, we wait."

She sipped at the cha, glanced from the rock to the wall. The defenders still there were watching the cliff, their backs to what might be happening behind them. "Think Kole will try hitting us now?"

"Why? All he's got to do is wait till the gate burns through, then he rolls over us." Rane bit off a chunk of bread and went back to watching the maneuvering of the tiny figures on the rock.

Overhead, the dragons began to change the patterns they were weaving, moving from chords to a powerful unity. Julia put a crick in her neck watching them. For a while she didn't understand what was happening, then she saw they were revving up to reinforce the little healer, magic dynamos resonating to a single beat. Magic merging with technology, power is power. She smiled, rubbed at her neck, nearly dropped the cup as the two figures were suddenly giants sharply limned against an apple-green sky. She squinted against grit-laden erratic winds, watching the figures circle about each other in a stately combat more like a dance than a battle to the death.

## 22

Nekaz Kole watched the circling giants and felt ice knotting under his ribs, failure sour in his mouth. He scanned the wall, seeing shadows in every embrasure he could look through; he suspected they were watching the drama on the mountain peaks and for a moment considered taking advantage. He twisted around, scowled at the Nor. The golden minark was staring transfixed at that deadly dance. "Ser Xaowan," he said sharply. The minark showed no sign of hearing him. Kole scanned his face, cursed under his breath and abandoned any thought of an attack. Frustrated and furious he settled back to wait, glaring at the giant figures, wondering how to incorporate the battle into his own plans once the gates burned through.

## 23

Tuli saw Ildas fade, turn cool and hollow as the giant figures swelled into the sky and began that dance of restrained violence. She held him in her lap and felt a hollow growing inside herself, a weariness that seemed the sum of all the weary days and nights she'd spent since this travail began. At least he wasn't lost completely this time, his ghost stayed with her, giving her a hope he'd be whole again as soon as . . . she didn't know as soon as what. The army sat on the hillsides, their usual clamor muted, the men gaping at the show. Coperic stood beside her, his eyes fixed on the green glass figure, shocked and afraid. He knew her, Tuli saw that, and she was important to him. His hands were clenched into fists, his wiry body taut, as if by willing it he could add his strength to hers. Tuli cupped her hands about the sketchy outline of the fireborn and fought with a sudden jealous anger.

And the dance went on.

## 24

Nilis sat with the other Keepers, throbbing with the power flowing through and out of her, barely conscious, blending into a single being with those others, concentrating on endurance, on lasting until the need was over.

## 25

Serroi caught hold of his sound wrist, another quick step and she held the withered hand. Light closed about them, beginning to dissolve them.

Ser Noris changed.

His mouth gapes in a silent scream, his body writhes, his skin darkens, roughens, cracks, turns fibrous and coarse. Eyes, mouth, all features, dissolve into the skin, vanish. His head elongates, bifurcates, the portions spread apart and grow upward, dividing again and again. His arms strain up and out, stretching and thinning, his fingers split into his palms, grow out and out, whiplike branches in delicate fans, twigs grow from the branches, buds popping out from them, the buds unfolding into new green needle sprays.

Serroi changes, her body echoing everything happening in his.

The cliff cracks, shatters, great shards of stone rumbling into the valley, an unstable ramp bathed in dust that billows up and up, drawn to the glowing, changing giants, shrouding them.

When the dust settled, the giants were gone. Two trees grew at the edge of the broken cliff, a tall ancient conifer, a shorter, more delicate lacewood.

A hush spread across the valley, a hush that caught mercenaries, exiles, mijlockers, meien, everyone, and held them for a dozen breaths, long enough for them to become aware of that stillness, to notice that the glass dragons had vanished, the sky was empty.

## 26

Ignoring the hush, the Kulaan closed around Nekaz Kole; two tossed a third up behind him, another trio dealt with the Nor. Before Kole could react, a skinning knife slid into him, piercing his heart. The Kual pushed him from the saddle and jumped after him. The Nor was down also, dead before he could know he was dying, so tangled was he in the battle on the cliff.

Without breaking their silence, the Kulaan started briskly away, one Kual leading the gold rambut. They didn't touch the demon macai.

The beast stood frozen, locked into place by the metamorphosis of its creator, Ser Noris. Locked into place and beginning to rot, the demon essence coming loose from the natural part. Before the Kulaan had vanished into the brush, the skin and bones collapsed out of the smoky black outlines. A breath later, the demon residue faded, vanished.

## 27

Warmth followed the hush across the valley, visible in eddies of golden light spilling over the walls, flooding over the army, waking the men from their daze, prodding them into movement, urging them away from the valley. The Ogogehians snapped into alertness, found Nekaz Kole dead, the norits dazed and helpless. They split into small groups, rifled the supply wagons and marched away, the Shawar shooing them on until they started down from the saddle of the pass.

They crossed the foot of the Plain, made their way through the Kotsila Pass and descended on Sankoy like a swarm of starving rats, looting and killing, working off their fury and shame at their defeat, paying themselves for the gold they'd never collect. They trickled into the several port cities, comandeered sufficient shipping and went home.

The Sankoise were slower to understand and react, but the unleashed Shawar nudged them from their lethargy and into movement. They began drifting away from their camps, abandoning much of their equipment, some of them even ignoring their mounts, moving slowly almost numbly at first, then faster and faster until they were running. They settled to a more conserving gait when they passed beyond the reach of the golden warmth, but they were a ragged, weary, starving remnant by the time they crossed Kotsila Pass and straggled down to a homeland in chaos with no time and less will to welcome them.

Few of the dedicated Followers were left on their feet, most were laid in the mud; those that survived huddled in dazed groups about the mindless norits. But the others, the tie-conscripts there because they had no choice, they needed no urging to leave. They followed the Ogogehians over the supply wagons, carrying off all they could stuff in improvised packs. They went home to starvation and raids from human wolves, young men roaming the Plain attacking anything that seemed vulnerable; they went home to a guarded welcome as chill as the winter winds sweeping the Plain, a welcome that warmed considerably when they joined the folk inside the walls, added the food they brought to the common store and helped fight off the raiders through the rest of the winter.

(Hern ranged the land with a motorized force of meien and exiles, gradually restoring order, bringing isolated settlements into the common fold, passing out the rescued grain.)

## 28

Tuli crowed with pleasure as Ildas plumped out and began vibrating with his contented coo. Cradling him against her ribs she got to her feet and moved to stand beside Coperic.

He was staring at the patch of green on the top of the ruined cliff, strain in his face and body as he fought to deal with the loss of a friend and perhaps more than friend. Tuli watched, angry again, jealous, wanting to strike at him for the hurt he was giving her. She remembered how much she needed him and kept a hold on her temper and her mouth so she wouldn't say or do anything she'd regret later.

Coperic sighed as he relaxed. He put his hand on Tuli's shoulder. "Looks like it's over."

"Uh-huh. Kole's dead."

"I saw." He lifted a hand, squinted against the gilded light pouring like water over the wall, washing over the army. "Rats are running for their holes. Time we was leaving too. Bella."

She stepped away from him and stood watching as he talked rapidly with the others, sending them out to scavenge food, mounts and anything that seemed useful. After a frown at Tuli that told her to stay put, he left. For a while she stood watching the army break apart and wondering what was happening inside the wall, then she settled herself on a bit of withered grass and arranged Ildas comfortably in her lap, and began brooding over her future. Coperic probably expected her to come back to Oras with him, and she was probably going to go. It looked like the best choice—if she could make him keep her and not send her home to her father. She frowned at the wall, thinking about the swarm of girls inside. Maybe she could have grown used to all that if she'd stayed there. What had Tuli-then thought? She tried to remember. It was only what? two-three passages ago. To much had happened since. She couldn't bring that girl back, she was just gone, that was all. And it didn't matter anyway. She scratched absently along the fireborn's elastic spine and thought about staying at the Biserica for weapon training. Rane wanted that. The ex-meie wanted Tuli to take over her run, and the idea appealed to her. Trouble was she couldn't go out right away, she'd have to spend a bunch of years being trained. A great wave of resistance rose in her. All

those girls, tie-girls, tar-girls, strangers from all over, she
didn't like them any better now than she had when she
was growing up at Gradintar or forced to mix with them
up in Haven. The thought of having to live in a herd of
them churned her stomach and soured her mouth. She
couldn't do it. Giggling, stupid, supercilious girls. No!
Maybe if she went back when she was older. She thought
about what she didn't want. She didn't want to marry
anyone; and she'd probably have to if she went back with
her family. She didn't want to go back and be shut behind
house walls like most mijloc women, tar-women anyway,
doing the women's work she despised. She didn't want to
be shut behind Biserica walls either, living by Biserica
rules. At least Coperic understood her and accepted her as
she was. He could teach her how to support herself, and
how to defend herself so no one could tell her what to do.
*Have to send Da word I'm not coming home.* Wherever
home is. *He's going to howl. Maybe.* She was Tesc's
favorite, she'd known that as long as she'd known anything
and had taken careless advantage of it. She scratched behind Ildas's pointy ear and smiled as he groaned with
pleasure. The smile faded as she remembered her father as
he was up in Haven, busy, vigorous, happy, absorbed in
the problems of governing that forced him to extend himself for the first time in his life. *He might be too busy now
to bother about her.* Tears prickled in her eyes. Impatiently she brushed them away. *Silly. Making herself feel
bad. Over nothing maybe.* If she'd learned anything during the past year, she'd found from painful experience that
she wasn't very good at understanding people or knowing
what they were going to do. She shrugged. *Didn't matter.
Coperic liked her. That was enough to go on with.*

## 29

Georgia and Anoike were up in the observation room of
the west tower, moving about from windowslit to windowslit, watching the power-dance on the mountain peaks,

looking out over the army, checking on the vuurvis fire eating at the gates.

Anoike pulled her head in. "Somethin weird happenin over here."

Georgia turned from the side slit where he was scowling at the fire. "Huh?"

"C'mon here, hon."

He brushed at the crumbling stone, then leaned out the slit beside hers. "What?"

"Them. There."

"Mercs. So?"

"Uh-uh." She lifted her binoculars, looked through them a minute longer, slipped the strap over her head and passed them to Georgia. "Look close, see 'f you see what I see." She went back to leaning in the slit, ignoring the carbon staining her thin strong arms. When she saw the Kulaan swarm over Kole and the Nor, she gave a low whistle. "Would'ya look at that."

"When you're right, you're right." He brushed at his arms, handed her the binoculars. "Got your wish, Annie Lee." He grinned at her scowl. "Someone took out Nekaz Kole." He sobered. "Better let Hern and Yael-mri know."

Hern stood very still, his eyes fixed on the crumbled cliff, on the paired trees blowing in a wind that didn't reach the valley floor. His face and eyes looked blank, rather as if he were unconscious on his feet.

Yael-mri put her hand on his shoulder. "Hern."

He shuddered, sucked in a long breath, exploded it out, sucked in another. He glanced at the trees one more time, then swung around, his back to them. "What?" The single word was harsh, strained. He cleared his throat, coughed. "What's happening?"

"The Shawar are loosed. They're chasing the Sleykynin from the valley."

Anoike was staring at the upwelling of thick golden light, spreading in slow waves out from the heart of the Biserica. Georgia watched her a moment, then turned to Hern. "Nekaz Kole is dead. Looks like some of the raiders got hold of merc leathers, just walked up to him and stuck a knife in him, pulled him out of the saddle and went off with his rambut."

Hern closed his eyes. "Then it's over." He looked down at himself. "I'd better get dressed. Georgia, collect your councillors. Yael-mri, you get the priestsu together. Where'd be the best place to meet? Not the Watchhall." He brushed at his face as if trying to brush away memory. "The library, I think, neutral ground of a sort." He started walking toward the hospital tent and the trucks parked there, talking as he walked, as idea after idea came to him. "Oras will be a rat-pit by now. Won't take long to tame it, though. Hang a few of the bloodiest rats, keep patrols in the streets a passage or two. Cimpia Plain. That'll be harder. Food. Have to work out a way to distribute what's left of the tithing, chase off any bands of majilarni still there, bound to be raiders hitting the tars and the villages. Reminds me, we'll need someone to talk for the tars and ties, a Stenda and a Keeper, one of those who came in with the last bunch of mijlockers. Suppose I'll have to stand watch for the others. Your folks can stay here at the Biserica if that's what you want. Probably should until spring. North of the Catifey the winters are hard on those without shelter. Some should stay at the Plaz in Oras, once we can get that cleaned out, advance party so to speak, it's close to the land you'll be getting, got maps there. Have to talk to you about the Bakuur, they have tree-rights to bottom land on both sides of the river. Have to work out some kind of government, I'm not going back to the way it was before, even if. . . ." He stopped walking, paused. Then after a minute he started on, continuing to blurt out whatever came into his mind, not bothering with any but the most rudimentary of connections, talking to hold off the loss that kept threatening to overwhelm him.

The golden light thickened about them and began pouring over the wall onto the army, waking them to defeat, prodding them away from the valley.

## 30

Julia wedged herself into an embrasure and frowned at the ugly trampled plain below. The grass will be thick and tall next year. So much fertilizer. She moved a shoulder out from the stone, slipped the rifle loose. She'd like to throw it in the muck with the bodies, but likes didn't seem to count much these days. She felt drained, old, yet oddly open. Open to the life ahead, the challenge of this new world, this newer, fresher community. It seethed with possibilities and hope. Much experience had taught her the fallacy of new beginnings made by the same old people; whatever the starting point, sooner or later the ancient problems showed up. Still, there was always the chance that this time would be different. She set the rifle beside her and looked at her hands. The one thing she wanted most was to get back to her writing, to put the words and ideas churning in her head into physical form where she could play with them, shape them into pleasing rhythms, be surprised by them, by what she didn't know she knew. She was tired of this immersion in activity, itchy at the lack of privacy, beginning to resent the meetings, the endless talk, the painful and complex melding of two disparate cultures and traditions, the acrimonious clashing of the adherents of the several ideologies the exiles had brought with them. Thank god for daddy Sam, she thought. If anything works, it's because he makes it work. Hern's almost as good; his tongue's got two ends and he knows his people inside out. She shouldn't be surprised, I suppose, the way he maneuvered us. His heart isn't in it. She glanced at the two trees atop the ruined cliff, sighed. They were an impossibility. They made her uncomfortable, yet there was no way she could escape their presence here in the valley. Even inside the buildings when she couldn't see them, she knew they were there. Magic. It permeated this place and she wanted out. She wanted paper and ink and quiet and, oh god, a place of her own where she could shut out the world and work.

She eased out of the embrasure and looked along the

wall; there were a few more solitaries like her up here, getting away from the hordes crowded into inadequate living space in the Biserica. Mostly Stenda. They were a touchy bunch, willing enough to pay their fair share for roads and guards to keep them free of robbers, and that part of the tithing they thought of as a bribe to keep the mijlockers busy with their own affairs and out of the Stenda holds. Willing as long as no one messed with them. They'd been an autonomous enclave under the Heslins and saw no reason to change that. She looked at the rifle again, set her mouth in a grim line and slipped it back on her shoulder. A day or two more and the draft constitution would be finished, printed and passed out to everyone, ready to be voted on. Dort had the press set up, working on battery power. Half the Biserica had crowded round during the trial run, fascinated, full of questions, speculating on the changes such a machine would make in the life they knew. She smiled as she thought of the exiles. They'd come largely from the artisan and artist classes. They'd been accustomed to working hard, not because they had to, but because they liked what they did. They were happily at work now, adapting Biserica knowledge and skills to their own requirements. Every day brought something new, converting the trucks to run on alcohol, a solar-powered pump and hand-made pipes—we will have those hot baths and flush toilets soon enough, though Liz. . . . Julia shuddered, remembering the blackened thing landing beside her. God knows what else they'd come up with by the end of winter. Michael and several other youngsters were arguing about how to make microchips in a society that didn't even have electricity; they spent hours at it, inventing an amalgam of their own language and mijlocker that seemed to work well enough, bringing into their circle a number of girls with a mechanical bent and an insatiable curiosity, and several of the tie-boys who'd developed a passion for the motorcycles and the other devices the exiles had brought with them. She looked out over the newly peaceful valley and worried a little about what her people were going to do to it. We almost wrecked

one world. God . . . no, Maiden grant we've learned enough
to cherish this one. Some of the older women watched the
ferment with interest and more than a little sadness because they saw the culture they valued changing in unpredictable ways. Julia gazed out across the valley, then shook
her head. *Going to be interesting, these next few years.* She
started down the ramp. *Interesting times. A curse back home,
may it be a blessing here. Hmmm. Wonder if they've got some
paper to spare. I've definitely got to get to work.*

# EPILOG

Hern stopped to catch his breath. He brushed off a chunk of stone and sat looking down through a haze of dust and heat that softened the contours of everything and intensified the ripe smell of prosperity rising from the busy scene. Grain ripened in broad swathes vanishing to the south; hauhaus, horses, and macain grazed in yellowing pastures, drank from shrunken streams; Posserim rooted in orchards where the trees bent under a heavy load of green fruit. Small dark figures swarmed everywhere, working in the fields, treading water wheels to irrigate vegetable crops, tending the stock, loading two-wheeled wains with goods of all sorts for Southport, Sadnaji, Oras, and the Summerfair at Sel-ma-Carth. Wains and riders were thick on the road running down the center of the valley, the northwall gates stood wide, fragile charred planks a puff of air would shatter. Yael-mri hadn't got around to replacing them yet, so many more important things to do.

The heat and exertion were making him sleepy. Somewhat reluctantly he got to his feet and went back to climbing, moving slowly and warily over the shattered stone. Winter had stabilized the scree, spring rains had washed soil and seeds into the stone, summer brought grass, vines, and brush seedlings. The air was thick with the smells of dust and pollen and a spicy green from the leaves crushed under his feet. From time to time he stopped to wipe sweat from his face and swipe at the black biters that swarmed about his head and settled on his skin to drink the sweat. He reached the top of the scree and worked his way along the mountainside until he reached the narrow flat where the trees grew. For a moment, he stood hands on hips looking up at them. The conifer was huge, gnarled, ancient, and in his eyes indecently vigorous. He glared at it, then concentrated on the lacewood. The openwork leaves painted patterns on the stone and drew dark lace on the satin bark. A capricious breeze sang through the leaves, a rising, falling murmur different in kind from the soughing of the conifer's needles. It seemed to him they were talking to each other like old friends sitting in a patch of sunlight whiling away the hours with memories and pleasant lies, comments and speculation, heatless disputes over this and that. "Nonsense," he said aloud, winced at the harshness of his voice. He moved into the scrolled shade of the lacewood, flattened his hand against her trunk. The bark felt like skin, smooth, warm, pliant, and he had to remind himself that what he was thinking was absurd, that all lacewoods with the same abundance of sun and water and nutrients would feel the same. His mind believed that but his hands did not.

Hastily he moved away from the trees, shrugged off his knapsack and began setting up for his meal. When he was ready to make his fire, he eyed the lower branches of the conifer then smiled at the lacewood. "I suppose you wouldn't like that."

While the cha water was heating, he set out the rest of the food on a thin piece of leather, slices of roast hauhau, a chunk of ripe cheese, some crusty rolls still warm from the baking and the first picking of the chays fruit. Taking a quiet pleasure in the simple task, he sliced open the rolls and filled them with meat and cheese, halved and pitted the chays and set everything aside to wait for the water to boil.

Some time later he sat with his back against the lacewood's trunk, sipping at the cooling cha. "Lot of changes down there," he said. The leaves above him rustled companionably. He smiled. A few late blooms fluttered down, one landing on his boot, the others on the stone beside him. "The exiles are settling in, north of Oras. Houses going up, no crops yet, not many farmers in the mix." He chuckled. "We've got a newspaper in Oras now. Not all the exiles went north." He closed his eyes, drowsed a moment, yawned. "Ummf. The energy of those people, vixen. It's exhausting." Eyelids drooping, he gazed out across the valley. "I keep busy. Wagging my tongue to keep the peace." He chuckled again. "Nothing new in that. Land's a problem. Taroms. Some of them want the old ways back, fighting us. . . ." He set the mug down, yawned, laced his hands behind his head. "You wouldn't believe the things happening down there in the Biserica." He closed his eyes, listened to the whispering of the leaves; a breeze teased at his hair, tickling his face, the sun was warm, the air balmy. There was a peace up here, a tranquility that contrasted sharply with the busy, noisy, acrimonious, often frustrating life he'd been leading the past months. "Change," he murmured. "The exiles live with it as an old friend. Harder for us. . . ." He fell silent and drifted into a light doze.

He awakened a short while later, a recurrent clicking in his ears.

Reiki janja sat on the stone, tossing jewel-bright dice into the air and catching them, rolling them out on the stone as the whim took her. She was a sketch of herself, patches of color painted on air, and the dice she threw had blank sides.

"How do you win with those?"

The janja turned her head. He thought she smiled. "No one wins, Dom. Both sides lose." Her voice was as hollow as her form.

"No Dom. Not anymore." He thought she smiled again. "I've a more impressive title, janja. Representative to the Congress of the Domains, Speaker for Bakuur and Kulaan." He chuckled sleepily. "Serroi said keep busy. That I do."

The janja nodded. "You've seeded a new age, Hern. My

time is ending." She looked up, squinting into the sun, a painted glass figure, the ancient paint faded and rubbed thin. She tossed the blank dice high, watching the glitters until the sun swallowed the tumbling dodecahedrons, then she turned her vanishing face to him, "Live long, dom Hern." Like the dice, she dissolved into the sunlight.

He sat awhile where he was, drowsing, at peace, listening to the trees sigh. Then he rose to his feet, gathered his things into his knapsack and walked back to the lacewood. He stroked his hand along her trunk, his fingers feeling skin that his mind tried to deny. "Well, Serroi. . . ." He looked up. Another late blossom brushed his cheek as it fell. A corner of his mouth twisted up. "Why not." He touched the trunk with his fingertips. "I'll be back, love, when the world gets to be too much for me. To share your peace awhile." He lingered a moment, then started back down the mountainside.